BACK IN THE SHADOWS

BACK IN THE SHADOWS

J.A. OWENBY

Podium

Cover design by Dawn Adams

ISBN: 979-8-3470-1890-1

Published in 2026 by Podium Publishing
www.podiumentertainment.com

To all my dark romance book girlies who couldn't get enough of a pitch black MMC

This isn't a story for the faint of heart.
This is for those who understand that passion has teeth, that desire leaves marks, and that true connection is never about being saved—it's about being claimed.

You know the rules have changed.
And you're ready to break them all over again.

BACK IN THE SHADOWS PLAYLIST

"Eat Your Young" by Hozier

"Breezeblocks" by Alt-J

"Prisoner" by Raphael Lake, Aaron levy, and Daniel Ryan Murphy

"A Piece of Your Shadow" by Roby Fayer and Melosun

"la di die" by Nessa Barrett and jxdn

"Disease" by Lady Gaga

Scan the code below to listen to all the titles
for the book on my Spotify playlist titled "D2"

CONTENT WARNING

Please visit https://authorjaowenby.com/pages/content-warnings for triggers and content warnings.

Please do not proceed reading if these are potential triggers. Your mental health is too important.

xoxo,
J.A. Owenby

BACK IN THE SHADOWS

CHAPTER 1

ELLA

I ceased the gentle swaying of the rocking chair and arched a questioning eyebrow at my husband. "Sebastian, is it really necessary to play 'Eat Your Young' while I'm trying to put Alaric down for his nap? If he doesn't sleep soon, Verity will wake up, and I won't have any time alone with you."

A silly smile eased over his handsome face as he danced across our living room to the beat of Hozier's song. He kissed my forehead before he gazed down at his sleepy nine-month-old son. Then he gently cupped my chin, gliding the pad of his thumb along my jawline, leaving goosebumps in its wake. "These are the moments that I'll hold in my heart forever. I love you so much. You're an amazing wife and mother."

My eyes misted over, and I blinked the tears away.

"Baby, I didn't mean to make you cry." He placed his warm palm against my cheek, and I leaned into his touch.

"I'm fine. It's just hormones." I wasn't sure if it was, but it would explain why I was so emotional. Besides, carrying twins for nine months had taken a toll on my petite frame. I'd spent the last four weeks of my pregnancy on bed rest, feeling bored and miserable. Thankfully, my best friend Cami had visited for a week, providing much-needed company and distraction. Unfortunately, those long days had given me a considerable amount of time to think, and I worried that my husband would tire of my constant moods and insecurities about the changes in my body. Our babies had been delivered by C-section, which left a scar, but it had started to fade. And not once had Sebastian made me feel any other way than beautiful.

Even though I hadn't gotten many, I now had stretch marks on my sides and belly. I was self-conscious at first, but then Sebastian called them my "warrior stripes" and told me I should wear them with pride. When we finally had sex again, he lovingly traced each mark and kissed it tenderly before saying, "I love this one . . . and this one." His deep Australian accent made me weak in the knees and nearly sent me into a hormonal frenzy. I hadn't realized how much I'd missed him until that moment.

Regardless of the exhaustion and changes in my body, witnessing what a wonderful father Sebastian was had made me fall in love with him even more. I never thought it was possible to experience that level of happiness, and my heart swelled with an overwhelming sense of contentment and joy.

I glanced at his ring finger, noting he wasn't wearing his wedding band. His headaches made him sensitive to jewelry and some days even clothes. He had let me know that on those days he put his ring in my jewelry box for safekeeping until he felt better.

Sebastian grunted and stepped away, reaching for the sides of his head. I'd learned to read the signs of a coming shift. It started with a headache and a slight tremor in his leg. The headaches had persisted for over a week now, and I couldn't help but worry about him.

"Are you all right?" I asked, my voice carefully neutral. But even as I spoke, I knew Sebastian would brush it off and try to convince me that everything was fine. But it was only a matter of time.

I stilled as my husband dropped to his knees. His handsome face twisted in agony as he held his cry in.

"It's okay. I'm here, baby." I quickly glanced at Alaric, who was still awake.

A sense of foreboding hung heavy in the stagnant air, and Alaric attempted to sit up and look around, his attention on his father. The bond between Sebastian and Alaric was strong, that much was clear. But as I watched them together, a cold fear crept into my mind. What if their connection wasn't just familial, but something darker? The thought of Alaric or Verity being bound to Death on a level beyond comprehension terrified me. But then again, maybe it wasn't just his father that he shared this deep connection with. Maybe it was . . .

My husband's head slowly rose as if trying to orient himself to his surroundings. His once piercing blue eyes faded into a cold, steely gray as he stared at me with a calculating and sinister gaze. But beneath the surface lurked a familiar hunger. A need to hunt. A need to claim—to claim me.

"There's my queen," he said, his Australian accent disappearing as he stood and squared his shoulders.

"Hi." I gave him a genuine smile. It had been three months since Death had appeared, and I'd missed him more than I could have imagined.

With a confident stride, he approached us, his jawline sharp and his stare intense. Tilting my chin up, he placed his lips over mine. His mouth was warm and commanding, making me moan softly as he tugged on my lower lip with his teeth. Sebastian was everything I could want in bed. He made me feel loved and sexy, which had helped me feel less insecure when Death had finally returned.

My tummy somersaulted as I recalled how Death had ravaged me the last time we were together. My body still tingled with the memory. Now that our children were older and I'd healed, I craved his demanding and sometimes brutal touch more than ever.

As if sensing my thoughts, Death's hand moved to caress the front of my throat, his thumb gently stroking my sensitive skin. He looked down at our son, who was excitedly grinning and kicking his feet. It warmed my heart to see them like this.

"Son." Death's voice cracked. Every emotion possible was wrapped in that one word. "Come see your father."

I held Alaric out to him and watched in awe at how Death, a savage killer, could be so gentle with his family. He held Alaric in his arms, lightly bouncing him while he walked the room. "Is it nap time for you, Alaric?" Death's attention scanned the area before it landed on me again. "Where's Verity?"

"She's already down for her nap. I think this little guy was waiting for you." I rose from the chair and approached them. "How are you?" I pushed up on my tiptoes and pressed a gentle kiss to his soft lips.

"Ready to bring my queen to her knees." He flashed me a wicked grin, and my legs turned to jelly.

I bit my lower lip before I responded. "Then I guess you should focus on getting your son down. The nanny will be here around two this afternoon to take them to the park for a few hours."

"Excellent. I need to handle some business, but I'll be back after the kids are gone."

I understood what he was hinting at, although he attempted to keep me away from his extracurricular activities. As a result, I didn't bother asking for any details.

"While you're spending time with Alaric, I'll clean up." I pointed to the baby spit-up that covered my lilac T-shirt. Eventually, I might be able to wear something nice again, but with the twins, there was no use in trying until they were older.

I hurried up the staircase, my feet light on each step. I paused as I reached the babies' room and gently pushed open the door. The soft sounds of Verity's breathing filled the air as she lay nestled in her crib, her tiny lips making small sucking noises as she slept soundly. My heart swelled with love as I watched her for a moment before continuing to my bathroom.

Ten minutes later, I was freshened up and wearing a black sundress with a pretty pattern of bright-colored flowers. My teeth were brushed, and I'd removed the hair tie, allowing my long dark locks to tumble over my shoulders. Feeling a little more human, I strode down the hall and stopped at the twins' room again. Death carefully bent over Alaric's crib and lowered his son to the mattress. He covered him in his blue summer blanket, then turned to Verity's bed. He remained still, watching her sleep.

My heart lodged in my throat with an onslaught of emotions—love, pride, fear, and excitement. Being married to Sebastian had its complications, but moments like these made me forget all my concerns. I had everything I could ever hope for: Sebastian, Death, kids, my parents, and friends. I lived in a beautiful home in upstate New York in the middle of nowhere, surrounded by the beauty of hardwood trees at the edge of the forest. It was quiet and peaceful. We also traveled whenever we wanted to. Sebastian's private plane allowed us to pack up the babies and fly anywhere we dreamed of. The kids would be well-versed in travel and different cultures, which made me happy that we were able to offer them those experiences.

As I stood alone in the quiet of my thoughts, I couldn't shake off the feeling that something was missing. It wasn't anyone else's fault . . . It was my inner darkness that I had tried so hard to suppress after I'd killed John, the man who had repeatedly molested me and other children.

But I'd had to push the forbidden craving away when I found out I was pregnant. My babies were more important than fueling that side of me. Even though I'd left my job at the lawyer's office, where the adrenaline rush of dealing with dangerous men had been a constant presence in my life, I was now married to someone even more powerful and potentially dangerous. So, what was it? The loss of adrenaline? Or had Death awakened something vile inside me? Were Alaric and I connected on a dark and twisted level? Was he more like me and craved the darkness? *Stop! You're a mother. You can't entertain those kinds of feelings or memories of what you did to John anymore.*

The barely audible sound of Death's footsteps approached. His stormy gray eyes held a fleeting moment of sadness before they settled on me. I reached out and placed my hand on his chest, feeling the softness of his silk shirt beneath my palm.

"They have grown so much already," he said, looking back at the sleeping twins.

"Yes, they do that. Grow up quickly," I replied, trying to ease the tension apparent in his shoulders.

"How long do they normally nap?" he asked, shifting his weight from one foot to another.

"Usually a few hours. Once Lulu picks them up, we'll have some alone time." I peered at him through my dark eyelashes, already imagining him inside of me.

He grabbed my chin, digging his fingers into my jaw as he ravaged my mouth with a desperate hunger. His lips crushed against mine with a ferocity that made my head spin and my breath catch in my throat. The bruising pressure only heightened the intensity of our kiss, but I didn't care. All I wanted was for him to return to me and never let go.

I stood at the edge of the porch and waved goodbye as Lulu drove away with the twins. When Sebastian had first mentioned a nanny, I'd objected. I wanted to raise our babies. As the months passed, we became so exhausted and couldn't spend any time together, so I gave in. She only worked a limited number of hours and didn't live with us, so it felt like a good decision. Plus, it helped when Death appeared.

I closed the front door and raced up the stairs, my pulse pounding so loudly I could barely hear my footsteps. Anticipation fueled me as I entered the bedroom, eager for Death's return. But my enthusiasm died in my throat when I saw Death perched on the edge of the bed. He turned his hollow gaze toward me, the darkness in his eyes swallowing any trace of light in the room. I froze in place, the air thick with a chill that seeped into my bones.

My bedspread was littered with newspaper articles, the sight of each one halting the beat of my heart, and a sharp gasp escaped me.

"What are you doing?" My voice quivered with fear and astonishment. "How did you find that?" I pointed to the papers strewn across the mattress.

Fury rippled off him in waves as he swept away the contents, and I watched it all flutter to the floor as he stood to the full height of his six-foot-two frame. His gaze narrowed as he shot off the bed and stormed closer before I could blink. Pushing me against the wall, Death wrapped his large hand around my wrist and dug his fingers into my skin.

Death's lips brushed my ear, and then he dragged them down the side of my neck. "You know better, little lamb." He fisted my hair and jerked my head back. "You thought you were keeping it a secret from me, didn't you?"

My blood froze in my veins. "I don't keep secrets from you." The tremble in my voice betrayed me. How had he found the file? I'd taken painstaking measures to conceal any evidence from Sebastian and Death.

"The manila envelope hidden in the floor beneath the rug. The pictures, the articles, the news clippings," he growled. "What part of no did you not understand when you asked if you could look into my past? Several years ago, when Kip and Dope wanted to dig into who killed my parents, I told them the same thing: it's risky and could lead to me. If they get to me, they get to you, so what makes you think you can fucking go behind my back?"

My heart felt like it was being crushed under the weight of my fear and desire, each beat hammering against my chest. The air around us crackled with tension as Death spoke. The truth was, I couldn't stop myself from digging. Death wasn't just my lover or the father of my children. He was a force beyond human comprehension, and that terrified me as much as it fascinated me.

Every time he appeared and disappeared, every mysterious moment when his eyes held secrets, I felt a gnawing uncertainty. Who was he really? What darkness lived inside him that could so seamlessly transition between gentle father and ruthless killer?

My past working with dangerous men had taught me one crucial lesson: knowledge was survival. And survival meant understanding every potential threat, even if that threat slept beside me, held our children, and kissed me with a passion that could consume worlds.

But more than fear, there was something else. A strange mirroring I saw between myself and Death. We both carried darkness. We both understood violence not as a horror, but as a language. My killing of John wasn't just self-defense. It was a calculated act of survival. And Death? He was survival personified.

I needed to know if either or both of our children would inherit this darkness. If they would understand this unspoken language of power and endurance that ran through our veins.

So, I collected newspaper clippings. Old records. Whispers from shadows. Not to expose Death, but to understand him. To protect my family from whatever powerful force he truly represented. If I ever found his parents' killer, there would also be a need for vengeance and answers.

"You betrayed me, Ella. And now you will face the consequences."

Fear clawed at my insides as I realized the gravity of my reckless actions and the severity of his intentions.

CHAPTER 2

DEATH

They'll tell tales of the lamb that strayed, but none will speak of how the darkness sang it sweetly home.
—Anonymous

My queen's defiance was a sharp blade that cut into my patience, but I also relished the power it gave me over her. As she scurried down the stairs and through the living room like a helpless fawn, a dark chuckle rumbled deep within my chest. I could see the fear and desperation swirling in her gaze as she looked over her shoulder at me, begging for punishment. Ella's insatiable thirst for submission was evident, but she had forgotten the consequences of crossing me. It was time to remind her with a harsh lesson that would leave her trembling at my feet. But there was something else that nagged at me. Why? Why did she do it? That was what I intended to find out.

I hurried down the stairs after her.

"One, two, whispers in the night. Three, four, stay out of sight. Five, six, a wicked fix," I chanted.

Although the house was a good size, there was nowhere that she could hide from me. The scent of her vanilla and peach body wash always gave her away, but I would never admit it to her.

"Seven, eight, accept your fate. Nine, ten, darkness reigns again." I entered the kitchen. The black granite counters were clean and void of any evidence of the twins. "There's no escape, little lamb. You should know by now that I always find what is mine."

A flicker of Ella's dress caught my eye as she bolted through the dining room and toward the back of the home. My heart pounded with adrenaline as I gave chase, thoughts of dominating her flashing through my mind.

With a smirk, I burst through the kitchen door as I followed the sound of her hurried footsteps. I knew every move she would make before she even thought of it. And I was well aware of exactly where she was headed.

I took the stairs two at a time, and my steps thundered through the hallway until I reached the twins' room. I stood in the entryway, savoring the anticipation and indulging in the power coursing through my veins. Memories of newspaper articles and files from the manila envelope danced in my mind, fueling my intense desire for vengeance. I clenched my jaw so hard that sharp pain shot through my head, but it only added to the pleasure of finally claiming her.

"Come out now, or I'll drag you out by your hair. The choice is yours."

Ella wouldn't surrender, but it was a piece of the game to her. I just wasn't sure if she realized it or not. That dark, beautiful part of her danced along the edge of sanity, taunting her. If she surrendered once again, maybe it would be for good.

With determination fueling every step, I closed the distance between us and flung open the closet door. Ignoring the mountain of stuffed animals she had barricaded herself behind, I reached in and grabbed a fistful of her hair.

Ella's yelp pierced the air as I hauled her out, her body rigid with fear and defiance. Despite her struggles, I forced her to stand before me.

"Why? Why did you do it?" I snapped.

Tears misted her eyes, but she refused to give me the pleasure of watching them fall. She pursed her lips together with perseverance. My little lamb was hiding something else.

I bent down, picked her up, and threw her over my shoulder.

"Put me down!" Her tiny fists slammed into my back.

I ignored her as I carried her to the bedroom. With my free hand, I opened the nightstand and rummaged through the items until I found the ropes I sought. I flung her down on the bed but held on to one of her arms.

"What are you doing?" She tugged against my hold.

I quickly secured one wrist to the bedpost and offered her a wicked smile as I grabbed the knife strapped to my calf. "What am I *not* about to do to you?" I hissed as I pressed the sharp tip against her smooth neck. With a quick movement, I sliced through her flimsy dress, leaving it in tatters. Her body was exposed, her large breasts spilling out of the remnants of her beige lace bra. In one swift motion, I cut through the delicate fabric, relishing in her gasp. She struggled to sit up, but she was wasting her energy.

"Lie down," I ordered.

Fear flickered in her eyes, but she didn't dare defy me again. As I reached for another rope, I couldn't help but feel torn. Part of me was still angry at her for betraying me, yet another part longed to forget it all and drown in her beauty. With each knot tied, my emotions battled inside me, unable to decide whether to punish or pleasure her.

As I finished securing her wrists to the headboard, I stood back and watched her struggle against the bindings. The room was heavy with anxiety, the air crackling with longing and resentment. She glared at me with a defiance that sent shivers of excitement down my spine, yet beneath that fire in her gaze, I sensed a hint of vulnerability.

I wanted to break her, to make her pay for what she'd done. But as she lay there, exposed and helpless, I couldn't ignore the little whisper in my head that reminded me that even though I was angry, I would be sorry if I hurt her. It was a dangerous game we played, one that blurred the lines between passion and destruction.

I leaned in close, my breath warm against her skin. "Do you regret it?" I asked, my voice low and rough. She remained quiet, her jaw clenched in stubborn silence.

I traced a finger along her jawline, feeling the rapid beat of her pulse beneath my touch. "You can't resist me forever," I murmured, more to myself than to her.

But as I looked into her dark and stormy eyes, which were mixed with emotions, I knew this battle between us was far from over. Whether it ended in flames or ashes, only time would tell.

One thing remained unchanged, though. I had to know why. Not only did Ella need to admit it to herself, but she had to explain to me what drove her to do it.

"If you tell me why, then I might forgive you." I climbed onto the mattress between her legs. Her pink thong was damp with her desire. I gripped the handle of the knife and slowly traced the sharp tip over her covered pussy.

"I had every right to look into what happened," she said between gritted teeth. "I need to know, Death. You can't deny me that anymore."

Anger pulsed through my veins, the darkness briefly consuming me again.

"My queen speaks so bravely."

"I wasn't trying to hurt you, but I'm a part of you now. I need answers even if you don't." The rise and fall of her breasts quickened, then she stilled as I used the blade to cut off her thong. I pressed the tip of my knife into her skin and remained riveted to each stretch mark on her stomach and hips as I traced one at a time. Ella's eyes widened as she glanced down, watching intently to see what I would do next.

Her scars were proof that she belonged to me. I had given them to her. When she had announced she was pregnant, I had accomplished what I'd set out to do—fill her with my seed and claim her.

"You don't need the answers, Ella." I crawled back down her beautiful curvy figure and pushed the fabric away from her sweet cunt. She was dripping wet for me, and I resisted the urge to lick and taste her. The tension in the room was thick enough to cut with the very same knife I held in my grasp.

Refocusing, I shoved the handle of my weapon inside her before she realized what I was doing. Her green eyes widened as she arched off the bed, a cry slipping through her full lips.

CHAPTER 3

DEATH

The lamb followed the darkness like a thread of song,
each step unwinding what it used to be.
—Anonymous

"Do you understand what would happen to you if you tracked him down?" I moved the weapon in and out of her slowly.

"Nothing. He'll never find out." Her little moan reached my ears, and I lowered my mouth to her throbbing clit and sucked her sensitive skin. She squirmed beneath me, her body begging for more as her juices coated my knife handle. I allowed my fingers to stroke her inner thighs, creating a sensual contrast from the knife's grip. The anticipation was palpable, almost tangible.

"Oh god." Her hips moved to meet the rhythm of my tongue.

Seconds before she came, I pulled the handle out of her and sat up. Her whimper of disappointment filled the room.

"If you tell me why you're looking for my parents' murderer, I will give you permission to come."

She tugged on the ropes restraining her wrists, then stared me down. "Why is this a problem for you?"

A feral growl escaped me as I hovered over her and unfastened my jeans. Once I freed my cock, I plunged inside her so hard her head hit the headboard, but I didn't stop. I wanted to feel her pain, her fear, her desperation for answers.

My hips pumped relentlessly, each thrust harder and deeper than the last. Ella cried out, a mixture of pleasure and suffering escaping her lips. She trembled beneath me, her muscles contracting around my cock with every stroke. It was intoxicating, like a drug that had taken hold of me.

But this wasn't just about pleasure. It was about power. I wanted to show her just how much control I had over her body, over her very being.

I pulled out of her and quickly undid the ropes before I flipped her over on her stomach. Digging my fingers into her hips, I jerked her up, her perky ass begging for my cock.

I ran the tip of my dick along her wet pussy, then over her tight asshole.

"I haven't fucked you here in a long time, little lamb, but you loved my dick inside you that night in the woods." I leaned toward the nightstand, opened the drawer, and removed the bottle of lube. Once I applied an ample amount around my shaft and her hole, I pressed against her. Ella's ass refused to give, and she sucked in an audible gasp.

"I'm going to take you either way, but if you're tense, it will hurt. Or is that what you crave—pain? You had to have known what I would do to you for crossing me."

"I never planned for you to find out," she said through gritted teeth.

I pushed the head of my cock inside her asshole, and a wave of ecstasy ripped through me. Her cry pierced my ears as I worked her a little at a time. Her greedy hole took me inch by inch until I was buried inside of my pretty little slut. Rocking gently at first, I claimed her, then picked up my pace. Finding her clit, I massaged her until her cries of pain turned into moans of pleasure.

"You're such a whore for my cock in your ass. Admit it. I want to hear those words."

"No. You're doing this to punish me, not make me feel good." Her fingers dug into the mattress as I moved in and out of her.

I pinched her clit hard enough to make her yelp, then stroked her to soothe the pain. When I was finished fucking her, she wouldn't be able to sit down for a week.

"Oh, Jesus," she squeaked.

"Say it."

"No."

I picked up the pace, sweat forming on my forehead as I continued.

"Then I'll deny you once again." I pulled out of her and climbed off the bed as she collapsed onto her stomach. Making my way to the bathroom, I discarded my jeans and shirt before I turned on the water and washed myself. I wasn't done with her yet, and by the end she would be begging me to let her come.

Minutes later, I returned to her. She turned her head away, but I saw her tear-stained cheeks.

"Denying me won't change anything, Death. I won't apologize for trying to find your parents' killer."

My little lamb was still feisty and refused to give me what I wanted. "Make no mistake, Ella. I broke you once, and I'll do it again. Apparently, I've been gone for too long, and you've forgotten who you bow to and serve." I grabbed her ankle and spun her around on the bed, then I flipped her onto her back. With a gruff tug, I brought her to the edge of the mattress and knelt before her. I placed her legs over my shoulders and buried my face in her pussy. She shoved her fingers in my hair, gripping it tightly as she rocked against me. My tongue danced around her clit, then dove into her sweet cunt over and over. Ella leaned back but didn't let go of me.

"If this is punishment, then punish me, Death." Her ragged breaths filled the room.

I licked her pussy, my chin slick with her juices. She bucked, and I knew she was about to lose control.

Without warning, I stood and chuckled as her expression twisted from ecstasy to anger.

"Fuck you," she spat.

"I intend to." I flashed her a feral smile while I stroked my cock. She lay back on the mattress, watching my every move as I towered over her, fear and lust dancing across her beautiful face. I positioned myself between her legs, then with one swift push, I plunged into her with such force that her body jolted up the bed, and a helpless moan escaped her lips.

Her eyes widened in terror as she struggled to break free from my grip. The room was a blur as she thrashed around, trying to escape my merciless assault. I grabbed her wrists tighter, applying just enough pressure to keep her still as I delivered violent thrust after violent thrust, her cries of agony echoing in the bedroom.

She wrapped her legs around me, pulling me deeper, desperate for more. Sweat dripped from our bodies, the scent mingling in the air between us. Each plunge brought me closer to my release, but I had to prolong the ecstasy, knowing it would only be more intense when it finally came.

With every pounding stroke, she convulsed beneath me. Her nails raked against my back, leaving trails of fire in their wake. My heart thumped in my chest like a drum as I surrendered to the primal urges that fueled our anger and lust.

With a newfound ferocity, I pushed into her eager cunt, and her moans filled the room.

Finally relaxing, her gaze locked with mine. "Tell me why you don't want me to look into who murdered your parents."

"Because the truth will put you in danger," I grunted.

Ella's cries reached a fever pitch as I pounded into her with unrelenting force, her body writhing and convulsing beneath me. Her slick walls clenched around me, gripping my shaft as if trying to pull me deeper. She was so close, but she hadn't earned her orgasm yet.

I pulled out, leaving her furious and panting.

"Tell me the truth, and I'll make you come." I smirked at her, relishing the control I had over her once again.

She shook her head, still refusing to give in.

I moved to the edge of the bed, and with a determined stride, I returned to the bathroom, leaving her.

"Where are you going?" she demanded in a panicked voice.

Ignoring her question, I snatched up a small white candle and lighter from the side of the claw-foot tub. I lit the wick and approached her once again. After waiting for the wax to melt to just the right temperature, I allowed it to drip onto her bare skin, starting from between her breasts and trailing down her stomach.

With a flick of my wrist, I gathered my glinting knife from the bed and dragged it across her, tracing the trail of wax as red droplets bloomed in its wake.

"Tell me why, Ella. Why did you dare to defy me?"

She quivered with fear as a lone tear escaped her eye, and she held her breath. I continued to cut around the candle drippings, relishing the sight of crimson blood seeping through her porcelain skin. As I reached the tender flesh of her inner thigh, her body convulsed in pain.

"Please, no more. I'll tell you," she pleaded between ragged breaths.

I withdrew my blade, allowing her a brief respite before forcing her to speak. She closed her eyes, steeling herself for what was to come.

"Because I want . . ."

CHAPTER 4

ELLA

A mix of agony and desire twisted my insides, threatening to tear me apart. But I couldn't deny the truth any longer.

"I want to . . ." My voice shook with fear. As I gazed at Death, a wave of darkness engulfed me, drowning out all rational thoughts. It was the same darkness that had consumed me as I repeatedly stabbed John's broken body.

Gritting my teeth before I spoke, I found the courage to share my secret.

"I intend to hunt him down like a rabid animal, ripping his secrets from his throat one by one. I will use every method at my disposal, no matter how brutal or cruel, to extract the truth from him. Why did he target your parents? What drove him to that fateful night? But once I have all the answers, I will make him suffer. Slowly and mercilessly, I will carve into his flesh until he feels every ounce of pain and regret. He'll never know a moment of peace until his final breath escapes his wretched lungs. And then, only then, will justice be served."

He froze in place, his eyes locked on mine, as my words pierced through the air like a sharpened dagger. A shiver traveled down my spine at knowing the weight of what I'd said and its impact on him.

Abruptly, he placed the candle and knife on the nightstand and positioned himself between my legs with a predatory grace. His tongue grazed along my thigh, then his teeth sank into my flesh with a ferocity that made me writhe in both pleasure and pain. "Tell me more, Ella," he growled, his hot breath tickling my core as he trailed kisses up my trembling body. "Tell me how you plan to destroy him."

Every inch of me quivered under the skilled touch of his mouth, my hips arching off the bed in search of release. But he held me firmly in place, his fingers digging into my sensitive skin as I gazed down into his intense stare.

I licked my lips, trying to form the words he wanted to hear . . . and I needed to say.

"I would slide the knife into his thigh and mangle him so he couldn't run. When he stumbled to the ground, I would target areas to inflict the most pain—but not death. Not yet. I would make him suffer just as he made you." I took a deep breath, my heart and mind racing with the images that bombarded my brain.

"He would scream in agony, writhing on the cold, hard floor. This is payback for everything he's done to you. Every tear shed, every sleepless night, every moment of fear and uncertainty. He has to pay."

"Keep going," Death urged.

"I would laugh at the pain etched on his face, his eyes wide with terror as the knife digs deeper into his flesh. I assume he would try to fight back, to scream at me to stop, but his whimpers would only be pitiful sounds that added to my fury. With each slice of the blade, with each new wound inflicted, it would be harder and harder to resist the urge to end his life completely. And then, just as suddenly as it started, it will be over, and the man will lie motionless on the ground." I cleared my throat before I continued. "I sometimes wonder, though. Will it be enough, and will I feel as though justice has been served? Or will my rage cloud my judgment?"

Honestly, I didn't know and didn't care. All that mattered was the knowledge that Sebastian's parents' murderer would have paid for what he'd done. And maybe, just maybe, my husband would be able to find some peace.

"My queen has arrived," he said against my core before he climbed over me. He rubbed the tip of his hard cock over my slick pussy, then slowly pushed inside me.

Pleasure shot through me like lightning splitting the sky as he rocked his hips against me. I wrapped my legs around him, holding his gaze as he stared into the depths of the darkest parts of my soul.

"I want to watch him bleed." I dug my fingers into Death's back, teetering on the edge of losing my body and my mind to him.

"Let it consume you, little lamb. It won't help to fight it. It's always there. Always clawing at your soul until you no longer recognize yourself. But I have always known who you are."

His words calmed me as we connected on a physical and emotional level.

"I will protect you even during the darkest moments." He leaned down and kissed me roughly as if our souls were merging, and he couldn't risk letting me go.

Death quickly rolled over, and I straddled him. Taking my time, I slid up and down his thick, long shaft and moaned.

"Ride my cock, my little whore." His fingers wrapped around my throat and tightened until I could no longer breathe. Death slammed into me and massaged my clit with his other hand as he fucked me.

"Once you kill him, I'll force you to your knees in his blood. My dirty slut will suck me off and milk me dry."

I clawed at his arm, black dots dancing in front of my vision, as my pussy clenched around him. He released me seconds before the orgasm ripped through me. I groaned and then screamed his name as I leaned forward and dug my claws into his chest.

"Goddamn, your cunt is so good." He lifted me off his dick and sat up, a wicked smile curving his mouth. He climbed off the bed and stood.

"On your knees."

I quickly obeyed even though my orgasm left me weak. He fisted my hair and jerked my head back. With a quick move, he shoved himself into my mouth until he hit my throat, and I choked around him.

"You're so beautiful with tears streaming down your cheeks, your mascara running, and my dick between those pretty little lips." He ran his knuckles down my face.

I struggled to breathe, but he held firm.

"Suck it. Worship me like it's the last time you'll have the chance. Show me how much you want my cum."

He pulled back enough for me to drag in a lungful of air, then he slid in and out. His gaze narrowed, and his lips parted. I prepared myself for his release. I sucked and stroked his shaft until his eyes slammed shut, and his hot, sticky substance filled my mouth.

Death stilled, then stared down at me with pride in his expression. He pulled out and knelt in front of me. He wiped my tears away with the pad of his thumb, and I swallowed over the soreness in my throat.

"So beautiful." He kissed my forehead, then dipped his head to my ear. "Tell me, little lamb. Have you found him? Is the man who murdered my parents still alive?"

The air was thick with tension as I struggled to find my voice.

"Yes," I managed to utter in a faint whisper.

In an instant, Death scooped me into his arms and rose to his full height, his gaze blazing with vengeance.

"Who is he?" Death's grip tightened like a vice around my waist as he carried me to the bathroom, a sense of primal urgency driving his movements. He sat me on top of the counter and turned on the shower. Despite our rough sex, Death always made sure to take care of me afterward. It was a twisted but deliciously necessary part of our dynamic.

He tested the water with his fingers before lifting me off the sink and pulling us under the hot spray. His lips crashed onto mine in an intense kiss, his hold on me unrelenting as he sat me down.

"I'm not sure. He has several aliases. I haven't been able to learn much more than what you already found."

He gripped my jaw and leaned my head back, allowing my hair to get wet.

"No more secrets, little lamb. I want to know everything you find out as soon as you do. If he's truly alive, then we will hunt him together."

My mouth went slack as my brows rose in surprise. "You'll let me join you in the . . . kill?" My breasts brushed against his chest as excitement bubbled to life inside me.

His eyes sparked with deadly ferocity and eagerness.

"As long as you're not in danger, you will be by my side."

His lips captured mine, and a surge of adrenaline coursed through my veins. The thrill of the chase and the hunt consumed me as his words sank in. I would finally experience what Death did, and I couldn't wait. I tightened my arms around his neck, pulling him closer as I eagerly surrendered to the unknown.

Each time Death left, my heart broke a little more. Thoughts bombarded my brain as I watched him vanish into the dense, foreboding woods. The babies would return soon, and I couldn't risk Lulu discovering the truth about Death and Sebastian's hidden identity. With every fiber of my being, I vowed to keep my husband and children safe. Lulu would only know the man who adored me and protected us with his life.

I rubbed my arms, trying to shake off the sadness that threatened to engulf me. He would return later that evening, but a sense of dread lingered in the back of my mind. The constant worry over him getting caught never left me. Thankfully, the kids would keep me occupied until he returned, which would ease my anxiety a little.

As much as I loved seeing Death, I was often a single parent due to his absence when he was eliminating sick, twisted men. Maybe I should give Lulu more hours this week and see how it went. I could use the extra help.

The soft hum of a car engine drew me away from my thoughts. My heart raced with eagerness to see the babies as I waited for Lulu's black Kia to appear in the driveway, but my frown deepened when a strange vehicle pulled up instead.

I squinted at the sleek vehicle as it parked, my senses on high alert. The door swung open and a tall, dark-haired man emerged, his expensive suit jacket perfectly tailored to his muscular frame.

"Hi, can I help you?" I placed my hands on my hips. No one had any business being here other than family and friends.

"You sure can." His broad smile reflected his cheery voice, and I tried to relax a little. "You're Ella McCloud, right?"

I gave him a tight smile. "McCloud is my maiden name. It's Fletcher now, but how do you know who I am?"

He tipped his chin up while he sauntered toward me with an air of confidence. The sunlight bounced off his designer sunglasses and temporarily blinded me. My gut twisted with unease as he grew closer, an unfamiliar aura of danger emanating from him. He only met my question with an eerie silence.

I cleared my throat, my pulse pounding in my neck. "What can I do for you?" I asked as I mentally reminded myself not to mention that my husband wasn't home.

He swaggered up the porch steps, stopping mere inches in front of me. The overpowering stench of his cheap aftershave choked me as I saw my stern expression reflected back at me in the dark lenses of his sunglasses.

"A friend sent me."

His cryptic reference to a friend had me nearly bolting into the house and grabbing the gun.

"Please, tell me why you're here or you'll need to leave. This is private property."

He chuckled softly, his gaze darting around as if he was searching for someone. "I personally don't mean you any harm, Ella."

I didn't miss what he'd said—"personally." Taking a few steps back, I edged toward the open front door. "Then who does want to cause me harm?"

After working at the law firm, I was aware that I'd made some enemies since my bosses represented several big criminals. I could easily be on someone's list, but the Safe Horizon Society could also cause issues for any of us helping to relocate families to safety. Hell, it wasn't that long ago that one of them had tried to kill me, and Death had stepped in and ended Stephen on my kitchen floor.

The man tapped the side of his head. "Smart girl, listening to what I'm saying and not just what you want to hear."

Each muscle in me tensed, and I became acutely aware of every sound. Suddenly, a chill slithered down my spine and goosebumps dotted my skin. The tiny hairs on the back of my neck stood on end as a feeling of unease consumed me.

My fingers curled into tight fists, knuckles white as I prepared for a potential fight. "Get out of here," I barked through gritted teeth.

The loose wooden board of the porch creaked ominously behind me. I whipped around to see a hulking figure looming over me. *Run!* My body instinctively kicked into flight mode, but before I could make a move, a meaty hand clamped down on my arm with a viselike grip, trapping me in place.

Suddenly, a searing pain shot through my entire being like a hot needle piercing my skin. My eyes bulged in terror as I stumbled backward, grasping for the railing to steady me. But my legs betrayed me, buckling under the intensity, and I crumpled onto the porch, helpless and at the mercy of the drug that pulsed through my veins.

The late afternoon sun cast long shadows across the yard as my vision blurred and faded in and out of darkness. With a last burst of strength, I turned to face my attacker, their twisted features taunting me as the world began to spin out of control. I desperately tried to fight unconsciousness, but it swallowed me whole as it sent me spiraling helplessly into the depths of oblivion.

CHAPTER 5

DEATH

White wool, black thoughts—a lost lamb carries both until one outweighs the other.
—Anonymous

The dried leaves crunched beneath my booted feet as I hurried through the forest toward my car. I'd jogged a couple of miles after I'd left Ella. By the time I slipped from the tree line, the sun hovered low on the horizon, streaking the sky in deep purples and fading gold. Shadows stretched long across the yard, the last traces of daylight clinging stubbornly to the world before night claimed it. Until then, I would remain hidden.

As badly as I wanted to return to Ella and my children, I had to extinguish the fire burning inside of me. Months had gone by since my last victim, and my bloodlust had returned full force. I needed to kill, to watch the life drain from some pathetic bastard's eyes. I had the power, the ability to play God when necessary, and I was ready. It was easy to murder a twisted son of a bitch for hurting his children, especially since I had my own kids. Even though I had to be careful not to get caught, the urgency to kill faster and to rid the world of evil had started to consume me.

I slowed my pace and listened to my surroundings, but only silence responded. I reached inside my jacket pocket to retrieve my burner phone and tapped out a text message.

Me: Do you have a target for me?

I waited impatiently for a reply, keeping an eye out for anyone that might accidentally stumble across my hiding place. It would be a very bad day for someone if that happened.

My phone vibrated in my palm, and I stared at the screen.

Dope: Are you sure you want one in that area, or a bit farther away from your home base?

I knew he was referring to Ella, and he had a point, but I wouldn't kill tonight. Not yet. I would stalk and prepare, drawing out the excitement and anticipation, then remove the victim from the vicinity. My cock hardened at the thought of taking my time before I devoured my prey.

Me: Give me the information. I'll draw it away from base.

Dope: I'll get details together and message shortly. Hang tight.

A wicked smile eased across my face as I waited for the darkness to descend. Dope, aka Hal, along with Kip set up my kills for me. It not only saved me time, but they helped me space them apart and across the country. But as the days moved on, I was finding it more difficult to leave Ella, Alaric, and Verity. I had to remind myself that I did this for them and for all the families who were suffering at the hands of a maniac.

A dark chuckle slipped from me while I toyed with ideas of how I might torture my next victim.

My cell vibrated again, and I looked at the screen, weeding through Dope's coded-keyword strewn message. A burner phone only protected you so much, but with Dope's hacking skills, we stood a better chance of not getting caught. Even then, he wasn't the best out there, and we weren't ever one hundred percent safe. If I was ever arrested, charges would never stick without evidence, and my men made damn sure there wasn't anything traceable.

Dope: I've let Kip know you're on a bender. Let me know when to send him your way.

Kip had been going off radar occasionally, and I had my concerns about his activity, but as long as he didn't land himself in hot water with the police, I wouldn't jump to conclusions . . . for now. For my peace of mind, I wanted backup, though. Over the years, my cop friend, Ryan, had helped clean up after my kills and had also pointed the detectives in the wrong direction, throwing them off my path.

Me: Will you be available in a week on the East Coast?

Ryan: As long as you fly me out, I'll be there. Give me a heads-up, though.

Me: Always. See you soon.

I tucked the phone into my jacket pocket and pressed my lips into a thin line. Ryan had been one of my closest people since college, when he tracked me to one of my early kills. I was young and dumb, and when he confronted me about my activity, I took him hostage. It didn't last long. He was on board with helping me any way he could since he believed in the cause. Ryan majoring in criminal justice and landing his first job as a cop was icing on the fucking cake. He watched my back and was a key player in my investigation. I just wondered how long he could keep it up without being exposed.

By the time I reached the road, the sun had nearly slipped below the horizon, streaking the sky in deep purples and fading gold. I slipped from the tree line and jogged up the dirt road to my car. I climbed inside and started the engine just as my phone vibrated again. I retrieved it, glowering at the screen before answering.

"What?" I snapped at Dope. He knew better than to call when I was out. The sound of the phone could give me away at any moment, jeopardizing my safety. At one time, I used to turn it off, but if Ella ever needed me . . .

"Man, you know I wouldn't call if it weren't an emergency," Dope said, his voice frantic.

My shoulders pinched as I spoke. "What is it?"

"I was just scrolling through the video footage at Ella's house like you asked me to, and normally it's boring shit I see."

"Get to the point, Dope," I snapped, losing my patience.

"Death, man, she's gone."

I gripped the steering wheel until my knuckles turned white, and I was sure that I would rip it out of the column.

"What the fuck do you mean by 'gone'?" I placed the phone on my lap and tapped the speaker option. "I'm on my way to her place, so you better talk fast."

I hit the accelerator, rocks and dirt spitting from my tires as I tore ass down the road.

"A Nissan Sentra pulled up and some guy in a suit was talking to her. There was another man too. He came up behind her and stabbed her in the neck with a needle. She dropped to her knees on the porch. A few men went into the house, but Ella was carried to the car and tossed in the trunk."

A roar tore from my throat as I tried to process what Dope was telling me.

"I backed up and looked at more of the footage, and the only good news I have is that the kids were still with Lulu. I think they're safe, but we need to make sure."

The car bounced along the dirt road as I sped toward her home, panic ripping through me as I realized that my worst fear had manifested. I'd pissed someone off, and it had put Ella and my family in danger.

"We have to act fast. Call the men and get to the airport. You know what to do. I'll reach out soon, but first I need to look for her. Maybe they didn't take her. Maybe they photoshopped the video or some shit." As soon as the words left my mouth, I winced. Why would anyone threaten me and not act? If someone pulled that crap, they would die the moment I found them.

As my mind raced with thoughts of worst-case scenarios, a tiny glimmer of optimism kept me going. Maybe they altered the footage or something. It wasn't likely, but I had to hold on to any shred of hope.

Silence crept over the line. I knew I was reaching, but she couldn't be gone. She fucking couldn't be.

Seconds later, I saw it. The house with its door wide open, taunting me with its emptiness. A surge of fury rushed through my body, igniting every muscle with blazing determination. My nostrils flared with contempt, and I gritted my teeth with a fierce resolve to prove Dope wrong.

"I'm here. I'll keep you posted."

"Yeah, we'll see you soon. Hang tight." Dope disconnected the call as I slowly approached the driveway. I pulled over and parked the car in the thick of the trees. I needed to note the tire tracks of the vehicle Dope mentioned, and if I drove over them it would be much more difficult to get what I needed. Proof, for starters. My thoughts teetered on the edge of insanity as I hurried to Ella's place on foot.

My knife strapped to my leg gave me little comfort as my mind and heart warred with each other. I refused to acknowledge Dope's words that she was gone until I saw it for myself.

Quietly, I took the steps to the porch and slipped inside her home. My eyes widened in horror as I took in the sight in front of me. Verity's stuffed bear had been ripped apart, stuffing bursting from its stomach. One eye dangled from a thread as the other stared directly at me. Alaric's blanket had been shredded, and the pictures of Ella and my children had been smashed and broken. The couch and chair were turned over, and magazines were strewn all over the floor. I removed my weapon and crept into the kitchen, hoping to catch the son of a bitch responsible for entering Ella's house without permission. A surge of primal satisfaction jolted through my body at the mere thought of carrying out my revenge, my fingers itching with anticipation. I forced myself to maintain composure, to stay laser focused on the task at hand.

The sound of me clenching my teeth reached my ears while I took note of the kitchen: cabinet doors were open, and food and broken dishes littered the floor. My nostrils flared as rage ignited inside me. No longer caring if I was quiet or not, I raced up the stairs and flung open the door to the kids' room. Empty. Hopefully, they were still safe with Lulu, but I had to check the rest of the house before I called her. If the kids were okay, I didn't want to scare the shit out of our nanny.

The beat of my heart pounded in my ears as I ran down the hall to Ella's bedroom. The papers that had scattered the floor and bed previously were gone, but so was she. I searched the bathroom, closet, and every fucking nook and cranny upstairs, then downstairs. There was no sign of her. A sharp pain shot through my head as sweat coated my forehead, the fear and anger of losing her ripping through me. I returned to the living room as the blinding agony dropped me to my knees.

"This isn't the fucking time for a migraine," I snapped as I pounded on the fucking floor. A feral roar ripped through me as the truth sank in. Ella was gone. Fear taunted me as images of her lifeless body took center stage in my mind's eye. I couldn't allow myself to go there. My hands clenched and unclenched as I said, "You motherfuckers better run because I'm coming for you."

I grabbed my head, groaning, as the room faded from sight.

CHAPTER 6

SEBASTIAN

The living room blurred in and out as I struggled to focus and stand. The headaches had grown more frequent, and I was worried something was seriously wrong with me. Since my parents had died, I tended to lose time and not be able to remember what had happened. I'd become a pro at masking those gaps, but maybe I should talk to Ella and see a doctor. My mind immediately went to worst-case scenarios. What if the migraines were a sign of something worse, like a brain tumor? I would need medical treatment. I owed it to myself and my family to take better care of myself, to be the best husband and father I could be.

I stood slowly and grabbed the top of the recliner as I found my balance. Frowning, I blinked several times as I attempted to clear my vision.

"What the hell?" Toys and books were haphazardly thrown on the floor, and the furniture was on its side. "Ella?" I called out. Confused, I walked toward the kitchen to find an even bigger mess. *What the fuck happened? Why don't I remember any of this?*

Fear shot through me as I ran down the hall looking for Ella and the kids. Not seeing anyone, I rushed upstairs to search for them. Once again, all I found were clothes and toys all over the kids' room and the same in mine and Ella's. Even with the twins, Ella and I maintained a clean place. This was out of the ordinary and nearly doubled me over with anxiety.

"Ella! Ella!" My voice grew frantic as a harsh possibility slammed into my chest. I dug my phone from my jacket pocket. I always carried a burner with me for the Safe Horizon Society. My first call was to Ella, but it rang and rang before it went to her voicemail.

My forehead creased as I waited for the beep. "Baby, it's your husband. Please call me as soon as you get this message." I hung up and swallowed over the lump in my throat.

I immediately dialed Lulu's number to make sure my babies were safe with her. With the house in chaos and not hearing from Ella, I needed to know if they were okay.

She answered on the first ring. "Hello?"

"Hey, it's Sebastian. How are the kids doing?"

"We're taking a walk in the park. It's such a beautiful day, I thought they would enjoy the fresh air."

I heard the kids babbling in the background, and my heart skipped a beat with the knowledge that they were unharmed. Fear tiptoed down my back as I suspected that, unlike my children, their mother wasn't safe.

"Could you keep them a few extra hours today? I'll Venmo you the cash."

"Sure. When would you like them home?"

I didn't miss the concern in her voice. We rarely asked for extra time, but I needed to make calls and find my wife. If I lost my shit, I didn't want to terrify my kids.

"I'll give you a call."

She agreed and we said our goodbyes. After I hung up, I tried to fit the puzzle pieces together, fearing the worst. Then I remembered when Ella had finally told me the truth about Stephen coming after her when I was out of town. She promised he was no longer an issue, but I wasn't clear on what she meant. No matter how hard I pressed her, she just assured me he wasn't a problem, and he was out of our lives. Jumping to the bleakest conclusion possible, I couldn't help but wonder if he'd found her. One thing I knew: he was a mean motherfucker with zero conscience. Unless he needed you as a means to an end, he'd rather slit your throat than spit on you.

My phone buzzed in my palm, and I answered without looking at the screen.

"Ella?" Hope burst inside my chest, then disappeared as soon as I heard Dope's voice.

"Bass?" I could almost hear him cringe.

Unable to hide my irritation, I said, "Who else would it be?"

"No, dude, my bad." He paused before he spoke again. "Are you . . . are you at home?"

"Yeah, and shit isn't right. Something is really wrong . . . I . . . I can't find Ella." My tone cracked with the confession.

"We're on the way."

My shoulders tensed as I realized Dope knew something.

"What is it, mate? Don't draw it out. Tell me where my wife is."

I visualized Dope holding up his hands in surrender. He was used to my temper, but this time it would be a lot worse if he stalled and hid shit from me.

"I was calling to see if she was there. A few minutes ago, I checked the camera footage, and some men showed up and wrecked your house and . . . took Ella."

My gaze narrowed. "You weren't watching live?"

"I can't monitor twenty-four seven, man," Dope admitted, guilt heavy in his voice. "I check recordings every few hours, run analytics for unusual patterns. But they knew our schedule, knew when I'd be focused on helping relocate that family in Oregon. They timed it perfectly, which means one thing: someone was watching. They could have hacked my system. I'm good, but shit happens, and there's always someone better out there. I'm sorry, man."

Tears pricked my eyes as I struggled to digest what the fuck he'd just said. "No way did I hear you right." I realized I was grasping at straws. The evidence was right in front of me, but I couldn't believe it.

"From the earlier video, I think the kids are with Lulu. I suspect she'll be home soon. I called everyone, and we're all on the way to the airport."

I shook my head, confusion settling over me like a wet blanket. "The kids are definitely with Lulu. I've already called her." I massaged the back of my neck, the sharp headache giving way to a dull pounding. "Why is my plane in Oregon?"

"Riley and I were heading out to help a family, Bass. You had your pilot fly over. It was actually perfect timing, but we're on our way to you. Well, Kip and I are." The tension dripped off his words. "I just pulled up and Kip is on the tarmac. We're on our way, man. We'll find her. I swear to fucking god we'll find her."

"You're sure you saw someone take her? The shit you smoked wasn't too strong and you hallucinated?"

"I'm positive. I watched the footage several times. We can go over it when I'm there."

"Screw that. I'll look at it while you and Kip are in the air."

Dope sucked in a sharp breath. "Then go straight to 1:23 this afternoon. There's nothing else to see, so don't waste your time."

"I'll see you in a few hours. Call if you find anything else." I didn't wait for him to speak before I hung up and tossed my phone onto the bed. Hurrying to my laptop, I flipped it open and retrieved the camera footage. I rarely looked at it since I didn't want Ella to think I was spying on her, but we had a lot of enemies, and I couldn't take a chance on not picking up danger.

I dropped onto the edge of the bed as I frantically pulled up the surveillance footage. My pulse pounded against my neck as I fast forwarded to the timestamp Dope had mentioned. And there it was, a black Nissan Sentra pulling up to my house. The hairs on my arms stood on end as a tall figure in a dark suit and sunglasses emerged from the car. I cranked up the volume, listening to every word of the conversation. The security system, meant only for outside threats, suddenly seemed useless as I cursed myself for allowing this to happen. I forced myself to focus: I needed to hear every last detail of what that son of a bitch said when he took my wife.

Horror slithered through my veins as I watched a man creep up behind Ella, then jab her in the neck with a needle. She stumbled; fear was etched into her beautiful face as she grabbed the railing of the porch. Within seconds, she slumped forward, and the man who had injected her scooped her up and carried her to the Nissan Sentra. I yelled at the video as I witnessed him put a helpless Ella in the car's trunk and close it.

Two other men entered my home while the guy in the suit swapped out both license plates on the car.

"You stupid son of a bitch. You think that will keep me from finding you?" I focused on the car and caught a glimpse of the license number. I hit the button to pause the feed and grabbed the notebook and pen Ella always kept on her nightstand. I scribbled down one letter and two numbers on the Wisconsin plate. Unfortunately, I suspected it wouldn't be the only time those plates would be changed. I had to act fast.

Once I located my phone again, I texted Dope that I was going to file a missing person's report with the police. Before I could dial 911, my phone vibrated.

"Yeah?"

"You can't call the cops, man." Dope cleared his throat. "Wait until we get there, but you have to trust me. Keep them out of it."

"You're not making any damn sense, Dope."

"What if those men are tied to the Safe Horizon Society? Every family we've worked hard to help might be jeopardized. Not to mention we'll all get arrested and put in jail. We can't do Ella any good if we're all behind bars."

"Yeah, you're right. I hadn't thought about that. I'm fucking out of my mind right now." I rubbed my temple.

"That's what you have us for. To help you think straight. I'll text you if I learn anything else."

"Later." I gripped the phone in my hand. A hitch in Dope's voice told me he was hiding something. He knew more than he was telling me. When the guys got here, I would pry it out of him one way or another. For now, I had to try to keep a clear head and focus on my twins.

CHAPTER 7

ELLA

With a sharp gasp, I snapped my eyes open, and my breath caught in my throat as I took in the dimly lit room that lay before me. The single light bulb swung back and forth, its flickering illumination casting eerie shadows that seemed to dance around the cramped kitchen. I scanned the space, taking in the tattered orange couch and ancient television set across from me. I was in the far corner of a living room, but whose and why? A combination of body odor and stale air smell filled my nose, triggering a violent sneeze that echoed off the walls. As I recoiled from the sneeze, my head collided with something hard behind me, sending a loud thunk echoing through the area and causing stars to skip across my vision.

"Shit!" My skull throbbed as I pressed against the spot where it had smacked the unforgiving glass. Taking a deep, ragged breath, I forced myself to survey my surroundings. The space was suffocatingly small, and as my eyes adjusted to the faint light, terror gripped my chest and squeezed until my heart stuttered in fear. Suddenly aware of the confining walls closing in on me, I frantically searched for an escape. My fingertips scrambled at the smooth surface that served as my prison: four glass walls and a cement floor. There were several openings—most were small but some large enough for a hand to fit through—mocking me. In a desperate attempt at freedom, I reached for the ceiling, but even standing was impossible in this cramped space. Panic consumed me as I quickly realized there was no way out.

"Let me out!"

How did I end up here? Flashes of memories came to mind—a man in a suit, another one sneaking up behind me on my porch. Terror and anger surged through me. *Fuck! Fuck! Fuck!* I'd been drugged and kidnapped. Tears threatened to spill down my cheeks, but I refused to let them fall. If I wanted to survive, I needed to keep a clear head. Forcing myself to remain calm, I reminded myself it would only be a matter of time before Death and our friends searched for me. With their help, I wouldn't be here for long. The thought of being stolen from my family intensified my rage, and I vowed to kill the motherfuckers who had taken me away from my babies and husband.

"Listen up, motherfuckers! You took the wrong girl. Let me out before you regret being born." I released an ear-piercing scream and kicked at the cage, hoping to find a weak point. "Let me out! Who are you, and what do you want from me?" Sweat beaded on my forehead from the exertion, and I wiped it away with the back of my arm. My pulse pounded so hard my ears rang as I smacked the wall until my fist throbbed with pain. Although I was terrified, I needed to save my energy and use my damn brain to get out of here. I forced myself to take in my surroundings, but all I could make out were rows of stuffed animals on the opposite wall. Most were clowns, but then my attention landed on a Chucky doll. Shivering from the cold temperature of the room, I rubbed my arms and stared at the creepy Chucky. That movie had always weirded me out, but this was on a whole new fucking level of weird.

Slamming my eyes closed, I forced myself to take several deep breaths. Panicking wouldn't help me get the hell out of here. I slowed my breathing, calmed my mind, and imagined myself and Death killing the pieces of shit who stole me. That anger would drive me and keep me sane. Revenge gave me a little something to look forward to as well.

A sudden sound pierced the silence, shattering my meditation. My head snapped to the side, and I saw a figure approaching, his dark hair standing up in wild tufts. He wore tattered jeans covered in dirt and a faded navy shirt that clung to his emaciated frame. Had he also been imprisoned in this underground cell? His gaunt appearance evoked pity and fear from me in equal measure. I needed to be careful around him, but my mind was already racing with plans to escape. If only I could break free from this glass prison. *Think, Ella! Pay attention to your surroundings and take notes.*

"She's awake. She's awake." He clapped his hands together as he chanted. The high pitch of his voice sent chills racing down my arms.

My throat suddenly grew raw and dry, but I forced myself to speak. "Who are you?"

He spun around, arms flung out like blades of a helicopter. His grin became manic as he spoke. "It's been too long since I've had company. So, when the boss called and said there was a package for me, I couldn't contain my excitement." He stopped spinning and his smile widened even further, revealing yellowed teeth. "Allow me to properly introduce myself, Ella McCloud Fletcher. I am Xavier Hyde."

"Like Jekyll and Hyde," I muttered. Anxiety set in as I scrambled to come up with a plan. Should I attempt to befriend him and gain his trust until I could make my move? Or should I resort to threats and fight off the son of a bitch? My mind raced with the few options I had, but one thing was crystal clear: I had to time it perfectly. I only had one chance, and I couldn't fuck it up.

My thoughts were cut short as he approached, and I gasped in horror. Crawling over his shoulder was a massive spider, its hairy legs inching closer and closer toward me.

Trembling, I pointed at him and stammered out, "There's a s-s-spider on you."

A cruel grin twisted his lips as he looked at me with large, wild eyes. "Yes, there are many here. You'll see them."

My heart dropped as I realized the gravity of the situation. "Many?" I croak out. "What kind are they?"

"My masterpiece! I have worked for years to breed the perfect spider, and here they are—big, hairy, and extremely venomous," he replied. "They love dark places to hide. Don't worry, Ella McCloud Fletcher. They only hurt if they bite."

My hands trembled uncontrollably as I prayed that the venomous creatures wouldn't attack. But deep down, I understood that my fate rested on their unpredictable nature and my quick thinking.

I gulped as I wondered how dangerous they were and what would happen if one bit me. If there were a lot of spiders like Xavier said, there could be more than one bite.

"Please, I'm begging you. Don't let them hurt me." My body shook with my pleas. "You don't understand, you don't want me here. I'm involved with very powerful people, and I don't want you to get killed." *I definitely want to hurt you, though.*

His maniacal laugh echoed off the cement floor and walls.

"Don't worry that pretty little head of yours. If you behave, then the spiders won't get near you. You have my word. I'll keep you safe."

Before I realized it, I opened my damn mouth and said, "You're holding me hostage, so what in god's name makes you think I can trust you?"

Xavier's smile fell, and he knelt next to me, the glass the only thing between us. The spider climbed down his arm as he placed his palm against the side of the cage . . . right next to a large hole that was definitely big enough for the creature to crawl through. I would kill that motherfucker the second he entered my tiny space. Thank god I still had my tennis shoes on. My sundress offered little protection from the frigid temperature or the critters, but by damn, I would beat the hell out of the spiders.

"My little pet wants to meet you."

The venomous spider scurried through the small hole and down the side of the cage. My mind was consumed with terror as I desperately searched for a way out. But then I saw it, my only chance. With a burst of adrenaline, I lifted my foot and brought it down with all my might, crushing the bastard against the glass with a sickening crunch. Guts and legs splattered across the floor and wall, creating a disgusting mess.

Xavier's face contorted in horror, and he released a bloodcurdling scream. His dark eyes locked on mine, filled with anguish and betrayal.

"Why would you do that? He was my friend."

I couldn't believe what I was hearing. "We clearly don't have the same definition of friendship." A wave of disgust washed over me as I wiped the remains of the spider off my shoe and onto the cold concrete floor. Meeting his gaze head-on, I delivered my ultimatum.

"If you keep me safe from these monsters, then we can be friends. Otherwise, I can't protect you when my husband comes for me."

His attention darted to the dark corner behind me, where two more spiders skittered closer to my cage.

"You'll be my friend?" His voice trembled with fear and desperation, tears glistening in his eyes.

My insides twisted in disgust at the thought of befriending him, but I had no choice if I wanted to survive.

"Of course," I replied, trying to ignore the spiders inching closer. "I bet we have a lot in common. And you'll definitely need me on your side when my husband finds me."

He nodded, his attention flickering back to the spiders. "I . . . I would like someone to eat dinner with." The misery and loneliness in his voice were palpable.

My stomach churned at the thought, but I forced a smile, unable to meet his stare or bear looking at the grotesque creatures any longer. "Then keep me safe, and I'll have dinner with you."

He nodded eagerly, his eyes wild with excitement. "I'll take care of you. Be right back." With that, he scurried away, leaving me alone with the unsettling presence of the little monsters and an uneasy feeling in the pit of my stomach.

Anxiety speared me, and I searched the floor and cage, but I didn't see the venomous beasts inside again.

Xavier's return was announced by the clanging of metal. My heart pounded in my ears as he approached holding several large plugs to seal the holes in the glass prison. Panic set in as I noticed them at the top—my only source of oxygen. With each plug that was secured, my breathing became shallower and more frantic. Finally, Xavier produced a key from his pocket and slid it into the lock on the structure. He unlocked the front panel, and hope surged through me. Was he going to let me out?

He reached in and held a palm out to me. "You've been sitting for hours, and your legs might be asleep."

How was this man vicious one minute and kind the next? I took his hand and allowed him to assist me out of my confined quarters. Slowly, I stood and stretched. My body rebelled at the sudden movements with a sharp spasm in my back and a searing cramp in my calf. But it was nothing compared to the slimy and chilling feeling that consumed my insides at his touch.

"Thank you. It feels nice to stand." If I broke through his distorted reality, maybe he would help me escape, but it would take a while to earn his trust.

"Not for long." His cackle filled the room, and I cringed. "Let's get ready for dinner." Xavier grabbed my biceps and pulled me along after him.

For being so skinny, he had a surprisingly firm grip, and I suspected he was much stronger than he appeared. I had to be careful and choose my time to run carefully, or I would only manage to piss him off.

"Do you cook?" I didn't give a fuck what he did, but I needed conversation.

"I'm an excellent cook." He nodded excitedly.

I scanned the little room and searched for a door of any kind, but I didn't see any yet. Three dirty windows lined one of the walls, but they were too small for me to crawl through. As night fell, the basement grew even darker. I had lost track of time since my watch was taken, but I estimated that hours had passed, judging by the sound of crickets beginning to chirp in the distance.

Nestled in the shadows lurked a kitchen table, its surface stained with dried blood. As Xavier flicked on another light, a swarm of spiders scattered and the true horror of the room was revealed. My pulse pounded wildly against my neck as I realized the gravity of the situation.

Panic surged through me as my desperate gaze darted around the tiny space, searching for any glimmer of hope. Suddenly, my attention locked onto the family seated at the table. Their once living bodies were now preserved and posed like grotesque dolls, their faces frozen in eerie twisted grins. A surge of revulsion ripped through me as I came to a horrifying realization—at one time these were real people. Had he slaughtered them like animals and saved them as trophies?

"Meet my mother, father, and little sister." His voice held a sickening pride as he gestured toward each figure.

My stomach churned as Xavier proudly introduced each member of his family with a nonchalant wave in their direction. Bile burned up my throat. I turned my head and puked all over the floor. A string of saliva clung to the corner of my mouth, and I wiped it off with the back of my hand, scared shitless to look at him. He was much more deranged than I'd initially realized.

"You don't like my work? It took me a very long time to preserve them." His tone was laced with disappointment. "I've practiced on animals all my life, so humans were a challenge, but one I loved."

What the fuck! He did all of this? No one else helped him?

I'd better talk fast. "I'm so sorry. No, your work is amazing. It's just that whatever drug they gave me is making me nauseous."

He blinked several times, and I suspected he was trying to figure out if I was giving him a line of shit or not.

"I suppose that would upset your stomach." He pulled out an empty chair at the table. "Sit. Let me get you some soup to eat. It will help."

Horrified at the thought, my legs trembled. I sank into the seat, then realized I needed to make sure no creepy crawlies were blending into the color of the wood. I jumped up and looked around the chair, table, and floor. Maybe our activity had scared the disgusting bastards off and they would leave me alone for now.

Xavier sang as he opened a small, dirty, and scuffed white refrigerator and then removed a large bowl.

"Tick tock, little gears spinning round. Each perfect piece makes such a lovely sound. I craft my machines with meticulous care. While your city sleeps, unaware, unaware.

"Oh, how they dance to my mechanical song. Never suspecting anything's wrong. My clockwork children will rise with the dawn. By then it will be far too late, far too gone.

"Ratchets and springs, such delicate things. Like puppet masters pulling invisible strings. Each calculation precisely designed to leave your precious order far behind.

"Wind them up tight, set them just right. Release them all on this wonderful night. My beautiful chaos about to unfold. A symphony of brass and tarnished gold.

"You called me mad, locked me away, but genius needs no light of day. In darkness deep my work was done. And now at last my time has come.

"The gears are turning, can't you hear? The moment of truth drawing near. My masterpiece about to start as all your world falls apart.

"Final tick . . . final tock . . . Let the clockwork madness walk."

The words of his song cast even more gloom over my situation. Each note pierced my mind like shards of glass, amplifying my already suffocating dread. The haunting melody painted a vivid image of death and destruction, leaving me paralyzed with fear. From the sound of it, he planned on killing more people, and I suspected I was one of them.

"Chicken noodle soup is good for the soul," he said, pulling me from my thoughts.

"I love soup. Thank you." I sat on my hands so when he turned his back to me, I wouldn't run over to him and slam his head against the wall. I would have to wait before I attacked him since I had to figure out an exit strategy first . . . like where the damn door was and what I could use as a weapon.

"It's good for the soul. Good for the soul." He busied himself and poured two bowls full, and then he put them in the microwave and warmed them up.

"How long have you been down here?" I had a million questions for him, but I had to be careful to not piss him off. I stared at his sister and cringed. How could Xavier stuff his own parents and sister after killing them? If he hated them enough to end their lives, why did he have them at the kitchen table? *To create the perfect family.* If that was true, what the hell was he planning for me?

My thoughts ran rampant as I tried to figure out why I was here. Maybe he'd been watching me and decided I would be a good addition to his group. A sharp needling sensation spread through my chest as I struggled to swallow, the feeling as devastating as an open wound.

"Not sure. Off and on for a few years. I needed a place to hide after . . ." He tilted his head toward his family. "They were going to leave me. Said I was fucking cuckoo. How can you leave your son? That's when it occurred to me to keep them alive forever . . . with me. They can't leave me now." The corners of his mouth curled up into a sneer.

"Is that what you're going to do to me?" My voice hovered above a whisper. I wasn't sure I wanted to know. "I have babies at home. You wouldn't want me to be away from them for long, right? You know what it's like to miss your family so much it breaks your heart."

His brows knitted together.

I continued, hoping to break through his twisted thinking. "Twins. They're nine months old, and they need their mother. Please, please let me go."

Conflict twisted his features as he stared at me. "Boss wants you alive for now."

His boss? If Xavier wasn't behind all of this, then who was, and how could I pull the information from Xavier? His words bounced around in my head as I tried to piece together the answers. Then my brain latched on to what else he'd said, and a big sigh of relief escaped me with the news he wasn't going to kill me . . . today. Maybe that meant I had time to figure out how to get away from Xavier, but only if the spiders didn't get to me first.

I tucked my hair behind my ears as he retrieved the bowls from the microwave and set them on the table. He hurried to a drawer, pulled it open, and removed two spoons.

"Eat, eat." He handed me the utensil before he sat down next to me.

I stared at the soup, wondering if there were spider legs in it as well as the few noodles I could identify. I stirred it, hesitant to take a bite until Xavier began to loudly slurp down the meal. If I wanted to keep up my energy, I had to eat. As I lifted a spoonful to my mouth, I glanced sideways at Xavier.

"Who had you kidnap me?" I took a tiny taste of my dinner, and to my surprise, it was good. My stomach growled in agreement.

He tilted his head toward my bowl. "Don't worry about that. Eat. Then you can tell me why you married a serial killer."

Thank god I had plenty of practice mastering my expressions while working for attorneys. My face remained stoic as I slightly tipped my chin and stared at him. "I have no idea what you're talking about."

He leaned in close, his body only inches from mine, his putrid breath assaulting my senses. His bloodshot eyes bore into me with an insane intensity, the manic darkness that possessed him now fully focused on me. I could feel his madness radiating off him in waves, suffocating me with its ferocity.

Then he said, "I know your secrets, Ella. All of them."

A loud cackle burst from him as he shifted in his chair, grinning like he'd just won the war. I had news for him—he wouldn't live long enough to see the end of it.

Time blurred in the cage. Without my watch, I was left with no way to mark the passing hours except the sporadic appearances of the spiders that seemed to dance at the edges of my vision. Sometimes I wasn't sure if they were real or if isolation was already breaking down my grip on reality.

"Do you know why I chose glass?" Xavier's high-pitched voice drifted through the darkness as he approached. He'd been watching me for what felt like hours, his presence a constant reminder of my captivity.

I remained silent, refusing to engage. My throat was raw from earlier screams that had earned me nothing but his amusement.

"It's because I want to see you change." He pressed his palm against the wall. Xavier's voice deepened as he spoke. "Watch as the woman who thinks she's strong enough to handle Death crumbles into something . . . more manageable . . . more moldable."

A spider descended on a thread directly in front of my nose. I jerked back and hit my head against the glass. Xavier's laugh echoed through the room.

"Did you know that one bite from my pet would make you very sick? It would take a week for the venom to kill you, though." He tapped the spot where the spider now rested. "But that's too quick. Too merciful. I prefer to watch the mind dissolve first."

"Fuck you," I spat, my voice trembling.

"Such fire." He pressed his face close to the wall that separated us. "But fire needs oxygen to burn. And in there? Well, let's just say I control how much you get to breathe." He clapped his hands and then threw his head back and cackled.

To demonstrate that he held all the power, he moved to the air holes I relied on and slowly began to plug them, one by one. My chest tightened as panic clawed at my throat.

"Please," I whispered, hating the weakness in my voice.

He uncovered the holes but kept his hand hovering near them. "See how quickly you break? How easily you beg? Death would be so disappointed." His words slithered through the cage like poison. "But don't worry. Soon you'll forget all about him. Soon you'll learn to plead for my approval instead."

How could he have possibly discovered the truth about Death? How could he have learned about the closely guarded secret that those who cherished Sebastian above all else had fought tooth and nail to keep hidden? The thought of everyone I loved being exposed to this evil man was enough to make my blood run cold.

My stomach churned as he pressed something against the glass—a photograph. It was me, sleeping in my bed, taken through our bedroom window. "I've been watching you for months. Learning your habits. Your fears." He showed another photo of me with the twins at the park. "Everything you think is yours? It was only borrowed time."

Tears streamed down my face as I realized the extent of his surveillance, of his obsession. How long had he been plotting this? How many times had he watched me while I thought I was safe?

"You're going to be my masterpiece," he whispered, his breath fogging the glass and his eyes wild. "My perfect bride, preserved forever in this beautiful cage. But first . . ." He gestured to the spiders gathering in the corners. "First, we have to strip away everything you think you are." His maniacal sneer sent me scurrying backward.

I curled into myself, trying to make my body as small as possible in the confined space. The spiders seemed to multiply in the shadows, their presence a constant reminder of my helplessness. Xavier's soft humming filled the air, a twisted lullaby that would haunt me if I ever slept again.

"Sweet dreams, my love," he sang as he dimmed the lights until I was left in near total darkness. "Tomorrow we'll peel away another layer of the woman you used to be."

As his footsteps faded, I pressed my forehead against my knees and tried to hold on to memories of Sebastian, Death, and my children. But in the suffocating confines of the glass cage, even those began to feel like dreams, while Xavier's psychological torture became my new reality.

CHAPTER 8

SEBASTIAN

Time stood still, yet it blurred past, cruel and merciless, until my friends finally arrived. Being alone in the house was maddening, and I desperately tried to make sense of the chaotic situation. A thick haze settled in my mind, like a foreign presence had taken up residence in my brain and was smothering all rational thought. It was almost as if someone else was in my head, but that was ridiculous. *Then why have I felt like that most of my life?*

I rubbed my face vigorously with trembling hands, hoping to shake off the overwhelming confusion, but it only amplified the intense pounding in my chest. My entire world had flipped upside down, and I was shaken to my very being. Everything was unraveling before my very eyes, and I felt helpless against it.

"We need to make a list of suspects." I paced the living room, moving some of the still scattered toys out of my way with my foot. Kip and Dope had finally arrived twenty minutes ago, and we were digging in and brainstorming to find my wife. Three heads had to be better than one panicked one.

"I've already started," Kip said, shoving his fingers through his dark hair. Many people had a difficult time telling us apart. We were the same height with dark hair and broad shoulders. Dope, on the other hand, was much shorter, thinner, and his red hair stood out in a crowd. "With Horizon, we've made several enemies, and the list is long."

Dope nodded in agreement.

"How the fuck did this happen?" I clenched my fists in frustration, digging my nails into my palms as I frantically searched for a solution to Ella's kidnapping. My heart pounded in my chest as I turned to my friends and ran my fingers through my hair, pulling at it in agitation, as I tried to see every angle of the situation. But no matter how hard I looked, all I saw was fear and despair reflected back at me from my friends' expressions.

I swallowed over the dryness in my throat. "Stephen . . . He came after Ella last year. Maybe he's pissed because he can't find his wife and kids, so he decided to take *my* wife. When we helped his family escape his sorry ass, he saw Ella when we were loading his wife and kids into the van and later paid her a visit. Ella promised me that he wasn't a problem, but I think she was just saying that so I wouldn't worry."

Kip rubbed his stubbled chin as he shifted in his chair. At least I'd had the presence of mind to set the furniture upright again.

"Let's go through the list," Dope suggested.

Kip nodded in agreement before he spoke. "I started eliminating people that didn't seem likely to be a huge threat or to know who we are, but I'll share those names too."

I urged him to continue. As Kip ticked off possible suspects one by one, then mentioned who they were and their families, nothing seemed to fit. No one other than Stephen.

"Why isn't Stephen on that list? We should put a tail on the sick bastard and see what we can learn," I said.

"He's not a suspect, Bass. I promise," Dope explained, his expression grim.

"What do you mean?" I pinned him with a glare. "Everyone is a suspect until we find my wife." My voice boomed through the room, my temper rising along with it.

Kip and Dope glanced at each other, then Dope said, "He's dead, Bass. That's why he's not on the list of people we need to look into."

My jaw clenched, and the muscles in my face jumped with the news. Anxiety and fear had consumed me, leaving me constantly on edge that he would come for Ella, and now I was hearing he was dead? *What the hell.* "Why didn't anyone bother to inform me?" My voice rose in a mix of shock and anger, causing those around me to recoil.

"Because it was managed, and there was no need to bug you when you needed to focus on your family. It's why you have us: to take care of problems so you don't have to."

I drew in a deep breath, calming myself as much as possible under the circumstances. "If this ever happens again, tell me right away. Stop trying to fix it all. That kind of information is critical for me to know about. It's a matter of keeping my family safe." Unease about the situation hovered around me. *What is he not telling me?* "How did he die?" I needed to know the answer since I had been so sure that he was the one that had taken Ella.

"Not long after he tried to hurt Ella, he was . . ." Dope shot Kip another look. "He was in a car accident."

My brow arched. "You're clearly blowing sunshine up my ass. What are you hiding?"

Kip leaned back in his chair and scrubbed his jaw with his fingers. "I think that we should talk about some stuff, Bass, but why don't you fly Ryan and Cami out to help? Lulu is fine, but she has no idea what we do in the society and . . . you know, other things. We need to keep her out of it as much as possible. I feel Cami would keep that secret safe. Plus, the kids need someone they're comfortable with, like their Aunt Cami. We have a lot of work to do."

My gaze narrowed on him. "If I bring Ryan and Cami over, will you two tell me what you're hiding?"

Kip and Dope answered "Yes" in unison. A lead ball dropped to the pit of my stomach as I reached for my phone in my back pocket. At first, I hadn't been a fan of Ryan, but as he and Cami spent more time with us, we'd become good friends.

My attention bounced between Kip and Dope. "Since Ryan is a cop, if I call him, he'll learn about the society and our work. Do you think we can trust him not to arrest us or share the information?"

Dope leaned forward and propped his elbows on his knees, and exhaustion flickered across his features. "Yeah, we're pretty sure we can. Besides, the most important thing is to find Ella. He won't turn us in and have us arrested at least until after she's home, safe and sound. It's a chance we have to take. My personal opinion? We can trust him with our lives, and Ella's too."

I chewed on Dope's words before I turned to Kip. "Your thoughts?"

"Yeah, I agree with Dope. Ryan is on our side. We don't need to worry about him right now. Let's just find your wife, and we'll deal with any consequences later."

I didn't miss the glint of uncertainty in his eyes. "Okay." I located Ryan's number in my contacts and placed the call. He and Cami were three hours behind us, which made it seven in the evening there. I had no idea if he was working or not.

After the third ring, he picked up. "Hey, man. How are things?"

I pinched the bridge of my nose, my temples throbbing with the sheer stress of the situation. "I need your help. Cami's too." I sucked in a breath. Once I told him, there was no going back, but my best friends were right: we needed their help, consequences be damned. "Someone took Ella."

An audible gasp filled the line. "What the fuck? Surely I didn't hear you right."

"You heard me. Someone stole her right off our front porch. It's all on video." My head hung down, and I massaged the back of my neck. "Can you two fly out? I'll need Cami to help with the kids."

"Yeah. I've got some vacation time I can take. Cami won't care if she has time off or not. It's an emergency, and I'm sure she'll make it work. I was just on my way over to her place, so let me talk to her, and I'll call you back."

"Perfect. I'll have one of my pilots meet you at the Portland airport."

"Okay. Talk to you in a few."

"I assume they'll be on their way shortly," Dope said.

"Yeah." I hung up and released a sigh. Everything was becoming so frighteningly real.

Lulu had dropped off the twins and they were safely tucked into bed. I had located the nanny cam and placed the teddy bear in their bedroom so I could keep an eye on them. If someone took Ella, they might come after the kids too. If so, I would be ready. Images of torturing and killing the person who came after my family flickered through my mind. Instead of being revulsed at the idea of someone's brains splattering against my living room wall, it gave me peace. Although I knew that revenge was best served cold, I wouldn't hesitate to eliminate a threat.

A soft knock sounded at my door, and I peered through the peephole. Relieved that Ryan and Cami had arrived safely, I let them in. "Hi, Bass." Cami gave me a big hug. "We're going to find her. I promise."

I returned her embrace, grateful to have her here. She was a big part of my wife's life, so in a small way, it was like having a little piece of Ella near me.

"Thank you for coming." My voice cracked with regret and guilt. It was my fault that Ella was missing, and once Cami learned the truth . . . I wasn't sure what would happen.

"Where else would I be?" She backed away, and I noticed her blue eyes and nose were swollen and red. Her blond hair was piled on top of her head in a messy bun, and strands escaped it.

"Hey, man." Ryan stepped forward and squeezed my shoulder. His hazel-eyed gaze flickered with worry and determination. "What can I do? I have some . . ." His expression grew even more serious. "I have some off-the-record contacts that might be able to help, but I wanted to talk to you about it first. They're not on the right side of the law, if you know what I mean." His voice was low and deadly.

"I wasn't planning on doing this by the books." I waited for Ryan's reaction to my words, but he just tilted his chin at me. "Can I trust you to help, or do we need to end the conversation now before it puts you in a bad situation?" My accent grew thicker with the stress of my question.

"I'm on your side. Right now, I'm not a cop, so don't sweat it. There are bigger issues at hand that need to be addressed. Plus, I didn't figure you'd deal with this legally. I sure as hell wouldn't if someone took Cami." His attention landed on her briefly and then returned to me.

"Can I check on the kids?" Cami asked, her words weaved with worry and fear.

"Yeah. I have the nanny cam in there to keep an eye on them. I've also adjusted the cameras to see the windows more clearly. Between the group of us, I feel a bit better about their safety."

I closed the front door behind my friends, feeling a tinge of relief that they were here and that Ryan had pledged his help and trust. Hopefully, he would still honor his word even after I explained about the society.

Ryan pulled Cami to him and placed a kiss on her mouth. "Hang in there, babe. We're going to get her back. I love you."

She grabbed the front of his shirt and nodded. "I know you guys will do everything necessary. Thank you for being here with me . . .

with us." She pushed up on her toes and kissed him again. "Love you too."

Cami made her way upstairs, and Ryan greeted Dope and Kip. "I'll make a pot of coffee for anyone that needs it. I don't figure I'll be getting any sleep, and the caffeine will help me keep a clear head." *I hope.* I disappeared into the kitchen and made the coffee, the scent of the fresh beans brewing keeping me in the moment. I gathered cups, milk, and creamer and set them on a tray. My mind raced with thoughts of Ella. Was she hurt or even alive? I couldn't think like that. Ella was strong and smart, and I had to trust that she could handle whatever she was going through with the assurance that I would be coming after the motherfucker who took her.

Entering the living room, I placed the tray on the coffee table. "Anyone hungry?"

"Always," Dope said.

"I should have known better than to ask." Dope's pot habit gave him the munchies on a regular basis. As much as he ate, he was still a skinny motherfucker.

I disappeared again and then returned with chips, beef jerky, nuts, and the carafe full of coffee. Once I had the snacks available, I placed my hands on my hips and glanced at my friends.

"Ryan, I don't expect you to keep this information from Cami. She should know as well in case there's more danger. I want you and her to make an informed decision about what you're getting involved in."

"About what?" Cami asked as she descended the stairs from the kids' room and sat next to her fiancé.

Kip laced his fingers behind his head but remained quiet.

"The society."

I waited for a reaction from Cami, but she didn't give one. "Ella hasn't told you?"

Cami snorted. "Ella worked on criminal cases with attorneys. She's tight-lipped even with me."

That news made me love my wife even more. I knew she was capable of secrets, but Cami was her best friend, and sometimes that line blurred. Apparently, it didn't with Ella.

"Several years ago, I created and started the Safe Horizon Society. We"—I tilted my head in Kip and Dope's direction—" help women and children escape dangerous situations and set them up with fake names and a new life. What we do is illegal, and we break a lot of rules when we transport the families over state lines if there's a divorce and custody decree, not to mention creating new identities and social security cards, but we justify it to keep people safe." There was no use in sugarcoating what we did.

Cami's mouth opened and closed a few times before she was able to form words. "You're criminals?"

"Yeah, but I won't apologize for it. Dope is a hacker and an expert on the dark web. He's already been searching for Ella while you guys were flying over. But if we're going to find her, you need to know what you're stepping into. You'll be guilty by association. If you're not okay with that, you're free to leave, but I ask that you don't give us up. Women and children are depending on you to keep them safe and so is your best friend."

Ryan rubbed his hands together, grinning. "I fucking love it, man. I'm in. Too bad I can't be a part of the society, but with being a cop, I don't want to jeopardize my career. I won't be of any help to anyone if that happens."

Dope snorted, and I shot him an inquisitive look. "Mate?"

"Sorry, I got a chip stuck in my throat."

Apparently, something that Ryan had said was funny. I wasn't sure why Dope was flat-out lying to me, but I would deal with him later.

"Ella knew about all of this?" Cami asked.

"Yeah, she actually helped us when she could. Once the twins were born, she worked more with Dope to help find the families than on the front lines. I've also taken a step back to keep my wife and kids safe. Guess that didn't work out like I planned."

Cami's forehead creased. "Oh, you think you guys pissed off the wrong person and he took Ella?"

"Yup," Kip chimed in. "Even though we go to great lengths to hide our identities, if one of the women got in touch with her husband or boyfriend, then it could have blown everything to shit. My guess is that something like that happened, and now a pissed-off husband is coming after us through Ella."

Cami hopped off the couch, her hands flying over her mouth with a mix of fear and shock on her face. I could only imagine the thoughts that were going through her mind. "I can't decide if I should thank you for rescuing those kids or throttle you for endangering my best friend."

"Cami, I know this is hard to digest, but Ella wanted in on the frontline action, and Bass said no. You've known her the longest, so you know how damned determined she is when she wants something. Bass didn't have a chance," Kip said, defending me.

Cami spun on her heel and glowered at him. "She is bullheaded for damn sure, but she never signed up to be kidnapped and taken from her kids." Fury rolled off her in waves.

"Cami," Ryan said gently, placing his hand on her lower back as if to contain her outburst of emotions. "Babe, we can be pissed later. Time isn't on our side, and we have to focus on finding Ella before . . ."

My gut twisted into painful knots. He didn't need to finish the sentence. We all knew what was on his mind.

Cami blew out a heavy sigh. "You're right. My feelings aren't important at the moment. I just want to find her and bring her home safely." She sank into her seat and rubbed her hands together. Ryan put his arm around her and kissed her forehead.

My burner phone vibrated in my pocket, and I quickly retrieved it, praying to a god I no longer believed in that it was my wife.

"Hello?"

"Death, oh Death, come out wherever you are. Your wife is missing you," the voice said in a high-pitched sing-song voice.

"Who the fuck is this?" I roared. "Let me talk to Ella."

A maniacal cackle shot through the speaker, and I wanted to reach through the phone and grab the son of a bitch through it and kill him slowly.

"Hold, please." Shuffling filled the line, and I quickly put it on speaker and placed my finger to my lips, indicating for my friends to be quiet.

"Sebastian?" She sounded far away, terrified.

"Ella!" My heart hammered in my chest as I frantically listened. "What's happening? Are you safe?" Every word was like a knife in my gut, but at least she was still alive.

"For now." Her voice was barely a whisper, filled with terror and anguish. "I'm underground, trapped in a cage, surrounded by stuffed animals—" Her next words were cut off by an ear-piercing scream.

My body stiffened as goosebumps dotted my skin, the hairs on the back of my neck standing on end like soldiers at attention. My eyes widened in fear, absorbing the horror of the situation.

"You fucking son of a bitch, if you hurt her, it will be the last thing you do alive!" I yelled.

"You'll what?" The man's laugh sent shivers down my spine. "Listen carefully, and there's a small chance you'll get her back."

A metallic taste filled my mouth, like I'd been sucking on a penny. It was the taste of fear and dread, my reaction to the horrifying situation Ella was in. "What do you want?"

"Death. I want Death."

What kind of fucked-up shit was this? "I'll give you fucking death, and you'll be begging for mercy as I end you."

"Wrong Death. Wrong Death," he chanted. "I'll offer you a clue while we wait for him."

Dope scrambled for a piece of paper and pen from my desk, ready to write it down.

"Born of silence, fed by fear, my walls have ears, but none draw near. I am nowhere yet everywhere found, where geometry and nightmare are bound." The line grew quiet, then he said, "Good luck, Sebastian. The clock is ticking." With that, the call was disconnected.

I stared at it. "Hello? Hello?" Everything inside me wanted to throw the cell against the wall, but then Ella wouldn't be able to contact me, and I would never forgive myself. My gaze traveled across the room and to my friends, their expressions ghostly white.

"Anyone know what the hell he's talking about? If he wants a different death, I'll give the son of a bitch a slow, torturous one."

Kip and Dope exchanged a worried look before they glanced at Ryan.

"We need to have a talk . . . in private," Kip said, his words heavy with concern.

CHAPTER 9

ELLA

I didn't have enough time to rub my stinging cheek before Xavier shoved me back into the glass box.

"This was a test, Ella McCloud Fletcher. You failed." His features twisted in anger as he slipped the key into the lock. The sound of the click clawed at my chest.

"I'm sorry. I'll be good. I promise. Just let me out." Tears spilled down my cheeks, each droplet carrying the weight of my actions. My heart had plummeted to the pit of my stomach as Sebastian's voice answered instead of Death's. The realization that my kidnapping had hastened his transformation, and he'd returned to Sebastian knocked the wind out of me. While I knew Sebastian would search for me with fervent desperation, it was Death who struck fear in the hearts of humans and mercilessly destroyed them. And in this crucial moment, I needed the viciousness and power of my husband's darker half to find me.

Xavier stomped off, his black combat boots smacking against the concrete floor.

"Where are you going? You can't leave me here. Xavier, please. I won't do it again. I swear." I smacked my palms against the cage, my hope withering as he walked away. Silence descended on the room, and I wondered how long it would take the spiders to reappear.

My pulse raced as I watched Xavier return, his expression dark. With a cruel smile, he began pushing pegs into the air holes, sealing my only source of oxygen.

"Xavier, please," I begged, my voice trembling with fear. "I'll suffocate. I'll die."

"You should have thought about that before you betrayed me," he spat, his eyes filled with a chilling fury. With each peg he pushed in, his rage twisted and contorted his features into something unrecognizable.

As I gasped for breath, he revealed his true plan. "Soon you'll be at our table as a permanent guest," he sneered. "As my wife forever."

A wave of revulsion washed over me as his words sunk in. Maybe this had been his warped revenge all along. I frantically searched for a way out, but it seemed there was no escape from this living hell. Was this really how I would meet my end, trapped in this claustrophobic tomb at the hands of a madman?

But maybe it was my chance to redeem myself before I ran out of air and fucking died.

"Xavier," I whispered. "If you'd only asked . . ." I gulped, coming to terms with the lies that were about to spew out of my mouth. "I'm leaving Sebastian. I was making plans to take the kids away from him. I can't live that life anymore. If you want me to be your wife . . . all you have to do is ask."

His hand hovered over the last hole, the peg catching the lone light from the kitchen.

"I didn't realize that you wanted me like that." Nausea churned in my stomach, and I prayed I wouldn't puke. I was desperate for him to believe me. It was life . . . and death.

He frowned, then his face shifted from fury to eagerness, and his arm dropped to his side. "You're a lying little bitch." His voice was low, sharp, and accusatory.

I held my breath, then reminded myself not to do that. Seconds ticked by as I waited to see if he would block the hole or if I had broken through to him.

The corners of his mouth kicked up in a sickening grin. "You've been lying to your husband?" He threw the peg over his shoulder, then jumped up and down, clapping his hands with glee. "I win! Ella McCloud is mine, mine, mine!" He danced around the room, and I watched and waited for his next move. Suddenly he stopped, his expression turning sinister again as he searched the small space. I knew exactly what he was looking for, and I hoped like hell he didn't find the little stopper. My heart pounded in my ears as I tried to anticipate his intentions.

"There!" He hurried across the room and snatched up the peg. Xavier rushed over, then shoved it in the last hole.

"Consequences, you lying little bitch."

A gut-wrenching scream escaped me as I beat against the walls, begging him not to do this. But my wails fell on deaf ears as he walked off and disappeared past the kitchen.

I gasped for air, the cruel truth slamming into me like a sledgehammer. As I wiped away my tears, I fought to keep my breaths shallow, knowing I needed to conserve every last bit of oxygen in case Xavier returned. But deep down, I knew it was futile. Time dragged on as spiders scuttled up the side of my cage and over the glass top, their legs tapping softly against the surface. The thought of slowly suffocating to death now seemed like a merciful escape compared to what Xavier might have had in store for me.

Visions of my babies flooded my mind, their cherubic smiles and little teeth peeking through. The tenderness of their soft skin against mine, and the warm weight of their bodies as I rocked them to sleep. The thought of losing them sent a wave of primal fear coursing through me, twisting my gut into knots.

"Verity, Alaric, I'm so sorry. I love you both so much." Tears streamed down my face as I realized I would never hold them or hear their infectious laughter again. My mind flashed back to all the precious memories we shared, and in that moment, I held on to them with all my strength. Never again would I kiss Sebastian and Death. Memories of our times together broke through my horror, and I embraced them. I hoped my husband knew I was willing to die to safeguard his secret. I'd told Death that before, but now . . . now it was happening. But there was no secret. Xavier had learned the truth already. Why did he want Death?

Brain fog clouded my thoughts as I coughed, my body fighting for air.

I curled into the corner as the minutes passed and desperation settled in. It was now clear that Xavier had left me to die, and no matter how close Sebastian might be, I was out of time.

CHAPTER 10

SEBASTIAN

I led the men into my office on the main floor of the house while Cami remained in the living room. Before I closed and secured the door, she flashed me a worried look, then started to collect the toys and items still scattered everywhere.

I stared at my friends, aware of the expressions of dread on their faces. Dope was full-on fidgeting like a little kid caught stealing a candy bar from a store, and Kip was vibrating with nervous energy. Dread curdled in my stomach as it clenched, the tension in the room feeding my growing agitation.

"What are you hiding? I need to know so that we can find Ella before . . . before it's too . . ." I couldn't say it. No matter what, I had to try to stay positive for our kids and my own sanity.

"He's baiting you," Ryan said. "Whoever the guy is that called is baiting you."

"To kill him? I'm happy to oblige."

Kip's pacing became erratic as he struggled to find the right words. "There's no easy way to say this, Bass."

My heart began to race as I braced myself for whatever news they were about to deliver. "Just tell me what's going on," I demanded, growing frustrated and impatient with their cryptic behavior.

"You know what? Maybe you should sit down for this."

"Just fucking tell me!" My words lashed out, reverberating around the enclosed space, and Ryan nodded once to Kip, signaling for him to continue.

Every tick of the clock on the wall seemed infinitely louder, reminding me how little time we had. I was crawling out of my skin with the need for fucking answers.

Kip took a deep breath before continuing, his voice thick with emotion. "Bass, we've known each other since we were kids, and we met Ryan in college. After your parents passed away, Dope and I had to make some tough choices. Choices that we thought were best for you."

My eyes widened in shock as I turned to Ryan, who avoided my gaze and looked guilt ridden. "What the hell do you mean?" I asked, my voice shaking with anger and betrayal. "I've only known Ryan since he started dating Cami." But even as the words left my mouth, a sinking feeling in my gut told me that there was much more to the story than what they were telling me.

Their heads shook in unison, and a silent understanding passed between them. "We met in college." Ryan finally spoke up, his voice strained with guilt. "But I didn't hang out with you."

My jaw clenched as irritation pulsed through my veins. "That makes no fucking sense," I snarled, crossing my arms over my chest. "We're losing valuable time to find my wife, and you're giving me some bullshit excuse?"

Kip stepped forward, his eyes full of compassion but also fear. "After you witnessed your parents' brutal murder . . . something inside you snapped. A darkness took hold, consuming you. Dope and I saw it happen, and we've been trying to help you ever since. But Ryan has seen it too."

"Everyone has a dark side," I spat out defensively.

"Not like yours," Kip countered, his tone grim. "I mean, not everyone in this room has taken a life in cold blood, but you . . ."

Confusion clouded my mind as I struggled to process his words. "I've never killed anyone," I protested. "Sure, I've beaten men bloody, but I've never committed murder." Suddenly, a terrifying thought sparked in my brain and realization dawned on me. "Did I accidentally kill someone, and you guys covered it up?" Chills rippled down my spine with the possibility, and the weight of potential guilt crushed my chest.

An oppressive and foreboding silence consumed the room, suffocating me as I scanned the faces of my three friends, hoping for some kind of explanation.

And then, with a grave voice, Dope finally spoke up. "It wasn't an accident. You have another side to you, Bass. His name is Death." The words struck me like lightning, my heart racing with fear and confusion. The mysterious caller had been trying to reach *Death*, not Sebastian. But who was this Death? Did they mean me? Did they mean someone else inside of me? All three men stared at me intently, as if expecting me to grasp what Dope had said. But how could I?

I scrubbed my face with my palms. "I don't know anyone named Death. And why the hell would he go by that name? It's stupid."

But before the guys could respond, Ryan dropped another bombshell. "Because he's a serial killer." His voice was calm, as if he were comfortable with the idea. "One of the most wanted in the country. Since we met in college, I've helped clean up bodies and evidence after he's killed."

"Me too," Kip added. "We've gotten our hands dirty to keep you safe."

My mind reeled with this information, and my stomach clenched as I fought to comprehend it all. Ryan had known Death since college and even helped cover up his gruesome crimes. And Kip, always the loyal friend, admitted to sacrificing himself for the sake of protecting me from this monster. How long had they been keeping this secret from me? And how would I stop this other side of myself from taking over completely? Even the mere thought that I was capable of such horrific acts sent me into a tumultuous storm of emotions; the weight of their words crushed me as I struggled to breathe.

"But also to protect the families we relocate in society. When I find the women and children we need to help, I choose sick, fucked-up men for Death to kill." Dope gulped, his confession twisting my neck and shoulders into painful knots.

"You help this Death character kill, and the other guys clean up?" I could feel the color draining from my face as I attempted to wrap my head around what they were telling me. I was a killer, and apparently, they had blood on their hands too. "If this is true, then why don't I remember any of it?"

"Because you and Death share the same body and mind, but you're not aware of each other. We know you've tried to mask it, but you lose time, don't you?"

Dope's voice was barely a whisper, but it cut through the fog of confusion in my mind. They were right. I lost time and made excuses for it, trying to ignore the truth lurking beneath the surface.

I shifted my weight from one foot to the other, desperate to understand even a fraction of what they were saying. Tears stung my eyes, and I blinked rapidly. "Yeah. I just put it off as my migraines and move on."

"Which would make sense because those headaches are bad. You're in agony when they happen." Dope folded his arms across his chest. "It's how we know you're going to change soon and Death will appear."

I shook my head, refusing to believe that there was something *that* wrong with me. Barking out a laugh, I waved my hands in surrender. "This is a really shitty time to joke. You guys can knock it off now."

No one returned my laughter or smile.

Dope shifted his weight from one foot to the other. "You killed Stephen. He forced his way into Ella's house and held her at gunpoint. Once you arrived at Ella's, you slit his throat and killed him in her kitchen. This side of you is merciless, but you watch our backs at any cost. When Death became obsessed with Ella, we knew there was trouble, but she handled it like the amazing person she is."

Shocked, my mouth opened and closed several times before I could form words. "*I* killed Stephen, and Ella knows Death?"

Ryan squared his shoulders and tipped his chin up. I'd learned his cop-mode body language from the time I'd spent with him and Cami. "She met Death first, actually. You stalked her and showed up at her home. I was one of the cops on the scene when she called 911."

"So, you're all in on it and have lied to me my entire life?" Rage churned my stomach, the acid threatening to travel up my throat. *Ella.* How could my sweet Ella be connected with a killer? Fight for and protect him? The weight of this information stopped me in my tracks, leaving my mind spinning with disbelief. My fingers clenched and unclenched while I fought to keep my breakfast down. "Why now? Why tell me now?"

"Because Ella is in trouble, and we need Death to . . . to come out." Kip's expression twisted with guilt.

"She was taken because of Death, not me?" I struggled with the idea that someone else was in my mind. Wouldn't I have known if it were true? The weight threatened to crush my chest as my mind began to sift through the numerous times I had experienced headaches and then experienced gaps of lost time. "I was worried I had a fucking tumor, not someone else inside my goddamn head," I growled. "Not to mention a killer. If what you're telling me is the truth, when did you meet him?" My heart pounded with dread as I waited for the answer. This wasn't about me anymore. It was about Ella's safety, and I needed to understand the darkness that lurked inside me to save her.

Dope's spine stiffened, and he took a deep breath. "The first time we met Death and hung out with him was the weekend we played Dungeons & Dragons at my place. You were living with us after your parents were . . . killed."

My eyes widened in horror. "Did I—did I kill my parents?" My legs shook with my question.

"No," Kip said quickly. Too quickly.

"Someone else did, but that's not important right now. Kip, Ella, Ryan, and I have known Death for a long time. We're the *only* ones that know." Dope shoved his hands in his jean pockets, looking guilty and nervous. Dope was much easier to read than Kip and Ryan. He wasn't afraid to show a softer side of his personality. Kip was a pro at hiding what he was thinking. In fact, I suspected there was a lot about his childhood he'd never shared.

I swallowed over the lump in my throat. "If the son of a bitch that called wants Death . . . how . . . how do I find him? How do I—"

"That's the problem. Death was here earlier with Ella. Normally he doesn't disappear so quickly, but when Death couldn't find her and saw the chaos in the house, it triggered Sebastian's return."

A surge of terror coursed through me as I attempted to come to terms with the weight of the situation. My mind whirled, struggling to comprehend how they now saw me as two separate entities. Death. And Sebastian.

The realization was like a physical blow to the chest, as if my heart was pounding in protest against what they'd said.

Kip shot a look at Dope and Ryan, and I suspected he was hoping they would say something. What, I wasn't sure. As far as I was concerned, they'd said enough.

Ryan cleared his throat before he spoke. "If I were in your shoes, I wouldn't believe us, but we're telling you the truth. If nothing else, understand that Ella is depending on you to bring out Death. Her life depends on it."

"He's right. Doubt us all you want, but Ella needs Death, and we have to figure out how to find him," Dope agreed. "I'll check on the kids and Cami, so you three can catch up and discuss how to handle this."

With the horrendous conversation, I'd forgotten Cami was here. "Yeah, I know she's scared too." Still looking at my friends, I reached for the doorknob and opened the door.

"Fuck," Ryan said.

Spotting a pair of sandals and pink toenails, I looked up and was greeted with a horrified and furious Cami.

"How much did you hear?" Ryan asked.

Her lips pressed into a thin line as her attention darted to me, then to the other three men. "All of it. Verity wants her favorite stuffed bear, and I can't find it, so I was going to see if Sebastian could help, but—" Her voice cracked as she stepped back, clearly terrified of me.

"Cami, wait." Ryan shot past me and hurried after her.

"Shit. Like we don't have enough to deal with." Kip shook his head, his brown eyes narrowing. "Well, there's nothing to hide from her, so let's get to work and see if we can figure out how to tell Death we need his help."

Dope rubbed his fingers over his chin, his thick stubble rustling beneath his touch. "Stress is a big trigger that causes the change."

I closed the door, wondering how long this would take. My friends were right. It didn't matter what I believed or how horrified I was. I had to do this for Ella. Once I brought her home and made sure she was safe, I had to . . .

CHAPTER 11

ELLA

I jerked awake as something cold pressed against my forehead. My eyes popped open, and the kitchen table blurred in and out as I tried to recall what had happened. *Xavier left me to die.*

He lowered his hand, and I realized he must have been trying to wake me up.

"Ella cannot die. The boss said, 'Ella cannot die.' Not yet. But he gifted you to me to take care of. I did not. I did not," Xavier chanted softly.

"You tried to kill me." If my body wasn't so weak, I would have punched him in his ugly face. "Your breath stinks." Clearly, I'd lost my mind from lack of oxygen.

"I'll get a mint. Stay put." Xavier laughed as he hopped out of the kitchen chair and hurried to the sink.

Panic surged through me as I struggled against the restraints—my arms were bound tightly behind my back and my ankles fastened to the chair legs. My head throbbed with a sharp pain, making it difficult to think clearly. "I-I didn't mean to be rude," I stammered, desperation creeping into my voice. "Maybe I suffered some brain damage." I didn't think I had, but I was definitely foggy headed. Hopefully, it would lift soon.

Xavier returned and popped a mint into his mouth, the little white disk slipping through his yellowed teeth. "Open."

I parted my lips, and he slipped one of the refreshing candies between them.

"It will help your throat too." He nodded and smiled as if he'd done the nicest thing for me. Maybe to him, he had.

"Who's your boss? Does he know I have kids waiting for me at home?" My voice sounded thin and exhausted from lack of food and sleep.

"In due time, my sweet Ella." He lifted his hand and gently stroked my cheek with his rough knuckles. "Everything will make sense."

"But he doesn't want me dead?"

"Nope. You're mine. He gave you to me to have and hold and . . ." An evil grin slid across his face.

"I'm married, Xavier. Plus, I'm a human being, not a possession." I kept my tone even and as soothing as possible. I didn't want to trigger him into another episode where he might actually kill me.

He shook his head, disagreeing with me. "You're mine. Can't you accept that you'll never leave? We're bound by fate."

It took every cell in my body to not cringe. It would be easier to welcome death than live the rest of my life with this monster.

"What are your plans for me? I mean, your boss doesn't want to kill me, but . . ." My eyes darted to his family that was still sitting at the table. I suspected he rarely moved them. "Will I join your parents and sister?"

Deep frown lines etched into his forehead. "You betrayed me by trying to tell Sebastian where you were. You had to be punished."

I swallowed my anxiety and thought through what I should say, choosing my words carefully.

"Is that what happened to you?" I tilted my head toward the stuffed dead people next to me. "Were you disciplined a lot?" One thing working in law had taught me was that many criminals had an abusive background, or their brains weren't wired like a lot of people's. That wasn't the case every time, but more often than I had thought before I landed the job at the law firm. Plus, I was married to a criminal, so I had a bit more insight than most. I wished resources were more widely available to study the brain and help people. I suspected it would cut down on a lot of crime and people would be able to lead happy lives. Maybe someday.

"Father and Mother . . ." He ran a hand over his wild hair. "They punished me for being different."

"I'm so sorry. That wasn't right. Tell me what happened. What did they do to you?" If my wrists weren't tied behind my back, I would have reached out and held one of his hands to appear more interested, when really I didn't give a shit about anything except getting out of here. It was clear to me I had to establish trust and make sure I didn't end up in the same situation as his parents.

A sharp hiss left him as he smacked himself on the forehead. "Locked me up for days without any light. It drove me mad."

My heart sank to my toes. How could anyone treat their child that way? Tears pricked my eyes as my thoughts returned to Alaric and Verity. I could never do anything like that to either of them, even if they took after Death with his craving to kill.

"It's one thing to be different, but it pushed me over the edge, Ella. I was fed through a slot in the door as if I were a criminal. I was alone for weeks, pissing in a bucket and sharing my food scraps with the rats so they wouldn't bite me." A heartbreaking wail escaped him. "I had plenty of time to plan exactly what I would do to my family." He nodded enthusiastically. "I had to be free. Free of their torture and brutality."

"What about your sister? She doesn't look like she was more than fifteen when she . . . died." I didn't want to say when he killed her, even though that was apparently what had happened. Someone had, but there was a little nudge in my gut that had me questioning if he was fucking with my head or if he really had murdered these people. People lied when they were backed into a corner, and if I posed any kind of threat to Xavier, he would try to scare me. So far it was working.

"She never helped. Instead, they treated her like a princess, with new clothes and birthday parties. Amber knew they kept me in that dark room, but not once did she ever try to help me get out."

"Do you think she was too scared? If she was younger, maybe she was terrified of being punished too."

Xavier shot out of his chair, sending it flying backward. "Are you sticking up for her? Taking her side?" The screech of his voice sounded like fingernails on a chalkboard.

"No. Not at all. I was just attempting to understand better. Get to know you a little. I mean, after all, we're going to spend a lot of time together, right?" I forced a fake smile onto my face, trying to suppress the anger and fear that were boiling inside me. Regardless of his past, I couldn't help but feel disgusted by his actions, trapping me in this creepy basement filled with spiders and disturbing clown dolls. It was no different from the torture he endured from his parents.

His shoulders relaxed as he slithered back into his seat. "Yes. Eternity, Ella." He fisted his hair and pulled it so hard that I was surprised he hadn't yanked a handful out.

"You're safe now, Xavier. I'm here for you."

I couldn't believe how convincing my performance was becoming, but I had no other choice if I wanted to escape.

"Why did your boss choose me? What does he want from me?"

"You're full of questions tonight."

I caught on to what he had said—it must be nighttime outside, and I estimated that I had been here for around twenty-four hours. However, it was impossible to determine the exact time.

"I'm sorry. I'm not very good at small talk."

He chewed on a short thumbnail, then his attention traveled to the wall. "My pets are coming out to play." Xavier clapped his hands, clearly thrilled with the idea of the only friends he seemed to have, the spiders.

"Please protect me. Don't let them—" The hair rose on the back of my neck as I felt multiple legs crawl over my skin. "Please get it off me. I'll do anything you want. Please." My body trembled as the creature crawled in my hair, and I slammed my eyes closed. Realizing the unknown would be worse than seeing the creepy crawly, I opened them again.

"Anything?" Xavier stood slowly and reached his hand out.

"Anything. Please hurry."

He placed his palm against the side of my head. Seconds later, the little brown bastard crawled up his arm. Before I could realize what was happening, he bent down and pressed his mouth to mine. Fighting the urge to jerk back, I kept my eyes open and watched the spider crawl farther away from me. My breath halted in my lungs and my nose stung as I struggled to hold back tears and nausea, horribly repulsed by his touch, but I couldn't allow myself to break down. I had to remember that survival was the only thing that mattered, and I had to play his sick and twisted games.

Instead, I focused on the fact that Xavier had just kissed me, but he'd also saved me. What the hell was I supposed to do with that? I already knew the answer. If I ever wanted to see Sebastian and the twins again, I had to reach him on an emotional level and pretend to fall for him. It was the only way I might make it out alive. Until then, I would learn everything I could about Xavier and his boss, then fucking kill them myself.

CHAPTER 12

SEBASTIAN

"I should go after her. It's my fault. I'm the one that she's terrified of." I scrubbed my face with my hands, exhausted. My wife was missing, plus my friends had revealed a dangerous secret that could destroy not only Ryan, but all of us. And now Cami knew the truth, putting her in grave danger as well.

"She can't turn us in, man." Dope stood and paced the small space, staring at the floor.

The high pitch of Cami's voice reached us from the living room. "You're fucking kidding me. This happens and you're feeding me a line of shit?"

The three of us stared at the door to the office, and once again I debated if I should talk to her.

"I know you think you'd be helping Cami understand, but you're the wrong guy for the job, dude." Kip grimaced, but we all knew it was the truth.

"I'll go." Dope reached into the front pocket of his black T-shirt and produced a joint. "I'll see if I can get her to relax and then talk to her. Maybe she'll understand that we're not the enemy."

I folded my arms over my chest. "If anyone can, it's you, Dope. Give it your best shot. You're the most levelheaded out of all of us."

"Probably all the pot," Kip added.

"I'll keep an eye on the kids while she's with you. We need to make sure she's not going to run straight to the cops. Even if she says she won't, we have to keep a close eye on her. She knows where we live, our schedules; she's Ella's closest friend." I rubbed my stubbled jaw, hoping for a quick resolution with Cami, but I understood it wasn't likely.

Kip blew out a heavy sigh. "Yeah, and maybe that will work in our favor. If she understands that Ella chose to be with you—both sides of you—then Cami might see a good reason to be on our side."

"I hope you're right, mate." I glanced at Dope. "Do your best, but I'm not expecting miracles. I gave up on those a long time ago."

When Ryan emerged, his usually composed expression was replaced with a grim, tormented look. He ran his trembling hands through his messy brown hair, making it stick up in every direction. "I hate myself for what I did to her," he muttered, his voice laced with self-loathing. "God, I hate myself for hurting her. I hate that I couldn't tell her sooner and that she found out like this. The look in her eyes . . . It was like I was a total stranger to her."

A deep sense of regret radiated from him, filling the room with an oppressive weight that hung in the air like a thick fog.

I approached him and placed my hand on his shoulder. "This wouldn't have happened if you weren't protecting me. I'm sorry shit went down like this. Give her some time and let her calm down, process what she heard. I'm sure everything will turn out."

Ryan's shoulders sagged. "Sorry, Bass. I'll have to deal with my mess later. I think we've got another problem, but she said she wouldn't go to the cops until we found Ella."

My gut fisted into painful knots. "Then we have to have a plan to get the hell out of here as soon as we find my wife. We all have to disappear."

"Ella won't like that one bit," Kip said.

"Might not have a choice if Dope can't get through to Cami. Maybe you can try to talk to her again once she's calmed down, Ryan."

Ryan shook his head. "Cami broke up with me. She said she didn't want to ever speak to me again. Guess she couldn't get over the fact that I was covering up crime scenes for a serial killer." Ryan shot me a look. "But I'll handle that later. We have to find Ella, then deal with the rest of this shit show another time."

"We need to talk to Death and see if he has any ideas of who took Ella. Do you think . . . do you think that"—Kip winced—"y'know, you could change and let us talk to him?"

My brows arched. "I've done that?"

"Actually, no. But maybe we can try it. Now that you're aware that he's there, maybe . . ." He gave me a half shrug. "It's worth a shot."

Once again, I was bewildered at the idea that I didn't have control over my mind or body. I just gaped at my friends. "This is real?" I choked on the words; I'd been hoping they were fucking around with me, even though I knew better. I'd known Kip and Dope my entire life, and they would never joke around in such a serious situation. I just wasn't sure how the hell to get a handle on all of this. If Ella were here . . . *Jesus, she married me and knew the truth. How could I have asked her to do something like that? I truly am a monster to involve her and now my kids.*

"How does it normally happen?" I stared at my feet, shame clinging to me like a second skin.

Kip's face darkened, and his voice took on a grim tone as he explained, "You get bad headaches for a week or two before Death shows up. It's our cue to know that we need to have some men lined up for you to . . ." He coughed and cleared his throat. This conversation wasn't easy for him either, apparently. "Death says he washes the earth with their blood. Bass, you've got to understand that Death only goes after some sick fucks. Men who sell their kids and beat their wives . . . sometimes worse, if there is such a thing."

"A vigilante?"

Ryan nodded at me. "Exactly. He can do what I can't as a cop. It's why I try to point the investigation in the opposite direction without giving myself away."

My attention traveled from Kip to Ryan. "How long can you keep that up? You're risking everything for a cold-blooded killer."

"But that's my choice. Maybe he goes about shit in his own way, but do you have any idea how many women and children he's saved? When you save them through the Safe Horizon Society, you're doing the same damn thing, just in a different way."

Kip's brows furrowed as if he were deep in thought. "Ryan is right. Each of us has chosen to be on this journey with you, protect you. You're our brother. Dope and I have watched out for you since your parents were killed."

A lump formed in my throat. "And now Ella is going to pay for it." I pinched the bridge of my nose, attempting to keep the onslaught of emotions at bay. I couldn't find her if I was a goddamn mess, but I wasn't sure how to be anything else. "Okay. Let's see if we can bring out Death."

"I have an idea, but I need Dope to hack into the FBI's ViCAP."

Kip shot Ryan a sideways look at his mention of the Violent Criminal Apprehension Program. "I think I understand where this is going. It might work," he said.

"It has to," I muttered. "Will . . . Do you think that now I know about my other side, I'll remember him or he'll remember me?"

Kip held my gaze. "I'm not sure. We've never been able to approach either of you about the other. But when Ella got pregnant, she had Death run a DNA test. She took some of your hair and had one run on you too. He was furious, but he did it. When the results came back showing your DNA matched and you were both the father, he . . ." Kip hesitated.

"What?" I urged him to continue.

"He promised Ella he wouldn't try to kill you anymore."

I rubbed my forehead with the heel of my hand, afraid to learn more. "What do you mean?

"Your car accident," Kip explained.

Memories of the wreck rushed toward me at top speed. "He . . . he was the one that I thought ran me off the road?"

"From what you were explaining, Death was fighting to appear, and you were driving. The fight to be front and center didn't go well. But there haven't been any more problems like that since Ella showed him the DNA tests. Plus, you both love her and those kids more than your own life. You've both always put them first."

"Jesus. It's as if you're describing another man violating my wife," I snarled, my teeth gritted so hard I could almost feel the enamel cracking. A deep rage boiled and churned in my chest, threatening to consume me whole.

"He thought the same about you. He's also not married to Ella, only you are. She takes off her wedding rings when he's around."

My eyes widened. "Fuck. I hate myself for putting her in that position."

Ryan took a step closer to me. "You can't go down that road, Bass. She *chose* you. *Both* sides of you. That's real love. You're a lucky son of a bitch. I can only hope to have that someday." Sadness flickered through his gaze. "While we're waiting for Dope, let's try to think of any other suspects. When he's back, we'll try to lure Death out. I have no idea if this will go sideways or not, so just try to stay calm. When Death realizes what's happened, he's going to flip the hell out. If you have any connection with him at all, you need to try and help him keep his head on straight so we can get Ella home safely."

I nodded, the gravity of the situation crushing me like a brick wall. "What do you think he'll do if I can't reach him and try to rein him in?"

The men glanced at each other before Kip said, "He'll burn the whole fucking world down until he finds her or he gets caught."

CHAPTER 13

ELLA

My jaw clenched as Xavier drew back, his touch turning my stomach. His long, dark eyelashes fluttered as his eyes opened.

"My first kiss. Ella is my first kiss." His expression lit up, and a sweet smile pulled at the corners of his mouth.

"Your first? You've never . . ." From my best guess, he had to at least be in his thirties.

"First." He sank into his chair and stared at me like a lovesick puppy. "No one liked Xavier."

What was happening? This was the only time I'd heard him refer to himself in third person.

"And to think, I'm the lucky girl," I managed to say with sympathy. Even though his touch revulsed me, maybe it was the key to talking him into letting me go. It might be beneficial if he thought he was in love with me.

"This calls for a celebration."

A flicker of hope sparked to life in my chest. "It does? What do you have in mind?" I offered him the sweetest smile I was capable of.

"Another riddle." Excitement clung to his words.

"I don't understand."

"Another riddle for Sebastian Fletcher. Another clue to where you are."

"Oh." I struggled not to ask him to let me talk to Sebastian again, but even hearing my husband's voice would help me hang on to the possibility of escaping or being found.

"Yes! I love riddles. Then, Ella . . . then we will have our first date."

"You're taking me out of here?"

Xavier wagged his finger at me. "No, no. We will watch a movie together. I have lots of choices. We can kiss and snuggle too."

My lips pursed into a thin line, but I managed to nod and lie through my teeth. "I would love a movie. Why don't you pick it, since you know what you have?"

He leaned forward in his chair. "*Silence of the Lambs*. It's my favorite movie ever."

I gulped. He would choose a twisted, fucked-up movie like that to be his preferred choice. "I love it too."

He clapped his hands, then removed his cell phone from the pocket of his flannel shirt. Even though it was summer outside, it was cold in his underground hole. He tapped the screen, then put it on speaker and set it on the table. "If you behave, I'll let you speak."

"I promise. I won't make you angry this time." I nodded for emphasis. The ring of a phone pulled my attention away from him, and my pulse kicked up as it rang again.

"Hello?" Sebastian said, his voice tight with stress.

My eyes snapped shut in a desperate attempt to contain the ocean of tears that threatened to spill over at the sound of his voice and beautiful accent. My heart wrenched with conflicting emotions. I wanted Death, not Sebastian. I needed Death to come find me, to rid this twisted world of the evil that had stolen me from him and our children.

Xavier's face fell. "I'm so sorry to hear it is still Sebastian Fletcher. I was hoping that Death would come out to play."

"It's only been twenty-four hours since you called last time. It doesn't work like that, motherfucker. He doesn't jump when he's told to appear," Sebastian barked. "Let me talk to my wife."

My hands trembled with Sebastian's words. Had I misunderstood what he'd said about Death not just appearing? If so, how? I couldn't handle thinking about it right now. He'd also let me know how long I'd been away from him and my babies. Around twenty-four hours. It seemed as though I'd been gone for days. Xavier glanced at me, jealousy flashing through his narrowed gaze.

"Please," I mouthed. "Then our date."

Xavier's expression changed as soon as I mentioned the word *date*. He moved the phone closer to me. "No clues."

I silently agreed. "Bass?" My voice cracked. "Hi, baby."

"Ella. I'm trying, honey. I'm trying."

"I know you are. I'm so sorry."

"Why in god's name would you apologize? I'm afraid it's my fault that you're . . . wherever you are."

In order not to start blurting out more details about my surroundings, I shifted the conversation. "Are the babies okay?" If we talked about the kids, maybe it would reach Xavier on some level, and he would let me go.

"They miss their mom, as do I." Sebastian's voice was tight, and I knew him well enough to realize he was fighting back tears.

I glanced at my captor. "I don't have any idea of who or why."

"It's all right. Just stay safe."

With that, Xavier picked up the cell and tapped the screen before he held it to his ear. "Here's your next clue." He waited and then he spoke again. "Bound by threads invisible, yet tighter than steel, I'm a puzzle wrapped in shadows. What secrets do I conceal? Count the heartbeats, measure the breaths. Her fate dances on the edge of depth." Xavier's high-pitched laugh echoed through the room, then he hung up. His gaze drifted to me. "Poor Ella, Death doesn't want to come out and play." He tsked while he slipped his phone back into his pocket. If I could reach it without him noticing, I could tap the redial button and call Sebastian . . . but what would I tell him? I had no idea where I was. Regardless, it was the only plan I had until I found the door that led out of this hellhole.

"Come, come." Xavier stood and held his hand out to me. "Oh, wait. I have to untie you." He laughed as if it were the best joke he'd ever told.

"Since you gave your word and didn't give Sebastian any more clues to where you are . . . I'll leave the ropes off. But first." He turned his back to me and strolled over to one of the kitchen drawers. He opened it and retrieved a pistol. The sound of the safety reached my ears. "Locked and loaded, so don't try anything. Even when you can't see my gun, it's always near me. Keep that in mind." His voice was low, threatening. "I would hate to have to shoot you. It messes up the taxidermy."

My heart hammered against my ribs. "I won't give you a chance to shoot me. I promise."

He studied me momentarily before he strolled in my direction, then untied my wrists and feet. I groaned as I rubbed my arms and legs, hoping they would wake up before I had to walk wherever we were going. Xavier waited patiently for me to stand, then he held out his hand again. I briefly hesitated, and then I placed mine in his, imagining it was Sebastian instead. I hoped like hell it would help me get through this nightmare.

He led me over to the couch and grabbed the remote off a little side table I hadn't noticed earlier. A loud bang sounded, then light spilled down a set of stairs that the darkness had been hiding.

"Xavier!" A deep voice called. "Now."

"No, no. It's date night," he called back.

Heavy footsteps traveled down the stairs and closer to us. "Boss isn't asking. He said now. Take care of her, then meet me outside."

The door. That's the path to my freedom. My heart jumped with hope as my mind began to form a plan. But there was an additional problem. Xavier wasn't alone. I just wasn't sure if there were men guarding the outside or if they'd just stopped by to tell him his boss wanted a meeting.

"Don't be sad, Ella McCloud Fletcher. We will have our date when I come back."

Before I could brace myself, he kissed me again. "In the cage. Hurry, hurry. I can't be late, or the boss will be angry. That's very bad."

I hurried toward the glass cell and crawled back in, checking for spiders as he secured me inside.

He briefly stared at me before he said, "You look tired. Be right back."

I frowned as I watched him hurry off. A minute later, he returned with a dingy yellow pillow. He unlocked the container and handed it to me. "Sweet dreams. I'll see you soon."

I took the pillow and hugged it to my chest, grateful for a softer place to lay my head. I hadn't realized how much I could miss one, along with the comfort of my bed, until I'd landed in this shitty hellhole. My gaze traveled to his, and for the first time since I'd been here, my words were genuine. "Thank you, Xavier. This means a lot to me."

His expression softened. "I'll be back as soon as I can." He stepped away, my attention trained on him as he hurried across the small room to the hidden staircase. Light and fresh air spilled in as he opened the door, then closed it behind him. The moment he was gone, my mind started to spin with ways to get his gun, shoot him, and then run. If there were more people waiting outside, then at least I could kill them and ask questions later.

I lay down on the cold cement floor and slipped the pillow under my head. The stench didn't bother me, but I wondered if the man knew how to use a washing machine. If he had one, maybe I could work my way into his heart if I offered to do his laundry. Maybe his walls would crumble if I gave him what he'd apparently never had before—care and love.

I wasn't sure how long I'd slept, but the sound of the door creaking woke me. After what must have been my second night in this hell, strange footsteps traveled down the stairs and closer to me. Sitting up, I waited to see Xavier appear from the staircase, but small black boots caught the edge of my eye, and I glanced up. My mouth gaped open at the sight in front of me.

"What the fuck?" the young blond-haired woman said as she stared at me wide-eyed.

CHAPTER 14

SEBASTIAN

Time had worn thin, and we were still no closer to finding my wife. Desperation coated my sweat-slickened skin while my nerves teetered on the edge of sanity. My world had changed on a dime. Ella had been taken, and my best friends had told me I was two different people in one body. Panic clenched its icy fingers around my throat, threatening to choke the life out of me. The weight of waiting coiled around my lungs, leaving no room for air or answers. I fought to stay conscious, straining to focus on the task in front of me and find a way to connect with this Death person. But what terrified me most was that I had no recollection of him. It was as if he had erased all memories of our encounters from my mind. And the realization hit me like a sledgehammer; those missing chunks of time were not just a coincidence. My brain was protecting me from him.

Dope finally returned with his laptop and settled in at my desk. "Give me a few." He opened his computer, and his fingers flew across the keys as he worked his hacking magic.

Ryan cleared his throat. "And?"

Dope continued working away, never missing a beat.

"Cami. Is she going to turn us in? Is she leaving?" Ryan's pitch jumped with his anxiety. Hell, we were all anxious.

"Oh. Yeah, she's cool."

"Dope, for fuck's sake. We're sweating over here. Tell us what she said," I demanded.

Dope sighed and dropped his hands to his lap. "She's not going to the cops, because we need to find Ella. She's terrified of meeting Death." The corner of his mouth kicked up. "Aren't we all?"

"Not the time to joke around, mate."

"Anyway, Ryan, she hates you. Not sure if you two will patch shit up or not. But she loves Ella and the kids, so she's on our side there. After we bring Ella home, I don't know how it will play out, but she gave her word on no cops or FBI. We can trust her."

"Goddammit. Why wasn't I more careful?" Ryan said, his head hanging down.

"None of us were. It's not on you," I added.

Kip walked over behind Dope and tapped him on the shoulder, urging him to continue. "Okay, that's one problem solved for now. Let's get to Ryan's plan to see if we can coax out Death."

Other than the sound of the second hand on the grandfather clock, a heavy silence fell over the room as Dope searched for what he needed.

"Ryan? Is this what you need?"

Ryan leaned over and stared at the screen. "Go here." He pointed at something I couldn't see since they'd blocked me from what Dope was doing.

"Fuck," Dope said as he winced and shrank back from the computer. "I've seen a lot of shit, but . . ." He swallowed hard and shot me a skeptical look. "You've always been so careful—except for the guy you left dangling from a hook in a warehouse a while ago."

Kip chuckled, apparently enjoying whatever they were looking for. "Death's a thorough motherfucker, that's for sure. I admire his work, though. I mean, it's skilled precision."

Ryan walked over to me. "Go check it out. You need to see what you do on your days off from being Sebastian."

I shot him a bewildered look. "Crickey, sometimes you have a real way with words."

Ryan gave me a half shrug.

I tried to prime myself for the worst, but nothing, and I mean nothing, could have prepared me for what I was about to see. A barely recognizable man dangled from a meat hook in an old warehouse. Blood pooled below him, and deep gashes erased his face.

His heart and stomach were on the floor next to the puddle. Revulsion shot through me like a shock wave as I stared at the image, speechless.

"That's Death's work," Kip said with pride in his tone. "And the knife you have from your father? That's Death's favorite tool. He just keeps it nice and clean. Bleaches the shit out of the blade to make sure there's no evidence."

"Show him some more, Dope," Ryan said.

Horror twisted my chest into knots as Dope showed me images from every angle of the victim. Somehow, I managed to find my voice. "Tell me he deserved that. Tell me that I'm not a stone-cold killer devoid of any empathy."

"I know this is hard to see, and hard to believe that this is your work, but his nickname was Dahmer Junior."

I stared at my friend in disgust. "He raped boys, then ate them?" Bile churned in my gut, and I pushed it down, unwilling to lose my lunch in front of my mates.

"Yup," Kip said.

Ryan ran his hand over his short hair. "I think it's one reason you left him there. I'm not positive, though. I'm pretty sure you were sending a message to let the cops know he wasn't a problem anymore. You should have heard the cheers at the station when they found him. At least you were careful and didn't leave evidence, but I'm guessing Kip had something to do with that since you didn't call me."

I staggered backward, my thoughts reeling from all the information. "Why are you showing me all of this?"

Dope leaned back in my office chair and folded his arms over his chest. "We're hoping to stress you out enough that Death comes out to play."

I resisted the urge to smack him upside the back of his head, my temper hanging by a thread. "Ella being taken, her life in danger—that's not fucking stressful enough?"

Kip chuckled. "We're short on time, man. We'll do anything we have to. I think Death might know who is behind Ella being kidnapped."

"Let's bring up some images of the real Dahmer's cases. See if that helps," Ryan said to Dope.

Dope's forehead scrunched. "Man, I don't even want to look at those. I barely kept my snacks down at the last ones. You and Kip are the ones in the field cleaning up the bodies and evidence. I don't have the stomach for it."

"Excellent. Maybe Sebastian won't either," Kip added.

Dope pulled up the crime scene images, then hopped out of my chair. "Sit. I'm going to go check on Cami."

Before I could respond, Dope practically ran out the door.

I cracked my fingers and attempted to find the courage to look at the twisted, sick pictures.

"Ticktock," Kip whispered and tapped the face of his watch.

I glowered at him while I reminded myself that Ella was missing, and we'd already lost a day. I gulped, then proceeded to shock myself with the horrible findings from when they arrested Dahmer. "The guy in the warehouse. He did the same things to his victims too?"

"Yup. He was a copycat. I mentioned him to Death a few times, just in case he got bored and needed something to do." Ryan folded his arms in front of him, grinning like the cat that caught the mouse.

"Good. I can see where Death could come in handy in situations like those." I hated to admit that out loud, but it seemed as though Death's intentions were good—or at least a little bit justifiable. *What the fuck am I thinking?*

"All the time," Kip chimed in.

I stared at the morbid, grotesque images and waited to feel a headache coming on, but there was nothing. Blowing out a heavy sigh, I said, "It's not working. I don't know what will work if that didn't. I'm literally sick to my stomach."

A soft knock at the door caught my attention, and we all turned to see who it was as Kip closed the laptop.

"Hey," Cami said softly. "Two little people want to see you." She adjusted Alaric on one hip and Verity on the other. "The twins know something is wrong. I mean, the tension is pretty thick around here." She glared at Ryan as she walked over to us.

I rose from my seat. "Come here, little man."

Alaric's eyes were rimmed with red, and a string of snot hung from his nose. "No need to cry. We'll bring her back. I promise."

"Alive?" Cami asked.

"You have my word." I gritted my teeth and hoped I hadn't just lied to her. In my mind, there was no other choice except to bring Ella home safe and sound.

Alaric grinned as he held out his pudgy little hands. Once I had him in my arms, he placed his head against my chest and grabbed a fistful of my T-shirt.

"Mama. Ma-ma-mama." Still in Cami's arms, Verity chanted, then sucked on her fingers, slurping loudly.

"I know, baby girl. She'll be back soon," I said while I sat down and rubbed my son's back. His little head popped up, total trust in his big green eyes. "Def." He slapped his palm against my arm. "Def."

Kip glanced over at me. "Jesus Christ. He knows the difference. Alaric, who is Death?"

I shot Kip a dirty look. "Do not ask my nine-month-old about that monster," I growled between clenched teeth.

Before Alaric responded, his sister piped up. "Da-da."

In response to Verity, Alaric nodded and kicked his feet with excitement.

"Nothing you can do. The kids know, Bass. And they clearly like him by how excited they are."

My heart sank to my toes. "Do you think they . . . that they have a connection because they're similar?" I stared into the sweet innocent face of my son and then my daughter, who was now pulling on Cami's hair, wondering if one of them or both took after a serial killer. A terrified shudder traveled down my spine.

"Ella has mentioned that to me. She has wondered the same." Kip ruffled Alaric's soft curls. "Tell Death to come out and play, little man. We need his help."

Alaric released a high-pitched squeal as he clapped his hands.

Verity's cry rang through the room as she leaned forward in Cami's grasp.

"Come here, baby girl," I said.

"Def. Def. Def," Verity chanted.

I handed my son to Kip before I gathered Verity in my arms, our gazes connecting as she stilled. She reached up and placed her warm palms on my cheeks and flashed me a big smile, showing off her four teeth. "Ma-ma . . . Def."

The room stilled as I looked into my little girl's eyes, which were filled with trust and excitement. She and her brother understood more than I'd realized, at least enough to know who I was at any given moment. Although every cell in my being wanted to continue to deny the truth, it was clear even my children knew I was two different people in one body.

A sudden sharp pain ricocheted through my mind, and I gasped as I grabbed the side of my head. I staggered backward, and my vision blurred as the agony intensified. Alaric's giggles filled the room, but they sounded distorted, warped somehow. Kip's voice seemed to echo from a great distance, his words muffled as if underwater. Panic gripped my chest as I struggled to focus, to fight against the overwhelming force invading my mind.

"Fuck," I whispered hoarsely as I tried to push the pain away, but it was like trying to hold back a tidal wave with my bare hands.

Alaric's joyful laughter turned hollow, sending a chill through the room. The air grew thick with an oppressive darkness that seemed to seep into my very bones.

"What's happening?" Cami hurried to take Verity as I fell to my knees on the floor.

"You should leave," Ryan said to her.

"No, you've all kept me in the dark long enough. I'm not going anywhere. If Alaric and Verity aren't scared, then . . ." But the expression on her face said otherwise.

CHAPTER 15

DEATH

It wasn't the wolves that took you, little lamb. It was the whispers of the wind promising adventures beyond the fence.
—Anonymous

A guttural roar erupted from my chest as I struggled to catch my breath. With fierce determination, I slowly rose to my feet and locked eyes with every person in the room. My senses heightened, I cautiously stood and scanned my surroundings, ready for any threat that may come my way.

"What the fuck is everyone doing here? The last thing I remember is walking into the living room, and it was a fucking disaster."

"Death, man, am I glad to see you," Kip said from behind me.

I turned to look at my friend, confused as to why everyone was in Ella's home.

"No shit," Ryan added.

Kip held Alaric as the little guy clapped his hands. "Def!"

"I'm helping take care of the kids since Ella is . . . missing," Cami said while she bounced Verity on her hip.

"We're all here, man. Dope is somewhere in the house too. When he called to tell you about the camera footage, we all hopped on a plane. Cami came, too, so she could help with the kids. Do you remember me calling?"

"Yeah, but barely. Those headaches are messing with my head . . . Everything's a damn blur," I said through gritted teeth. I rubbed my temple in hopes to ease the pain. "She's for sure missing?" The words fell from my lips like lead, heavy with frustration and confusion.

Ryan's expression twisted into a grimace, mirroring the turmoil in my mind. "Yeah, she's gone. Dope has footage of men taking her right off the front porch. They trashed the place too."

My hands instinctively clenched into fists, knuckles turning white as I struggled to process the news. Then a tidal wave of anger and helplessness crashed over me and engulfed my entire being as I desperately tried to grasp onto any memory of the events. Each passing second only stoked my frustration. This was becoming unbearable, the constant loss of time and missing crucial moments. And worst of all, how could I have failed to keep her safe? Guilt gnawed at me like a savage beast, threatening to consume me whole. I should have been here instead of chasing my own bloodlust; my selfish desires had led to devastating consequences. The lump in my throat threatened to choke me as I refused to even entertain the thought that I may have lost Ella forever.

I glanced at the laptop on the desk, and my dark chuckle filled the room. "That was a good day ending that son of a bitch." I grinned. "Give me my son," I said to Kip. My tone was firm, but not unfriendly. My attention landed on Cami, who I knew from Ella, but this was the first time I'd met her face-to-face.

Cami's arms shook as she held Verity. It was clear that I scared her, which wasn't an unhealthy response.

"Well, if there was any doubt that you and your kids are deeply connected, it's gone now." Ryan smirked. "They're the key to bringing you around. At least now we know."

I wrapped my son in my arms. "You are *my* boy." I smoothed the dark peach fuzz on his head and placed a kiss on his pudgy cheek.

"Welcome back. We need to know what happened when you returned to the house. Did you see anyone around?" Ryan asked.

Fear flickered in Cami's gaze, and I couldn't help but flash her a sinister smile. "Rest assured that I will find my little lamb and bring her home."

Cami tipped her chin. "Make it fast." With that, she spun on her heel and left.

"Send Dope in," Kip yelled after her.

I paced the room with Alaric. "I don't want the kids to leave here. Whoever took Ella, they might be back."

"If we could figure out who *they* are, it would really help." Kip rubbed his stubbled jaw. "Um, and not to piss you off as soon as you show up, but Ella told us that she's mentioned Sebastian to you before."

The tension around his name was so thick, I could have cut it with my knife. I pinned him with a glare and snarled. "We don't talk about it . . . about him."

"Hell, I wouldn't want to either, but we're going to have to in order to find Ella," Ryan said.

"Dude, never been so fucking happy to see you." Dope walked into the office and closed the door behind him. "Sorry I missed that entrance, but I had to take a piss."

"It was the kids that brought Death out, so here we are," Kip said.

"Very fucking cool! I guess the twins are the key to bringing you around. I kind of wondered if you all were two peas in a pod. I'm only guessing, but we might have to keep an eye on them." Dope rubbed his hands together as if he were up for the challenge.

"Def," Alaric said again.

Dope's light red brow arched. "And that's my point."

"About Sebastian," Ryan said, bringing the topic back around. "You knew about the paternity and DNA tests, so you know he's around. Somewhere in your head, you realize that you and Sebastian reside in the same . . . body."

"I don't have to know anything. I hate that son of a bitch for touching what belongs to me." I was seething.

"I would love to play this game with you, but we don't have time, so I'm going to cut to the chase," Kip said, approaching me with his features full of compassion. "You and Sebastian are the same man. You look exactly the same, live with Ella, have kids with her. You're a serial killer and Sebastian isn't. His dark side comes out in other ways, like cage fighting in the old days. He's calculated and smart, just like you. But you're his dark side and live with a bloodlust that drives you to kill people. The reason you lose time and memories is because Sebastian comes out and vice versa."

I shook my head at his directness. "And if I don't believe you?"

"Then remember who has hung around with you since middle school—Dope and, later, me. Have we ever lied to you about something this important? Would we do this just to fuck with you? Think, man. Ella is depending on you and Sebastian working together to find her. If for no other reason, accept the truth for her."

My eyes darted around the room, landing on each of my friends in turn. Kip's words hit me like a punch to the gut. They had never lied to me about anything important. I trusted them with my life and, more importantly, with the lives of Ella and our children. Everything they were saying was overwhelming, but I pushed it aside for the moment. Right now, all that mattered was getting to Ella and making sure she was safe. The rest could be dealt with later, when my mind wasn't clouded with fear and urgency.

"Fine," I snarled.

A collective sigh of relief exploded from the group, their tense bodies finally releasing fear and anxiety that had been building up. My thoughts raced with questions about Sebastian and our complicated relationship, but for now all I could focus on was getting Ella safely back home. Failure was not an option, and the thought of anything happening to her filled me with a searing rage. I would stop at nothing to find her.

"We finally took a chance and told Sebastian about you. We need any help we can get to find Ella. Plus, we think her being taken has more to do with you than Sebastian."

"You mean *my* enemy, not Sebastian's?" The hair on the back of my neck prickled with his name on my tongue.

"It's more likely since you tend to piss people off when you kill a family member." Dope shrugged with his comment. "I mean, no offense, but Sebastian is a nicer guy than you are."

I smirked. "If he's here to stay, that will have to change." I glanced at Alaric. "Son, I've got work to do. Someone took your mom, and I've got a mess to make." I hugged him before I handed him to Dope. "Take him to Cami. There's a nanny cam in one of the stuffed bears in the living room. Ella turns it on when Lulu is at the house with the kids by herself. Be discreet, but flip the switch on the camera so we can keep an eye on Cami. I clearly scared the shit out of her, but something isn't sitting right with me, and I don't want her taking off with my kids."

The guys grew quiet, but Dope took Alaric and left the room.

"She overheard that Sebastian is also you and that we've been covering up for you." Ryan shifted his weight. "She promised she wouldn't turn us all in to the FBI or cops so we can focus on bringing Ella back."

"Ah. That would be a big problem. One that I couldn't allow." They understood what I was implying.

Ryan's hands flew up in front of him. "Hey, she's off limits. You do not get to hurt her or even scare her. She's Ella's best friend. That has to count for something."

"And you're in love with her," I snapped. "Should have thought about that before you brought her into our fucked-up world."

Kip cleared his throat. "Yeah, well, Ella is missing and that's most likely on you, so we can point fingers another time. Besides, we're all choosing to be here, so man up and let's get down to business."

As much as I wanted to punch him in the nose, Kip was right. If anyone could help me bring her home, it was these guys.

Dope returned and closed the door behind him. "The camera is on."

I removed my phone from my back pocket and pulled up the app. Cami was on the floor with Verity and Alaric, playing with them.

"Who did you piss off recently? Or maybe a better question is who hates you enough to take what you love the most?"

My eyes narrowed as I sifted through a very long list, then I recalled the letter left for me in Portland.

"Someone knows who I am, and they're fucking with me."

Kip moved to the couch and sank down on it. "Care to explain?"

"The last time I was in Oregon at the warehouse . . . when I walked into the building there was an envelope on the floor with my name on it."

"Just to clarify, was it addressed to Death or Sebastian?"

I whirled around and stalked toward Dope. "What the fuck does that mean?"

Ryan stepped between Dope and me, playing interference. "Hey, we'll deal with that later. This is about Ella. You've gotta stay focused, Death."

I hated to admit it, but he was right.

"Sebastian is a part of you, Death. You're going to have to wrap your head around that idea. We're going to need both of you to find Ella. A part of you knows this, or you wouldn't have stuck around after Ella gave you the DNA results for the twins." Kip's voice was calm, soothing.

"Later," I barked. I stepped back and gained some space between Dope and me. "It was addressed to Death. As I said, someone knows who I am." I walked over to the window and looked out across the property; the tree line was heavy with fog. "When I opened the envelope, there was a letter inside. I pulled it out and there were messy words scrawled on the paper." I turned to look at the men. "It said, 'I'm watching,' but no signature."

The color drained from Kip and Dope's faces.

"Fucking hell," Kip said. "Was there anything else?"

"No, that was it."

Dope shoved both hands through his red hair. "Why in the hell didn't you mention that to us? Do you realize what this means?"

"Of course I understand what it means, but that was about seven months ago, and I haven't had any additional contact. I had other pressing matters going on that took up a lot more time and . . . *energy*. It slipped my mind." The possibilities spun out in my head as I recalled a conversation with Ella about my parents' murderer. "Ella." I nearly choked on her name. She was gone. Someone had taken her from me. Stolen her from her own home. "Ella has been looking into who murdered my parents. I think she stumbled onto some information that's put her in danger."

"Fuck!" Dope slapped his palm over his face. "Again, you didn't think to share this with us so we could protect her?"

"I literally just found out. She had newspaper articles and an entire manila envelope full of details hidden under the floor. I was so pissed that she'd crossed that line after I told her to leave it the fuck alone." Images of my little lamb tied to the bed as I fucked her with my knife pulled my attention away from them. The sight of her tear-stained cheeks, choking on my cock, sent a rush of twisted gratification through me. Despite the conversation happening around me, all I could think about was bringing her back to safety so I could claim her again. To erase the trauma of those dark days and replace it with unbridled pleasure. She would beg and scream and moan my name as I showed her what true submission meant. My little lamb would serve me, making up for causing me worry and fear. And in return, I would ravish her, pleasuring her like never before for putting her in danger.

"Where's that information?" Ryan asked while he walked toward the door.

"In her bedroom. Come with me."

The knowledge that my knife was strapped to my leg was the only thing that gave me comfort. When I hunted down the motherfuckers who took Ella, they would find out exactly who I was. A fucking monster.

CHAPTER 16

ELLA

I stared at the pretty woman in front of me. My best guess was that she was a few years younger than I was.

"Help me," I pleaded in a hushed tone as I pressed my palm against the cold glass between us. My frantic gaze darted around the room as I searched for any sign of Xavier, but he was nowhere to be seen. "I'll give you anything," I promised, desperation coating every word as I begged for her aid. "My husband is wealthy. I can pay you." The weight of my plea hung in the air.

Suddenly, a blinding beam of light illuminated the space, followed by the thud of heavy footsteps. The woman's expression turned to fear as she backed away from me and shook her head.

"Fiona, what are you doing here?" Xavier asked, his tone pinched.

Fiona turned her back to me as Xavier entered the kitchen.

He fidgeted with the front of his shirt before he continued. "I wasn't expecting anyone."

"Clearly. But even if you knew I was coming, how in the hell would you have hidden that?" She pointed in my direction. "Are you fucking out of your mind? You're smarter than that."

Xavier stalked toward her, fuming. "Watch your mouth, or I will close it for you."

She snapped her mouth shut so hard I heard her teeth click together.

Fiona reached out and gently touched his shoulder. "I'm sorry. That was mean to say. It just caught me off guard. Does the boss know you've kidnapped someone?"

Xavier sneered at her. "Oh, he knows. It was his idea. He gave her to me to love and protect."

"So you're keeping her in a cage against her will?" Fiona frowned. "Hon, you can't do that. It's not okay."

Xavier turned on his heel and stomped away. "Who says? Society? What the hell do they know?" He ran his hand through his messy hair, his expression bewildered.

Please, please get through to him. My hope was dangling by a thin thread as she continued to talk to Xavier.

"You know I love you and I don't want to see you hurt. I don't think the boss thought this through. I mean, what if she escapes? They'll come for you and lock you up for the rest of your life. It would break my heart. You deserve better than . . . this." She motioned to the shitty living quarters. "You deserve to be happy and see the sunshine."

Xavier blinked at her as if she were speaking in a different language. "You've never said those things to me before. Fiona is usually catty." He narrowed his eyes at her. "What do you want?"

Fiona's chest heaved with her deep breath. "I came by to see if you needed food or supplies since you rarely leave this place."

His expression brightened immediately. "Twinkies. I would love a Twinkie." He clapped his hands like a little kid. Xavier strolled over to me and leaned down. "Ella, do you want a Twinkie too?"

I gave him a soft smile. "And milk?"

"Yes! And cookies so we can dunk them during date night. What's your favorite?"

I pretended to think for a minute. I needed protein, not sugar, to keep my strength up. The measly soup he'd been feeding me wasn't cutting it.

"Chocolate chip, but even more than that . . ."

He looked at me expectantly.

"I would give anything for a hamburger and fries. Do you know how to cook that? Maybe we could have a proper dinner on date night?" I suggested.

"He makes the best hamburgers I've ever eaten," Fiona said from behind him.

"Really?" My mouth watered at the idea of a fat, juicy burger. "And do you like lettuce, tomatoes, and mayonnaise?"

Xavier nodded, clearly excited with planning our meal and evening. At least for the moment, I was dealing with an innocent child. I wish

I saw this part of him more often. It might be easier to talk him into letting me go.

"Xavier, I'll help you make a list." Fiona reached into her handbag for a pen and paper.

"I'll go. I'll shop for my future bride. The produce has to be perfect like she is."

Fiona's eyes widened. "Are you sure? You rarely leave here."

"But I do. Just to see the boss most of the time. I can still drive, though."

My pulse fluttered. Was he leaving? Now that I knew where the door was, it was just a matter of figuring out how the hell to get out of this goddamn cage.

As if Xavier read my thoughts, he trained his attention on me. "Be a good girl, Ella. You don't want to know what happens to people who don't mind me." He looked behind him at the kitchen table where his family stared at me with their faraway expressions.

"I wouldn't miss our date night for anything." I beamed at him, wondering how the hell I'd become so efficient at lying. Nearly barking out a laugh, I reminded myself that I lied every day to hide my husband's secret as well as the Safe Horizon Society. I'd become a professional and hadn't realized it until my life depended on it.

Xavier and Fiona turned their backs on me and left without a single glance in my direction. With a deep, shuddering breath, I tried to calm my racing heart and tense muscles. I knew the danger of being near him, always on edge for the next outburst that could result in my death. Every moment with him was a ticking time bomb.

I allowed my thoughts to drift to Sebastian and the kids, my chest squeezing so hard it was painful. In my mind, there was no other possibility than to live through this horrid nightmare. As I imagined Death showing up and carrying me out of this hellhole, I frantically ran my fingers along the cold glass walls, desperate for any chance of escape.

Even though I would be surprised if one were there, I was hoping to find a vulnerability. My pulse raced as I desperately searched for a way out. My thoughts turned to a conversation I had had months ago with Cami and Ryan, where they mentioned using forensic experts to locate weak spots in materials. The memory came flooding back to me as I frantically chewed on my lip and stared at my wedding band and engagement ring. I wondered if I could use an everyday metal to break the thick glass near the lock and escape. The thought gave me a glimmer of hope amidst the panic and fear that consumed me. With newfound determination, I moved to the door and began to test my theory, hoping like hell it would work before it was too late. I removed the platinum band and held my breath as I tapped the glass, then paused.

The light from the entryway spilled into the room, and I quickly placed my wedding ring on my finger again. Footsteps traveled down the stairs, and to my shock, Fiona emerged from the stairwell. She glanced over her shoulder as if she were making sure she wasn't followed before she came over to the cage.

"I'm not here to let you go if that's what you're thinking."

I sank my teeth into my lower lip in order to not scream at her. Since I wasn't aware of her intentions, I didn't want to dig my own grave, so I made myself remain calm.

I crawled closer to the side of the container and looked her in the eye. "I understand. Xavier is . . ."

"You can say it." Fiona sank onto the floor and crossed her legs.

"You know there are a ton of spiders out there, right?" I rubbed my arms, shivering at the idea of them crawling out of their hiding places to investigate the visitor.

"Yup. They don't scare me."

I swallowed over the ball of anxiety in my throat. "I can't say the same."

A silence fell between us, and I wondered why she was here.

"How do you know Xavier?" I asked, hoping to get some answers.

"We work together. Well, that's not really true. I work for his boss. But Xavier and I have known each other for years."

"Did you know his family?" I pointed behind her at the stuffed humans.

She frowned and glanced in the direction I was pointing. Fiona started to giggle, and I wondered if she was unstable like Xavier.

"His family?" She held her belly as she laughed. "Is that what he told you? That those dolls are his family? Oh my god, well played, Xavier."

"Not exactly. He implied that he killed and stuffed his parents and sister." I found nothing funny about the situation.

She wiped tears from her cheeks. "Sorry. I have a twisted sense of humor, and sometimes I can't help myself." She snorted.

I stared at her, trying to understand what she was saying. "Are you laughing because those people aren't real or because they aren't his family?"

"Oh, they are . . . well, were real. He's a very skilled artist, don't you think? His mom, dad, and sister were his first victims. You should see the others."

My legs trembled with the revelation. "Others?" I asked, my voice hovering above a whisper.

"He's found his calling. The next families got even better. What do they say? Practice makes perfect?"

My stomach churned and my heart dropped with lightning speed to my toes with her confirmation that Xavier wasn't only dangerous but had no problem with killing and stuffing me. "I just don't understand why me." I had a sneaking suspicion that it had to do with Death and my research on his family, but I wasn't going to offer that information.

"You can't repeat this, and if you do, I'll make sure you pay dearly, so don't forget that."

I raised my hands in surrender. "I won't say a word."

"After I saw you and Xavier, I talked to the boss. I wanted to know who you were and why you were stuffed in a glass box. Apparently, the boss asked Xavier to babysit you, get you out of the way, but . . . but *you* are bait, Ella. The boss gave Xavier strict orders not to inflict serious harm—like, he could cut you up, but not badly enough that you bleed out. Y'know, shit like that. I thought if the boss knew you were in a cage, he'd probably blow a fucking gasket. I was wrong since he doesn't think there's another way to contain you, so . . ." She gave me a small shrug.

I couldn't wait to meet Xavier's boss for myself and shove a knife into his heart and twist it slowly. Later, I would give myself permission to entertain that thought, but I needed to get as much information out of Fiona as I could. "I'm bait for who?"

Fiona glanced over her shoulder again, then she leaned closer to the glass. "Your husband."

I pursed my lips together, ensuring I kept my mouth shut. If she didn't know about Death, then that could work to my advantage.

"So, some goons snatched me off the front porch of my home as payback from someone whose family my husband helped?"

She smacked her lips loudly, as if I'd guessed correctly. *This is about the Safe Horizon Society?*

"There are some very twisted and dangerous men he's pissed off. I'm guessing your boss is one of them."

"Something like that, yeah."

I tilted my head, still confused why she'd returned.

"Fiona, why did you come back if you weren't going to help me escape?" A creepy crawly moved across the floor, and I pointed near the couch. "One of your friends is coming to say hello."

I watched in disgust as Fiona extended her hand and let the critter crawl up her arm like Xavier had. Sucking in a breath, I looked away. "I just can't get used to that."

"It takes awhile." She cooed at the spider as if it were the cutest little kitten she'd ever seen. "And to answer your question, I'm not sure. When I saw you locked up and realized that Xavier was in love with you . . . I guess I felt sorry for you. Having a date night with Xavier is kind of gross." She scrunched up her nose in disgust.

"And I'm married, but that doesn't seem to bother him."

Her brow arched. "Why should it? In his mind, you're never leaving him."

"Do you know that I have nine-month-old twins? They need me home, Fiona. Please. I'm begging you, just open the cage, and I'll do the rest."

She set the spider on the floor, then stood slowly. "I can't. Xavier and my boss wouldn't hesitate to kill me. I'm not suicidal." She pursed her lips, her eyes flickering with regret. "I'll try to stop by again soon. At least you'll have a good meal when Xavier returns."

"How long will he be gone?"

"He should be back any minute. I should go." She hopped up and then spun on her heel and practically ran out of the underground hole, leaving me behind once again. I couldn't help but think about what Fiona had said regarding Xavier being a killer. She was clearly having a good time fucking with my head. I stared at the lifelike dolls again. One thing was confirmed from her visit— Xavier was a murderer and dangerous, and I couldn't afford to let my defenses down.

I drew my knees up to my chest and rested my chin on them. Deep inside me, I understood that my time was running out. Xavier was growing more obsessed with me, and my chances of escaping were dwindling. I stared at my wedding rings. Maybe, just maybe my band would be what set me free.

The sound of the door creaking let me know that I'd have to wait until I was alone again to try my idea. I just hoped it would be soon enough.

CHAPTER 17

DEATH

The flock moves as one, but solitude moves through the lost lamb's bones like winter.
—Anonymous

I led the men up the stairs to Ella's bedroom. The rug had been haphazardly replaced over the loose board, and I wondered if whoever had broken into the home and stolen her had also found the information she'd been working on. I knelt, then pried the floor up, revealing a dark hole.

I reached for my phone, flipped on the flashlight, and shined the light into the floor. To my surprise and relief, the contents were still there. Maybe Ella had cleaned up after I'd left. I reached in and hesitated. "Hang on, I see something else." I adjusted the light and spotted a white envelope.

"Don't touch it," Ryan ordered. "Do you have gloves somewhere?"

"In the bathroom, second drawer."

"What is it? Can you tell?" Kip asked.

"A white envelope. I'm not sure if it was in the original manila envelope or not. I don't remember seeing it, but I haven't been myself lately." I held out my hand to Ryan as he returned with the latex gloves. Ella always kept a box around for when I returned from a kill and required some medical attention. The first aid kit was loaded with anything needed to patch me up.

"Thanks," I muttered as I slipped them on. Silence hung in the air as I reached in and retrieved the unfamiliar item. Carefully, I lifted the unsealed flap and pulled out a little piece of paper. My nostrils flared. "This is the same cream paper that was used for the note in the warehouse." I glanced at the men before I read the words out loud. "'Hello,

Death. Glad you could join us. Just because I'm so happy you're here, I'll give you another clue to where your precious Ella is: Some ghosts never leave. Some rooms remember everything.'"

"What the hell is that supposed to mean?" I muttered. "And how did the bastard get into my home undetected?"

"Let me see the note." Dope reached out for it. "My guess: if it wasn't here last time you looked at the contents, then he was here when those men grabbed Ella. They came into the house and trashed it, remember?"

I grunted at him; the memories were dark and faded.

"Whoever kidnapped Ella and left this for me must have put the papers under the floor and then taken a chance that I would look through this information again." I stood and paced the bedroom, ready to tear someone apart.

"We should search through the manila envelope to make sure they didn't leave anything else for you," Ryan said. I hadn't noticed earlier, but he'd also slipped on a pair of gloves.

"I need my laptop. I'll be back." Dope rubbed the back of his neck as he left, then proceeded down the stairs.

"If anyone can figure out that clue, it's Dope," Kip said, walking the length of the room.

I reached into the hole and removed the manila envelope. "I'll have to look at it all again. I remember most of the contents, but I was so angry that Ella had gone behind my back, I don't recall all of it." I walked to her bed and opened the flap, then pulled out the newspaper clippings, notes she'd made, and photos.

Ryan released a low whistle. "She's been busy from the looks of it."

"No kidding," I grumbled as I began to sort the items by what I knew I'd seen and what I wasn't sure about. "I doubt the piece of shit left any other clues other than the riddle."

"Even so, you might see something important that you didn't the first time." Kip pointed to the pile. "Since I won't be of much help here, I'll find Dope and make sure he's staying on task."

Ryan tipped his chin at Kip. "Good idea. I'll help Death."

"Check on Cami and the kids, Kip," I snarled. "I don't trust her right now."

"Same." Kip nodded and then left us to our work.

Over the next half hour, Ryan and I sifted through everything Ella had gathered. Even though there were some notes I hadn't seen earlier, nothing stood out to me as important. I collected the information and slipped it into the envelope, my mind spinning with the riddle in the note.

"Ella must still be alive, or whoever has her wouldn't have risked leaving a hint." I glanced at Ryan before I walked to the bedroom window that overlooked the back of the property.

"It's a good sign. In fact, he might not want to kill her at all. You've gotten a phone call and a hidden clue. I don't think this is about Ella."

I turned slowly, the impact of his words weighing on me. "It's about me."

"Somewhere out there, you've pissed someone off."

I glowered at him. "Not helping, asshole. I've pissed off a lot of people."

A flicker of anger registered in his eyes, then disappeared.

The sound of footsteps running up the stairs caught my attention, and I hurried to the hall as Dope and Kip joined us again.

"I have an idea. I haven't confirmed it yet, but as soon as I heard you read the note, I had a sneaking suspicion. And I think I'm right." Dope coughed as he struggled to catch his breath. He must have made a mad dash up here, but he needed to lay off the smoke for damn sure.

"What is it?"

"The clue said 'Some ghosts never leave. Some rooms remember everything.'"

"Yeah, and?" I asked impatiently.

"What if they're talking about the kitchen in your childhood home? The one you lived in before you moved in with me and my family."

I shot him an inquisitive look. "What about it?"

"For being a genius, you're kind of dense sometimes." Dope's voice was filled with exasperation. "Dude, your parents were brutally murdered in that kitchen. If the walls had eyes, they would remember everything. And the ghost . . . It's haunted you and Sebastian your entire life."

"How the hell did you get all of that?" Kip asked.

I was glad Kip spoke up because I was wondering the same thing.

Dope rocked back and forth on his heels. "Since the first phone call, when the caller asked for Death, I suspected this was all about him, not Sebastian and someone pissed about the society helping their family escape. I mean, I could still be wrong, but I don't think so. Then, once

Death read the new note, it started to make sense." He tapped the side of his head. "Death, one room changed your entire life. Nothing has had that kind of impact on you again . . . until Ella, but she's the good part of all of that."

"Keep going," Ryan said.

The excitement in Dope's gaze dwindled as we just stared at him.

"Okay, I can tell you think I'm reaching for anything concrete, and maybe I am, but it's literally the best hope we have." Dope turned to me. "We need to go to your childhood house, especially the kitchen. I suspect your next clue is there."

A heavy knot formed in my gut at the mention of returning to that scene. I'd worked hard to block out that home and everything that had happened there. Now I was about to rip that nightmare open again.

"Ryan and I will go. Kip and Dope, you stay here with Cami and keep looking into any other ideas."

"Got it." Dope hurried down the stairs.

Kip ran his hand through his hair, hope in his expression. "I think he's on to something. Let us know what you find at the old place."

"Ryan, you up for a walk into my personal hell?"

"Let's go." Ryan patted my back as he passed by me.

Only time would tell if Dope was right, and I had a sickening feeling there was very little of it left.

The flight on my plane from New York to Minneapolis, Minnesota, where my childhood home was located, seemed like an eternity instead of only three-and-a-half hours. Once we landed, I sent the plane back to New York in case there was an emergency and I needed to get the twins to safety.

The old neighborhood was another forty-two minutes from the airport, but Ryan offered to drive the rental car, a black Camry, which blended in well enough with the other cars on the road. When I grew irritated that he was driving the speed limit, he reminded me that being pulled over could be very problematic for me. He had a point. The FBI was trying to solve the Portland serial killer puzzle, and I couldn't take a chance on one of them getting too close to me. I couldn't risk some cop having a gut feeling something was wrong and sticking his nose where it didn't belong.

My blood boiled as I reluctantly returned to Minnesota, a place that held nothing but fucked-up memories. I hadn't been back since I'd moved away. There wasn't any reason to . . . until now. The thought of stepping foot in the place that stole my childhood and parents ripped me apart like a dog with a stuffed toy, but it was the only hope I had at saving Ella.

My heart skipped a beat with worry for her safety. Had that son of a bitch hurt her? The mere notion of another man laying a hand on her ignited a blazing fury within me, sending electric currents of rage pulsing through every fiber of my being.

"I wish we knew what the hell we were looking for," Ryan said.

"It's not like this guy has been forthcoming other than the fact that he has Ella. I suppose we will figure it out when we get there."

Ryan glanced at me, then his attention returned to the road. "Going back to the house has got to be fucked up, man."

My brow arched. "I wouldn't know. I haven't returned since leaving for college."

"Not sure I'd want to go back either." He paused before he continued. "We're almost there."

I stared out of the passenger-side window as the houses grew more familiar. Young seedlings that had just started to grow when I lived there were now huge oak and maple trees. Cars lined the streets next to the sidewalk, and a few dogs safely ran alongside the Camry behind their chain-link fences.

"It used to not be so busy. Dope and I used to walk up the middle of the street at night." I rubbed my jawline, my fingertips tingling with my anxiety.

The sound of the turn signal filled the car, and then Ryan made a left onto Madison Avenue. He slowed to the mandatory twenty-five miles an hour as I stared at the changes in the neighborhood. A handful of memories flashed through my mind, some good and some bad.

"Slow down." I pointed to the two-story navy-blue home with brown trim. "That's Dope's old house. It used to be yellow. I lived with him and his parents after mine died. But you know that already."

"Did you have good times there?" Ryan asked as he pulled over and parked the car. He shifted into park and let the engine idle.

"I had a few, but not many."

"Makes sense. I think Sebastian was here most of the time, and you were just starting to appear from what Dope and Kip have told me."

I resisted shoving my friend's head into the passenger window. The mere mention of Sebastian sent me into a tailspin, and if I ever met the motherfucker, I would end him. There was only enough room for one of us in Ella's life. When she needed us most, I was the one who was here. *Fuck Sebastian.* A pain shot through my skull, and I grunted while I massaged my temple.

Ryan's eyes widened. "This is not a good time, Sebastian. Don't fucking do it. Ella is counting on you staying put for now."

"You're a crazy motherfucker if you believe I'm buying that shit that he and I are the same person," I snapped.

"Doesn't matter what you think right now. We have to find Ella, so deal with it." Ryan shifted the car into drive and slowly steered the car to the end of the street.

I glanced at Ryan, then said, "The pain in my head is gone."

"Good. That means he heard me. I've never been able to talk to him before when you're Death, so something is definitely changing with the two of you."

Ryan could think whatever the hell he wanted about Sebastian. I had other plans for the fucker who thought he could share a bed with my little lamb.

CHAPTER 18

ELLA

Xavier sang as he descended the stairs and into the kitchen. "I'm back. Are you hungry?" He set a few overflowing bags on the dirty counter.

"I'm starving." My legs were cramped up, and I hoped he would let me out soon. "Can I help you put the groceries away?" It was strange how an ordinary chore meant something special to me now.

He turned slowly, a grin tugging at the corners of his mouth. "I'll let you help, but not yet. I have a surprise!"

Dread settled like a heavy weight in the pit of my stomach as his words sank in. I could feel my insides churning, flip-flopping with unease. But I forced myself to nod, then watched helplessly as he put away groceries and then disappeared into a hidden room that I hadn't been shown before. Time crawled by as I waited and wondered what else he had kept secret from me. When he finally reemerged, he set down glasses and filled them with milk, then grabbed cookies from the cabinet with an eerie calmness. My heart raced as he set everything on the table, his every movement calculated and deliberate. My body tingled with an odd sensation as I realized that something was off, but I couldn't quite put my finger on it yet.

After what must have been my first full day in captivity, my stomach growled painfully. I hadn't eaten since Xavier fed me soup yesterday.

"First, a snack . . ." He rubbed his palms together as if he were planning to take over the world. Sweat dotted my forehead, and I wiped it away with the back of my hand while my pulse raced and I waited for him to make his next move.

His brows creased and he nodded as if someone had just asked him a question, but I didn't see anyone else. I suspected he was having a conversation with himself. He raced across the room and clapped before he turned on a small stereo. "Breezeblocks" by Alt-J played through the old dusty speakers, making the song sound tinny and far away.

"I love Alt-J." His eyes lit up with the music.

"Me too. I guess it's something else we have in common." I gave him a warm smile, hoping he was beginning to trust me. The second he let his guard down, I planned on kicking his ass and running for my life. I just needed the right moment to present itself.

Xavier produced the key and slipped it into the lock on my glass cage. Once it was open, he extended his palm, and I took it. I crawled out of the small area, and he helped me to my feet.

"Thank you." I hated that those words held so much weight. I was truly grateful that I was out of my confined quarters.

He tapped his foot to "Left Hand Free" as Alt-J continued to sing to us. Xavier led me away from the cage, then gently spun me around.

"Dance, Ella. I know you love to." He cackled as he insisted that I join him.

"How do you know I like to dance?" I asked as innocently as I could while fear and dread consumed me.

"I have eyes everywhere. The cameras that your friend installed? Child's play," he explained, pride seeping through his tone. "Signal jammers, loop feeds . . . Your security was good, but I'm better. I spent months learning your routines, your blind spots. My boss taught me everything about staying invisible, plus my childhood instilled that in me as well."

The music slowed and he pulled me flush against him. I fought back the need to retch as he pressed his hips to mine. A cold, hard knot formed in my stomach, and I wondered how long he'd been watching me. He must have been a pro because Xavier would have been easy to spot, and I definitely would have recognized him if I'd seen him before. Not to mention that Dope would have detected someone piggybacking off his camera system. Then it dawned on me that he'd mentioned his boss was behind all of this. Somehow, I had to learn more.

He stopped dancing and tugged on my arm as he walked over to the table where the milk and cookies were waiting for us. To my surprise, he pulled out a chair for me.

My stomach gnawed at itself as I collapsed onto the seat, desperately craving sustenance.

"Eat," he commanded, sitting next to me at the table.

I shoveled three cookies into my mouth and gulped down the milk, feeling its nourishing effects spread through my body like a jolt of electricity. My eyes flickered to him as I remembered how my dark lashes and innocent gaze had affected Sebastian in the past. "Can I have some more?" I asked, wiping my lips hastily with the back of my hand. "I'm so thirsty."

He snatched up the glass and returned to the kitchen, where he filled it once again with creamy goodness, his actions almost frantic.

"Thank you," I murmured before grabbing another cookie and chugging the milk down without pause. I set the empty glass down with a satisfied sigh.

"That was . . . amazing," I managed to compliment between bites. When I finally looked up, I realized that Xavier hadn't touched his milk. My gaze returned to my empty glass and plate, and fear and suspicion bloomed in my stomach. Something was wrong, and I'd allowed my hunger to take over my common sense. "Are you not hungry?"

Xavier stared at me, his expression unreadable.

A sudden wave of dizziness hit me like a freight train, causing the room to spin violently and my body to collapse onto the floor with a loud thud. Gasping for air, I tried to focus on the figure looming over me, but my vision blurred, and I could only make out the distinct smell of chocolate chip cookies on his breath.

"Why?" I managed to choke out, my voice strained with confusion and fear.

He leaned in closer, and his eyes flashed with anger and disappointment. "I know you went behind my back and begged Fiona for help." He tsked, wagging a finger in front of my face. "Just when I thought maybe I could trust you, you betrayed me yet again. Well, if I can't trust you to stay by my side willingly, I'll have to take matters into my own hands."

My mind reeled as I tried to piece together what he was saying. "You . . . you drugged me . . . ," I muttered weakly, struggling to remain conscious.

His face twisted into a cruel smirk. "Not enough to knock you out permanently," he sneered. "But just the right amount to keep you under control. You may be clever, Ella McCloud Fletcher, but you're not clever enough."

Through the hazy drug-induced fog, I wondered what his plan with me was.

"Come, come." He grabbed my arm with a surprisingly strong grip and jerked me up off the floor.

I stumbled behind him as he led me through the kitchen and into the dark area he'd never shown me. He flipped on the overhead light, and I shrank back from the brightness.

"Look! It's your surprise!" He released me and bounced up and down on the balls of his feet like a little kid.

The room moved in slow motion as I looked in the corner. Next to a table, on a headless mannequin, was a white wedding dress.

I licked my lips, suddenly feeling parched. "Who's that for?"

"You, of course! I need to make sure it fits before our big day."

Unable to move, my feet remained rooted in place. Somewhere in the back of my mind a little voice whispered to play along. Reminding him that a wedding wouldn't be real since I was already married would only send him into a rage, and I didn't have the strength to defend myself.

My limbs grew heavier by the minute, and Xavier strolled over to me. He gathered my dress at my hips and began to pull it up.

"Lift your arms."

"I can't. It's hard to move."

"Hmm, maybe I gave you too much. I'll adjust the dose next time."

My body turned to stone. Every muscle was frozen in terror as his rough hands grabbed at my shaking frame. My mind screamed for him to stop, but all I could manage was a pitiful squeak of protest. He roughly removed my dress, leaving me vulnerable and exposed. Goosebumps traveled over my skin as I stood shivering in only my panties and bra.

His tongue darted over his dry, cracked lips, and I tried to pull back and cover myself, but it was as if my limbs were moving through quicksand. His gaze darkened as his eyes raked over me from head to toe, a twisted expression taking over his features. Regardless of the date night talk and innocent kisses, there was something much darker and deviant lurking inside of him.

The wedding gown hung on the mannequin next to us, mocking me with its pure-white lace and delicate fabric. As he guided me into the dress and pulled up the zipper, hot tears welled up in my eyes. It hit me then with a cruel force—he had been planning this all along. Keeping me drugged and helpless, a prisoner in his sick game. I wanted to push him, to run and never look back, but my body refused to move. He stepped away to admire his handiwork, and a sinister smirk spread across his face. My stomach twisted in revulsion as I realized what he truly wanted—to possess me, to own me. Without warning, my gag reflex kicked in, and I vomited down the front of the pristine white dress. A hysterical giggle bubbled up from my throat as the warm bile soaked through the fabric and onto my skin.

"You've ruined it!" He reared back, and his open hand connected with my cheek.

Unable to defend myself, I stumbled backward and hit my forehead on the corner of a table as I collapsed. Something warm trickled down the side of my head as I peered up at him.

"No, you ruined it by drugging me. It's making me sick." As soon as the words left my mouth, my stomach cramped.

"You fucking bitch! How dare you ruin my plan. It was supposed to be perfect!" Furious, he grabbed a fistful of my hair and dragged me toward the bathroom, my head screaming with the movement and pain. I attempted to dig my heels into the floor, but he was too strong, especially with the drug in my system.

"You're a fucking mess, and you ruined your beautiful dress," he sneered at me. "On your knees."

Too weak to argue, I did as I was told. The cold cement floor bit into my skin as he jerked my head backward, nearly hitting the edge of the rust-stained toilet. His bony fingers pried my jaw open, then he shoved a finger in until it hit the back of my throat. He moved away just in time for me to puke again, this time into the toilet with a splash. Before I could recover, he repeated the vile action. My stomach muscles cramped and strained to get rid of any leftover remnants, but I was only puking up clear bile.

He washed his hands, then grabbed a green washcloth and wet it. The rough material scratched over my skin as he wiped me off. He rinsed it, then placed it on the side of the sink.

"Get changed, and I'll get rid of the dress tomorrow." He stared at me, sadness in his gaze. "The drug should mostly be out of your system. I'll get something else that won't make you sick." Xavier knelt in front of me, cupped my chin, and ran his knuckles down my cheek. "I suppose it's my fault since I didn't dose you properly."

Exhausted, all I could do was nod.

"Sleep now. We will have to resume our date tomorrow." He traced his fingers down my neck and to the top of my breast that was peeking out of the dress. "You're more beautiful than I could have imagined. The second you stood in front of me in your bra and panties, I knew our wedding night would be even more special once I was inside you."

Suddenly, my body contorted in agony, and I vomited violently, spewing bile all over his face. Enraged, he stood up and roughly wiped his cheeks with a washcloth before turning to me with disgust. With a swift backhand, he struck me so hard that I fell backward, my ears ringing and vision blurring.

"You will learn to mind me and be more respectful, or you'll end up at the table with the rest of my family, you stupid little bitch." His expression twisted as his cheeks burned red.

I struggled to sit up, my head reeling from the impact of his hand.

Xavier grabbed my fingers and tugged on my wedding rings.

"No." I managed to clench my fist so he couldn't remove the jewelry, but I didn't have enough strength.

With a sharp tug, he jerked them off and stuffed them inside his jeans pocket.

"There's no need for those anymore. Soon you'll—" His jaw clenched, and he stormed out of the tiny bathroom.

Grabbing the lid of the toilet, I lowered it, then used it to pull myself off the floor. My vision blurred through my tears. Then I spotted what I hoped was an answer to prayers I was sure had fallen on deaf ears. I glanced over my shoulder as a burst of adrenaline cleared my foggy brain long enough for me to do what I needed to.

A few minutes later, he stomped back in and took my hand again. He shoved a black wedding band onto my finger.

"Whenever you look at it, you'll remember who you belong to. Forget your past life, Ella. It's over. The sooner you admit it to yourself, the happier you'll be with me."

My mind wasn't working quickly enough to fire off a smartass remark, but it was for the best.

Ten minutes later, I was out of the wedding dress and wearing my sundress again. He shoved me into the cage and locked the door behind me. I crawled across the cement floor and collapsed, landing on the pillow he'd given me a few days ago, or at least what felt like a few days ago. I wasn't sure anymore.

The sound of banging pots and pans penetrated my aching head. I wasn't sure how long I'd been asleep. My best guess was a few hours, and I was relieved that I was feeling better than I had earlier. My stomach seemed to be a lot calmer as well. Slowly, I sat up and looked around and winced from the light in the living room. For some reason, Xavier had all the lights turned on. He was furiously scrubbing something at the kitchen sink. The wedding dress. He was trying to save it. A wave of disgust washed over me.

"It's useless!" He picked up the gown and threw it on the floor before he marched over to me. "This is your fault!"

I cowered away from him even though the glass wall of the cage was between us. Earlier, he'd admitted he was to blame for drugging me and making me sick, but it seemed as though he'd changed his mind.

"You'll pay for this." He stared down at me as he removed his cell from his back pocket and tapped the screen.

A phone ringing filled the speaker before a familiar man answered.

"Little lamb?"

Death! His voice was music to my ears. My emotions stumbled over themselves as I shifted from fear to imagining the sweet taste of revenge. A sadistic smile eased across my face as I glared at Xavier, wondering if he knew who he was talking to this time. "One, two, he's coming for you," I whispered, the sound barely audible but filled with hate.

Xavier stared at me, and he clucked his tongue, his expression filling with understanding as he rubbed his hands together like a greedy child waiting for dessert. "I have what you want." He cackled. "No one calls Ella 'little lamb' except for Death. Welcome back."

"Death!" I yelled. "Please hurry."

Xavier's features twisted in anger as he pinned me with a look full of hatred.

"It doesn't seem you're as smart as I thought you were," he said to Death. "Your time is running out and so is hers."

"If you hurt her, I'll fucking spend the rest of my life hunting you down. When I get a hold of you, I'll cut your goddamn dick off and stuff it down your throat. Then, I'll cut off each finger and toe. I'll make you suffer slowly until you bleed out and you no longer see my face. But I promise you this, I will be the last thing you see before you fucking die."

"Promises, promises." Xavier rolled his eyes. "You have eight hours to find her, or she'll be joining my family."

Fear gripped my heart as my attention landed on the three stuffed people at the table. Xavier was definitely capable of killing. Fiona had confirmed that they had at one time been his family—alive. The thought of her pissed me off. She'd visited just to fuck with my head, nothing else. For all I knew, it was her idea to drug me in case I tried to run since I'd asked her for help. Fucking bitch. She better hope I died because if I made it out of there, I'd come back for her and bury her alive.

"Here's your last clue. Remember, you have only eight hours left."

A feral growl filtered through the phone, and a maniacal grin eased onto Xavier's face.

"Where your childhood screams still echo, she whispers her last goodbye. The wall between memory and salvation is thinner than you know."

"That doesn't make any fucking sense," Death yelled. "The—"

Xavier disconnected the call in the middle of Death's sentence.

"I have something very special planned for tonight."

My head was reeling with the riddle, and I missed what he'd said.

"Huh?" *Holy shit.* An idea tickled the back of my brain, trying to piece together where I was, but I had to be certain before I said anything.

"You'll see. For now, enjoy your day. I'll be back soon."

"Don't leave me here!" I yelled as he walked away and picked up the dress from the floor before climbing the stairs and disappearing.

Hope bloomed to life inside my chest. I was grateful he was gone, but I couldn't let him know that. My attention landed on the wedding band that encased my finger. I slid it off and held it in the palm of my hand while I offered a meager prayer to the heavens that my plan would work.

CHAPTER 19

DEATH

The shepherd calls it straying, but the darkness calls it pilgrimage—
every lost lamb is just a shadow being born.
—Anonymous

"What did he say?" Ryan asked.

My hands clenched into tight fists as I imagined choking the life out of him. "Another goddamn riddle, but I heard Ella in the background. She's alive, but the motherfucker only gave me eight hours to find her. From the riddle, I think we're on the right track with the house. He said, 'Where your childhood screams still echo, she whispers her last goodbye. The wall between memory and salvation is thinner than you know.'"

Every second was crucial, and I couldn't bear the idea of failing to save her. My pulse raced with adrenaline at the possibility that we were finally close to her, but I didn't dare speak it aloud for fear of jinxing our chances. Even as I pushed away the thought, my pulse quickened with anticipation and dread. Time was running out, and we had to act fast.

Ryan's brows shot up. "Let's get to the place where it all went down." He glanced at me, his expression hopeful. Ryan was probably thinking the same thing I was. Ella was nearby.

The car tires screeched as Ryan made a sharp turn onto Tully Lane, my childhood street. My stomach clenched with fear and anxiety as each familiar yard we passed ignited a memory—most of them involving Dope and the neighborhood kids.

I leaned forward, my heart jumping into my throat. "What the fuck?"

Ryan slammed on the brakes and pulled over to the side of the road, then killed the engine. We unclipped our seat belts and jumped out of the car.

"Holy shit." Ryan proceeded toward where my old home once stood. Now, it was reduced to nothing but rubble.

"I can't believe it's gone," I whispered, shaking my head in disbelief. "But . . . where's Ella!" Panic rose in my throat as I frantically scanned the debris for any sign that she had been there.

"I don't get it." Ryan walked across the dirt where my yard used to be, kicking at it as he moved. "It's fresh. The house was demolished recently. I wonder why, though." He looked down the street, and I followed his attention. "Someone is coming. Keep your mouth shut and let me see if we can learn anything."

I wouldn't have a problem staying quiet. At the moment, I was messed up in the head about Ella. The second I saw that the home was gone, I realized the caller was fucking with me. For a fleeting second, I had thought we would be leaving Minnesota with her in my arms. Clearly, I'd allowed my emotions to muddle my judgment, and this was just a game of cat and mouse to him. He was probably laughing his ass off.

A man who appeared to be in his mid-sixties approached us with a German shepherd.

"Afternoon," he said, slowing so his dog could take a piss on the dirt.

"Afternoon," Ryan replied. "You have a beautiful dog."

The man glowed with pride as he introduced Dixie to us. Her tail wagged happily as we pet her.

"You're not from around here," the guy said. "By the way, I'm Chester. I've lived in the area for more than twenty years. I'm about three streets over, but Dixie and I walk this way twice a day."

"Nice to meet you. I'm Jack, and this is my brother, Hugh. We grew up in the neighborhood and thought it would be fun to see how much it's changed. We weren't expecting this, though." Ryan motioned to the empty lot.

"I was shocked to see a crew tearing down the structure a few weeks ago. They just finished cleaning everything up yesterday. It seemed sudden, but the house had been for sale for years. No one wanted to buy it."

He had my attention now.

Ryan looked at me before he spoke. "You moved into the area after we left. We were pretty little. Grade school, actually."

"Everything has changed around here, that's for sure." Dixie sat next to her owner, panting.

"So, they tore down the place because no one would buy it? Why was it difficult to sell? Hugh and I loved the place."

Even though Ryan had suggested I stay quiet, I had details about the home that he didn't. "There was a door under the stairs and a small storage space. When I was supposed to be in bed, I used to hide and then watch television when our parents thought I was sleeping." I managed a smile and Ryan chuckled. "There were definitely some unique features about the place."

"There were rumors that the house had a weird vibe, and the creepy basement was filled with toys, stuffed animals, and dolls. Something along those lines, anyway. They were too old to clean up and donate, but I wonder if any were yours?" the guy asked.

"We were G.I. Joe kids, not stuffed animals," Ryan said with a smile.

My jaw ticked as I tried to recall any of the toys, but my memories were few and far between. The only reason I knew about hiding under the stairs was because Dope had mentioned it to me a while ago.

Kip's words echoed in my mind as I remembered him telling us all about the initial phone call, when Ella had given clues to her location—a cage, underground, surrounded by stuffed animals. If my old basement had toys . . . Something in the back of my brain nudged me. I wasn't remembering an important piece of the puzzle, but how could I with so few memories?

"What happened there that no one wanted to buy it after we left?" I asked, repeating Ryan's question.

Chester cleared his throat, then said, "It was before I moved here, but rumor has it the couple that owned the place were brutally murdered. They had a son, and apparently, he witnessed the whole thing. Poor kid was traumatized by that, and child services put him in foster care right after. I bet he was a mess. No child should have to see that, and lose everything too."

"What happened to him?" I asked, shoving my hand into the pocket of my jeans.

"A family took him in and helped him through the hard times. Gave him a safe place to stay. I heard they were really good people.

After that, he graduated and moved out of the area. No one knows what happened to him. It would be interesting to find out, though. See how he turned out."

He didn't want to know how it had all turned out. I was a killer and one of the most wanted in the country by the FBI.

"Yeah, it would be intriguing to see what he made out of his life," Ryan agreed.

"Well, it's nice to meet you both. I better get Dixie home and feed her." Chester offered us a wide smile. "Take care."

We said our goodbyes and patted Dixie as they walked past us. A few seconds later, Chester turned around.

"Y'know, I almost forgot. I chatted with one of the crew last week. He mentioned that even though this place was gone, there was an exact replica of it. Struck me as really weird."

My ears perked up. "What do you mean?" I was well aware of what a replica was, but I had to be certain I'd understood what he'd said.

"Apparently, some guy knew the family and was obsessed with the story of the murders."

Ryan folded his arms, his stance unwavering. "That's pretty obsessed if he rebuilt the home."

"I agree. Definitely strange, and it stuck in my brain, y'know?" Chester tapped his chin.

"Did he say where the place was located? We'd love to see it," I said. He had no idea how much I wanted to see it.

Chester scratched his balding head and frowned. "He said it was tucked away somewhere. Where was it?"

My patience was wearing thin, but I couldn't tell him to hurry the fuck up because the love of my life was being held captive and most likely at that house.

Chester snapped his fingers. "I got it. He said it was at the base of Mount Casper and hidden in the woods. It's about an hour north of here. I bet the owner would let you see it if you asked nicely and told him you used to live in the original place."

I closed the gap between us. "You seem like a good guy, Chester. But a word to the wise. If anyone knocks on your door wanting to see the inside of your house, don't let them in. You could be inviting the devil in and not realize it until it's too late."

His bushy gray eyebrows rose in surprise as he stared into my eyes. "You . . . You're . . . I knew there was something familiar about you, but I couldn't quite place it." He took a few steps back as Dixie barked at me. "Sebastian? The boy who lost his parents? I've only seen pictures of you when you were in high school. My stepdaughter attended with you before I married her mother. You've grown up and changed, or I would have placed you sooner."

"Wrong guy. As I said, this is my brother, Hugh," Ryan said. "Chester, it's been a pleasure chatting with you, but you should listen to Hugh. Don't let strangers into your home. The world isn't safe anymore."

He nodded and tugged Dixie's leash as she pulled on it to leave. "I won't. You boys have a good day." He started to walk away, then glanced over his shoulder at us one last time.

"Let's go . . . now." Ryan headed back to the car, and I was right behind him.

Once we were safely inside and the doors were closed, Ryan started the engine.

"I'll look for directions." I grabbed my phone and brought up the map of the area that included the mountain, then I zoomed into Google Maps. "Guess Sebastian is a legend around here," I muttered.

"I can see that. Not many nice areas like this have murders go down, but it happens more than most people realize."

"Thanks for covering for me. Even though he was wrong about me being Sebastian, I have a feeling Chester is chatty and will tell anyone who will listen."

A mix of anger and hope tightened my chest. If a stranger thought I was Sebastian, I clearly looked like him, but I still wasn't willing to admit we were sharing the same body. I would deal with that later. It was time to find my little lamb and bring her home.

I searched the address of the house that was no longer standing and located images of the exterior and interior. It was the same one I remembered. Then I looked on Google Maps at the base of the mountain and zoomed in. I spotted the structure that looked like the one that had recently been torn down. "I think I found it."

Ryan's expression turned grave. "Do you have directions for me?"

I tapped the button, and the voice floated through my speaker. "If she's there . . ." A lump formed in my throat, reminding me to remain cautious about finding her this time.

"You've got backup. You know I'm always armed, and I'm guessing you have more than one blade strapped to your person."

My nostrils flared at the thought of finally getting my hands on the son of a bitch who took her. "Damn straight."

I sucked in a lungful of air, and excitement stirred deep in the pit of my stomach as I began to plot out how I would end anyone who was involved with Ella's kidnapping. It was going to be a fucking bloodbath, and I couldn't wait. But first, I had to make sure Ella and my children were safe and sound, tucked away from any more harm.

CHAPTER 20

ELLA

As I watched Xavier disappear up the stairs, followed by the creak of the door to the outside world, my father's words echoed in my mind. He used to tease me that I was born into this world with a contingency plan. My entire life had been spent meticulously planning every move, always having a backup option in case things went awry. It was a survival instinct that constantly consumed me, and the thought of not having a plan B sent me reeling.

My mind was hazy and disoriented from the drugs coursing through my system, but a primal instinct for survival had sparked to life inside me. When Xavier had carelessly left me alone in his bathroom a few hours ago, I had spotted the prescription bottle he had used to drug me sitting on the sink. With trembling fingers, I had opened the container to find its contents crushed into powder. I had discreetly coated his damp toothbrush with the powdered pills. Would it work? I had no idea how often Xavier brushed his teeth or if enough of the drug would remain after adding toothpaste and water, but I'd had to take the chance. Not only was it the best opportunity that had presented itself, but my future depended on it.

The door at the top of the stairs opened again, and I waited to see if it was Xavier or someone else.

"What the fuck did you do?" Xavier roared as he stumbled into the kitchen as if he were drunk off his ass.

He brushed his teeth!

"What's the matter?" I feigned worry as he tripped over his feet and caught himself before he fell. A few spiders skittered away with the racket. "Are you okay? Xavier, talk to me. Let me out so I can help you." I pounded on the glass. "I can't help you from inside here."

"I know what you did, you little bitch." He staggered closer to me.

"I don't have any idea what you're talking about." I had to retain my innocence in case my plan didn't work. "Hurry, you need help. Let me out so I can reach you."

Xavier's eyes rolled to the back of his head as he dropped to his knees, and a sickening crunch echoed through the room. If I had to take my guess, he just broke both of his kneecaps on the concrete floor.

"Fuck, that hurt," he muttered, looking at me. "All I wanted to do was protect you, Ella. Protect you from him."

"Who is him?" *Pass out, you stupid motherfucker. Pass out!*

"Too many to name. But there's something you should know, Ella."

I frowned. He wasn't making any sense at all, but as the next words slipped through his lips, my mouth dropped open. There was no way he was in his right mind and telling me the truth. The drug was messing with him. Puzzled, my brows furrowed as I tried to understand the impact of what he'd just shared . . . If it was true, that is.

Suddenly, he gave me a stupid grin right before falling forward face-first. Wincing, I remained still and watched if he moved or got back up. The rise and fall of his chest told me he was still alive, but even if he woke up, there was no way he could get up off the floor and run after me with busted knees.

I opened the palm of my hand and studied the wedding ring he'd given me. My two days of captivity had sharpened my focus to a deadly point. Unlike all the other shit in his personal hellhole, the band didn't look cheap. Not wasting any time, I traced my fingertips along the cage. Each time Xavier left me alone, I constantly searched for the right tension in the glass.

I began a deliberate rhythmic tapping, barely perceptible, as I tried to target the microscopic imperfections near the bottom corner panel. Tap. Pause. Tap-tap. If I remembered Ryan and Cami's conversation correctly, a precise cadence that built harmonic stress was critical for this to work. Even so, I wasn't sure if the ring was made from the right kind of metal, but it looked like platinum.

Sweat beaded on my forehead as the minutes passed. Each controlled strike created near-invisible microfractures. The glass, seemingly impenetrable, was slowly being compromised. Who knew a physics conversation had the ability to save my life?

With a final strategic tap, the glass fractured in a precise pattern, creating a weakness I could exploit. I pressed the ring against the weakened point, applying the perfect combination of pressure. A small section gave way silently, just large enough for me to reach through and manipulate the lock mechanism. A loud click echoed in my ears as the cage finally released, and then I pushed the door open. Adrenaline surged through me as I scurried out of the cage, my heart racing with fear and desperation. With shaking hands, I approached Xavier, and my fingers curled into fists as I flipped him over. Blood gushed from his broken nose, staining the floor red like a macabre painting. I didn't care that he was hurt, though. All I cared about was retrieving my stolen wedding rings. My breath hitched in relief as I found them still in his front pocket, glinting mockingly at me. I quickly slipped them back onto my finger, feeling their weight like a comforting anchor. But then, with a triumphant smirk, I placed the ring Xavier had given me on his chest like a sick joke. A reminder that he could never truly possess me again.

"Thanks for the help in getting the fuck out of here." I rose and forced myself not to kick him in the side until his ribs cracked; time wasn't my friend, and I needed to leave. I was well aware of the fact that just because I'd managed to get past Xavier didn't mean there weren't men outside guarding the entrance. At least I thought there were the other day.

My heart thudded as I frantically searched the kitchen for a weapon. My legs shook as I finally found a small knife and gripped it tightly, feeling its sharp edge digging into my skin. With sweat trickling down my temple, I crept out of the room and located the stairs leading upward to the outside, steeling myself for confrontation. I couldn't afford to hesitate. If anyone was on the other side of that door, I needed to catch them off guard and use every ounce of surprise to my advantage. They would never expect me to burst through it, armed and ready for a fight. But I had to push all doubts and fears aside and take the only chance I might have.

I wiped my brow with the back of my hand, inhaling deeply. My pulse cruised at Mach speed as I reminded myself that this was what

I'd been waiting for. If I got caught or failed to kill someone who tried to stop me, they would make sure I never had another opportunity to run. Death's voice filled my mind as I took each step. *Go for the jugular. If you can't get to it, cripple them so they can't chase you.* My breaths came in short gasps as I approached the door. I reached for the handle, my heart pounding so hard I couldn't hear anything else. On the count of three, I burst through the doorway and stepped outside for the first time in days.

The bright sunlight temporarily blinded me as I staggered around and attempted to find my footing. Dead leaves littered the ground, and I searched for any pair of shoes that belonged to the enemy, but I didn't see any.

"No one is guarding the place," I said quietly. I shielded my eyes and lifted my head, trying to identify anything that seemed familiar.

"What side of the tree does moss grow on?" I had to stop talking out loud in case someone showed up and heard me. Recalling that moss liked the north side, I turned in that direction. The slope of a mountain greeted me, and I turned and ran in the opposite direction, nearly stumbling down a hill. I hoped like hell I was going toward civilization and not away from it.

I picked up my pace, still gripping the knife in my hand as I remained alert for any other people or any wild animals that might be interested in feasting on me. From the corner of my eye, I saw something bright green. An old beat-up car was parked at the bottom of the hill. Then I remembered Xavier and Fiona's conversation about him still knowing how to drive. Dammit, why hadn't I looked for car keys? Even though it was a shot in the dark, I hurried to the vehicle and glanced through the filthy driver's side window. I swore when there weren't any keys dangling from the ignition.

The sun cast an eerie glow through the pine trees, and I realized it would be setting soon. I would have to run like hell if I hoped to find help before it got dark. Sprinting as fast as my legs would carry me, I darted through the woods, trying to watch where I was stepping, but the snap of the sticks and dried leaves on the ground were definitely giving away my location. Suddenly, it dawned on me that mine weren't the only footsteps I was hearing.

"Hey! It's her!" a man's voice said from behind me.

"Don't let her go!" another yelled.

My heart jumped into my throat as I ran for my life, no longer giving a shit about the noise I made. I glanced over my shoulder and spotted two big men barreling after me. *Maybe I should let them catch me so I can slit their throats.* But I was afraid I might be outnumbered. As fast as they were approaching, I quickly understood I couldn't outrun them. My lungs burned as I ducked behind a tree and waited.

As the men approached and stopped within a few feet of where I was hidden, I could see the anger etched on their faces. They were determined to catch me and, quite possibly, do much worse. Gathering every ounce of courage I could muster, I jumped out from behind the tree and charged at the man closest to me with a ferocity he wasn't expecting. My fists connected with his nose, causing him to stumble back in surprise and pain. I took that fleeting moment to shove the knife into his neck, sinking past flesh and tendons, the pressure singing up my arm in a wave of perverse pleasure. His eyes widened as he staggered backward and grabbed at the blade jutting out of his skin.

"You little bitch," the other snarled at me. He lunged at me, but I dodged him and used his buddy's body to hide behind. I pushed his friend into him, knocking the second man off balance. As they both tumbled to the ground, the second man's head hit a rock with a sickening thunk. I hurried over and quickly pulled my knife out of the first guy's neck, making blood arc and spurt from his wound. It was close enough to his jugular that he would bleed out in seconds. I seized the opportunity and sprinted in the opposite direction. If the guy who had hit his head got up, I needed to lose him in the maze of pine trees. The sun was now setting fast, casting long shadows that made it even more challenging to navigate through the dense forest. As I ran harder than I ever had in my life, I heard footsteps growing fainter and fainter until they vanished completely.

Taking a deep breath, I tried to compose myself. My pulse slowed down, and my lungs finally stopped burning so badly. The adrenaline rush from almost being caught was still coursing through my veins. I only allowed myself a minute to recover before I continued running until the sun had disappeared well below the horizon. Now I was in near-total darkness save for the faint moonlight that managed to pierce through the canopy of trees above.

The sound of a car approaching caught my ears, and I peered down the small hill. To my surprise, a narrow dirt road wound through the area. A chill shot down my spine as I feared someone might be checking on Xavier. The drugs had probably worn off and he'd called for help.

I ducked behind the trees and watched the car drive by me, the headlights breaking through the darkness. As soon as it disappeared around the corner, I continued to walk but made sure to stay off the road. It was too dangerous, and I couldn't risk being caught by Xavier again.

I wasn't sure how much time had passed since I'd escaped, but exhaustion sank into my weary bones. I was dehydrated and weak from lack of food, but if I could keep going . . .

My foot snagged on a branch, and I lurched forward. The impact of the hard ground knocked the air out of me as I rolled down the hill. A cry burst from me as a sharp pain shot through my leg and head at the same time. I struggled to remain conscious as I was catapulted over rocks and sticks and then onto the dirt road. The woods spun, and I teetered on the edge of consciousness before the world slipped away completely.

CHAPTER 21

DEATH

Night after night, darkness polished the lamb's bones
with velvet promises until its wool grew black as dreams.
—Anonymous

"That guy must have been fucking with us," I grumbled, pissed the hell off that we hadn't located the replica of my house.

"Maybe it was another riddle or that old man was paid to feed us that information," Ryan replied.

"But why? I even saw a structure on Google Maps, so I know it's around here."

"It's dark, and we're in unfamiliar territory. Let's turn around and find somewhere to stay for the night. We can begin the search again in the morning." Ryan pulled to the side of the dirt road and hooked a U-turn. From his grim expression, he was as worried and upset as I was.

"We will find her. Alive," I snarled. "I refuse to accept anything else. And I swear to fucking God, or Lucifer, or whoever claims my fractured, black soul, I will hunt down every last person involved in this, and I'll flay the skin from their goddamn corpses and display them at The Met as a warning to anyone who dares to cross me or those I care for."

"He won't kill her, man. He's enjoying the game way too much to end it. He's a fucking twisted motherfucker, but don't forget, this isn't about Ella either. It's about you. He wants you."

The road ahead stretched on for what seemed like an eternity, empty and mocking, while she stayed hidden from us. Ryan drove in silence, taking the bumpy road slowly. My mind raced with thoughts of Ella. I couldn't let her down. She couldn't . . . die. Anxiety coursed through me with every beat of my frantic heart. There had to be something I could do. There was always an answer if you wanted it bad enough.

"What the hell?" Ryan slowed and then came to a complete stop.

"Stay here." I jumped out of the car before he had a chance to argue with me. Grabbing my knife from the sheath on my calf, I approached the person in the middle of the road. It could be a trick. Hell, I'd played it myself, then snatched the unsuspecting victim.

The torn and dirty dress was barely recognizable, but the black hair hiding the person's face made my pulse skip a beat. I stilled and scanned the body. Blood pooled beneath the person's leg and a knife protruded from the thigh. The rise and fall of the chest told me they were still alive. From the looks of the curves and petite form, the person was female. Slowly, I knelt, then moved the hair from the face.

My eyes widened in shock, but there was no mistaking her—my Ella.

"Ella," I whispered. "I'm going to pick you up." If she could hear what I was saying, I needed her to understand she was with me. "You're safe, little lamb. Your wolf is here to bring you home." With care, I scooped her into my arms and carried her to the Camry. Ryan hopped out of the car and opened the backdoor for me.

"Jesus, is it her?" He popped the trunk and then placed a jacket on the seat for her. "I have a blanket. Lay her down, and I'll cover her up. She might be in shock."

My arms trembled with the realization that she could be badly hurt. We weren't out of the woods by any means.

"I'll stay back here with her." I gently placed her on the back seat. I slid in, then placed her head on my lap and stroked her hair. "Little lamb, come back to me," I whispered.

Once Ryan was settled in, he drove like a bat out of hell down the road. I wanted to argue with him bouncing her around like a rag doll, but we were both probably thinking the same thing. Would Ella live long enough for us to get her help?

I leaned down and pressed my lips to her dirty forehead. "The kids have missed their mother, and I have missed my queen. Hang in there. We're on the way to the hospital."

Ryan glanced in the rearview mirror, studying me. "Have you considered not going into the hospital in case the cops are around? If any police have even a hint of who you are, you could be arrested. If you're worried about it, I can take her in."

Four days of searching, of not knowing if she was alive or dead, had driven me to the edge of sanity. Now that we'd found her, I couldn't let her go. "I'll do it. She's mine to take care of." There was no way I was letting her go again. I would take my chances. I stroked her cheek and continued to talk to her quietly, hoping that she would wake up and know she was safe.

It seemed like an eternity later that Ryan pulled up to the emergency room. After getting out and picking up Ella, I walked through the sliding glass doors. The hustle and bustle of sick and crying people in the ER didn't faze me. I was used to it when I tortured a victim. Besides, everyone else would have to wait. Ella needed immediate care.

A nurse approached me as she took Ella's wrist and began checking her vitals.

"What happened?" She glanced at me briefly.

"I'm not sure. My buddy and I found her in the middle of a dirt road about forty minutes ago. She hasn't been conscious, either."

"Do you know her?"

A far away voice answered the nurse's question in my head.

"I'm her husband. We were out hiking when she got lost." I wasn't her spouse, but the nurse didn't need to know that.

"And how did she end up with a knife in her leg?" The nurse glared at me, and I suspected she thought I'd abused Ella.

"She has a nasty habit of running with sharp objects," I snarled. "Get her admitted and do whatever you have to do to make sure she's okay." Glancing at her name tag, I arched an intimidating brow at her. "I'm holding you responsible, Nurse Jones."

A gurney caught my attention, and I hurried over and placed Ella on it.

"Sir, that wasn't for her. There's another patient—" some guy said behind Nurse Jones.

Before I could wrap my fingers around his throat, Ryan stepped up.

"You'll treat her now. She's a witness to a murder, and we need her to stay alive. Do you understand?" Ryan flashed his badge at the nurse, but not long enough for her to realize he was an out-of-state cop.

She placed her hands on her hips. "I treat all my patients equally. You'll have to wait just a minute."

I left Ella on the gurney and stomped toward the nurse. "Now. Take fucking care of her now," I growled as I jabbed a finger into her face.

The woman took a step back and nodded. "Okay." She glanced around, then called for help. "You can have a seat in the waiting room."

"Not happening." My patience was wearing thin.

"Then let us examine her and see how much blood she's lost. You can't be there. It's a sterile environment, and she's already at risk for infection. If you love your wife, sit your ass down. You have my word that I'll call you back as soon as she's in a room."

Ryan placed his hand on my shoulder. "Come on, man. They have to be able to do their job."

My gaze narrowed on Nurse Jones. "If anything happens to her . . ." I didn't need to say anything else. She got my meaning.

I stood rooted in place as the guy and Nurse Jones wheeled Ella through the doors. There were only a few times in my life when I experienced true, deep terror. One was in the memory of my parents lying on the kitchen floor covered in massive amounts of blood. It was as if I'd faded in and out of reality when I realized I was holding a butcher knife. I had been responsible for their deaths, but I hadn't ever told anyone that. It was only a fleeting recollection, but there was a knowing in my gut that I'd had something to do with it. The second time was now as I watched Ella get wheeled away. I had no idea if I would ever see her alive again, or if I would ever hold her or hear her voice. Sucking in a slow breath, I slammed my eyes closed against the dark fears that plagued me. She had to come back.

My palms burned and itched, and I rubbed them on my jeans. I had to keep busy one way or another while they tended to Ella. Otherwise, I would lose my fucking mind. Strolling over to Ryan, who was on his phone, I paced in front of him. If I didn't keep moving, I would rush down the hall after Ella. Every cell in my body craved her, needed to see with my own eyes that she would be okay, because nothing that I'd seen told me otherwise.

A minute later, Ryan hung up. "I called Dope and Kip to let them know we found Ella and where we were. They'll let Cami know."

"Thanks." In all the excitement, it hadn't dawned on me to call them. At least Ryan was a voice of reason to me for now.

My arms folded tightly against my chest, I replayed the memories on repeat. A quiet and seething rage ignited inside me, pulsing with a deadly intensity. Every fiber of my being was consumed with a burning desire for revenge. I swore that if it was the last thing I did, I would hunt down those motherfuckers who had laid a hand on my little lamb and make them pay with rivers of their blood. With each clench and unclench of my jaw, the familiar cold drive to kill surged through my veins, pushing me toward vengeance with relentless force.

Ryan stood and closed the gap between us, speaking in a hushed voice since we were in a public area. "You've got that look, man. Can you keep your shit together or do we need to find you someone—"

I glanced around, making sure no one could overhear our conversation. I would have preferred to talk elsewhere, but we had to stay here in case the doctor came out with an update. "I already have someone, but I have to find the son of a bitch first."

Ryan nodded. "I can have the guys fly out, and we can go hunting. The woods are perfect for it. Cami can stay with the kids. I can call in a few favors and have Ella's room guarded to keep her safe until she's well enough to travel home."

I mulled over his words. "I won't leave Ella until I know that she's going to recover. But call the guys and have them get here as fast as they can. Can you call in a favor and have someone watch the house and Cami? I don't trust her to not take off with my twins, but I also need to keep them safe. Those fuckers might come back, and I can't leave Cami and the kids vulnerable."

Ryan tipped his chin. "Of course. I have a buddy that knows how to be discreet and is well connected. He'll be great for the job and keep his mouth shut with any shit he sees."

"What's his name?" I wasn't too keen on the idea of a stranger learning my secrets, but at this point I had to trust Ryan's call.

"Zayne Wilson. Good guy, ex-military, and has gotten his hands dirty several times. He's on the East Coast, so it won't take him long to get to your place if he's available. If not, he has very qualified men on his team."

"If you trust him, then I will too." I shifted my weight from one leg to the other, restless as hell.

"I know you don't want to hear it, but Sebastian knows Zayne too. He trusts him, and you can too."

He was right, I didn't want to hear that shit. Changing the subject, I asked, "How fast can Kip and Dope get here?"

Ryan's forehead creased before he spoke, as if he were weighing his words. "I'm not sure. I'll check in and see where they're at."

Terror and anxiety consumed every fiber of my being, leaving no room for rational thought as I frantically worried about my little lamb. The words he had spoken barely registered in my brain, drowned out by the pounding of my heart and the overwhelming sense of dread that gripped me.

"For the record, Sebastian sounds like a spoiled rich motherfucker that depends on his plane too much," I snapped. "I prefer to drive or travel by foot. It depends on how heavy the load is. I have more important shit to worry about right now than him anyway." I sneered and imagined throwing the body of a victim over my shoulder.

Ryan smirked. "You two are definitely different, but one thing remains the same. You love Ella and will destroy anything and anyone that is a threat to her. Same for your kids. At some point, I hope you and Bass can coexist together. You could each teach the other a few things."

My gaze narrowed on his. "You're a bold son of a bitch, aren't you? You think you can rattle me with this bullshit about Sebastian?"

"Nope. It's just the truth. I've known you both since college, so I'm a good man to have on your side. We've tiptoed around you, afraid that if we told you, it could push you or him into madness. We weren't willing to risk it, but the moment Ella went missing, it changed the game. She's back now, and I'm trusting that she's going to be okay. That means we have work to do, and you need to get your head in the game as soon as you know she's alive and going to make it through this shit."

My tortured soul absorbed his words. A heavy silence fell between us as we settled in for what I assumed would be a very long wait.

Hours ticked by as I stared at the second hand on the large clock that hung on the wall in the emergency room. Finally, a female voice grabbed my attention.

"Sir? We have an update on your wife," a petite, dark-haired woman said as she approached me.

Ryan and I turned to her at the same time. "And you are?" I needed to know if I was talking to a doctor or someone who had secondhand information.

"I'm Dr. Neely. I operated on your wife." She took a deep breath, her shoulders slumping.

My legs trembled as I witnessed her body language. It wasn't good. Jesus fucking Christ.

I struggled to form the words, my tongue thick and heavy in my mouth.

"Is she alive?"

CHAPTER 22

DEATH

Sweet was the shepherd's call, but sweeter still the midnight whispers that promised to unmake innocence.
—Anonymous

The doctor shoved her hands in her white coat pockets, her expression grim and tight with sadness.

"I'm so sorry, but your wife didn't make it."

At that moment, the devil knocked on my door, and the second we stared each other down, the son of a bitch ran. Hell hath no fury like Death scorned. I shook my head, refusing to believe what she'd said.

"No." I moved back, my heart pounding so fucking hard my skull rattled.

"How?" Ryan stepped forward.

The doctor gave him a tight-lipped smile. "I can't discuss the details if you're not family."

I growled out a response for him. "He's her brother. Now answer his question."

"I'm so sorry. Her heart stopped. Whatever trauma she went through was just too much." She reached out to touch my arm, and I jerked away. A tsunami of grief and rage flooded my body, contorting my stomach into a twisted mass of knots. With a primal scream, I unleashed the caged beast, picked up a chair, and hurled it with all my might into the center of the room. Chaos erupted as people scattered and shrieked, but I was consumed by a grief-fueled frenzy as I continued to grab and throw chair after chair until the emergency room was torn apart in a violent show.

"Stop!" Ryan attempted to calm me, but it was too late. There was no returning from the darkness that had completely claimed every part of me. Two security guards ran toward me, and I threw them off and sent them sprawling across the floor.

Ryan stepped between me and additional chairs as everyone turned coward and hid the best they could. "Goddammit, get the fuck out of here before you're arrested!"

I blinked at him as if he was only a figment of my imagination.

"The kids still need you. Alaric and Verity are waiting for you at home. Don't do this, man. If they arrest you . . ."

He didn't need to say anything else. Somewhere inside my mind I heard Sebastian's words. *Get the fuck out now!* I stilled, knocked off guard by the voice. It seemed familiar, as if it were my own thoughts. A sharp pain split through my skull, and I grabbed my head as I dropped to my knees. A man's voice with an Australian accent broke through my agony. *I'm here.* Shit, it was back, and my sanity was teetering, barely hanging on a thread. I'd heard him before but shoved it into the corner of my mind. I hadn't ever told anyone, but I'd thought I was losing my mind when it appeared. Then I'd learned to tune it out. It didn't happen often, so it had been easy to ignore it. But now . . .

"Shit. Not now. Sebastian, not fucking now," Ryan said between gritted teeth.

"Sir, you're under arrest for . . ."

I couldn't make out the words as my breath halted in my lungs, the room in and out of focus.

Ryan stepped between us. "No. I've got this. You need to back up. Here's my badge. This man is under my protection. You need to back the hell up."

I placed my palms on the cold white-tile floor, trying to grip reality, but it all began to fade into oblivion.

A firm hand jerked me up, then rushed me out of the hospital and into the cool evening air.

"Hurry up." Ryan refused to let go of me as we hurried into the parking lot. "I'm going to kill the motherfuckers that did this to Ella."

"Where are we? What's going on?" I asked, disoriented.

"Shit. Sebastian, is it you now?"

"Yeah. Ryan, what are you doing here? Where the hell am I?" My skull filled with pain again and I stumbled forward. My voice changed, sounding foreign to my ears. "Get the fuck out of my head, Sebastian. I have to take care of some shit, and I don't need your lame ass hanging around."

Ryan stared at me in awe as he unlocked the car and practically shoved me into the passenger's side. He closed the door and hurried to the other side.

"Jesus, I've never seen you change . . . Are you Death or Bass?"

CHAPTER 23

SEBASTIAN

I stared at him blankly. "This is fucked up. I haven't felt anything like this before." I glanced around, and then I looked at him again, trying to understand what was happening. "Both are here. I can feel both inside my head. What the fuck is going on?"

Ryan started the car, then hurried out of the parking lot. He fumbled for his phone in his back pocket, then slapped it on the seat next to him.

"Siri, call Kip Lytton." He shot me a sideways glance as the cell began to ring through the phone's speaker.

"Hey, man, how's everything? How's Ella?"

"Uh, pretty fucked up. How close are you?"

"We are just about to take off, so it will be a few hours. I'm assuming something else has happened since you're calling?"

"Ella . . . She didn't make it, and Death went crazy and started tearing up the emergency room. He almost got arrested, but I was able to get us out of there. At the moment, he and Sebastian are aware of each other."

Silence filled the line as I blinked and wondered if what I was hearing was correct. This had all happened while I was Death? My Ella had died? Tears welled in my eyes. My phone buzzed in my back pocket, but I ignored it. Nothing could be more important right now.

"How?" I asked. "How did my wife die?"

"Bass?" Kip questioned, his voice tight with emotion.

"Yeah, it's me. I don't remember how I got here or what happened."

Ryan turned left, then continued toward the outskirts of town. "A shit show. Death almost got you arrested. Is he still around?"

I stilled for a moment, the world blurring, then I heard his voice. A chill traveled down my spine with his words. *I got her killed, that's what happened.*

"He's here and says he got Ella killed. She's . . . Is . . . is that how it happened?"

"Her heart stopped from the trauma. Death and I found her in the middle of the road. A knife was in her thigh, but the back of her head was also bloody. I think she must have hit her head at some point. I need to get back to the hospital and see what I can find out. Death told the doctor that I'm her brother, so I should be able to learn more. I just had to get Death out of there before they arrested him and discovered who he really is. But then Bass started to appear."

"Fuck," Dope said. "She can't be gone, dude."

I struggled to comprehend the magnitude of my loss, but I wasn't sure how I was supposed to digest everything. The sound of sniffles filled the car, and I realized tears were running down my face. "What the hell did Death do? If this is my fault . . . how will my kids ever forgive me?"

"I need to find a hotel room where Bass can lay low. I'll tell you guys where to meet us, and as soon as I have him settled, I'm going back to the hospital to demand some answers. Plus, I probably have to talk to the cops and try to get Death off the hook for his outburst."

"Okay, keep us posted," Kip said before he disconnected the call.

Minutes later, Ryan turned into the parking lot of a seedy motel. "It sucks, but at least if Death reappears and loses his shit, they won't call the cops, because they'll lose all the drug and prostitute business. I think you're safer here than anywhere else."

Ryan whipped the car into a parking spot at the side of the motel. "Hang tight, I'll get a room. Do not fucking leave this car. Are we clear?"

"Yeah." I wiped my eyes.

"Are *both* of you clear?"

Death muttered his agreement in my head, then I responded to Ryan. "Yeah."

I watched as Ryan hurried to the entrance and disappeared inside.

"Why are you here?" I asked the person everyone referred to as Death. "Why am I aware of you suddenly?"

A voice with an American accent filled my mind. *Because Ella is dead, and it was too much for us to both block out is my guess. It's my fault, but you need to get the fuck out of my way because I'm going to hunt the motherfuckers down and kill them all.*

I winced at the knowledge of being able to communicate with the dark side of me.

"Do you know who took Ella?"

Not yet, but we were close to finding out. Ryan and I were making our way to a place where we suspected she was being held, but then it got too dark. On our way back down the mountain we found Ella unconscious in the middle of the road.

A soft wail escaped me, imagining her beaten, bruised, and all alone.

You've gotta let me take over, Sebastian. I'm not fucking asking. We can do this the nice way, or I will shove you aside and take control.

Deep inside me, I knew he was right. If we wanted to learn the truth about who was behind killing my wife . . . I stared out the window, trying not to lose my shit. The car door opened, and Ryan climbed in.

"We're in the back where it's a little quieter and more private. I'm going to get you settled, then head to the hospital."

Ten minutes later, I'd gone to the bathroom and Ryan had gotten some snacks and bottled water from a vending machine he'd located in the hall.

"Sorry to do this, man," he said. I frowned at him as he produced his handcuffs. "It's for your own good, unless you want to land in prison and lose your kids too." He tilted his head and indicated for me to sit on the mattress.

I sank onto it, a spring poking me in the ass cheek as I did.

"Scoot back and get comfy."

"Are you sure you have to do this, mate?" My voice sounded sad and foreign to my ears.

"Yup. I can't take the chance of you disappearing on me. When we go after the fuckers that are responsible, I'll be right by your side, but I have to take care of . . ." He swallowed as he grabbed my wrist and secured me to the headboard.

As if that will hold us. A sinister chuckle echoed through my mind.

He stepped back and pocketed the key. "You can have your phone, but you have to promise no calls outside of me, Kip, and Dope."

"Sure." I snatched up the remote control and pushed the power button, hoping for the noise to drown out the voice in my mind.

"I'll return as soon as I can."

I stared at the television, desperately needing a moment alone to process what had happened. I still couldn't fathom the idea that Ella was gone. "Take your time."

Ryan nodded, his mouth pursed into a thin line. He'd always been one to hide his emotions, but with the news about Ella, it seemed as though he was struggling as much as I was. Something inside me required proof. To see her body and to say goodbye. It wasn't going to seem real until I could do that. I needed closure.

And when we have it, I'll turn this world into a fucking blood bath. I'll cut the bastard's cock off and shove it down his throat while I fillet him alive.

I winced as the voice in my head continued sharing in graphic detail what was going to happen.

"I can't listen to that right now. I need answers, so tell me everything you know, you piece of shit." I scrubbed my face with my free hand.

The voice responded with a gruff snarl, then explained the calls and riddles, and what he and Ryan had figured out so far. It was strange to realize that I had retained bits and pieces of Death's conversations with others. Not much, but more than ever before.

I glanced at the clock. Ryan should be back at the hospital by now. My phone vibrated, and I pulled it out of my back pocket and looked at the screen. I had three missed calls. Frowning, I ignored the call since it wasn't from a number I recognized. I placed the cell on the nightstand and stared into space as my mind and emotions sank into a pool of numbness.

CHAPTER 24

ELLA

Hairy legs traveled over my body, and I stilled. If I moved, the spiders would bite, and I would be left alone to die a slow death. Xavier would never give up his location to save me. He'd probably encourage my quick death in order to stuff me and place me next to his family at the table.

"Ella?" A panicked voice broke through my terror.

Too terrified to move, I uttered a tiny cry of help. Fear paralyzed me as the creatures covered nearly every inch of me.

"Ella? Can you hear me? You're safe."

The sounds of beeping and hushed voices penetrated my foggy brain. Where was I? How could I be safe locked in a cage with spiders covering every inch of me? A sharp pain traveled from the back of my skull and through my entire being. Unwillingly, I jerked, followed by a scream as the creatures swarmed me.

"Ella, I'm Dr. Neely. You just came out of surgery. We thought we lost you, so please try to be still and breathe."

Doctor?

"Doctor, her heart is beating again. I don't understand," a female voice said.

"Thank god. Let's get her stable, and then I'll call her husband. He was escorted out of the emergency room due to his violent response to her condition."

My brows furrowed. "Sebastian?" I winced. My throat was so sore it felt like fingernails were dragging their way down my esophagus.

"Hang on, hon. Don't try to talk yet. I've got an ice chip I'll place on your lips to help."

A cold sensation rested against my mouth, and I parted my lips, allowing the droplet of water to hit my tongue. The fog in my brain began to clear as I focused on the sounds and smells around me. Beeps, hushed conversations, cleaning products. Something beneath me felt much softer than the cement floor I'd been sleeping on. With a rush of memories, I suddenly recalled that I had drugged Xavier, and he'd passed out. I'd gotten out of the cage and had run for my life. It had grown dark and cold, and I remembered tripping over a log or rock, then falling and falling. My eyes slowly opened, the bright light blinding me. I closed them, then tried again.

A dark-haired woman stood over me with a concerned expression.

"Hi, Ella. Can you hear me?"

"Yeah," I whispered.

"Good. You gave us all a big scare, but it's nice to see you with us again."

"What happened? Sebastian?"

"We're trying to reach him. He made quite a scene when we told him you . . . well, you died."

I couldn't believe what I was hearing. Died? A surge of panic and confusion washed over me as the doctor's words echoed in my mind. I tried to wrap my head around the idea of being dead, but it just didn't make sense. And Sebastian . . . He must be devastated. My heart ached at the thought of him finding out I was gone.

As the reality of the situation started to sink in, a whirlwind of emotions engulfed me. Fear, disbelief, sadness—all jumbled together in a mess of conflicting feelings. But amidst the chaos, a tiny flicker of hope ignited within me. Sebastian. I needed to see him, to reassure him that I was here, alive and well. The thought of him mourning my death tore at my soul, and I had to tell him I was all right.

Fear ripped through me as my skin crawled, and I attempted to kick off the blankets. I dug my fingers into them, feeling the texture between my fingertips. "Spiders."

"No spiders, honey. I think your mind was playing tricks on you. It's okay, though," one of the nurses said as she slipped a white device on my finger.

"Sometimes the drugs from surgery can do a number on you. But I assure you that I am terrified of spiders and I would not be in here with you if there were any." She attempted a sweet smile.

I turned my head slowly, the nausea from the pain in my neck and skull nearly paralyzing.

"Let me see her. She's my sister," a voice said from down the hall.

"Ryan?" I tried to sit up, but the doctor firmly pinned my shoulders to the bed. "You can see him, but you have to promise me that you won't try to sit or get up. We need to make sure you're stable. You've been in and out for the last hour, and we can't have you dying on us again." She squeezed my fingers.

"I promise." At that point, I would tell her anything to see a friend.

"Let him in," Dr. Neely said. She stepped away from my bed and patted my foot.

"Ella? Jesus, Ella?" Ryan's eyes were rimmed with red as he rushed over to me. He grabbed my hand and knelt next to the bed. "We thought we'd lost you. How are you here?"

"It's good to see you too." I gave him an exhausted smile. "Sebastian? The kids?" I choked on my words, overwhelmed with the idea that I would be able to see them again—touch and kiss them.

"Bass and . . . He's a mess. I need to call him and let him know. Hell, Kip and Dope are on the way too. Cami is with the kids." Ryan stood and placed a sweet kiss to my forehead. "He's going to want answers, but we'll get to that in a bit." He leaned down and whispered, "Death made a huge scene in the emergency room when the doctor told us you'd died. He was almost arrested, and now he can't come see you."

The news jolted me upright. "Keep him safe, Ryan. Please."

"Ella, lay back down or Ryan will have to leave," the resident said.

"He's okay. I just had to handcuff them to the bed in the motel room," he said so quietly I strained to hear.

"Them?" My hand flew to my mouth. "Are they aware of each other?"

Ryan nodded. "More later, though." He removed his cell from his back pocket and gave it to me. "I don't think anyone else but you should make the call."

My heart lodged in my throat as I held out my shaky hand. "Can you dial for me?"

"Yeah." Ryan tapped a few buttons, then gave me the phone.

"Tell me you know why she died." Sebastian's voice cracked, and my stomach sank like a stone with the pain in his voice.

The line crackled with static, drowning out my cries as I desperately tried to hold on to the connection. "I-I didn't die, baby," I gasped into the phone, tears streaming down my face. "I'm here." The sound of rustling filled the line, and I glanced up at Ryan, my pulse pounding in my chest. "I think he dropped the phone."

"Ella? Oh my god, is it really you?" His voice was tortured, desperate. "Or have I finally lost my fucking mind and I'm hallucinating."

"It's me, baby," I choked out, trying to control my trembling voice. "I've missed you so much."

"I need to see you," he pleaded, his words laced with panic. "I have to make sure that he isn't playing a sick joke on me."

Sebastian didn't need to explain to me who *he* was talking about. I knew what he was saying.

"I understand, but he would never do that. He loves me as much as you do." I bit my lip, reminding myself to be careful what I was saying. I wasn't alone. "Ryan told me you had to leave the hospital, so you'll have to wait to see me in person, but hang up, and I'll have Ryan FaceTime you as soon as we have the room cleared out."

"Yeah, that would help, baby. I'm terrified to think this isn't real, that I'm asleep and dreaming."

"I'll call you back in a few minutes. They want to monitor me some more, and I need to know what happened."

"Can you ask them now and put me on speaker? My mind needs to make sense of it all," he pleaded.

"Hang on." I held the phone to Ryan and glanced at the doctor. "We're going to put my husband on speaker. He's much calmer now, but it will be best if you explain what happened and how I'm here now."

Dr. Neely walked toward me. "Sure, then I can help with any questions too."

Ryan tapped the screen and held the phone to where Sebastian would be able to hear everyone.

"Go ahead, doctor." I closed my eyes, overcome with exhaustion.

"It's rare, but it's called Advanced Shock State, where extreme shock triggers a protective response in the body. The metabolic process slows, and the cardiovascular system enters a near-complete shutdown.

Cellular preservation mechanisms activate as a last-resort survival tactic. Your vital signs were undetectable, and your blood pressure approached zero. We announced the time of death after we tried to bring you back without any success. But by the time I talked with your brother and husband, you were with us again." Dr. Neely motioned the resident forward. "Dr. Thompson is the one responsible for taking a chance and administering a high dose of epinephrine to you through your IV. It worked. If I'd been in the room, I would have never allowed it, but I wasn't. Lucky you, huh?"

"What made you try it?" Ryan asked Dr. Thompson. "To you she was dead."

"We're required to have continuing education, and just last week we talked about Advanced Shock State. I didn't have the right equipment to help me determine if that was in fact what was happening, and I didn't have time to locate what I needed. I just took action. At that point, it wouldn't have mattered if it hadn't worked—she was already gone."

"Bass, did you hear all of that?" Ryan asked.

"Yeah, mate. Thank you, Doctor . . . I'm sorry, I didn't catch your name."

"Dr. Thompson, and you're welcome. We're just glad that Ella is still with us."

I chewed on my lip as I watched Dr. Neely's expression shift from relieved to quizzical.

"I don't remember you having an Australian accent when we spoke," the doctor said.

"When he's really upset it kind of disappears," Ryan chimed in quickly. "Clearly he's calmer now."

Sebastian cleared his throat but remained quiet otherwise.

"When can I go home?" The only thing I wanted was to have my husband's arms wrapped around me.

"In a few days, but we need to know what you remember so we know what to keep an eye on."

I closed my eyes as if struggling for the right words. I couldn't admit that I'd been kidnapped and held captive by a lunatic. "We were out camping, and I took off by myself. I got lost, then when it got cold and dark, I tripped and fell. That's the last thing I remember."

"With a knife in your hand?" Dr. Neely gave me a skeptical look.

"I always have a knife on me when we're camping. You never know when you'll need it. I ran into a hungry wolf one time, and the knife saved my life." I hoped my lie was believable.

"The fall would make sense. You must have rolled over the knife because we had to remove it from your thigh and repair your leg. You're lucky it didn't hit a main artery." She patted my shin. "You should make a full recovery. Other than that, you have a concussion. The rest we've already explained."

"Thank you all for taking care of my wife," Sebastian said.

"You're welcome. Ella, we will check on you in a few minutes. Press the call button if you need anything before then."

"I will." Then to my husband, I said, "I'll FaceTime you in a minute." Ryan ended the call and passed the phone back to me.

When the door closed and the staff had given me a moment of privacy, I pushed the button on the bed and raised the head up enough for me to be able to hold the phone better. Seconds later, Sebastian's face filled the screen.

I choked on my tears as we stared at each other in silence. His once vibrant blue eyes were now haunted by dark circles, and his pale skin showcased the physical strain of the past few days. Yet, even in his exhausted state, he was more handsome to me than ever before.

"I didn't think I'd ever see you again, Ella. I'm so sorry. I'm so sorry. I love you so much, and I'm glad you're safe."

I shook my head. "It's not your fault. I should have been more careful." My hand shook as relief flooded my system.

"Are you okay? Is . . . is Death okay?"

Sebastian gave me a sweet smile. "He's the devil, baby. He's ready to deal with matters his way, but we will talk about it later."

I couldn't help but laugh. "I love you. I love you both, don't forget that."

Sebastian frowned. "I don't understand how. He even said what happened is his fault, but he's been beside himself. Not sure if he's just blaming himself like I am or if he really is responsible. If so, what am I supposed to do with that?" He looked away, shame flickering through his expression.

Everything inside of me wanted to reach out and touch my husband, comfort him. "We will get through this. All of us will, but I think Death will want to set the world right again. You'll need to let him."

"What does that even mean?" From the look in his eyes, he already knew.

Ryan cleared his throat. "I don't mean to interrupt, but is there anything that you can tell us about where you were? Who took you? It's important in case we can track them down."

I looked at Ryan. "His name is Xavier, but he wasn't the one that took me off our front porch. He was my gatekeeper, so to speak. Apparently, his boss wants Death, and I was bait . . . and promised to Xavier as a reward." My skin crawled with the words. "I never learned who his boss was or what he wanted with you." I hesitated after my slip up, but Sebastian didn't seem to be bothered by it. Maybe he and Death had finally met and come to terms with sharing a space. It was too soon to tell.

"Did he—" Fear twisted Sebastian's features. "Did he *hurt* you?"

CHAPTER 25

ELLA

My insides shook with his question. Thank god Xavier hadn't violated me, but I wasn't sure how much longer he would have waited, since he was planning our wedding night.

"Are you asking if he raped me?

He nodded.

"No."

A pinched expression twisted my husband's face as he tugged on his handcuffed wrist. "You promise me he didn't? No one raped you, baby?" As hard as he tried, Sebastian couldn't hide the tremor in his voice.

"You have my word, Sebastian. He did kiss me a few times and touched my breast, but the abuse was mostly psychological. I was locked in a glass cage, and there were spiders everywhere. They were like his pets." I slammed my eyes closed, but images of the disgusting creatures bombarded my mind, and I quickly opened them again. "He also—" I took a deep breath, filling my lungs with the clean air I'd missed so much. "He killed his family, but he kept them with him at the dinner table. I sat next to stuffed dead people."

"Shit, that's fucked up," Ryan said. "I've seen some messed up stuff, but that's on an entirely different level."

"As I said, there was more psychological abuse than physical."

"Do you know where you were held?" Ryan asked.

"It was a basement of some sort, but . . . even though I have my suspicions, I haven't been able to put it all together. There was a little kitchen and living room. I think there was a bedroom, but I never saw it. It was dark and musty. What was really odd were all the stuffed animals. It was like the place was staged and not real, but I can't explain why I felt that way."

"What kind of stuffed animals?" Sebastian asked, his voice low with a sharp edge of anger.

"Mostly clowns. Though, there was one that resembled a Chucky doll, which didn't bother me as much as the spiders did." An involuntary shudder racked my body. "I tried to tell you that over the phone that day, but Xavier hit me the second I started to give you clues."

A growl worked its way up Sebastian's throat. Maybe he would allow Death to handle Xavier and his men after all.

"Did the doll have anything in its hand?"

I didn't miss the anxiety in Sebastian's voice.

"A bloody knife."

Sebastian sucked in a breath. "I never told anyone, but a Chucky doll clutching a bloody knife showed up in my bedroom a few days before my parents were murdered."

"What?" Ryan hissed. "Like, you never told Kip, Dope, or the cops? No one?"

Sebastian shook his head. "No one. I thought Mom or Dad was playing a joke on me, then I forgot about it. Losing my parents took precedence over a damn doll. Again, I figured they were messing with me. Dad was a practical joker at the time, so I just assumed . . . But something is telling me it wasn't them."

I looked at Ryan, then my husband. "Did you have stuffed clowns too?"

His shoulders slumped forward. "It was a collection from my grandpa, but all the clowns except for a few terrified me when I was little. Mom moved most of them to the basement." He swallowed and then said, "The downstairs had a kitchen table and sink. There was an old dirty white refrigerator that Mom kept extra food in when we ran out of space upstairs. Dad liked to go down there sometimes and watch television on an old beat-up couch. He joked it was his man cave. It literally was since most of the room was underground except for a few tiny windows at the top."

I could feel the blood drain from my cheeks as the puzzle pieces started to fit together. "Sebastian, I think I was kept in your childhood basement."

"Not possible since Sebastian's home is no longer standing. Are you sure it wasn't the replica? Death and I went to visit after whoever called and gave us those riddles."

I nodded. "It was Xavier. He loves riddles and fucking with people." I leaned back against the pillow, trying to sort through the conversation.

"Bass, man, I'm starting to think that, with the setup of where Ella was held and the riddles, maybe the man that killed your parents wants your attention."

Sebastian grabbed the side of his head, the phone jostling as he moved.

"What's wrong, babe?"

"All these years I thought I had a brain tumor that made me hear someone else's voice, but apparently it's another part of me." He released a sad sigh before he continued. "Death says the basement and riddles make sense, but why would someone want to draw him out now after all these years?"

"Wait, what? You can hear him?" I gave Sebastian and then Ryan a bewildered look.

"It's a new development since you were taken. All the stress had him changing quickly, and we had to tell Sebastian the truth," Ryan explained.

"We definitely need to talk when you're better," my husband said.

From the tone of his voice, I wasn't sure I would like what he had to say, and I wasn't ready to deal with anything except catching the men who took me. I redirected the conversation and said, "They must have learned that I was trying to find out who killed your parents." Guilt gnawed at me. "Death learned the truth, and he was furious. They must have been tipped off or learned about my investigation somehow. Xavier said he had eyes everywhere. He knew that I loved to dance and that I'm married to Sebastian."

Ryan scratched his chin, pondering. "Maybe you were being followed and didn't know it. Did you talk to anyone about the case? Ask questions to anyone that had lived in the area or anything?"

"I tried to be discreet, but I did reach out to a few people. Unfortunately, they didn't want to talk too much about it other than how horrible it was for the family."

"I'll need the names and any details that you can think of. Dope and I can look into it while you're getting better." Ryan patted my shoulder, his expression grim.

I'd been around Death and Sebastian long enough to be able to tell when someone was hiding something from me, and Ryan was definitely hiding something. I just had no idea what it was . . . yet.

The door to my room opened and Dr. Neely reappeared. "Let's get some bloodwork done and see how you're feeling, Ella. You also need some rest."

"I need to take care of a few things, Ella, so I'll be back later. Call if you need anything. Glad you're back." Ryan gave me a warm smile.

"Me too."

I looked at the phone still in my hand and realized Ryan was waiting for it. "I'll talk to you in a little while. I love you." I blew Sebastian a kiss as we said our goodbyes before I gave the cell back to Ryan. I knew Sebastian was worried about me, and I'd tried my best to let him think I was mentally unscarred. But it was a lie. I was struggling to keep it together in front of everyone when what I really wanted was to sob, scream, and hit something. With everything going on with Sebastian and Death, I was afraid to add any more emotional baggage that might tip him one way or the other. Death had to lie low for now.

"I need security outside of her room," Ryan explained to the doctor. "I won't leave until someone is there. No one other than you and a nurse can enter. Are we clear?" Ryan flashed his badge.

Exhausted, I gave him a smile. "Maybe I can get a little sleep before you leave."

"If you need me to stay, I will. Bass isn't going anywhere." He chuckled at his joke.

"Just until I can fall asleep. I'm . . . I'm afraid I'll have nightmares."

Ryan pulled up a chair and sat next to me. "I'll be here."

"Cami is lucky to have you," I mumbled through a yawn.

Ryan's expression stuttered at the mention of Cami. His gaze darted away from mine before he looked at me again. "More on that later too," he said, his tone subdued. He patted my arm while the nurse drew blood from the other one. "I'm going to call Dope and Kip and give them the good news about you, but I'll talk to them after you get some rest."

As soon as she was finished, my eyes fluttered closed. I slipped into a fitful sleep and dreamed Xavier was hunting me.

CHAPTER 26

SEBASTIAN

The next few hours dragged on as Ryan stayed with Ella. I was mad as hell that Death had caused a scene and if I stepped foot back into the hospital, I would immediately be arrested. Under no circumstances could that happen.

A loud pounding from outside jolted me out of my daze. My pulse thundered in my ears as I struggled against the restraints, desperately trying to free myself. With each knock, I heard my best friends' voices shouting for me on the other side.

Seconds later, the door opened slowly, and Kip and Dope walked in, their eyes wide as they surveyed my situation.

"Don't just stand there. Pick the lock on these fucking handcuffs."

Kip chuckled as he approached me and began to work on the lock. With a soft click, I was free. Relief flooded through me as I rubbed the raw skin on my wrist.

"Thanks, mate."

"Nice digs." Dope chuckled as he looked around at the red bedspread that matched the worn red carpet. To my surprise, he gave me a hug. "Glad Ella rejoined the living. I sure did miss her."

I slapped him on the back a little too hard for his comment.

"Me too. I don't think I've ever been so happy to see her face in my life. We talked some, but I can tell she's trying to hide how bad things were while she was . . . gone. I'm worried about her. I don't want her to be left alone until I can spend more time with her, gauge where she's at emotionally. I failed to protect her, and I won't do it again."

Kip gave me a quick hug too. "Anything she needs, we're all here for her. When Ryan called to tell us, it was a huge relief. I never thought I'd get a call saying someone had died, then a little later that they were alive. The brain is a powerful thing, man."

I winced, but the pain in my head when Death wanted to be heard was growing less intense as I became aware of his presence. "Death agrees."

Kip sat on the rickety black leather office chair, and Dope made himself comfortable at the foot of the bed.

"So, what's next? What has Ella told you so far?"

I hadn't noticed at first, but Dope had his laptop bag with him. He unzipped it and removed his computer.

I explained everything Ella had shared with Ryan and me about the home and how we suspected that the person who killed my parents had been keeping tabs on me. He was clearly aware of Death and his activities from the note at the warehouse. Plus, if Xavier was keeping an eye on Ella, it meant he was keeping an eye on me too. How had we not been more careful?

"Did Ryan tell you my childhood house is no longer there, but there is a replica of it near the mountain?"

"Yeah, that's some fucked-up shit. Someone clearly is obsessed with you and what happened." Kip rubbed the back of his neck, a clear sign that he was thinking hard.

"And the riddles made even more sense when we learned that. I'm telling you, I feel it in my gut that whoever killed your parents is behind this. Ella was just a means to an end . . . You and Death."

I grunted. "I think it's more about Death than me since he's the one killing people."

Kip barked out a laugh. "We'll have this conversation again after this is over. If you have a chance to get your paws on that fucker, then I suspect you'll put him in the ground."

I shoved my hands in my pockets, unsure how I would feel about that scenario, but I suspected Kip was right. At least these guys knew how to cover my tracks.

"On the plane ride over, I was able to dig into this house. It's set up under a shell company, and it took me awhile to find out who bought the property and built a place there."

"But you found a name?"

"Yeah, but I suspect it's an alias."

"What is it?" I urged him to continue.

"Xavier Manatee."

"Shit, that's not an alias. Ella mentioned Xavier was the man that held her captive." A lump formed in the pit of my stomach at the idea of the bastard keeping her in a glass cage.

"Hmm, maybe he's not as smart as he thinks he is if I found out who he is and that he owns the replica of your home." Dope frowned.

"Or he *wants* you to find him," Kip said.

"That's what I was thinking too." I paced the small motel room, ready to see my wife, then go look for the motherfucker. A sudden chill skated over my skin. "Ryan said he has some men guarding the place in New York. I think we need to move Cami and the kids and put them somewhere else. Even with security, I don't feel right about leaving them there. From what we've been able to learn so far, Xavier has been watching us for a while. Dope, we need to make some changes to your methods and security measures since Xavier snuck in undetected." I massaged the back of my neck, the tension slithering through my muscles and down my back.

"Where do you want Cami and the kids to stay?" Dope asked.

"Let's move them to the penthouse in Portland. They won't be as accessible there. Plus, there's security at the door to even get into the building."

"I'll call Cami if one of you reaches out to the pilot and tells him to meet her and the kids at the airport." I scooped up my phone from the nightstand and called Ella's best friend. Even though I wasn't Cami's favorite person, she would do whatever was needed to protect the kids.

Ten minutes later, everything was set into motion, but I wouldn't feel good about their safety until they were inside the penthouse, locked away from the rest of the world.

"We'll go there, too, as soon as Ella is released from the hospital."

"And what about Xavier? We're here in the same state, so I think we should see what we can find while Ryan and Ella aren't involved," Kip said. "I'm guessing that Ella has been gone long enough that Xavier knows she escaped and he's pissed. It would be a good time to strike."

"What you're saying makes sense. I was just hoping to see Ella first."

"All we're doing is sitting around, waiting, and you know how I feel about that," Dope said. "It's overrated. I'm sure Death would agree."

Within a split second, a blinding pain shot through my skull and dropped me to my knees. I moaned and grabbed my head as the room blurred in and out.

"Looks like Death wants to join us on this one," Kip said.

CHAPTER 27

DEATH

In the shepherd's tales, darkness always devours. They never tell of how it cradles, how it crowns its lambs with stars.
—Anonymous

Alive. The word echoed in my mind like a deafening thunderclap, shattering the numbness that had consumed me since I'd learned of her supposed death. My body trembled with a mixture of relief and adrenaline as I frantically searched for her, desperate to see her, touch her, and devour her with my all-consuming hunger. The thought of losing her again tore through my soul like a blinding white-hot flame. But she was alive. She had come back for me, defying death itself to be by my side once more. A surge of fierce protectiveness and unwavering love flooded my being, propelling me forward with determination to go to her and never let her go again.

I rose slowly, thankful that this time I'd been aware of Sebastian talking to Dope and Kip and that I remembered the conversations. I squared my shoulders as I stood to my full height and Sebastian's words returned to me. There was no way in hell I was sitting this one out. Sebastian would fuck everything up if I allowed him to take the lead with Xavier.

"Welcome back." Dope reached into his computer bag and then tossed something at Kip. "I came prepared." An ornery grin lit up his face right before he pulled on the skeleton mask I'd given him a year ago. Kip followed suit and situated his devil mask over his head and neck.

"My mother would fucking love this one," he mumbled as he adjusted the eye holes.

I chuckled at his comment. "Let's get going. I assume you have a rental car?"

Dope and Kip removed their masks, and Dope produced a car key. "I have the map and directions already brought up on Google. We should be able to make it in about an hour and a half, right before dusk, which will help us stay hidden."

"I know part of the way since Ryan and I were there when we found Ella. I'll let him know we're leaving." The mention of her name brought back the image of her limp and battered body in the middle of the dirt road. A feral rage reared its ugly head, and I swore I would get revenge on everyone responsible. In fact, it would be my pleasure.

The drive had taken a little longer than we'd anticipated due to the winding and bumpy road that climbed up the base of the mountain. The conversation had been mostly about how we wanted to approach the area. If Xavier was there, we should knock him out but not eliminate him . . . yet. I definitely wanted to play with my prey before I moved in for the kill.

I'd be surprised if the fucker was even there, but you never knew what someone unstable might do.

Dope parked the car on the side of the road behind a cluster of trees. When the sun set, it would be nearly impossible to see the vehicle, which would allow us to sneak up on Xavier unannounced.

We hurried through the woods until the replica of my childhood home came into view, and I removed my knife from the sheath on my calf. Careful not to step on the dead leaves that were scattered across the ground, we slipped our masks on and circled the house. It was eerily quiet as we split up and each took a side.

"Watch my back, but let me handle it unless I call you in for help," I said to Kip and Dope.

They nodded, understanding all too well that I could easily take out a number of grown men on my own. Bloodlust was a powerful tool when I needed it.

As I crept closer to the house, my heart quickened in anticipation. The adrenaline coursed through my veins, fueling my every move. The shadows of the late afternoon sun cloaked me like a shield. I could hear faint whispers on the other side, and their hushed voices added to the tension in the air as I approached the first guard stationed near the back entrance.

Peering through a dusty window, I caught a glimpse of movement inside. My grip tightened on the knife as I prepared to strike. Suddenly, a figure emerged from the door, and my body tensed, ready to attack. He strolled lazily outside, unaware of the danger lurking only steps away from him.

He never saw me coming.

I moved with swift precision, and my blade sliced through the air before plunging into his unsuspecting flesh. A gurgled gasp escaped him as I watched the life drain from his eyes, and a twisted smile curled on my lips. The metallic scent of blood mingled with the crisp air, sending a shiver of pleasure down my spine.

Three more guards remained, unaware of the fate that awaited them.

I ghosted through the semi-darkness, a silent predator stalking its prey. The second guard fell with a choked cry as my knife found its mark, carving a path of crimson across his throat. His body crumpled to the ground, a lifeless heap at my feet. I rolled him face down in the dirt in case the fucker had the audacity to take another breath.

The third guard put up more of a fight. His eyes widened in terror as he realized the danger he was in, but it was futile. I was fueled by my rage, unstoppable and merciless. With a savage ferocity, I overpowered him, relishing in the desperate struggles that drove my hunger for revenge even more. As he gurgled and clutched at his neck, I watched with detached interest.

"That's for Ella, motherfucker. See you in hell," I said quietly.

With a final shudder, he went limp and collapsed at my feet. Another one down.

Only one guard remained now, his breath ragged with fear as he witnessed the carnage around him.

I advanced toward him slowly, savoring the moment before delivering the last blow. His pleas for mercy fell on deaf ears as I struck without hesitation, ending his life with ruthless efficiency.

A soft bird call came from the back of the house, and I recognized it as Dope and Kip signaling that more men were approaching. Good, I hadn't met my quota for the week, and I was ready. The thrill of the hunt was in full bloom, my entire being on edge, eager for more.

It was over in seconds. A swift blow to his head cracked his skull open like an egg, splattering blood everywhere. A rush of energy and the buzz of excitement surged through me, wild and untamed like a raging bull. The sweet taste of victory filled my mouth, and a sick smile spread across my lips as I watched him crumple to the ground like a sack of potatoes.

Three more men came running toward me, their faces twisted into expressions of shock and fear as they took in the area littered with bodies. With a wicked grin, I signaled to Dope and Kip, who flanked the unsuspecting men in a well-coordinated move. It was like a dance—a deadly ballet of violence and death. One moment they were rushing toward us, the next they were pinned down by our merciless attacks.

My target turned to look at me. His eyes were wide with fear as he realized he wasn't going to walk away alive. He lunged at me with a desperate fervor, but I was too quick for him. With a swift motion, I slid my weapon between his ribs and into his heart. A satisfying crunch of bone reached my ears as I twisted my knife twice and then removed it.

"I think we're all clear," Kip said. "When we got here, I only saw the original three, but they must have called for backup."

I wiped the blood from my blade onto my pants, grinning.

"I'm going in. You two guard the door and fucking end anyone else that shows up."

Kip grinned and rubbed his hands together. "It's been awhile, but it feels damn good to be back in the fight."

I glanced at Dope, who shifted uneasily, gripping his weapon tighter. "I don't have the stomach for this shit, but adrenaline's a hell of a thing," he muttered.

My skull throbbed as Sebastian weighed in on the situation, urging me to hurry. Even though he remembered the layout better than I did, and I needed it for our advantage, I wasn't sure I would ever get used to hearing him talk in my head. He probably felt the same way, so I promised myself to give him a hell of a time with brutal ways to kill Xavier when it was my turn. The thought made me happy.

Go to the back of the house. There's a door to the basement.

I would have to take Sebastian's word for it. I didn't remember the area very well or how to access the home. I crept around the corner, then spotted what appeared to be an entrance. Hopefully, it would open without any noise, but I wasn't holding my breath.

Spiders. Ella said they're everywhere, so watch out.

"More things to kill," I responded out loud to my other half.

A noise pulled my attention away, and Dope tipped his chin at me to signal it was clear on his side. Seconds later, Kip appeared and gave the same signal.

We'd agreed that Dope and Kip would stand guard while I went down alone. There was no need to have them follow me into a spider den when I needed them to make sure we didn't have any more surprise visitors.

As suspected, the door creaked open and the little remaining daylight spilled into the basement, illuminating the stairway that sloped downward. I scanned the area, waiting to see if anyone would appear, but it was deathly quiet. With my knife in my hand, I descended the steps one at a time. Finally, I reached a small hallway with a room to the right. Still not hearing any movement, I moved forward.

Sebastian's thoughts entered my mind as I continued. *Holy shit. This looks just like my childhood basement.*

My cold, calculating eyes scanned the place, taking in the three lifeless figures slumped over a grimy kitchen table. The putrid odor should have made me recoil, but I was numb to such things after years of inflicting pain and terror upon my victims. I stomped through the kitchen, relishing in the crunch of spiders under my sturdy black combat boots. My gaze landed on a small glass cage that sat on the cement floor, hardly large enough for a small adult, and I knew Ella had been held captive in there.

In my mind, I could see Ella lying motionless, her porcelain skin marred with bruises and cuts. A surge of rage boiled within me as I squeezed my fists, the anger pulsating through my veins like a raging river. How dare they lay a finger on her—my sweet little lamb.

A guttural growl erupted from deep within my chest as I surveyed the room, the knife clenched tightly in my hand, eager to slice through flesh and bone. The sound of a low moan caught my attention, and I turned. My gaze narrowed at the figure on the floor.

"Help," the voice pleaded weakly.

My grip on the weapon tightened as I cautiously approached, unsure of the intentions of this intruder. "Who are you?" I demanded.

"I live here. Please help me. I was attacked, and my knees are busted. I can't get up," came the pitiful response, filled with desperation and pain.

"What's your name?"

There was a long pause before he finally answered, his voice scratchy and whiny. "Xavier. And I'm guessing you're Death."

I strode over to him and knelt, the light from the kitchen glinting off my blade.

"You'll be begging for death by the time I'm done with you. You'll be praying to me in your final moments for forgiveness for what you've done to my Ella." My words dripped with venom.

Xavier whimpered, fear evident in his trembling voice. "I'm not the one you truly want. It would benefit us both if you spared me."

My lip curled in disgust at his pathetic attempt to bargain for his life. But as much as I wanted to end him right then and there, a small part of me wondered if he might have some information that could lead me closer to avenging Ella.

A sharp whistle sounded from outside, and I realized it was my warning signal. I hurried to the first stair and looked up to where Kip was waiting by the door. "We need to go. A car is driving up the dirt road."

Without hesitation, I kicked some more spiders out of my way and walked back to Xavier. A large spider crawled down his leg, and I flicked it against the wall with the blade of my knife.

"It's your lucky day, motherfucker. Someone is coming." I sheathed my weapon, then knelt down and picked him up off the floor and slung him over my shoulder. "One word out of your mouth . . . Nah, fuck that." I swung to the left, and a hard, loud thunk from Xavier's head meeting the wall made me smile. Now that he was unconscious, I wouldn't have to deal with the bastard screaming for help like a little girl.

I rushed up the stairs and into the fresh evening air, where Dope and Kip were waiting for me. Kip closed the door, and Dope led us through the trees to the back of the house.

Men's voices weren't far behind us, and once we were out of sight, I stopped and watched as two men approached the basement.

"You know how he gets, man. He's probably in bed with his new girl. What's her name? Ellen? Something like that, but who cares?" One of them chuckled. "She's fine as hell and a good fuck, I bet."

"Yeah, but it's so much better when they're trying to fight you off."

He would be the first one I killed for that remark about Ella.

The men continued to talk as one of them opened the door.

"It's him," Dope whispered. "The one that went down the stairs first. He's the guy that drove up to the house when Ella was taken. He was wearing dark sunglasses, but I recognize his voice from the video."

Rage surged through me as I dumped Xavier on the ground and commanded my men to stay put. With fierce determination, I strode toward the entryway to the basement, my knife clenched tightly in my hand. This was more than business. It was fucking personal.

As I descended the stairs with deadly silence, a wicked grin spread across my face. "Well, well, well. Look who decided to join me tonight," I taunted, my voice dripping with malice.

Startled, both of the men spun around to look at me with wide eyes.

"You're . . . you're Sebastian Fletcher," one of them stammered, visibly trembling in front of me.

"You only wish it was him. And you are?" I asked with mock politeness. "I always like to know who my victims are before I torture them."

The larger man spoke up, his voice shaking. "They call me Tiny Tim."

I narrowed my eyes at the guy who had played a part in capturing Ella. "And you?"

I reached behind me and quickly withdrew my second knife. With a flick of my wrist, I flung the weapon at Tiny Tim. I hit my target and watched Tim weave, then collapse to the floor with the blade protruding from his neck. Blood poured from his wound as I grinned at his friend.

"I asked for your goddamn name," I said again.

Horror twisted his friend's face as he witnessed his buddy bleed to death on the floor next to his feet.

"John," he said, his voice trembling.

"What the fuck is it with assholes named John?"

"I-I don't know. It's a common name."

I stalked toward him, closing the gap between us. I towered over him and grabbed the back of his neck with my free hand. "Who is Xavier to you?"

His tongue flicked over his cracked lips, a nervous tic before he spoke. "No one," he stammered, sweat beading on his forehead. "My boss sent me to check in on him is all."

"Who is your boss?" I demanded, my voice cold as ice as I towered over him. "And why did they send you to my home to kidnap Ella Fletcher?"

John's entire body trembled, his eyes wide with fear as he struggled to form words. I tightened my grip on his arm, the coppery scent of blood filling my nostrils.

He pursed his lips tightly, and I knew in an instant what he was trying to hide. I pressed the weapon deeper into his flesh, drawing a thin line of blood along his neck.

"Are you willing to die for your boss?" I snarled, my fingers tightening around the handle of the knife.

"If I tell you, I'm a dead man anyway," John choked out.

I laughed darkly, the sound echoing off the cold walls of the basement. I snarled, knowing damn well his answer didn't matter. His fate was sealed the moment he stepped into my home.

With a steady hand and precise cuts, I sliced his right eyeball out of its socket, relishing the agonized screams that filled the room. The warm blood sprayed across my face, and I smiled, feeling a rush of exhilaration at the sight of it.

His eyeball fell to the floor, staring up at me.

"You'll never look at my Ella again," I said as I carved the left one out.

He went limp as I finished. I had wondered how long it would take him to pass out from the pain. I released him, and he dropped to the ground like a ton of bricks.

I strolled to the kitchen and located a Tupperware bowl with a lid. Then I rummaged through the drawers until I found a soup spoon. Returning to John, I used the spoon and bowl to collect his eyeballs, then sealed them.

I grabbed the back of his shirt and proceeded to drag him as I left the basement and walked up the stairs, his body thumping along behind me. Once I was outside, I dropped him on the ground and signaled to Dope. He hurried over to me, and I handed him John's eyes.

"A gift for Ella."

Dope frowned, lifted the lid, and peered in. His face immediately turned gray, and he resealed the container.

"That's the man who dared lay eyes on my little lamb and helped them take her from me." I pointed at the pathetic heap of human. "Let's take him along with Xavier. One of them will give me the answers I want."

"Where do we need to take them?" Dope asked.

"California for now. While you and Kip handle their travel

arrangements, I'm going to spend time with Ella and my kids. Then I'll be back for them."

This was just the beginning of what I had planned for Xavier and anyone who dared cross me or harm the ones I loved.

CHAPTER 28

SEBASTIAN

After three agonizing days, Ella was finally released from the hospital, and Ryan brought her to me at the rundown motel. As soon as I laid eyes on her frail figure, we crashed into each other's arms, tears streaming down our cheeks in a torrent of emotions. Ella's touch was a lifeline, grounding me in reality after the nightmare we had endured. All the terror and uncertainty of never being able to hold one another again melted away as our lips met in a desperate kiss, grasping onto each other as if our survival depended on it. It did.

I whispered against her mouth, "I thought I had lost you forever."

Her eyes shimmered with tears as she cupped my face in her hands, her voice barely above a whisper. "You'll never lose me. I promise."

As we held each other close, the world outside faded away, leaving only the two of us holding on to each other.

Ryan, Ella, and I headed to the airport. Dope and Kip said they would catch up with us at my penthouse in Portland once they finished some things. Cami and the kids were already waiting for us there. I didn't bother asking for details, since Death and I connected occasionally.

As I neared the entryway to the penthouse, I slowed and turned to my wife. "It was hard to find the right time, but you're going to find out."

Ella took a step back, fear flickering through her gaze.

I reached up and placed my hands on her shoulders. "No. No. It's okay. It's not bad like that."

"What is it?" she asked, her voice shaking.

"Baby, Cami knows about . . . him."

She frowned at me and then said, "I'm confused. What are you talking about? Ryan?"

Before I could respond about Death, the front door opened, and Cami stared us.

"Hi," she said, her voice cracking and her chin trembling. Big tears flowed down her face as she pulled Ella inside and flung her arms around her best friend. Ella's body visibly tensed and trembled slightly with Cami's sudden hug. I was about to step in and ask Cami to give her some room when my wife finally spoke.

"I'm home."

Cami moved back and dabbed at her eyes. "Don't you ever fucking die on me again."

That was the Cami Ella needed, cracking jokes at the shitshow we'd all somehow managed to survive.

Cami stepped out of the way and avoided looking at me as she motioned for us to come inside.

The moment we walked into the penthouse, Ella's shoulders visibly relaxed. It was hard seeing her afraid of every unknown sound, and I hated myself for putting her and the kids in jeopardy. At least we had more security here, and I was making sure they were safe instead of returning to New York. My wife was strong, but what she'd endured had the ability to break even the strongest people.

As I entered the living room, a rush of emotions hit me like a tidal wave—love, overwhelming gratitude, and an unbreakable determination. It was a moment I thought would never come: bringing my children's mother back to them.

Ella looked up at me, tears glistening in her eyes as she said, "Thank you for bringing me home." And with those simple words, she rose on her tiptoes and planted a kiss on my mouth that was both sweet and powerful and was filled with all the love and hope we had fought so hard to hold on to.

"Ma-ma-ma!" Verity bounced up and down in her playpen that Cami had set up in the living room.

"Verity!" Ella dropped her handbag on the floor and rushed to our daughter. She scooped her up in her arms and kissed her as tears fell down her cheeks.

myself a decent drink. Working in the bar and having access to alcohol on a regular basis had built up my tolerance, so slamming down a few drinks wouldn't have the same effect on me as it would on someone like Ella. I just needed some peace to untangle this mess and figure out what to do next.

As the liquor hit my tongue and traveled to my stomach, the clutter in my mind began to settle down, but I knew Death was still around. Over the last week and a half, I had felt him getting stronger, and I wondered if he had the ability to push me out altogether. It messed with my heart to think he might be the one that was present with Ella and my babies. I massaged the back of my neck and walked to the kitchen entrance. I leaned against the door frame and watched the kids play and throw soft toys at each other. They had a special bond, and I wanted to do everything possible to protect them and their relationship.

My cell buzzed in my back pocket, and I snatched it up and glanced at the screen.

Ryan: B or D?

I hated that the guys were starting to ask who they were texting, but I would do the same if I were in their shoes.

Me: Bass. What's up? Anything new in the investigation on who took Ella?

Ryan: Working on it. Have some leads we're looking into. How's she doing?

Me: She and Cami are talking.

I knew Ryan was going nuts about Cami breaking off the relationship with him and hoped that Ella might talk some sense into her. I wanted that for all of us. Otherwise, we'd constantly wonder if Cami would run to the cops and blow everything up.

Ryan: Hope that goes well.

Me: Me too. I'll let you know. But message if one of those leads pans out.

I approached the couch and set my phone on the coffee table. I had a sneaking suspicion Ryan, Kip, and Dope had more than just a lead, but even Death had kept that from me. It was time to take some action myself. I had never been good about sitting on the sidelines waiting for shit to happen.

CHAPTER 29

ELLA

Cami sniffled, then blew her nose and tossed the tissue in the small wastebasket. "I'm so relieved you're home."

When she patted the mattress next to her, I couldn't move. My heart pounded against my ribcage as my eyes widened in terror—the bed was alive with thousands of writhing spiders. The room swirled around me, and I tried to convince myself that it was just an illusion, that I was safe in the presence of my best friend. But every fiber of my being was on the verge of complete panic, teetering on the edge of a breakdown.

"Ella, I've known you for a long time, and you're not okay. You're hiding it well but not well enough. There's no way that you're okay after being kidnapped."

My hand shook uncontrollably as her voice brought me back to the present, and I spilled my terrifying ordeal to Cami. The memory of Xavier, his deranged family, the claustrophobic cage, and the scuttling spiders made me feel like I was suffocating all over again. As her expression twisted into one of pure horror and pity, a heavy weight settled in my chest. I didn't want anyone's sympathy. I just wanted to forget it all, but the trauma had a tight grip on me. The guys were on high alert, determined to keep me safe from any potential threats, but I couldn't shake off the constant fear. Every little sound sent shivers down my spine and sleep had been elusive as I relived the nightmare in my dreams. But even though I desperately needed to talk about it, I couldn't bring myself to revisit those memories anymore.

"I'll get through it. No one has really said much, but I'm sure they're looking for Xavier." I was happy to redirect the conversation from me to him at least.

Cami wrapped her arm around my shoulder. "Who is? Sebastian or Death?"

My head spun so quick my neck popped.

"What?" My pulse spiked fast and hard with the realization that Cami had mentioned Death. Maybe that's what Sebastian had been trying to tell me before Cami opened the front door. But this was really important, and I didn't understand why the guys hadn't talked to me about it. Maybe because I'd been kidnapped, died, and hospitalized. They probably wanted to protect me and hoped Cami would wait until I'd settled in back at the penthouse.

"Death. Sebastian's alter . . . the serial killer. Why didn't you ever tell me? Do you know how terrifying it was to see Sebastian turn into a cold-hearted monster right in front of me? And . . . Son of a bitch, Ella. He was the reason you were taken in the first place. Then . . ." She hopped off the bed and paced, her legs shaking. "Kip, Dope, Ryan, and you have all been covering for him. He's a killer. Like, how long have you known? Before or after you married him and had his kids?" She threw her hands in the air, exasperated.

My heart lodged itself in my throat as I struggled to form coherent words. I wasn't expecting this, and she'd completely caught me off guard. The room spun, and I rubbed my arms, reminding myself I was safe at home. If I could deal with Xavier, I could deal with my best friend being an insensitive brat. We'd all been through hell, and I needed to remember that so I didn't slap her upside the head. Irritated with her timing, I prepared myself for her questions.

"Cami, before we have this conversation, you have to promise me that you won't turn us in. Not any of us. No cops, no FBI, or anything close to that. If I tell you, then you're in this with us. Hell, you already are. You were with the kids while I was kidnapped and you learned the truth, but you stayed, which now makes you an accessory. You understand that, right?"

"I stayed under duress, afraid for the kids' lives!"

"And you're still here, so that won't hold up in court," I spat. My patience had worn thin with this woman who dared to threaten the safety and stability of my family. A twinge of guilt nudged me. *But she took care of your kids, so maybe you're the one being a brat?*

She stared at me, her mouth agape in shock as she struggled to form a response. "You wouldn't," she finally managed to choke out.

"But you would? You're angry at me for even mentioning the idea of us testifying against you, but you wouldn't hesitate to testify against all of us?" My body shook with rage as I confronted her.

I couldn't believe that after everything we had been through, she would be willing to tear us apart. As if I hadn't already been through enough hell, now she wanted to discuss my husband and his involvement in this mess.

I collapsed onto the bed, my head hanging low as waves of frustration and exhaustion washed over me. Cami's need for answers was understandable. Sometimes I forgot that my life wasn't the norm, and I couldn't expect Cami to get on board with it. She was scared for me and my children, but her careless words only added fuel to the fire. How could I handle such a bombshell on top of everything else?

Cami grabbed my hand, and her eyes filled with fear and concern. "Tell me the truth, Ella. Are you being held against your will? Do we need to get you and the kids out of here?"

I looked at her, my heart softening as I realized how much she didn't grasp. How could she possibly comprehend? "It's not like that," I choked out, my voice shaking.

"Then what is it like?" Her grip on my hand tightened even more. "Explain it to me, Ella. Help me understand why you're still here."

"Give me your word, unbreakable and ironclad, that this conversation will never leave this room. No authorities of any kind, and no way for us to be put in even more danger than we already are. Think of my children, Cami. They could be taken away from me any second." Tears spilled down my cheeks, my soul shattering into a million pieces at the thought of losing my twins.

My entire world hung in the balance, and it all depended on Cami's decision at that moment. The weight of her influence over my future was suffocating.

Cami's leg bounced nervously as she considered her options. Time seemed to crawl by, each second dragging on like an eternity. I stood up, ready to leave if her silence was an indication of betrayal. We needed to get out of here, and fast. She had the power to turn us in, and I couldn't afford to stick around and find out if she would. We had to flee immediately.

"It seems your decision is already made. Take care, Cami. No matter what, I'll always love you like my sister. I'm sorry it's come to this." I turned away, holding back the tears. I wasn't sure how I'd escaped my kidnapper and then returned here to lose my best friend. If I'd said it once, I'd said it a thousand times: I would do anything to keep my family safe. I opened the door and left the room, my feet taking me straight to my husband and children, who were playing in their playpen together. "Babe?"

"Hey, how did it go?" Sebastian asked.

I wrung my hands. I dreaded telling him that we had to leave and hide for the rest of our lives. That our babies wouldn't know their grandparents or grow up at our beautiful home in New York or the penthouse. That we would be looking over our shoulders even more than we already were. A sob lodged in my throat.

"Not good. We should—"

"Wait."

I turned to see Cami staring at me and Sebastian, then her attention landed on the kids. "You have my word. Besides, I'm already involved, as you said. But I have to know the kids are safe from . . ." She cleared her throat and looked at my husband. "Death."

Sebastian rose and approached her. Cami's fingers clenched and unclenched, and from her body language, she was trying not to take a step back from him.

Sebastian shoved his hands in his pockets, as if trying to defuse the situation with a non-threatening stance. I'd seen him do it with some of the women he and the society had saved. "He loves them, Cami. That's one thing I know for sure. He loves Ella and the kids, and he'd never hurt them. You have my word on that."

Cami nodded and turned to me. "Okay, I really thought I could call the FBI, but I can't, Ella. I'm so sorry. I guess I'm just as messed up in the head as the rest of the group. If you're with him, there has to be more to it, so come back and talk to me. You have my word that I won't turn on any of you."

Verity squealed and giggled her approval.

"Forget it, Sebastian. I thought we were going to have to run, but Cami changed her mind. I'll be back." I crossed the room and kissed him. I'd missed his kisses more than I'd allowed myself to admit.

He slipped his arm around me and pulled me to his side. "Let me know if you need anything."

"Okay."

I followed Cami back into the bedroom. The second we were alone again, I burst into tears. "I'm sorry. I really thought that was goodbye." I leaned against the door to steady myself. "So much has happened, and I'm struggling to get my footing again."

"I'm a bitch for bringing everything up right now. I'm sorry. It's a lot to process, and I need answers. I've had days to dwell on this, worrying about you and the kids and trying to understand what was going on . . . why everyone was just going along with it. It's not like I can say, well, he might kill someone today, but I'll ask questions later. These are people and families he's destroying."

I pushed off the door and sat down on the edge of the bed again. "You don't understand. We make sure he's only killing criminals. Bad ones. The men who sell their children or buy kids to use as sex slaves, murderers the cops can't catch, and other horrible situations. Sebastian helps relocate the families to keep them safe, and Death, well, he deals with the men."

Her forehead creased as she chewed on what I'd just said. "Men who sell their own children?" Her tone was gentle, and compassion flashed across her pretty features.

"Yeah, and worse, if you can imagine that."

She rubbed her shoulder. "When did you find out?"

"Remember a while back when a masked man appeared at my house, and I called the cops?"

"Yeah. Ryan was one of the ones that showed up."

"I didn't realize you two were interested in each other at the time. Anyway, it was Death. He started appearing more often, and then I was attacked and almost killed by a bastard named Stephen. Death saved me. I wouldn't be sitting here with you if it weren't for him. He's not a bad man. He's just . . ."

Cami laughed and rolled her eyes as if she couldn't believe that we were actually having this conversation. "He's a good guy that kills bad people. I get it. A vigilante."

"His parents were brutally murdered in front of him. Dope explained it all to me after I'd fallen in love with Sebastian and . . . and Death. I love them both. They're very different men, but they will do anything for me and the kids. It's a life I won't apologize for having, and I'll do anything to protect my husband and family."

"You proved that a few minutes ago. I think that's when it hit me how much you love and trust them. And somewhere inside me, I still trust you, even though you hid this dark and twisted secret life from me. And Ryan hid it from me too." Her voice was laced with sadness that tugged at my heart strings.

"Sometimes it gets really lonely hiding this side of me from everyone. There have been so many times that I needed to talk to you about something, but I had to lean on Kip and Dope instead. I tried to keep you out of all of this, Cami. We all did."

"I'm sure I'll have questions, if it's okay that I talk to you about it all."

I took her hand in mine. "It will be nice not to have secrets anymore."

"Agreed. But . . ."

My heart jackhammered against my ribs, waiting for the other shoe to drop. "What is it?"

"I broke up with Ryan. I couldn't get past the idea that he helped throw the cops off Death's trail and also cleaned up the crime scenes with Kip."

My body relaxed, and the tension drained from my neck and shoulders as I realized she hadn't changed her mind just now about turning us in. But a gnawing doubt remained, plaguing my thoughts with a relentless question. Could I truly trust her as we moved forward, or would I always be watching her every move with suspicion?

"Oh, Cami, I'm sorry. Are you sure, though? You love Ryan so much."

Her chin trembled. "I do, but he lied to me."

"So did I. We all did to protect you and ourselves too. From what I can tell, Ryan would never intentionally put you in harm's way. You have to believe that."

She wiped the tear that had snuck down her cheek. "I don't think I can get past it."

I slipped my arm around her shoulder and hugged her. "Maybe you just need some time. When I mentioned your name, he seemed so sad, but no one said anything about you two breaking up."

"I shouldn't have brought it up tonight either, but clearly I did." A flicker of regret flashed over her expression.

"It's okay. I'm glad it's out in the open and we can talk. It feels better than keeping things from you. You're my best friend, but even more than that you're my family. I will always try to do what's best for you, even when you question my choices. In this case it was to keep you out of the chaos I call my life. But don't get me wrong: I wouldn't trade it for anything in the world," I said gently.

"Love ya, bitch."

"Love you too."

Over the next several hours, Cami and I talked, laughing over old times, and she asked more questions. I answered them honestly, and as the time ticked by, I watched her smile return, which made my heart sing. I didn't want her to live in fear of Death or Sebastian. And I hoped like hell she would be able to forgive Ryan at some point. I understood how horrible it was to be separated from the people you loved most in this world.

Once Cami and I were caught up, I glanced at my watch. It was time to put the babies to bed for the evening, and I wanted to sing to them as Sebastian and I tucked them in. I promised myself to never take the little moments for granted again, no matter how tired or frazzled I was.

CHAPTER 30

SEBASTIAN

I sensed Ella's presence behind me before she even spoke. Her arm slid around my waist and her body pressed against mine as we stood at the window in our bedroom, looking out at the serene scenery below.

"It's all an illusion," I said to her. "Everything appears to be peaceful and beautiful below us, but underneath it's dark and chaotic." My gaze dropped to meet hers, and her emerald eyes filled with understanding. I wrapped my arms around her and pulled her close. "What can I do? How can I help you feel safe again?" I asked, my voice heavy with concern. I leaned down to kiss the top of her head, feeling a sense of comfort and security wash over me now that she was near.

"I need to stay close to you," she admitted, her voice strained from the intensity of her emotions. "The flashbacks are overwhelming, but when I'm with you or the guys, they're not as bad."

"I wish I could have kept you safe. This shouldn't have ever happened. I was lulled into a false sense of security out on the property."

She ran her warm palm up and down my back in a futile attempt to soothe me.

"Me too. I should have been more alert and aware. We can't spend time pinning the blame on someone when we need to find Xavier. He's still out there." She shuddered against me, and I brought her closer.

"Never again, Ella. You're safe. You have my word . . . and his."

She glanced up at me. "I'm not used to you referring to him. Are you talking with him? Has he told you what he knows?"

"Some. We're not connected all the time, and I haven't adjusted to the idea that he's in my head."

"I'm back now, so I can help. I'm so sorry you had to deal with my kidnapping and then connecting with Death on top of it."

My body trembled with pent-up emotion as I turned to her. "Losing you was too much, and it triggered everything," I confessed, my voice barely above a whisper. "We both thought we'd never see you again. But he was . . . is planning revenge." The words tasted bittersweet on my tongue. I wanted to be a part of whatever he was plotting, to avenge my wife.

Ella nodded slowly, understanding the gravity of the situation without needing any more explanation. "I know him well enough to understand that he will do anything to keep our children and me safe," she said confidently.

I reached out and smoothed a stray strand of hair from her face, tucking it behind her ear. "Is that why you love him?" My tone was laced with anger at the thought of anyone else being able to protect her.

Her response was hesitant, as if she were choosing her words carefully. "There are times that he scares me. But it's kind of our thing."

The sound of her confession made my blood boil. "What do you mean? Does he hurt you?" I gritted my teeth with the question. How dare he hurt her.

She placed her warm palm on my chest directly over my heart. "There are two parts of you. One is gentle and loving, but the other is fierce and unpredictable. Death can be rough with me . . . but I like it. I crave both sides of you." She moved her hand to my tense jaw, trying to ease the anger bubbling inside me. "I love both sides of you. In my mind, I'm lucky enough to experience all of what you have to offer. Sometimes it's hard or confusing, but I chose to be here with you. I chose to have your children. I chose to marry you." She looked into my eyes with unwavering love and determination. "Sebastian? Are you going to be okay? I'm worried about you. I can't imagine how horrifying this is."

I leaned down and pressed my mouth to hers, ready to stop talking about him. "This is what I know, Ella. I love you more than I ever thought possible. I love our babies. That's all I can tell you right now. Just try to be patient with me."

She slipped her arms around my neck and pushed up on her tiptoes, kissing me gently. "I love you too." Ella bit my lower lip and tugged on it.

"Baby, you should stop before I can't."

She nipped on my lip again. "Promise?"

"You've just been through a traumatic experience and in the hospital. You died. It's too soon."

"The doctor didn't say anything about not having sex. Please, I need you to remind me that I'm alive and safe at home with you. I need to kiss you and feel you inside of me, to erase the horror I lived through for just a little while."

I couldn't help but smile. She wasn't going to let it go, and I was okay with that as long as there wasn't a risk.

"Then relax and let me show you how much I missed you."

Her laugh went straight to my cock, and he was giving her his undivided attention. I cupped the back of her neck and placed a soft kiss beneath her ear. She shuddered against me, her hips pressing into mine.

"My girl likes that." I pressed my lips to the curve of her neck and across her collarbone. I traced down her side, then slid my hand beneath her shirt, my knuckles skimming her bare skin. She arched into me as I brushed her hard nipple through her lace bra.

"You're playing dirty." Her voice was breathy with desire.

I chuckled as my fingers traced circles around her sensitive peak. "I'm just making up for lost time."

Her body trembled beneath my touch as I treasured every moment, knowing soon the world would intrude once more. For now, though, it was just the two of us.

Slowly, I lowered my hand and trailed it down her stomach until I reached the waistband of her shorts. She gasped as I slipped my fingers beneath the material and felt the heat of her skin against mine. My dick strained against my jeans, begging to be released as I explored her soft curves. Then my fingertips brushed against her wet pussy.

Her breath hitched as I gently massaged her slick opening. She moaned softly and arched into me again, desire plainly written on her face. Her eyes were dark with passion, reflecting her longing. It was all I needed to spur me onward—to push further, to make her forget everything that had happened in the last week . . . to forget him.

I hooked my thumbs into the waistband of her pants and gently tugged them over her hips and slowly over the curve of her ass, careful not to hurt her. The wound from the knife in her thigh was healing nicely, but I took time to pepper soft kisses on each bruise and cut, my chest tightening as I mentally noted how many times she was hurt. Death stirred inside my mind, and I understood that he was also taking note in order to inflict pain on the men who did this to her.

"Be a good girl and part your legs."

Once she did, I nipped at her creamy thigh, her scent nearly driving me over the edge. Placing a soft kiss through the material of her thong, I moaned against her.

"I've missed you so much, baby." I cupped her ass cheeks as I ran my tongue over her pussy, teasing her.

She grabbed the short strands of my hair as I helped her step out of her pants and then her underwear. Ella leaned against the wall for support as I lifted one leg and placed it over my shoulder, allowing me the access I wanted while I spread her apart.

She cried out, her hips bucking, pushing herself closer to me. "Oh god, yes," she breathed, her voice filled with need.

I couldn't resist the scent of her as I savored every inch of her soft skin and explored the tender folds of her pussy. I flicked my tongue over her clit, feeling it harden under my touch. Her taste was intoxicating, and I lost myself in it.

Her hold dug into my shoulders as I continued my exploration, teasing her with languid licks and nibbles. Her moans filled the room while she trembled above me, and I knew that she was close to release.

I slid two fingers inside her wetness, feeling how tightly she gripped me. I curled my fingers and stroked that sweet spot inside her, eliciting a loud gasp from her. Her hips began to move, matching my rhythm as I finger-fucked her in earnest.

"That's it," I whispered against her skin, "be my good girl and come for me."

She cried out again, and her body arched as she climaxed. The feel of her muscles clenching around me made my desire all the more intense.

I slowly retracted my fingers from her slick pussy and raised them to my mouth. She watched me hungrily, desire still shining in her gaze.

I hesitated for a moment and allowed her time to catch her breath. Her eyes never left mine as I stood, leaned in, and claimed her lips with a searing kiss. She moaned as she tasted her arousal on my tongue.

As our kiss deepened, I reached up to undo the buttons on her shirt. Her skin was warm and smooth beneath my fingertips.

Ella's lips tasted like mint, and her breath came in quick gasps as we continued. I reached behind her back and unclasped her bra, releasing her full, perky breasts into my waiting hands. Her rosy nipples hardened with my touch. My lips trailed down her chest, tasting the light sheen of sweat on her skin. When I took one nipple into my mouth, she sighed and tangled her fingers in my hair.

She released a low moan as I sucked, my other hand trailing down her body to her wet pussy.

"That's my good girl, Ella. So wet for me."

An emotional charge connected us, and her eyes locked on to mine as I reached down to unzip my pants and step out of them. My cock bobbed free, grateful it was no longer restrained. Seconds later, I'd removed my shirt and tossed it on the floor.

I led her to the bed, and she lowered herself, then scooted up the mattress and parted her thighs for me, anticipation and arousal dancing across her face.

I crawled on top of her, ready to feel her tight pussy around me.

A moan escaped me as she wrapped her fingers around my thick cock.

"I've missed you so much," she whispered, the emotion clinging to her words as I lowered myself over her.

"You too, baby." I rubbed the tip of my dick over her wet slit and coated it with her juices. "You feel so damn good." I lined my cock at her entrance and slipped the tip inside her. Her eyelids closed as her lips parted. I shifted my hips and allowed myself to enter her a little at a time, drawing out her pleasure. "You're so beautiful."

Her fingernails dug into my ass cheeks, pulling me closer, as she wrapped her legs around my waist. I leaned down and licked her bottom lip, eliciting a soft moan. Our bodies moved in perfect sync, her back arching as she met my thrusts with eagerness. Her heavy-lidded eyes were filled with desire, and her skin was flushed. Ella's moans grew louder and more urgent, encouraging me to continue.

I reached down and found her sensitive clit, rubbing it gently as she clenched me tightly with her inner muscles. She clawed at my back, leaving marks with her nails as she cried out in pleasure. The heat between us was electric as we rode the waves of ecstasy together, our bodies tangled and lost in each other's touch.

"Sebastian, don't stop," she whimpered, our gazes connecting.

I increased the pace, driving myself deeper inside her each time until I could feel her inner muscles pulsating around me. I slowed my movements and focused on savoring the moment, every inch of my body screaming for release.

Ella slowly and gently flipped me on my back and straddled me before she lowered herself onto my shaft.

She began to rock against me, her rhythm nice and slow. I reached up and grabbed hold of her ass to help guide her deeper onto me with each thrust. Her breasts bounced as she rode my cock, and I palmed them, playing with her nipples. She leaned in close and kissed me passionately while never breaking our connection.

Sweat dripped down our faces as we continued to kiss hungrily. Despite her best efforts to remain in control, she pulled back, panting heavily.

It was time for me to take over and give her what she so desperately craved. With one smooth motion, I carefully flipped us over, keeping an eye on her wound as I positioned myself above her once again and drove inside of her like a man possessed. I was. I'd almost lost the love of my life, and I wanted to feel her come undone beneath me.

I leaned over and my nose grazed the outer edge of her ear. "Be a good girl and come for me."

Her back arched off the bed as her nipples brushed against my chest. I eased my hand between us and massaged her clit as she bucked against me.

"That's it, Ella."

She cried out loudly with her release, her muscles clenching my shaft as she rode wave after wave of her orgasm.

With one final powerful thrust, I let go, filling her completely as I exploded inside her.

CHAPTER 31

SEBASTIAN

We stilled, our bodies still intertwined and our breathing ragged. My gaze found hers, and I kissed the tip of her nose. "Nothing in this world compares to being with you."

Her eyes misted over, followed by a hiccup and rush of tears.

"Baby, what's wrong. Did I hurt you?"

"No. I—I love you so much. I thought I would never see you again."

She clasped her hands around my neck as I gently rolled over on my back and then wrapped my arms around her, holding her tightly.

"You can't get rid of me that easily. You are my shining star, and I will always find you, baby. I promise you that. Not even hell can keep you away from me."

Her hot tears landed on my neck, and she buried her face into my skin, her cries shaking her petite body.

Suddenly, I heard his voice in the back of my mind. *Tell her. Tell her this: Ella McCloud, you're the flicker of light in my dark, dark world. The color in my grayscale existence. I yearn for you like the night yearns for the stars.*

The words left my lips, and she lifted her head, her eyes rimmed with red.

"Death?"

I nodded. "He's here."

She sat up slowly, continuing to straddle me. "It's been so hard to protect you, but I don't regret a single minute of it."

My brows furrowed with her words. "I'm still trying to digest the idea that there are two different parts of me. I can't imagine how difficult it was for you to hide things from Death, like the wedding rings. Or remember what you'd said to which one of us."

She pursed her lips into a tight line. "Or that I'd flown in your plane before you ever told me about it. You flew me to Seattle to meet you at someone's sex club for a private show, but you had to cancel. That was my first time on your plane."

My gaze narrowed on her. "Holy shit. A sex club? I paid you for a private show?"

"It was supposed to be fifty thousand, but when you cancelled you sent me half. I used it for Dad's medical bills."

I shook my head as I tried to grasp those memories with her, but I didn't have any. "I thought there was something off the day I told you about it. There was a subtle hint in your expression like you recognized the interior, but then you realized you couldn't let me know." I smoothed the stray hair away from her tear-stained cheek. "You'll never understand how sorry I am for putting you in such a horrible position."

A sad smile eased across her features. "You don't ever have to apologize. I hated lying to you, but once Dope told me the truth, it was as if a thousand-pound weight was lifted off my shoulders. I was so torn between two men, in love with them both." She leaned forward. "Did Death ever tell you how we met?"

I placed my hands on her hips, still inside of her as we talked.

"Fucking camera," I growled. "Once I found out why you were working as a cam girl . . ." I hesitated, wondering if my strong-willed wife would be angry with me if I told her the truth.

"What? No more secrets between us. Please."

"Okay. I got insanely jealous and paid your dad's medical bills so you wouldn't have to continue entertaining men to pay for his treatment. But that moment when I was putting it all together, my heart filled with pride that you'd found a way to take care of him. Plus, no one had to touch you, and you had control over the situation."

To my surprise, she laughed. "I wouldn't call it control. I mean, Death found me and manipulated the circumstances and was incredibly possessive and jealous." Her features softened. "Thank you for paying the bill. If I'd known before we were married, I would have worked to pay you back. I thought it was Death, though, since he arranged the clinical trial that saved Dad's life." She grew silent, and I assumed she was skipping down memory lane. "He also made sure that no other men had access to my videos. He was my only paying client. The two of you went out of your way to protect me, just differently." She kissed me tenderly.

"And we will again." A sharp pain shot through my skull, and my wife climbed off me.

"Are you okay?" She placed her warm palm on my shoulder. "What does he need to say, Sebastian?"

The pain left as quickly as it had arrived, and I lifted my head, our eyes connecting. "He's ready to deal with Xavier. I won't have much time with you, baby. Death won't take no for an answer."

She took my hand in hers. "I need to go with him."

I shot off the bed so fast we nearly butted heads. "No. That is completely out of the question. You just came home and haven't even started to deal with the aftermath of what Xavier did to you. Not to mention that he's not even the one running the damn show."

My body froze in shock as Death shared the memory of Ella viciously plunging a knife into a man's chest until he stopped breathing. The scenes played out in vivid detail, searing into my mind as if burned by a branding iron.

With my legs shaking uncontrollably, I tried to process what I'd witnessed. A chill shot through me as I struggled to accept the truth.

"You . . . you killed him?" I stuttered, unable to comprehend the monstrous act that had just been revealed.

Ella winced at my accusation, her eyes flickering with pain and regret. "Death should have let me tell you instead of sharing that with you. John abused me when I was younger, and other little kids. When Death found out, he tracked him down and took justice into his own hands."

A calm storm brewed to life in my chest as I imagined Ella, a sweet innocent child, being violated by a twisted grown man. A monster and pedophile lurking in the shadows, preying on the most vulnerable. My blood boiled at the thought of such unspeakable depravity.

"What if someone hurt Verity? What would you do?" Her voice was soft. "I know what I did was to keep our children safe. John would have continued to hurt more and more kids. I couldn't let him get away with it any longer. I'm sorry if that changes how you see me." She tucked her hair behind her ear. "Honestly, it's one of the reasons I understand Death. Understand you. I rid the world of one more pedophile, and I won't apologize for that."

A war consumed me, one between right and wrong, but the protective father and husband inside me would have done the same. Hell, I wanted Death to torture Xavier for what he'd done to my wife. My emotions bounced back and forth, wrestling with the idea that my Ella had brutally ended a life.

The question on the tip of my tongue scared me, but I had to know. I had to know if Ella was more like Death than me.

"Did you enjoy killing him?"

She stood up from the bed and walked toward me. "Yes, it brought me closer to Death. He promised that if we found the man responsible for your parents' death, I would be there with him when he took his life."

A thick silence filled the space between us. I shoved my hand through my hair, grappling with the horrible reality that refused to release me from its grip.

"Sebastian, you're scaring me. Please, say something. Anything."

I searched her beautiful face, my gut churning with acid at the thought that I didn't know Ella at all. Who was she? My wife and the mother to my children was suddenly a stranger to me but not to him. My heart hammered against my ribs, and my head buzzed with his voice and my thoughts, stealing my breath. Moments later, I was finally able to speak.

"What the hell have I done to you?"

CHAPTER 32

DEATH

Shadows whispered secrets sweeter than salvation, teaching the lamb that being lost was just the first step to being found.
—Anonymous

The moonlight filtered through the penthouse bedroom, casting an angelic glow around my little lamb. She'd cried herself to sleep after I'd told Sebastian about John Bordeaux. His shock was palpable, but I wanted to throat punch him for making Ella feel bad. I had to remind him that I was about to go on a manhunt, and whether he liked it or not, he'd be along for the ride. Pissed wasn't even the right word for how I felt, and I promised to make the experience extra gory now that he was in my head more often than not.

Ella had tossed and turned all night but had finally settled into a fitful sleep. She would wake up in a few hours and look for Sebastian, but he was gone for now. The night outside waited, patient and merciless, while I lingered, torn between leaving her or staying. But it was my turn to be in the driver's seat, and I had some shit to take care of.

The rise and fall of her chest caught my attention, and I muffled my growl at the thought of Sebastian being inside my little lamb. When I returned from my trip, there were so many things I wanted to do to her. My cock strained against my jeans as I toyed with ideas of tying her up and licking her pussy until she begged me to fuck her. Or maybe . . . A thought stirred inside me, but it would have to wait until I took care of business.

I'd reached out to Dope and Kip and asked Dope to fly to Portland to stay with Ella, Cami, and the kids while I tended to Xavier and his buddy, who were being held in an abandoned building in northern

California. I placed a kiss on Ella's forehead, and then I slipped out of the room and then the penthouse, ensuring the entrance was locked and firmly closed before I made my way to the elevator.

Once I left the building, the sounds of the Portland nightlife came to life. I had hesitated at leaving Ella, but she was safe and tucked away at the top of the building. There was no way anyone who wasn't approved would be able to even make it to the elevator. After I'd had a little chat with the head security guard, I promised he would be compensated to make sure my wife and children were well guarded. Mike was a good guy, and over the years he'd turned a blind eye to some of my activities, so I was sure I could trust him.

A limo pulled up to the curb. The door opened, and a long jeaned leg appeared.

"I'm here," Dope said, gathering his backpack and laptop. He handed me a brown paper bag. "Burners."

"Good. I didn't want to leave until you arrived. Plus, I'll use the plane this time." I unzipped my bag and stuffed the phones into it.

"Might as well. I'll scrub the flight plan after you've landed. Kip is waiting for you." He adjusted his backpack on his shoulder. "You're all set up for your trip too. Kip will fill you in when you arrive."

I tipped my chin at him. "I'll be in touch. Hopefully, with some fucking answers."

Dope slapped me on the shoulder. "Later."

I slipped into the back seat of the limo and closed the door.

"Airport," I directed the driver. My palms itched as I mentally checked off the weapons strapped to my body. I was grateful for my own plane so I didn't have to try to get through security. I was ready to find out who Xavier and his boss were and what the hell they wanted.

"Time to play, motherfuckers," I muttered under my breath as the limo pulled away from the curb and headed toward the Portland airport.

The flight was just over an hour to California, then I rented a car and changed the plates as soon as I was out of the city. They could have it back once I didn't need it, but they'd also be looking for Scott Harrison, who had rented the car, not me.

After driving and then hiking to the abandoned building, I finally arrived as the sun was coming up. I used one of the burners to message

Kip that I was there. I didn't feel like getting shot if I startled him walking into the building.

The door creaked open, and I stepped inside, then secured it properly again before I made my way to Kip, who was sitting with his shoes propped up on an old, scratched desk.

"Comfortable?" I frowned.

He grinned as he placed his feet on the dirty tile floor. "Welcome to hell." Kip chuckled. "It's pretty boring around here. I poke the prisoners on occasion to make sure they're still breathing, but other than hanging around waiting for you, there's not a lot to do."

I set my bag on top of the desk. "How are my new friends?"

Kip smirked. "Ready and waiting." He rose from the chair, and I followed him out of the room and down the hall. He pointed to the first door. "Behind number one is our first victim, John, who somehow is still alive, but I suspect the onset of an infection from you plucking out his eyes will kill him shortly. He's in and out of consciousness, which might be useful if you can get any information from him." He strolled down the hall, then slowed in front of another door. "And the grand prize is our good friend Xavier, who is fully conscious but will never walk again due to broken kneecaps. He got a bit smart-assed with me, so I gave him a swift kick and broke them a little more." Kip's dark brow rose. "It's a shame I'm having so much fun inflicting pain . . . or is it?"

My wicked chuckle echoed through the hall. "Let's start with number one, since that son of a bitch is barely clinging to life." I stalked back to John's dingy room and flung the door open. The stench of urine and feces assaulted my senses, and I couldn't help but smirk at John's pitiful state. He cowered in the corner like a wounded animal.

I rolled up the sleeves of my black button-down shirt, ready to toy with my prey before I ended his pathetic existence. My boots scuffed across the floor as I approached him, fury rippling off me in waves as visions of my little lamb broken and lying in the middle of the road returned and fueled my fire.

"Who . . . who is it?" His voice quivered as he stared at me with wide, terrified eyes . . . or what was left of them.

"We meet again, John." My lips curled into a cruel smile as I relished in his fear.

He began to tremble violently at the sound of my voice, which only heightened my sadistic pleasure.

With a swift kick to his foot, I taunted him, "I have some good news for you." I knelt in front of him, allowing him a glimmer of hope before crushing it mercilessly. "If you tell me who your boss is and why they took Ella, I'll end your miserable existence quickly. Isn't there honor in being able to choose your own death?"

"And if I don't?" His voice cracked as sweat beaded on his forehead.

"Then prepare for a slow, agonizing death where you'll beg for mercy until your very last breath. Those are the only options I'm willing to offer you."

"Like I can believe you," John whined.

"I'm offended. I'm definitely a man of my word, and when I say I'll kill you, make no mistake. I absolutely will kill you."

John's face contorted with disgust as he spat on the floor in front of me. "Then I'll take my secrets to the grave. It's a matter of honor for a man to choose how he dies." He sneered. "And I'll die with my fucking mouth shut about your little piece of ass getting kidnapped." He chuckled, as if his words were the funniest thing in the world.

The sound of his laughter triggered a primal rage inside me. A feral growl erupted from my throat. "Don't you ever speak about her like that again." I stood up and walked toward one of my favorite tools for dealing with troublesome individuals. Kip, always prepared for any situation, had made sure it was within arm's reach. I picked up the small yet effective tool and ran my hand over the handle, savoring its cold metal against my skin. "Are you familiar with combing or carding, John?" I asked in a low voice.

"Like being carded at a club?" he replied, attempting to mask his fear with a feeble attempt at humor.

I let out a cruel laugh. "You wish it were that simple. It's an ancient form of torture where iron teeth used to prepare wool are instead used on human flesh."

John's Adam's apple bobbed frantically as my words sunk in, and sweat trickled down his temple. As I reveled in his terror, a twisted grin spread across my face.

"It's one of my most effective methods of torture," I hissed as I grabbed him by the throat and hauled him to his feet. "And you're about to experience it firsthand." I dragged the sharp comb down his arm, slicing through skin and muscle until bone was exposed. Blood spurted from the wound, painting the floor in a macabre display.

John's screams were muffled by my hand as I squeezed tighter, relishing his agony. "Who is your boss?" I demanded, my voice cold and emotionless.

John's cheeks reddened as he gasped for air. "I'll tell you!" he pleaded.

"Speak," I said, tightening my grip.

"They call him the Pied Piper," John sobbed. "He's a notorious killer with a legion of followers. He doesn't want Ella . . . He wants you. You and he are tied together."

My pulse raced with both fear and excitement at this revelation. The Pied Piper had been after me all along. And now, I finally had a name to put to the monster who haunted me.

My gaze narrowed on his grotesque eye sockets. "Why have I not heard of him before if he's so notorious?"

"He stays well hidden and only reveals himself to people he's chosen as his followers."

"He's a cult leader," I stated rather than asked.

"Call it whatever makes you fucking happy."

"When I found Xavier, he was holding Ella in a duplicate of the home that my parents were killed in. Why the obsession with them?"

John smirked. "Are you really that stupid?"

"The blood loss must be clouding your judgment," I retorted coldly as I pressed the iron combs hard against the side of his face. If he had still had eyes, they would have bulged from their sockets at the sight of the metal. "Apologies for my bluntness, but I am not in the mood for games," I growled as I slowly dragged the combs down his cheek just enough to prove my point, eliciting screams from him.

"I'm sorry!" he cried out, trembling under my grasp. "I didn't mean it!"

But it was too late for apologies. The pain and rage coursing through me consumed any trace of mercy or forgiveness.

"He's your man. He's the killer that left you an orphan. But you probably don't remember all of that, do you?"

"I remember enough," I snapped.

"But not what happened directly after. Just that your buddy found you huddled in the corner of the kitchen." He licked his dry lips.

"If you're asking if I recall stabbing my father, I do vaguely. I wasn't sure if it was a dream or real."

"Real. The Pied Piper had several hours with you, though. He told me all about it."

I paused, desperately trying to recall any memories from that night. But there was nothing. No flashes of violence or screams for help. Just a gaping black hole in my memory.

Now would be a good opportunity to weigh in, Sebastian. The asshole wasn't anywhere around, though. He was probably hiding and feeling sorry for himself after how he treated my little lamb.

"Where can I find the Pied Piper?"

John shook his head. "He'll find you when the time is right. Rest assured, it's soon."

With a sinister grin, I started to sing "Mary, Mary, Quite Contrary."

"What the fuck is wrong with you? You're singing a fucking nursery rhyme now?" John asked, his tone thick with disbelief.

"How does your garden grow?" I sang. "Lucky for you, you'll get to help fertilize her garden." I chuckled at my joke, and then with a quick flick of my wrist, I peeled the flesh and muscle off the side of his face. "Thanks for the information, motherfucker. This is for Ella." I dragged the tool down his throat and ripped out his larynx as he screamed for the very last time.

Blood spurted across my once clean shirt and soaked me to the skin.

CHAPTER 33

DEATH

They searched the hills with torches, never knowing darkness had taught their lamb to love the void.
—Anonymous

A half hour had passed as I remained in the room, my mind plunging into the dark depravity of my soul. The metallic scent of blood filled my lungs as I dragged my fingers through the crimson pool beneath John's corpse. With methodical precision, I began writing on the concrete wall in his blood:

I COUNT THE WAYS I'LL MAKE THEM SUFFER

My hand trembled, not from fear, but from the pure ecstasy of imagining their pain. Below it, I added:

FOR EVERY TEAR SHE SHED

The blood dripped down the wall like macabre tears. Kip watched from the doorway, his expression impassive. He'd seen me like this before.

"You're slipping," he said quietly. "Sebastian's fighting to surface."

"Let him try." I dipped my fingers in more blood. "Sebastian needs to see this. Needs to understand what we're capable of when someone takes what's ours."

I began drawing symbols beneath the words of ancient things that lived in the darkest corners of my mind. Patterns that spoke of torture and vengeance.

"Should I be worried?" Kip asked, his voice carefully neutral.

I turned to him, aware of how I must look covered in John's blood, my eyes wild with barely contained violence. "Worried? No. But they should be. Anyone who touched her, who made her feel fear . . ." I dragged my bloody fingers across my face, marking myself. "I'm going to take them apart piece by piece while she watches. And she'll love me for it."

"Jesus," Kip muttered.

"No." I smiled, knowing it wasn't a kind expression. "Just Death. And I'm going to show them exactly why they should have feared that name."

I pressed my palm flat against the wall, leaving a perfect bloody handprint. "This is my promise to her. Written in the blood of those who dared to cage my queen."

I could feel Sebastian's horror in the back of my mind, his desperate attempt to stop this display of madness. But he needed to understand—this was who we were. This beautiful violence was our true nature.

I whispered, more to myself than Kip, "I'm going to lay their bodies at her feet like offerings. Paint her skin with their blood. Show her that every drop spilled was for her."

I turned back to John's body, already planning how to display it when we found the others. It would be my gift to her. A tableau of vengeance that would make her understand the depths of my devotion.

"You think this will make her feel safe?" Kip asked.

"Safe?" I laughed, the sound echoing off the walls. "No. This will make her feel powerful. When she sees what I'm willing to do for her"—I dragged my bloody fingers across my lips, tasting copper—"she'll finally embrace her own darkness completely."

Kip pursed his lips together. "I should go check on Xavier and make sure the fucker hasn't figured out how to escape. I'll find you later."

I grunted at him as he left, then I closed the door as images of Ella flooded my mind. My cock hardened with visions of her on her knees worshipping me as we reveled in John's death. With her hand wrapped around my dick, stroking me, she worked her hot mouth up and down my length. I briefly closed my eyes and unzipped my jeans, my skin sticky with John's blood. I released my throbbing shaft and stroked as I imagined looking down at my little lamb, her green-eyed gaze full of reverence. As I continued to stroke myself, blood-soaked, I imagined Ella climbing onto a bed beside me. She would straddle me, her body glistening with sweat, her expression hungry and full of desire. She would lean forward, her breasts brushing against my chest and her lips meeting mine in a desperate kiss. Her hands would grip my hips tightly, pulling me toward her as she placed my cock at the entrance of her wet pussy. With a moan, she would slowly lower herself onto me, feeling me stretch her out and fill her completely.

I could almost hear her soft sighs as we moved against each other, our bodies slick with sweat and blood. She would ride me hard, her hips thrusting up and down, my cock sliding in and out of her as we lost ourselves in each other's pleasure. The thought of Ella's wetness enveloping me sent waves of ecstasy through my entire being.

As I approached my climax, I imagined Ella's fingers digging into my flesh, urging me to go faster, harder. She would call out my name, her voice hoarse with desire as she reached the peak of her orgasm. With one final thrust, I would pulse inside her, filling her with my hot cum as she shuddered beneath me, her body trembling with pleasure.

Still breathless from the intensity of my fantasies, I could see Ella's face clearly in my mind, glistening with sweat, lips swollen from our harsh kisses, eyes full of satisfaction as she looked at me.

A sharp pain stabbed me in my skull as the room came back into focus. My hands shook as I stared at them, coated in John's blood. The metallic scent filled my nostrils, intoxicating and familiar. I tucked myself into my jeans as Sebastian attempted to push his way forward.

Stop. This isn't who we are.

"Shut up," I growled at Sebastian's voice in my mind. I dragged my bloody fingers across the wall, painting it crimson. "This is exactly who we are."

You're going to destroy everything: our family, our life. Stop this madness.

I laughed, the sound echoing off the concrete walls. "Madness? This is clarity." I wrote on the wall in dripping letters: DEATH COMES FOR THEM ALL.

A sharp pain shot through my skull as Sebastian fought for control. I staggered, catching myself against the blood-smeared wall.

Think of Ella. Think of what this will do to her.

"I am thinking of her!" I roared, slamming my fist into the wall. "Every drop of blood is for her. Every scream is vengeance for her fear."

This isn't vengeance. This is you losing control.

I pressed my forehead against the cool concrete, leaving a bloody mark. "You don't understand. You never have. This is who we are. Who we've always been. The sooner you accept that, the stronger we'll be."

I won't let you destroy us.

The pain intensified as Sebastian pushed harder. I grabbed my head, gripping my hair. "You can't stop me. You're weak. You always have been."

And you're a monster.

"Yes," I whispered, a smile splitting my face. "That's what they need me to be." I dipped my fingers in more blood and continued writing: THEY TOOK OUR QUEEN. THEY'LL PAY IN BLOOD.

Please, Sebastian's voice grew desperate. *There are other ways.*

"No." I dragged bloody fingers down my cheeks. "This is the only way. The only language they understand." I turned in a slow circle, admiring my work—the walls covered in crimson promises of violence. "When Ella sees this, she'll understand. She'll see the beauty in it."

You'll terrify her.

"No, I won't. You don't know her like I do. I'll empower her." I pressed my palm against the wall, steadying myself. "She has the same darkness in her. She just needs permission to embrace it."

The pain in my head became blinding as Sebastian made one final push for control. I dropped to my knees, blood soaking into my clothes.

"You can't win," I snarled through clenched teeth. "I won't let you cage me again. Not until they've all paid for what they did to my little lamb."

Then we'll both lose everything.

"No." I forced myself to stand, fighting against Sebastian's influence. "We'll become what we were always meant to be. And Ella will love us for it."

I could feel Sebastian's horror as I added one final message in blood: FOR MY QUEEN—A SYMPHONY OF SCREAMS.

"See?" I whispered to Sebastian. "This is true love. This is devotion. This is who we really are."

His silence was answer enough. He was still there, watching, horrified, but powerless to stop what was coming. Just as he should be.

I stepped back to admire my work, covered in blood and grinning. Let Sebastian hide from our true nature. I would paint the world red for Ella, and she would finally see us for what we were—beautiful monsters, perfectly matched.

CHAPTER 34

ELLA

I folded my arms across my chest and impatiently tapped my foot against the hardwood floor of the living room. "I'll ask again, Dope. Where is Death?"

He reached for the rolled joint in his flannel shirt pocket and popped it into his mouth.

I gave him a pointed look. "Not in here with my kids."

"Yeah. I got it." He stood and headed toward the door.

With a few quick strides, I stepped in front of him and blocked his exit. "Not so fast. You can smoke your joint on the balcony if you behave and tell me where my husband is."

"Ella, I can't tell you. It would put you in danger."

I put my hands on my hips and glowered at him. "You're in danger now, so you better talk, and quick, dammit."

"All right. I'll make you a deal. I'll tell you where he is only if you give me your word that you're not going after him."

My eyes widened. "Does he have the guy that kidnapped me?"

Dope's gaze darted away from mine. Bingo.

"Who is it, Dope? I deserve to know. I lived through hell." I wasn't lying, but I hoped some guilt would also work in my favor.

"We don't know who is behind it, but Death has the guy that drove to your house when you were taken. He, uh . . . may or may not have eyeballs left in his head."

"Oh shit." I barked out a laugh, then slapped my hand over my mouth, hoping I hadn't woken Verity and Alaric, who were sleeping in their room. "Serves the son of a bitch right."

"I think . . . if it helps you feel better—" Dope stopped abruptly. "You didn't give me your word that you wouldn't go after him. I've already said too much."

A fierce battle raged within me as my conscience and heart fought for control, tearing me apart. One part of me thirsted for revenge and longed to join forces with Death against the men who had captured me. But the other part, the primal instinct to protect my children, roared through my veins like a raging inferno. If I abandoned them and something happened to both Death and me, my precious babies would be left without either parent to guide them.

I chewed on my lower lip and debated my answer, but I already knew what it was.

"You have my word. I won't go after him. I'll let him do what he does." My chest ached with my promise.

"Perfect. In my opinion, Death should have told you already, but for some reason he didn't. Sometimes I don't understand his reasoning. Do you?"

I resisted the urge to smack him, hard. Instead, I grabbed his joint from his hand and threatened to snap it in half.

"Go ahead. I'll just unroll it and smoke it in a bowl. No skin off my back."

"When I'm done with it, you won't have anything left to smoke." I waited for that to sink in. I hadn't told anyone how terrified I was that Xavier would heal and come after me again. I kept the truth hidden, too afraid to speak it aloud. The mere thought of Xavier seeking revenge made me break out in a cold sweat. How could we have been so blind before, unaware of his watchful attention constantly on me? The memory of him tracking me like a wounded animal after I'd escaped assaulted my senses as the memories rushed back.

"Why wouldn't Death tell me?" My chest heaved with my question in a lame attempt to control the emotions that were threatening to spill over.

"Because he didn't want you to find him until he sent for you. He needed time alone with Xavier and to make sure that you were safe."

I closed my eyes, trying to silence the rising panic that was wrecking me. "Okay. That makes sense." I looked at Dope again. "But I need to see Xavier again. I have to."

Dope gave me a quizzical look. "Why?"

I glanced around the room to make sure no one was in earshot, but Cami had left to go to the grocery store, and the kids were asleep. Dope and I were alone. Regardless, I leaned in and whispered what I'd learned.

Dope staggered backward with the news. "Fucking hell, do you think he was lying?"

I shrugged. "There's only one way to find out."

"Death can't kill him, Ella. I mean, not yet." He drew in a sharp breath, a desperate look on his face.

"That's why I want to know where he is. I want to give him the choice of whether we need Xavier alive for a little while longer. Please, Dope, tell me where they are."

He threw his hands up and stepped back. "Ella, he'll kill me. I feel letting Xavier go is a much better option."

I rolled my eyes. "I agree with you, but don't you think that should be Death's choice? Besides, he would never hurt you. You're his family." I glanced at my watch. Death had been gone for approximately twelve hours, according to Dope. "We're running out of time. What if he's already killed Xavier?"

"Fuck." He paced the living room, then reached for his joint. "I need that right now."

"Tell me where he is, and I'll buy your next bag."

Dope blew out an exasperated sigh. "Promise me you'll have me cremated and buried next to my grandparents if he kills me."

"You have my word. I'll make sure your wishes are respected."

"He's in California. There's an abandoned building he likes to use. He's holding Xavier and John there."

I flinched at the name John.

"Who is John?"

"The man that wore the dark shades and drove to your place."

I groaned and shook my head. "What's the deal with all these horrible men named John?"

"Dunno. But if you want to make it in time, you need to get the hell out of here."

I threw my arms around him in a big hug. "Please tell Cami I had to . . . find Sebastian, and that I'll be back as soon as possible." Before he could answer, I hurried to the bedroom to change into jeans and a sweater and to pack. A part of me wanted to call Kip and Death and let them know that I was on the way, but I didn't want them to tell me no. I would show up and ask for forgiveness later. Twenty minutes passed, then I kissed my sweet babies goodbye and left to find Death before it was too late.

Walking out the door of the penthouse had nearly ripped my heart out. The last thing I had wanted to do was leave my babies again. I wasn't ready. A part of me kicked and screamed as I boarded the commercial flight. I just wanted to return to my safe cocoon and forget the agonizing nightmare I'd lived. But I had to move forward. I refused to allow myself to live in bondage to Xavier . . . or anyone else.

Once I landed at the airport and rented a black car that would blend in well with others, I followed Dope's instructions to the abandoned warehouse, checking often to see if anyone was tailing me. Finally, I reached the building Death and Kip were supposed to be in. I fired off a text to both of them that I was there so they wouldn't attack me when I walked in. My breath caught in my throat as I realized that I was about to face Xavier once again. A messy ball of emotions bloomed in my chest—fear, horror, and a fury I hadn't experienced before.

The door swung open, and Kip stepped out to greet me.

"You're an unexpected surprise, but I'm glad you're here." He looked around outside, and then he held it open for me. "Watch your step. This used to be an old mill, and there are nails and shit still around."

"I will. I'm not sure that was the reaction I thought I'd get when you guys found out I was here, but I have to talk to Death. Please tell me Xavier is still alive."

Kip frowned. "You're concerned about Xavier after what he did to you?" He slipped his arm around my shoulders.

"Yes and no. I need to talk to Death."

Kip's steps echoed on the creaking floorboards as he led me through the abandoned building. The air was thick with a sense of foreboding, and my pulse raced in anticipation.

"You'll have to wait on that one." His tone was gentle. "We have a much bigger issue to deal with. That's why I'm happy to see you."

As we reached the doorway to a room, a wave of dread washed over me. Kip's cryptic words added to the unease gnawing at my stomach.

"Kip, I don't understand," I called to him as he walked away.

"Open the door, Ella," he responded.

Trembling, I slowly pushed it open and braced myself for what lay ahead.

CHAPTER 35

ELLA

My eyes widened as I took in the horrific scene before me. The man I had always known as strong and kind was now a blood-soaked, broken figure lying on the cold cement floor. His arms were wrapped around his head in a futile attempt to protect himself from an unseen enemy.

Ignoring the bile rising in my throat, I rushed to him.

"Sebastian?" I asked, not positive who was in front of me, but my instincts told me it was him.

"Go away," he whispered.

I reached for his arm, and he grabbed my wrist. His grip was strong as he squeezed.

"You're hurting me, Sebastian."

"I don't want you here. You can't see this . . . see me."

"I'm not leaving you. Tell me what happened." I refused to leave him alone in this state. But as I sat down next to him, the sheer amount of blood surrounding us made me dizzy. The metallic stench filled my nostrils, and I fought against the urge to vomit. I had killed before, but for some reason the aftermath was different.

Still shaking, Sebastian slowly sat up and turned toward me. His hands gripped some unknown object covered in crimson. His hair was matted with blood, and it stained his clothes and skin.

"What happened? Who did this to you?" I asked, desperation laced through my voice. I was pretty sure that I knew the answer already, but I needed to hear it from him.

He could barely meet my gaze as he whispered, "It was me." His head hung with shame.

My entire being cried for the agony he was going through, but I had to remain strong for him. "Tell me what you remember." I reached for his hand and held it in mine.

Horror twisted his expression as he stared at me. "How can you touch me right now? I'm a monster. I brutally killed a man and yet you're sitting with me."

I pursed my lips in an attempt to not let the tears fall from my eyes. "That body behind you . . . He was one of the men responsible for taking me. Death was dealing with him, and I'm guessing that you reappeared at the end."

Disgust twisted his features. "It was horrible how he . . . we killed him. I can't do this." He climbed to his feet and staggered backward.

I jumped up and reached for him before he lost his balance. "Can't do what, baby?"

He frowned, his brows knitting together. "Be the man that you need me to be."

The words hung in the air, stretching between us like a thread pulled too tight, threatening to snap.

I shook my head. "You are the man I need you to be. You keep me safe at all costs. I would do the same for you."

He snarled as he glared at me. "No man should ever ask his wife to protect him when he's a fucking monster."

I took a cautious step forward. My voice trembled with worry and fear of what he might do. "You're in shock. You've never seen Death's true power. It's grisly and gut-wrenching, but he only takes out the scum of society. If he had told me about John, I would have begged to join in. I would have relished the chance to make him suffer for what he did to me." My fists clenched so tightly that my nails pierced the skin of my palms, drawing blood. I raised my chin defiantly. "I knew exactly who you were when I said 'I do.' This"—I gestured toward the mangled corpse on the ground and the words on the wall—"was all part of the deal. You killed Stephen in my kitchen because he tried to kill me. And then you presented his heart to me as a token of love."

Sebastian stared at me with an appalled expression. "How could you choose me after that?"

"Because I love you. I love both of you. Now that you and Death are aware of each other, it's making it more difficult on you. The rest of us have already adjusted to who you are. Kip, Ryan, and Dope—we made our choices. I would choose you all over again if I had to." Dread washed over me as I said that. "But I have a feeling that's not the issue right now."

With a deafening roar, Sebastian grabbed his hair and pulled, his anguish pouring out in waves. My soul shattered into a million pieces, bleeding on the floor along with his suffering. I was helpless to ease his torment. All I could do was stand by him and love him through it all.

My pulse pounded in my ears as I neared him, tears blurring my vision. With a desperation I couldn't contain, I threw myself into his arms and clung to him like a lifeline. His body was drenched in another man's blood, but I didn't care. Even as he struggled against me, pushing me away with bruising force, I refused to let go. In that moment, all that mattered was showing him how fiercely I loved him and how unconditionally safe he was with me.

"You're my heart, baby. I've never loved anyone else. It's always been you."

Slowly, he wrapped his arms around me. A quiet sob escaped him as his knees buckled and we sank to the floor, holding each other.

His heart beat erratically against mine, matching the chaos that raged within me. How did we end up here, covered in blood and tears, clinging to each other as if our lives depended on it?

Deep down, beneath the layers of pain and betrayal, there was a flicker of hope that refused to be extinguished. Maybe, just maybe, we could find a way through the darkness that threatened to consume us whole.

As dawn broke over the horizon, casting long shadows across the floor, he finally lifted his head and met my gaze with an intensity that seared my soul. In that moment of raw vulnerability, I saw his walls crumble, revealing the shattered pieces of a man who had endured too much for too long.

As we held each other in that dimly lit room, I felt the boundaries of our reality distort. The line between right and wrong, between love and fear blurred until all that remained was us—two broken souls seeking solace with each other.

I knew then that our love was a battlefield, a war we fought against the world and ourselves. And as we stayed locked in that embrace, I wondered if we were each other's saviors or each other's damnation.

"I can't do this alone," he whispered, his voice barely above a breath, yet echoing with unspoken truths.

I looked up at the man I adored, my stomach in knots. "What do you mean?" My mind raced with the unthinkable. Was he going to turn himself in? Admit himself for mental treatment? Leave me and the kids?

His eyes, once filled with fire and determination, now held nothing but a profound weariness that weighed heavily on my shoulders. The silence between us stretched taut, heavy with fears and doubts that threatened to devour us whole.

"I mean, I need you with me. Through all of it. The darkness, the pain, the uncertainty. I can't face it alone anymore." He swallowed and hesitated, then he continued. "I was going to leave you. Leave the kids. I'm learning what I've done to you, and the twins have a connection with Death. The idea that Alaric loves Death terrifies me. How can I stay and destroy everything that I love?"

His words hung in the air, heavy with the weight of our shared past and the unknown future that loomed before us.

"But I'm not strong enough to abandon the only light in my world. I won't give myself over to Death completely, and I have to fight for you and the kids. I can't be a pathetic excuse for a man and leave all of you alone with him."

Tears welled up in my eyes as I struggled to comprehend the depth of his words. How could I be the anchor he needed when I felt adrift in a sea of uncertainty myself?

But as I searched his face for answers, all I found was a desperate longing for salvation, for redemption in the arms of the one person who had always believed in him against all odds.

In that moment, a new resolve ignited within me, pushing aside my fears and insecurities. I reached out and took his trembling hands in mine, intertwining our fingers in a silent vow of solidarity.

"We'll face this together," I whispered, willing my voice to remain steady despite the storm raging inside me. "Whatever comes our way, we're in it together." But something in the back of my mind told me this conversation wasn't over.

CHAPTER 36

SEBASTIAN

I hated myself. I hated myself for being weak and allowing Death to rule my life, to ruin my marriage and relationship with my children. If I was strong enough, I would walk away and let them find someone who could love and protect them, not make them lie and live a double life.

The hot spray of the shower cascaded over me, and I stared as red water swirled down the drain. The abandoned building had a shitty bathroom, but it worked, and I had to wash the man's blood and guts out of my hair. Ella wanted to join me, but I said no and let her clean up first.

You're feeling sorry for yourself, asshole.

I gritted my teeth and slammed my fist against the shower wall. "Fucking stay out of my head, Death. You've done enough damage already. Leave. You're not welcome here."

His laugh echoed through my mind, pissing me off even more.

You think there's a choice because you're strong-willed? We've shared this body since the beginning of time. It just took your parents' murder for me to fully evolve and appear.

I stilled with his confession, and water streamed down my forehead into my eyes, but I barely noticed the burn.

"Have you been aware of me all along?" I grabbed the bar of soap and lathered my face while I waited for him to answer.

No. I only learned about you when I found out Ella was pregnant. I was going to kill you for fucking her.

I flinched at his crude words. "She deserves more than to be fucked, you son of a bitch."

She likes it. She likes when I chase her through the woods and fuck her so hard she can't walk.

His words were difficult to digest. She deserved to be worshipped and not treated badly.

But . . . she also likes it with you. The way you touch her and care about what makes her feel good. He grunted. *It kills me to admit it, but I suppose every once in a while, we're going to have to get along. Not because I like you, but for her.*

"That's the first time I've ever heard you put her first."

I always put her first. She is my queen. I just have a different way of showing it.

We were definitely night and day. A part of me wondered if I could ever accept him. Accept that part of me, the pitch-black darkness. The other part of me wanted to fight it with everything I had, but what if it was futile?

Now. Are you finished with your fucking pity party? Can we get down to business?

I'd nearly forgotten that there was another prisoner waiting for him. Closing my eyes, I braced myself for what he was about to say. I didn't ever want to be around again while he was killing someone, but I wasn't sure after witnessing John's death if I would be able to disappear. Death's emotions and vile anger were so strong that lately, they were triggering me to appear.

"What do you have in mind?"

Before we move on, I need to make sure we're on the same page.

"About?" I rinsed the soap from my face and lathered my body as I continued to have a conversation with the other part of me.

Are you planning on leaving Ella and my children?

I snapped at him, "Clearly, my private thoughts aren't private anymore."

Answer the goddamn question. I'm not sure all the pretty words about needing her and not being able to do this without her were the truth.

My head hung low, the muscles in my neck and shoulders aching from killing John and the weight of the emotional aftermath.

"I was planning on leaving, yeah. I'm a danger to her and my kids. I love her enough to leave them and allow them to heal and have a better life without us. It's never even crossed your mind to be that selfless, has it, asshole?"

Pain shot through my skull so hard it dropped me to my knees.

If you hurt her by leaving, if my kids grow up without you around, I will find a way to kill you. I will take you over, and you'll never see the light of day. I will fucking end you.

His words echoed in my mind as I gripped the sides of my head, gasping for air.

"So, you're going to hold me hostage? Seems like it's your go-to," I grunted through the pain.

If you don't want her, then just give in and let me have her.

CHAPTER 37

DEATH

In the end, every lamb is lost—some just discover it sooner than others.
—Anonymous

"I knew you were a weak son of a bitch," I said as I stood in the shower. I'd won. I'd pushed Sebastian aside and had taken over. Soon, I would be in control and finally end his relationship with my little lamb. I refused to share her with anyone. Ever.

Turning off the water, I opened the door and grabbed the towel off the toilet. It was damn good to be back and in control. The first thing I needed to do was find my little lamb and promise her that she would never be alone. I would always be by her side as she would mine. Leaving had never been an option. The second Sebastian had considered the idea, I realized I had to do something, and fast.

My attention landed on a few specks of blood on my arm, and a dark laugh filled the small room. Sebastian had nearly puked all over the fucking corpse when I'd finished ripping out John's throat. Hopefully, I could keep the weak bastard at bay while I dealt with Xavier. Now that Ella was here, I would offer him to her to do as she wished. I wanted to see how dark and twisted my queen had become. This would encourage her to release her darkness and take her place with me once again.

Once I dried off, I quickly dressed in clean jeans and a black T-shirt. I hurried out of the bathroom, eager to visit Xavier. I wanted a word with him before I brought Ella into his room.

Silently, I headed down the hallway and halted as I reached the area where I slept when necessary. From my duffle bag, I retrieved a small offering for Xavier, then made my way to where I was keeping him. Kip had been instructed to keep him nourished and hydrated. It was crucial that Xavier remained lucid as I slowly inflicted torture upon him over the next week, possibly even longer if he refused to cooperate.

I pushed open the door and flicked on the overhead light. Xavier had been forced to sit in darkness for the past twenty-four hours. I hoped the isolation had driven home the gravity of his situation, but we would find out soon enough.

"Hello, Xavier. How nice of you to stop by," I sneered as I approached the emaciated man huddled in the corner. "How are your knees holding up?" From my pocket I produced a tiny white pill and dangled it in front of his face. "If you tell me what I need to know, this painkiller is yours."

He attempted to snatch it out of my hand, but he was too slow. I tsked as I stood and towered over him.

"Your friend John said to tell you goodbye."

Xavier peered up at me, squinting. "You let him go?"

"No. I carved him up like a fucking turkey on Thanksgiving Day, then ripped out his larynx."

Xavier trembled in his little corner as he stared at me, speechless.

"You kept my Ella in a goddamn cage." I paced back and forth in front of him. "Do you know how it made me feel when she told me how you planned on marrying her and keeping her in that glass cage? It fucking pissed me off. Bad. And, if you haven't guessed this about me, I have a nasty temper. Plus, I like to kill people slowly. It makes my heart happy." I laughed. "So, is there any reason that I should show any mercy and kill you quickly?"

"Y-yes." His pitch was high and his eyes wild.

"And what would that be? Go ahead and state your case. If it's a good enough reason, then I'll consider it." I folded my arms across my chest, enjoying watching the little pissant squirm.

"I . . . I can tell you everything. I'll spill every last detail about my plans for Ella and the trap my boss set for you." He gulped, looking as though he was genuinely terrified of what was to come. "Please, don't kill me. I could be very valuable to you."

I narrowed my gaze at him. "You really expect me to believe that? After everything you've done?" Skepticism dripped from each word.

Xavier trembled more, his hands twitching nervously. "I swear it," he said, almost begging. "I'll even give you the names of people connected to this mess. I know that you won't find peace until they pay for their parts in this."

I hesitated, considering my options. Xavier was a coward and a liar, but he wasn't wrong about one thing. There were others involved in this twisted game. If I could bring them down too . . . then perhaps there might still be some semblance of justice served for what they did to Ella.

"All right," I conceded, stepping closer to him and kneeling so we were almost nose to nose. "Tell me everything."

His tongue darted over his lower lip in a nervous gesture. "Do you know who your parents are?"

I arched my brow at his question. "Of course I do."

"Who, then?"

"Martin and Emma Jo Fletcher. If you know so much about me and my childhood house, you should know that already." Maybe this fucker was crazier than I initially thought. "I would think very carefully before you continue."

His Adam's apple bobbed up and down. "My boss knows your real family. He said you were stolen when you were a baby, then placed with Martin and Emma Jo."

Without hesitation, I pulled out the knife from its hiding place, feeling its weight and sharpness reassuringly in my palm. "You're lying," I hissed as I pressed the tip of the blade against his throat. "Why are you lying?"

He whimpered and urine soaked his pants, but it only stoked my anger more. The mention of Martin and Emma Jo's names sent a surge of Sebastian's memories flooding through my mind—memories of the horrors I endured in that childhood home. And this man seemed to know more.

He stuttered and trembled, but I refused to back down. "Tell me everything," I demanded, pressing the blade harder against his skin.

But he remained silent, his eyes bulging with terror. It made me more determined to get the truth out of him.

I stared at him, repulsed by his cowardice. "I have a confession," I began. "I don't really need you alive. I'll find the answers one way or the other. The biggest reason I have you here is for Ella. I thought she might enjoy ending your pathetic life. I just came here to watch." I stood slowly.

Suddenly, the door to the room flew open and Ella burst inside.

"Don't hurt him," she yelled, waving her arms.

I turned, shocked at her demand. "What is this about, little lamb?"

She hurried over to me. "Before we kill him, there's something you need to know."

I cupped the back of her head and my lips crashed against hers with an urgent hunger, my tongue plunging into her mouth, desperate to feed my addiction—Ella. I ravaged her, tasting the sweetness of her breath and feeling her body tremble beneath me. As my desire threatened to consume me, I tore myself away from her, leaving her gasping for air. But she wouldn't let me go, clutching at my shirt with fierce determination as she pulled me closer. Our bodies pressed together, and our gazes locked. "Tell me so we can be finished with him."

Her attention darted over to Xavier, and she took my hand in hers. "Hello, Xavier. I'm not here to spare your life, but when I drugged you, you told me something I don't think you planned to."

His eyes glazed over as a silly smile eased across his features. "Ella? I thought I would never see my beautiful bride again." He clapped like a little kid. His behavior with her caught me off guard. It was as if he were five years old. Then his expression grew serious. "You left me."

"Of course I did. Keeping a human being hostage in a cage isn't love. Plus, I belong to someone else. But do you remember what you told me?"

He gave a half shrug. "Don't know."

This motherfucker was playing games all the way to the end.

"Tell me." Ella approached him and then crouched down. She reached up to his cheek and dragged her knuckles down his face. "Please. We had some good times together, didn't we?"

I watched in awe as she played him. It appeared my little lamb had learned a few things while in captivity. Her manipulation skills had certainly grown. Pride burst in my chest.

He nodded, excited. "My first kiss." Xavier sighed like a lovesick puppy, and I forced myself to stand back and not fucking rip out his heart then and there. I hadn't had time to interrogate Ella over what that son of a bitch had done to her. But I bet that sniveling coward Sebastian knew everything. Even that this sick fuck had kissed her against her will. That was another point in favor of getting rid of both Xavier and Sebastian.

"And we had a date night planned. Remember the movie?"

"Yes!" His features grew grim. "I was really looking forward to that, Ella, but you left me."

"I did, but I'm here now. Talk to me. Tell me what you said right after you fell and hurt your knees."

His body trembled with fear as he slumped against the wall, struggling to catch his breath. "I didn't mean to let it slip, but you drugged me," he gasped, his voice hoarse and desperate.

She took his hand in hers, and I wondered how she didn't vomit with his proximity after what he'd done to her. But she was resilient, my little lamb, and she would see this through to the end.

"You're not supposed to know," he whispered, darting a fearful glance in my direction. "If my boss finds out . . ." His sentence trailed off as if his boss had magical abilities and could reach through the wall and kill him right there.

"I'll make a deal with you. If you tell me what you said and how you know, then I promise Death won't kill you."

His face lit up like a fucking Christmas tree, but I hadn't missed what she said. I guessed he had, though.

A heavy silence hung in the air around us. Finally, keeping his attention on Ella, he said . . .

CHAPTER 38

DEATH

The darkness didn't hunt the lamb—it hummed a lullaby until wandering felt like coming home.
—Anonymous

"Are you sure?" Ella's gentle voice broke me out of my fog from Xavier's confession. "How do you know?"

"My boss doesn't lie. He's brutally honest." Xavier's head bobbed for emphasis, and then he turned his attention to me. "You're my brother. Boss found a bit of your DNA left at the warehouse when you strung up Dahmer Junior by a meat hook. Once he got what he needed, he had the rest of the evidence scrubbed before the police showed up. He's on your side."

Ella straightened, her expression calm. She walked over to me. "Death, do you believe him? Is it possible that he really is your brother?"

My jaw clenched as a storm brewed to life and fury took center stage. If this piece of shit was my brother, I wanted no part of him. There was no love here. No familiarity or any kind of attachment. He was still scum to be interrogated, tortured, and disposed of. He was a means to an end, nothing more.

"I don't know. Tell me more," I demanded and kicked his foot.

He screamed in pain, and I held up the medication to remind him he could have relief if he wanted to. His eyes rolled in the back of his head, and for a minute I thought he might pass out, but then he seemed okay again.

"The family that raised me, they locked me in the basement for weeks at a time. I was a dirty secret, a shameful sin that needed to be hidden away. And then they tried to kill me too." His features glazed over as he recalled the horrors of his past. "He broke my mind, and my mother did nothing to help me. It's why they had to go." He seethed, his voice trembling with a mixture of rage and pain. "They're nothing but lifeless bodies stuffed and sitting at my dinner table." A menacing grin spread across his face as he stared at me from cold, dead eyes.

"I don't really give a fuck about your family or what you lived through. All I want to know is how are we brothers?"

"Not my story to tell. Not my story," he sang.

"Whose story is it, then?" I growled. The little shit was stomping on my last fucking nerve.

"You'll understand soon enough." His cackle split my eardrums. The fucker needed to shut up so I could think.

"And did it occur to you that your boss was playing you and that we're not brothers at all?"

Xavier nodded. "I'm not stupid. Of course it did," he spat, his entire demeanor changing on a dime.

"Where do I find him? Your boss?"

Xavier pursed his lips together. "When the time comes, he'll find you. He wants to meet his prodigy face-to-face. But he's interested in something else too. The boss wants . . ." He slammed his mouth closed and hesitated before he said, "I can't tell you what he wants. The boss tells me everything, though, and I can't break his trust, you know. But you should ask him when you see him." He licked his dry lips.

"I have enough information to find him on my own." I was bluffing, but Xavier didn't realize that. I tossed the little white pill at him, and it landed on the floor out of his reach.

He stretched as far as his body would let him and attempted to crawl to it, his fingers grabbing for it like a greedy child.

"That should keep him busy for a while. Let's go." I took Ella by the arm and led her out of the room. Once the door was shut, she looked up at me.

"Do you believe him?"

"I'm not sure. I need to chat with Dope and tell him what I've learned between John and Xavier. If anyone can find the man I'm looking for, it will be him."

I leaned down and kissed my little lamb before I brushed my nose along her ear. "As soon as I know where to find him, I'll give you another gift."

She grabbed my biceps and nipped at my neck. "Really?"

I straightened and placed my finger beneath her chin. "Yes. Xavier is yours to kill."

"Even if he's your brother?"

A chuckle rumbled through my chest. "Especially if he is my brother."

"As long as you're sure." She pressed her hips into mine. "I've missed you. I've missed what we share."

I slid my hand around her neck, my thumb rubbing up and down her sensitive skin. My cock hardened with the fantasy I'd had earlier about her in John's blood, sucking me dry.

"Come with me." We walked down the hall to where I'd killed John just hours ago. When I entered the room, his body was gone, but the blood had congealed on the floor. I closed the door behind us and grinned at her. "You were here earlier with Sebastian."

She nodded. "Yes. I was."

"Do you think he'll ever come to terms with who I am?" I strolled over to the partially dried blood and swiped my fingers through it, staining them red. I motioned for Ella to join me. She did as she was told, and I smeared the blood over her throat. With a quick jerk, I ripped her shirt open, the buttons flying across the room and pinging off the cement floor. Her chest heaved, the swell of her full breasts peeking out from the black satin bra.

"Would you miss him if he were gone?" I asked, my voice hovering above a whisper. The smell of her arousal mixed with fear about Sebastian was intoxicating. I stepped closer to her, our bodies touching, and I could feel her heart pounding. "Or would you welcome the freedom that comes with his absence?"

Ella licked her lips and locked her gaze on mine. She didn't answer, but the look in her eyes told me everything I needed to know. I traced the line of her jaw with my bloody fingers, feeling the heat of her skin under my touch. "You don't want him to be gone," I whispered, my breath warm against her ear. "But you also want me."

She shivered, the desire and desperation tangible between us. I pressed myself against her, the evidence of my own desire straining against my jeans. "I can give you what he won't." Nipping at her earlobe with my teeth, I added, "I can give you everything you need."

Ella moaned softly, a low sound that seemed to reverberate through my entire body.

"I want both of you. I can't choose."

It wasn't the answer that I wanted, but her response hadn't surprised me either. Threading my fingers through her long, dark hair, I gripped it and forced her to her knees in the pool of blood.

I stepped away from her, allowing some space between us. "Do you remember who you serve, my little whore?"

She looked up at me, her green eyes full of longing. "Only you."

"That's right. Crawl to me, Ella. Show me how much you want to worship the only man that sees who you truly are—my hungry slut ready to serve her god. I have the power to give you anything you want, but you'll have to earn it."

She glanced at the floor, then got on all fours and crawled through the thickest part of the congealed blood. Her hands grew slick with John's sin, and the corners of my lips twitched as I watched her. Once she was before me, she stopped.

I cupped her chin and tilted it up. "Undo my jeans and free my cock."

My little lamb flipped open the button and lowered the zipper. I wrapped my fingers around my shaft and stroked myself.

"Open your mouth and suck me."

Her lips parted, and I rubbed the tip of my dick along her lower lip. She ran her tongue across the smooth skin. She sucked lightly, coating my skin with her saliva. I grabbed the back of her head so she couldn't jerk away as I shoved my shaft into her mouth and down her throat. Her cheeks turned red as I mercilessly fucked her. Tears gathered in her eyes as she attempted to breathe around my girth, but it wasn't helping.

"I am the one who will allow you to breathe, not him."

Her eyes widened as she pressed her blood-stained hands against my jeans in an attempt to push me back.

"I alone can give you life or death, little lamb. I see your darkness and encourage it. He stifles everything you are." I thrust my cock in and out, pulling out enough to give her a quick chance to breathe. "You want this, don't you?" I asked, my voice low and dangerous. My hips moved faster, driving myself deeper into her throat. She whimpered, her tears now mingling with the saliva that coated my dick. "Admit it," I demanded, pulling out to the edge of her lips before thrusting back in with a rough groan. "Admit you need only me."

Her gaze turned fierce and unyielding as it met mine, and she mumbled, "Yes."

A surge of triumph coursed through me at her surrender. "That's my good little cum whore," I praised, driving harder and deeper. "Show me how much you need me."

She complied immediately, wrapping her lips tightly around my dick and sucking eagerly. Her tongue flicked across my skin, sending jolts of pleasure through me.

I pulled her head away and tilted her chin up while I wrapped my hand around my shaft, stroking it. Heat zipped up and down my spine as my balls tightened. Seconds later, I shot my cum all over her mouth and breasts as I marked her.

I tucked myself back into my jeans, enjoying seeing her face wild with desire and a hint of submission. She eagerly licked her lips clean, savoring the taste of my climax.

"Put your face against the floor and bow down to me."

She silently obeyed, and I ordered her to stay until I told her otherwise.

While my little lamb was remembering how to submit, I walked to the small closet and searched for what I needed. Within a few minutes, I had everything in place. I returned to Ella, who was still in the same position.

"Stand up."

She raised her head, and I extended my hand to her. Her palm was cold against mine from the cement floor. I helped her stand, suspecting that her knees were sore from the concrete. Walking around her, I nuzzled her hair from behind, then reached around and grabbed her breasts. Squeezing, she yelped. I moved the left cup, freeing her nipple. I gave it a hard flick and nip as she squirmed against me, her ass pressing into my once again hardening dick.

My hand traveled up her chest and around her neck. I gripped her throat, but not hard enough to cut off her air while I removed her shirt and bra. My fingertips danced across her skin and stomach and to the waist of her jeans. I quickly flipped open the button, unzipped them, and tugged them down over her ass and hips. I nipped at the smooth flesh of her ass cheek as I lowered them to her ankles. My little lamb stepped out of them, and I tugged her satin thong down next, leaving her naked and exposed to me.

Slowly, I turned her toward the swing that I'd attached to the ceiling over John's blood. With a swift movement, I lifted her off the ground, wrapping my arms around her waist and carrying her to it. Once I'd secured her, I stepped back to appreciate her beauty while she remained vulnerable and exposed to me. I spread her legs wide, showing off her wet pussy to me. Her clit was visibly swollen, begging for attention.

I knelt between her thighs and ran my fingers through her slickness and teased her lips. She moaned softly as I slid a finger inside her, feeling how tight and hot she was. Pumping in and out of her, I flicked her clit with my tongue.

"Your cunt is mine to fuck until you're raw and begging me to stop." I spread her apart and gained better access to her pussy and asshole. I wrapped my arms around her legs and pressed my nose against her slit, her scent nearly driving me over the edge. With each nip and suck, I applied more pressure and pain, making her squirm. I reached with one hand and ran it through the puddle of blood and rubbed it over her belly and inner thighs, noting the scar from her knife wound. A fleeting sense of calm flooded my senses as I reminded myself that I had exacted my revenge. Smiling, I continued to feast on her.

Her feeble attempts to grind against my face were easily stopped as I held her hips and dug my fingers into her skin.

"Oh god. Fuck me with your tongue, Death. Do what only you can do to me."

There it was. Her plea for me—not him.

CHAPTER 39

ELLA

I wanted the pain, the constant guessing of what Death would do to me next. He pulled away, his mouth and chin coated in my juices. He flashed me a wicked smile as he reached into his jeans pocket and produced a thick butt plug. Death massaged my clit with it, then slid it into my pussy, fucking me slowly. Once it was slick, he began to work it into my ass.

"Oh." My eyes widened as the long and thick curved plug stretched me. His thumb swirled around my sensitive flesh.

"I bet your cunt is begging to be fucked, isn't it?"

"Yes," I answered breathlessly.

"Beg for it, my little bitch. Make me believe you." He buried his face in my pussy again.

"Death, please. I need you to fuck me hard. Shove that big cock in me and fuck me until I can't take anymore. Then fuck me some more."

He moaned against my slick flesh before he bit my bundle of nerves, sending pain through me.

"More," I screamed.

His teeth plucked my sensitive bud until my screams became cries of agony and pleasure as I neared my orgasm.

"That's it, little lamb. Ride my face until you come on my tongue and lips." He placed my legs on his shoulders and pulled me closer as if he were a thirsty man in the desert.

As his fingers worked their magic on my swollen clit, my climax began to build, a wave of ecstasy spreading through my entire being.

My hips bucked against his mouth, eagerly seeking the release I desperately craved.

"Oh, fuck yes!" I screamed, my voice echoing loudly in the room.

He was relentless, skillfully manipulating my sensitive skin. Every nerve ending in my body was on fire. As I convulsed and shuddered beneath him, he continued to assault me with his skilled tongue, lapping up every drop of cum that flowed from my soaking pussy.

Finally, as the last waves of ecstasy began to subside, his hands left my hips and reached between my legs to cup my pussy. As he traced the inside of my swollen lips, he withdrew them and lifted them to his mouth. His tongue flicked at my juices with a craving that sent chills down my spine.

"You taste so sweet," he growled, making eye contact with me as he licked his lips clean. "Are you ready for more?"

I looked into his eyes and saw a hunger there that matched mine. Silently, he lifted me out of the swing and then turned me away from him. He placed me into the swing again with my ass tipped up in the air.

His palm landed on my butt cheek, and a sting zipped through me as I cried out.

"You belong to me." *Smack.* "You will always belong to me."

He wasn't wrong, but I also belonged to Sebastian, and it seemed as though he was disciplining me for that. As he continued, it was clear that Death was no longer willing to share, which terrified me.

My flesh stung with each slap as he told me that no one else could touch me. No one else owned me. His tone was clipped and cold, and I knew he was angry with my love for both sides of him.

"You're hurting me," I cried. "Please, stop." Even with my cries, he knew me well enough to know that I fed on the pain. He relished his power over me, but I reveled in being the one who could push him to lose control. The darkness within us both was a twisted dance, and I craved every moment of it.

He gripped my hair with his large hand, forcing my head back. The rustling of his jeans filled the room, and then he shoved his dick inside me. The butt plug made him feel tighter, and I moaned as rapture replaced the pain.

He fucked me relentlessly, showing my body no mercy. His hips banged against me as I gripped the handles of the swing, breathless from his brutality.

"No!" he said between gritted teeth as he slowed. "I said fucking no!" His angry words bounced off the walls, and I glanced over my shoulder at him.

"Death, are you okay?" The moment I saw him, I knew he wasn't okay.

His features twisted in agony, his cheeks turning beat red with his struggle.

"Ella." His eyes rolled in the back of his head as he continued thrusting into me. "Little lamb," he growled.

Pleasure zipped through me as I realized that both men were present, pounding into me as they shifted and shared their consciousnesses. I grabbed the straps of the swing, completely at their mercy and feeding off the idea they were both fucking me at the same time.

My eyes fluttered closed, lost in the sensations. Death and Sebastian inside me, stretching me to my limits and driving me closer and closer to the edge. It was a raw, animalistic experience—but I basked in every second of it.

The room filled with our grunts and moans, punctuated by the rhythmic slapping sound of skin against skin. Our bodies moved in sync, fueled by pure lust. They possessed me entirely, commanding my every move as I crashed into waves of ecstasy over and over again.

A sudden surge of power bloomed from within and took over the swing's speed, making Death and Sebastian go faster and deeper. Their grunts echoed through the room, sending me into oblivion as my pussy spasmed around their cock.

"That's it, little lamb." Death's voice was strained as Sebastian took control.

"Ella, it shouldn't be like this," Sebastian said, grunting as Death controlled their physical actions.

"Stop fighting it. Let yourself go. Fuck me. Both of you. Fuck me harder. Fill me up with your cum." I arched my back, lost in the sensation of being consumed by both of them at once.

Sebastian's hips moved in smooth, deliberate circles, while Death's thrusts were rougher and more erratic—a perfect complement to each other.

In that moment of heightened ecstasy and connection, they both reached their peak simultaneously, each slamming into me with renewed vigor until they erupted deep inside me. Every fiber vibrated with pleasure as I screamed out their names in surrender.

Time seemed to slow, stretching out the pure bliss until it felt like an eternity.

Slowly, he dropped his hands and looked at me.

CHAPTER 40

SEBASTIAN

"Ella," I said breathlessly.

"Sebastian?"

"Yeah, baby. It's me. I couldn't stand by and watch him hurt you any longer. I had to make him leave." After pulling out of my wife, I removed the plug and tossed it aside before I tucked myself into my jeans, horrified at the bruises and marks he had left on her body. But what frightened me more was the way she craved his brutality, reveling in it like a twisted addiction. Waves of pleasure still coursed through me, but this time they were laced with guilt and disgust with his actions toward her. Ella deserved to be adored and cherished, not used and abused like this.

"Are you okay?" I gently helped her out of the swing and set her feet on the floor.

"Yes. We just like to play rough. I promise he wouldn't really hurt me." She reached up and traced her fingertips along my jawline.

I leaned down and kissed her, shed my shirt, and wrapped it around her, making sure she was decent before I scooped her up in my arms and carried her out of the room Death thought was appropriate to fuck her in. It hadn't escaped me that her stomach and thighs were covered in blood. He disgusted me, but even more, I had a difficult time digesting that she enjoyed it.

I opened the door and peered into the hall, ensuring Kip wasn't going to round the corner at any second.

"I wasn't sure you were coming back." Ella leaned her head on my shoulder as I walked her to the bathroom. Once we were safely tucked away, I turned on the shower and tested the temperature. The small space filled with steam. I removed my shirt from her shoulders, then removed my jeans. I held out my hand and led her beneath the running water, droplets streaming down her face and over her full breasts.

I leaned down and gently sucked on her nipple, erasing Death's touch on her skin. "I'll always come back, baby."

Her gaze locked with mine, filled with desire and gratitude, as we stood there in the shower, our bodies entwined. I gently guided her against the slick tile, feeling her shiver.

With a soft moan, she pressed closer to me, her body's heat enveloping me like a warm embrace. I slid my fingertips slowly down her back and over her spine before I traced the curves of her ass and hip. My heart raced as I felt her pulse beneath my fingertips, matching the rhythm of our breaths mingling in the steam-filled room.

I brushed my mouth against hers, tasting the water and the salt of her skin. Her lips parted under my touch, and as our kiss deepened, my hands roamed further, exploring every inch of her that I could reach.

"You're everything I need," I whispered against her skin as we continued to savor each other in this sanctuary where no one else could find us. "Everything I want."

I moved my palms down her hips, gently urging her to turn around. She complied, her eyes filled with trust and desire. I reached for the soap and lathered it up in my palms before gently massaging it into her shoulders, working my way down her back. My fingertips traced every curve, every dip, every peak that she possessed.

As I continued to wash her, I couldn't help but marvel at the beauty in front of me. Her black hair was plastered to her head, the water running down her cheeks in rivulets. Her lips were slightly parted in a silent plea for more. And I was happy to oblige.

I grabbed her hips and turned her around to look at me again. My hands found their way back to her breasts, this time with a more urgent pace. I teased the erect nipples with my thumbs, causing Ella to let out a soft moan of pleasure.

"You taste so sweet," I murmured against her lips, "like the sweetest nectar." My words were like wildfire, igniting a passion within us both that could not be extinguished by a mere showerhead or bathtub.

I lifted Ella gently off the ground and wrapped my arms around her waist as hers circled my neck and her legs wound around my waist.

I positioned her just right as I slid into her tight pussy while I cupped her ass cheeks. Her soft moan sent pleasure rippling through me. Her muscles clenched my shaft as I buried myself deep inside her.

"That's my good girl."

I pressed her back against the wall in order to gain a better angle as my pace quickened. Ella's moans grew louder and more urgent with each thrust, her nails digging into my neck as she clung to my wet skin for support. Her eyes locked on mine, her expression a mix of need and love. I leaned in, and our lips met in a kiss as I continued to move inside her.

The steamy bathroom filled with our combined breaths, the only sound being our bodies slapping together and the gentle splashing of water. Her wet hair stuck to her face, her heart racing wildly beneath my touch. I felt her tighten around me—the telltale sign that she was nearing her orgasm.

"That's it," I whispered, my voice hoarse with desire, "be a good girl and come for me."

Her moans started as soft sighs, but as I trailed my fingers along her body, they grew into deep, guttural, desperate sounds. She grabbed my back, her nails digging into my skin as she climbed higher and higher toward her climax. I matched her every movement, our bodies moving in sync until we were both on the edge.

Finally, she cried out, "Sebastian, baby!" She seized, and her pussy pulsed and gripped me as she released, sending waves of pleasure through me. I couldn't hold back any longer and I exploded deep inside of her.

We stayed locked together for what felt like blissful eternity before I finally set her down against the wall. As we leaned against it together, catching our breaths, I kissed her tenderly, the feel of her warm lips against mine giving me a moment of peace. One that I'd needed for a long time.

I ran my knuckles down her cheek and kissed the tip of her nose. "I love you, Ella Fletcher."

She turned to me, her gaze full of love. "I love you too, Sebastian Fletcher."

I glanced down and noticed the blood that had once streaked her stomach and thighs was now washed clean. I inhaled a deep breath as I claimed the small victory that I'd forced Death into the background and had appeared when Ella needed me, needed to be loved and cherished, not brutalized by a monster. But somewhere inside me, I knew I hadn't won the war to rid myself of his presence. Yet.

CHAPTER 41

SEBASTIAN

Once Ella and I had cleaned up, she wanted to catch a quick nap in the room Death had been using. The cot wasn't much, but it was enough to keep us off the floor and warm. I hated leaving her, but I had things to sort out.

My emotions churned and my chest hurt at the thought of who Death was. What he'd done and planned to do. I had to find a way to keep him at bay. I dug my fingernails into my palms as I walked down the hall of the abandoned building and opened the door to where Kip was hanging out.

He glanced up as I entered the room.

"Hey, man."

"I notice that you guys don't call me by my name as much anymore. My guess? You're trying to figure out who you're dealing with."

Kip gave me a reluctant nod. "Especially lately. You're changing a lot. I'm guessing it's all the stress."

I rubbed my chin, the stubble scraping against my fingers. Shit had gone south so fast that I'd forgotten to shave. Hopefully, I hadn't scratched Ella too much.

She likes it.

"Shut up," I muttered to Death.

Kip arched a brow at me. "You two are talking back and forth now?"

"We always did. I just didn't realize what was happening." I sank into an old metal chair near the desk and blew out a heavy sigh. "How have you put up with him all of these years?"

Compassion flashed across my friend's face. "I won't give you a line of shit. It's been hard to deal with both of you. You're loyal, and I can never guess what your intentions are. You save women and children—that's impressive. Your temper gets a bit out of control sometimes, but it's usually . . . Well, in the past, that happened when Death was going to reappear. And he—uh, sorry, Bass, but Death is a fucking badass. Honestly, I wouldn't get rid of either of you."

Shocked with his response, I leaned back in the chair and stretched my legs in front of me. "It's too much for Ella and the kids. He's too rough with her, and he brings out a side of her that is startling."

Kip drummed his fingers on the desk and waited for me to finish, but I wasn't sure what else to say.

"Ella has that darkness in her, regardless. Look at how she loved working with criminals. She loves the danger and intrigue. Death gives her permission to be that woman. We've all accepted her. All of us except for you."

"That's because you all have known the truth for years. I'm just figuring out who I am, both sides of me, mate. I don't know how to fucking deal with it. I'm around him more and more, so my awareness of what he does is much stronger, and it's . . ." I pulled my legs back in, frustrated and terrified of that part of myself.

Silence hung in the air before Kip said, "You could go to a shrink and see if there are meds to help suppress Death, but you need to understand that you might end up committed and never be a free man again. Dope and I had to make that decision for you for a long-ass time, but now that you know . . . it's up to you."

My heart hammered against my ribs. I'd put everyone through hell. They lied and covered up my crimes because they believed in me. Both parts of me. It still baffled me why.

"Listen, I know you well enough to realize that this is really fucking with you, and that's fair, man. Let me ask you this." He leaned forward and rested his elbows on his knees, piercing me with his intense gaze. "If it were me or Dope in your situation, what would you do?"

I folded my arms over my chest as I chewed on his question. "You guys are my family. I would do anything in my power to protect you. I would stand by you."

Kip grinned and snapped his fingers. "Exactly. To us, you're family. We've all gone through hell and back together, and we'd do it again.

You'd do the same for us, so quit beating yourself up for our choice to cover your tracks and keep you out of trouble. Bass, you do a helluva lot of good. Stop sweating it. You have the Safe Horizon Society, and those women and children get a fresh, safe start all over because of you. Death, well, he helps the cops get rid of some really bad men. I mean, be real with me. Don't you feel just a little bit better knowing that some of the people that kidnap kids and sell them won't be around the twins? You're protecting them and all the other kids who are too small to take care of themselves. As far as I'm concerned, Death is a fucking hero."

I stared at the floor, tension snaking through my shoulders. "I hadn't thought about how Death's actions would keep the twins safe . . . all children, actually."

"Yup. He's not as bad as you think he is. Ryan and I are used to the blood and gore, but part of that is due to my uncle. He's a damn good cleaner."

I leaned my head to the left, then the right, and stretched the tight muscles in my neck. "Crickey, this shit is heavy. All I know is that I either have to gain full control so Death isn't around or learn to live with the bastard."

"My vote? Learn to deal with him. There's no guarantee that you'll be able to suppress him, so you might as well embrace that part of yourself, and him you."

I barked out a laugh. "He hates me too."

Kip grinned at me. "I don't think he hates you. I think he hates that you're with Ella. You're married to her, and he isn't. You sleep with her, and he does part of the time too, but he's a possessive son of a bitch, and he hates sharing. He's a selfish prick; it's just not in his nature." Kip chuckled.

From the conversations that Death and I had had, I knew that Kip was right. Death wanted the same with Ella. I stood and shoved my hand through my hair. "I've never said this before, mate, but thank you for watching my back all these years. I hope I've done the same for you."

Kip nodded. "Hell yeah, you have. That's what family does, man. My parents and relatives are all sorts of fucked up, so when I met you and Dope in middle school, and Death made some appearances, Dope and I agreed that no matter the cost, we'd make sure you stayed out of a mental institution and help direct you toward kills that were at least productive. For the first time in my life, I felt like I had a real family.

Anytime I needed a place to crash, you and Dope were always there for me. If I was in a fucked-up mood, you and Dope always made me laugh. As Death appeared more often, it gave me something else to focus on other than my own dark shit. So, yeah, you've done more for me than you'll ever realize, and so has Death."

"I'm glad to hear that." I massaged the back of my neck. "You've never told me that much about when you were growing up. I know it wasn't a good home life, and your mom was intense, but not much else other than the work you did with your uncle. Did you talk to Death about it?"

Kip pursed his lips. "Nah. It's not anyone else's problem."

"Not true. You just said we were all family, so I'm here if you need anything." I walked toward the door, then said, "Keep Xavier alive. Give him a few pain pills to keep him comfortable if you want to. I have a feeling I'll need him later on. Death is ready to end his life, but I'm not. I need answers."

"You got it."

"I'm going to get out of this dark-ass building and get some fresh air. Maybe a walk will clear my head. I'll be back in a few."

"All right. It's pretty secluded out here, so you should be good to roam around without running into anyone, but just keep your eyes open."

"I will." With our conversation heavy on my mind, I made my way through the old warehouse and to the front entrance. I pushed the door open, and sunlight filtered through the trees and onto my face. Maybe Death was used to hiding in dark buildings, but I wanted some air and the freedom to walk the fuck around outside.

The door closed behind me, and I walked to a trail that led north. The sun wouldn't set for several hours, which would give me the time I needed alone to process what my next step should be. Kip had seemed genuine when he told me he wanted Death to stick around. Plus, the thought of being committed to an institution made me physically sick.

You have to trust Ella, Kip, and Dope and what they say to you. They've chosen to stay. Let it go.

"Of course you'd say that, Death. You don't want to disappear. You still want to get rid of me, though. Not sure where that leaves us."

It's a battle of the strongest. We know that's not you.

"You really are an asshole." I moved a low tree limb out of my way as I continued walking. The leaves were mostly still green, but a touch of yellow rimmed their edges, introducing a hint of fall.

An odd sound caught my attention, and I stilled as I tried to identify it. The hair on the back of my neck stood on end as I glanced around, but I didn't see anyone. A sharp sting pierced my neck, and I reached up ready to slap the bug that had just bitten me, but it wasn't a bug that I felt.

"Motherfucker. Who shot me with a tranquilizer dart?"

Goddammit. What was I just saying about who the stronger one was? You were supposed to keep your eyes open in case anyone had located you and Ella.

"Son of a bitch." The world spun as I dropped to my knees before it completely faded away.

CHAPTER 42

ELLA

After a nap that lasted longer than I'd wanted it to, I made my way to the designated office in search of my husband and Kip. However, as I peeked through the entryway, I saw no sign of them. I made the rounds through the building and still hadn't found them. Maybe they were with Xavier. It was the only other place I could think of unless they were outside, chatting. It was difficult to stay in this dingy place all the time, but I understood Death couldn't make it more livable or it would look suspicious to anyone who wandered upon it.

As I flung open the door to Xavier's prison, my nostrils were immediately assaulted by a putrid stench that almost caused me to gag. He sat in the corner, his body covered in grime and filth, desperately in need of a bath and clean clothes. I hadn't noticed it earlier since I was trying to stop Death from killing Xavier.

I glowered at him as I remembered all he had done. The kidnapping, the emotional torture with those goddamn spiders and cage—and just like that, my fleeting moment of compassion disappeared, replaced by seething anger and hatred toward this man who had caused me so much pain and fear.

My heart pounded in my chest as I cautiously approached Xavier, keeping a safe distance from him. Death had left him unbound, relying on his broken knees to keep him in place. But I knew better than to underestimate his resourcefulness.

"Xavier?" My voice cracked as I spoke, trying to maintain an air of control. He looked up at me with bloodshot eyes and a lazy smile, clearly high on pain pills.

"I really like these," he slurred, his movements sluggish and clumsy.

I couldn't help but feel a twinge of pity for him, knowing that even if his knees somehow healed, he would never walk properly again without medical care.

"Have you seen Death or Kip?" My question almost made me laugh. Here he was, drugged out of his mind and locked in this room with no hope of escape or interaction with anyone else, and I was asking if he'd seen my husband. Unless the guys had recently visited him, he was completely isolated.

"Kip gave me this pill, but that was a while ago." His head rolled, and he continued to grin.

My hands balled into fists at my sides and my eyes narrowed into icy daggers as I imagined the different ways I could rip him apart and revel in his pain. My mind raced with sadistic pleasure and a sickening desire to torture him when the time came. But when he'd revealed he was Death's brother, something inside me snapped. A primal urge to learn more about this twisted family consumed me, overpowering any thoughts of violence. Maybe I could extract some valuable information from him while he was under the influence.

"Xavier?"

"Yup?" He popped his lips.

"Who is your boss? You call him the Pied Piper, but who is he?"

"My boss, my boss." He peered at me through squinted eyes. "I bet he's looking for me. We're very close, you know."

"I bet that's nice to have a friend." I wasn't sure I was going to make any headway with this conversation, but I had to keep trying. He'd always fallen for my kindness, so maybe it would work again, especially with the help of a pain pill.

"How did you meet him?" A thought had been buzzing around in my brain since Xavier had revealed to Death that they were brothers.

"My family." He snickered. "The ones still at my kitchen table, waiting for me to come back."

I kept my mouth shut. He wouldn't be going home, but he would find that out soon. Even if I didn't kill him for what he'd done to me,

Death would because Xavier knew too much and was crazy enough to not keep our identities to himself. Eventually, he had to die. I didn't see any other option.

"Boss would come over to my parents' house for dinner and be nice to me. Sometimes he would even bring a game over and we would play chess or checkers. My family never did that with me. They just locked me in the basement."

"Kind of like what you did to me, huh?"

His expression fell. "It wasn't the same, Ella. No. Not the same."

"And how is that? I couldn't leave. You held me captive. Fiona said that your boss would have been mad if he knew that you kept me in a cage. Would he have been upset?"

"Nope. It was his idea." He cackled. "Fiona is a compulsive liar. Nothing that comes out of her mouth is the truth. But me, me you can trust. Death and I are brothers."

"How, Xavier? How are you related? How in the hell would you even know all of this?"

"Not my story to tell, Ella. But . . ." He winked at me as if he were a sexy beast.

I stifled my laugh. He was almost entertaining on the pain pills.

"I'm trying hard to understand, but I just don't. Please help me." I gulped as I attempted to force the next words from my mouth without throwing up. "I need you, Xavier."

His expression morphed into awe and excitement before he leaned in closer. "You know, Ella, you're not as innocent as you pretend to be. You've got secrets too, don't you? Dark shadows lurking in the corners of your mind. You and I are the same."

I raised an eyebrow, intrigued despite myself. "What do you mean?"

He threw his head back and laughed like a damn hyena. "You married a serial killer. You have to be as twisted as he is in order to do something like that."

I resisted the urge to punch him in his already fucked-up nose. It didn't take a genius to figure that out. He was toying with me, and I was growing impatient.

Xavier leaned in closer, his eyes gleaming with a mixture of mischief and madness. "You want to know the truth, Ella? The truth about Death, about me, about everything?" His voice dropped to a conspiratorial whisper.

I glared at him, unsure if he was playing another twisted game or if he was finally going to reveal something substantial. Despite my better judgment, I couldn't help but be lulled almost into a trance by his cryptic words. "Tell me, Xavier. Tell me everything."

He sang a few lines of "Prisoner" by Raphael Lake, Aaron Levy, and Daniel Ryan Murphy. Goosebumps pebbled my skin with the haunting lyrics.

Once he was finished, he flashed me a manic grin. "Sebastian thinks he killed his pa-paaa." He said "papa" like a crow cawing, and I wanted to reach over and wrap my fingers around his scrawny neck and choke the life out of him. I was sick of his riddles, but this . . . I hesitated and realized what he'd just said. This riddle might change everything.

"Yeah." I didn't want to say too much to encourage Xavier to continue.

"The man he killed wasn't his pa-paaaa," he said again with the crow-like pronunciation. "We." He tapped his chest. "We were . . ."

"You were what? You can tell me, Xavier."

His gaze narrowed on me. "But if I do, you'll run to tell Death. Boss says it's not my story to share."

I gritted my teeth together in an attempt to gather my words and not blurt out what I really wanted to say. "Is this the entire picture or just a tiny detail?" Working in law had helped me rephrase questions and form a loophole or skirt the truth. Maybe it would serve me now.

He held up his first finger and thumb a little bit apart. "Just a dollop."

"Then you're not going against what your boss has asked of you, right?"

He leaned against the wall, pondering what I'd said. "You're a smart one, Ella. But are you smart enough?"

"Are you?" I fired back at him, furious at his nonsense.

He sneered at me. "I'm not the one in question here. Are you smart enough to play the game and walk away with your mind intact?"

I refused to answer him. Stepping backward, I spun on my heel to leave him alone with his pathetic thoughts.

"Sebastian Fletcher was . . ."

CHAPTER 43

DEATH

Night after night, the dark traced the lamb's heart with silver whispers until its pulse beat black as sin.
—Anonymous

I groaned. My neck was fucking killing me. As I reached up to rub it, I tugged on the restraints and realized my hands were bound behind my back. The rough material over my face stifled my breathing. Where the hell was I, and how the fuck did I get here?

Kidnapped. Fucking kidnapped.

"You stupid prick, you got us kidnapped?" I muttered to Sebastian.

Footsteps caught my attention, and I slowly lifted my head and attempted to peer through the potato sack, but it was useless.

"So happy you've joined me this evening," a man's voice said as he abruptly jerked the bag off my head.

I squinted at the bright light as it assaulted my vision. My gaze landed on his black dress shoes and slowly traveled up his black slacks and white dress shirt. His short dark hair was peppered with gray, and it matched his well-trimmed beard. He rolled up his sleeves, smiling as if I were a long-lost relative.

"Who the fuck are you?" I growled.

He chuckled. "I'll make you a deal."

"I'm waiting."

"I'll untie you if you give me your word that you won't kill me. I just want to talk. When we're finished, I'll make sure you return alive and unharmed to the abandoned building we tracked you to."

I suppressed my grin. Of course I would promise not to kill him.

And, since I was a man of my word, I wouldn't kill him . . . tonight. "How do I know you're not lying?"

"Well, I just offered to untie you so you could walk around and take a piss if you need to. I'm not interested in harming you."

My attention scanned the room, and my pulse kicked up a notch as I laid eyes on a Chucky doll sitting on a coffee table . . . holding a bloody knife.

That's the damn doll that was in our house! What is this fucker up to?

I mentally told Sebastian to hush. Now wasn't the time for his questions.

The man's eyes followed mine, and he flashed me a sinister smile. "You recognize that Chucky?"

Yes! This is what you need to ask him.

I wanted to shrug off Sebastian's request, but I needed answers too. "You?" I growled. "You put that fucking doll in my bedroom?"

"I've always been around, even when you were younger. I thought the doll might stick in your mind even after what you were about to live through. It was my way of planting that seed in your mind's eye."

Son of a bitch. He was in my home before he killed my parents.

As much as I hated to admit it, Sebastian was right. This motherfucker had apparently always been lurking in the shadows. I studied him, watching every calculated move as he waited for me to answer his earlier question. "Okay. You have my word. I won't fucking gut you." I offered him a sneer along with my words.

"Or harm me in any way."

I shook my head. "Yeah, that too."

He walked behind the chair, and I braced myself to have my throat split wide open, but he only untied my wrists.

Slowly, I brought my arms to my lap and rubbed them.

"You can stand and walk around. The bathroom is down the hall to your right if you need it." He pointed in that direction. I took a deep breath and stood, wobbly at first from the effects of the tranquilizer. As I turned to take in my surroundings, I scanned the luxurious living room complete with leather furniture and floor-to-ceiling windows that offered a stunning view of the lake outside. I couldn't see any other houses nearby, which made me wonder where exactly we were and why he had taken such precautions. A wave of anger washed over me as I thought about how he had drugged me, but my curiosity kept my temper in check. I had questions for him. A lot of them.

I stared at the man who had the audacity to take me in broad daylight. Must be his MO since he'd done the same to Ella. "You didn't answer my question. Who the fuck are you?"

He gave me a warm smile and sat on the gray leather couch. "They call me the Pied Piper."

Pursing my lips together, I folded my arms over my chest. "I've heard about you from Xavier. Why the name?"

"Simple really. I like to groom potential people with the same . . . darkness you and I have. Once I do, they follow me blindly."

Except for me.

He narrowed his eyes on me for a split second. "And I'm sure he mentioned that when the time was right, we would meet."

I nodded. "Yeah, but he's not a very trustworthy source of information. I don't believe most of what comes out of his mouth."

"So, he's still alive?"

I didn't miss the hope in his question. "For now. I can't guarantee for how long, though."

"Well, I'd love to take him off your hands."

My arms lowered to my sides. "To kill?"

He chuckled as if I'd told a good joke. "No, no. He's very dear to me." He leaned back on the couch and crossed his legs. "And so are you."

"Awesome. If I'm important to you, then tell me what the hell this all is about. Why put a tranquilizer in my neck and bring me here?"

"Because I want to make it more difficult for you to return here. Since you didn't see anything on the ride over, it will be impossible for you to trace the drive. It's self-preservation. You know all about that, Death."

I did. "Xavier said you're the man that killed my parents. Is that true or has he just gone off the deep end and made shit up?"

The Pied Piper rubbed his jaw before he said, "Xavier is special, but he's not a liar. I am the man you've been looking for."

I sneered at him. "I haven't been looking for you. Ella is the one that wants to know more. She's a very curious woman. It gets her into trouble sometimes."

"She's beautiful. You've done well for yourself."

My eyes narrowed at him. "Leave her out of this. Whatever you want, this is between you and me."

"Fair enough. I truly have no use for Ella. That was a kidnapping gone wrong and only a tool to draw you out. Unfortunately, Xavier fell in love with her and got careless. Ella was supposed to have been delivered to me after a few days of being held at Xavier's, but he begged to keep her longer. I agreed, and then she got smart and escaped his home."

"You mean the basement in the house that's an exact replica of where I grew up and you murdered my parents? What the fuck is that all about?"

"I know you have a lot of questions, and it would be best if I just started at the beginning. Would you like something to eat or drink? You're going to be here for a while. It wouldn't be right of me not to offer my guest some refreshments."

I clenched my jaw and then forced myself to relax so Sebastian wouldn't fucking pop out for a visit at the wrong damn time. "You're fucking nuts too."

He grinned at me, my words having zero effect on him.

"If I were you, I would want answers to why my parents died and who killed them. You were young, but I saw the darkness inside you. It was easy to mold you while I helped you kill your father. The fury that came out of you toward that man was intense. If you want to call it murderous, that's a more accurate description." He arched a salt and pepper eyebrow at me. "But the truth is, he's not your biological father."

My heart pounded against my ribcage like a drummer gone mad, matching the beat of my racing thoughts.

"You didn't kill your real father, so if you have any guilt left over it, let it go." He waved as though he swatted his words away.

"I don't understand. Of course they were my parents. I have memories with them when I was little, and in that home."

"You were with them at a very young age, but you and your brother were separated when you were stolen."

His words struck me like a physical blow, causing a whirlwind of emotions to flood through my body. I was torn between the anger and hurt at being lied to by people who I had thought were my family, and the overwhelming hope and disbelief that my real parents may still be alive. How could I trust a single thing I had ever been told? I needed answers, but how did I know that the Pied Piper wasn't lying to me as well?

You can't believe anything he says. We'll have Dope research it all.

For some reason, Sebastian's voice in my head helped ground me.

"Who is my brother?"

The older man draped his arm on the back of the couch, more comfortable than he should have been.

"Xavier is your brother, Death. Same mother and father, and you were both stolen by the same person."

"Jesus fucking Christ. I do have a kook for a brother."

"Yes. It's another reason that I want the boy back all in one piece."

"He's alive but has two very broken knees. Not sure he'll walk again. He hurt Ella, and no man can get away without suffering the consequences of touching what's mine, even if he is my brother." Xavier was alive for now, but his future was uncertain. But at that moment, another thought consumed me.

The Pied Piper's words lingered in my mind like a festering wound, each one stabbing at my sense of self. The idea of tracking down my parents and uncovering the truth sent a chill down my spine, yet an insatiable hunger for answers burned within me. After all this time, I had accepted that my parents were dead, but now, if he wasn't lying, his information had the power to change my life.

"Who are my real parents? Are they alive? Did they learn who stole us?"

"You were almost two and Xavier was a baby when you were taken. Not long after, your parents got into a bad train accident. They didn't live through it."

"They didn't survive? Are you implying it wasn't an accident?" All I wanted was answers and to finally put the past behind me.

"Yes, just not by my people."

I didn't miss what he said, and I wondered how many people he had working for him. Clearly the men who took Ella were some of them. I smirked. After I'd dealt with them, the Pied Piper now had four fewer on his team. "Okay, so let's say this shit is true. How did I end up with the Fletchers, and what did they do to you?"

"That's where this gets a bit more complicated. Are you sure you don't want something to drink before I continue?"

CHAPTER 44

ELLA

Irritated wasn't the right word for what I was feeling for Xavier at the moment, but I was done being played. Plus, I wanted to find my husband. Something felt off, and I couldn't put my finger on it. Stepping backward, I spun on my heel to leave Xavier alone with his pathetic thoughts.

"Sebastian Fletcher was . . ."

I stopped in my tracks and waited to see if he was going to finish his sentence or not.

"Stolen. Stolen. Stolen." He cackled and clapped his hands together.

His words slammed into me so hard that I gasped for air. I faced him again.

"His parents weren't his real parents?" I asked, trying to mask the eagerness in my voice.

"Nope. We were both stolen, Ella. Stolen, stolen, stolen," he sang.

"By who?"

Xavier sighed. "I gave you a piece of what you wanted, but the boss will tell Death the rest. I've already said too much." He held up a shaky finger in the air. "But the pain pills make me gabby. The boss will understand."

If what Xavier was saying was true, then maybe Sebastian's parents were still alive. I needed to find him and tell him the news so Dope could dig into the information and find out if Xavier was telling the truth.

"If you tell me, I'll make sure you get another pain pill in an hour."

Eagerness twisted his expression. "Yes, please."

I tapped my foot on the cement floor. "I'm waiting."

"Very bad people took us. Sebastian and I were supposed to go to a family together, but we were separated instead." Xavier sniffled, his eyes welling with tears. "Do you think I would have turned out differently if Sebastian and I had grown up in the same home?"

A fleeting twinge of compassion hit me, then disappeared as quickly as it had arrived.

"There's no way to know." Even though he hadn't really given me the information I wanted, it was easier to get it out of him while taking the medication. "I'll be back in an hour with a pain pill."

"Yeah!" Xavier clapped his hands together.

I left the room and secured the door behind me. Instead of searching the building again, I pulled out my cell and called Sebastian, but after two rings it went to voicemail. That rarely happened.

Maybe Sebastian would be in the office now. I hurried in that direction, but to my disappointment I only found Kip. I leaned on the door frame and asked, "Have you seen Sebastian?"

"He went for a walk a few hours ago. We talked for a while, and he's wrestling pretty hard with the Death idea. Bass wants to silence him for good. I'm a little concerned he might try to turn himself in for Death's crimes."

My mouth dropped open. "Kip, he can't do that. They'll lock him up for the rest of his life."

"I know. I told him that, but Bass isn't a killer, and he doesn't want you to have access to Death. He didn't say it, but he's worried about the kids growing up with a serial killer as a father."

I crossed the room and sank into the chair. "Me too, but he would never hurt them."

"I think he's concerned about Alaric and Verity being too much like their dad."

Sighing, I leaned back in the chair. "Yeah, me too. They definitely have a connection. But it's not just Death. Sebastian needs to understand that I am looking forward to ending Xavier. John was good practice." I flashed him a grin.

"I tried to tell him that, but he thinks Death is the one that made you that way."

I shook my head. "I think I was fighting that part of me for a long time. Death just saw it sooner than I did."

"Hell, Ella, I get it. Ryan and I are the same. I have no problem cleaning up bodies and covering up Death's mess. It's second nature to me."

"How so?" I asked.

"My uncle was a cleaner, and he taught me everything I know about how to dissolve a body and destroy any evidence. It's as if no one was ever there in the first place."

"That's a rare talent." I laughed, then grew serious again.

Kip picked up a cup of coffee and took a gulp.

"Xavier told me that he and Sebastian are brothers."

Kip's eyes widened, and he spewed his drink all over the desk. He broke into a fit of coughing before he was able to compose himself. "What the fuck? No way, man. There's no fucking way."

"I wanted to tell Sebastian what I've learned, but I can't find him. Do you think Dope could find out the truth?"

"Hell yeah, that guy can find out anything given enough time and resources. Tell me what you know, then I'll call Dope."

Over the next few minutes, I relayed what Xavier had told me about the boys being stolen and separated.

Kip remained quiet and then grabbed his cell phone off the desk and frowned. "That's some juicy shit. I wonder if it would ease Sebastian's conscience if he knew that it wasn't his real father that died in his kitchen."

I shrugged. "Does Sebastian know that the Pied Piper forced him to knife his father or whoever that man was?"

"As much as he and Death have been talking, I think so. Death always knew, so it wouldn't be a stretch that he said something to Bass. It's probably another reason he's fucked up in the head about Death being a part of him."

After my intense workout with Death in the sex swing, my muscles were achy, and my legs trembled as I got up. Kip's silence added to the weight of unease in my gut. I removed my phone from my pocket and checked for any missed calls. My heart sank when I saw the empty screen.

"No word from Sebastian." Despite wanting to give him space, worry gnawed at me after several hours of not hearing from him. The only time he didn't answer immediately was when Death had claimed another victim. I dialed his number and listened to it ring, each tone a deafening reminder of his absence. But all too soon, it went to voicemail, leaving me to dread what might be keeping him from answering.

"Maybe I should go look for him. I can't help but feel something is wrong, Kip. A few hours is a long time for him to be gone."

"You think so? I just wanted to give him some space, but maybe you're right." Kip rose from his seat and walked to the door. "I'll call Dope while we're looking for Bass."

"Thank you."

I followed him down the hall and double-checked that I'd locked Xavier's door from the outside. With the pain pill in his system, I wouldn't put it past him to drag his body across the floor and try to escape. I trusted nothing about him.

Over the next half an hour, Kip and I talked about how to help Sebastian come to grips with Death and his history as we looked for him. Sebastian under no circumstances could turn himself in. I would lose him, and the kids would lose their father. If he was set on that decision, I had to figure out a way to change his mind.

"Ella, it's starting to get dark. We should head back. Bass would kick my ass if anything happened to you again."

I didn't miss the worry in Kip's tone. In fact, the longer we'd looked for my husband, the more my anxiety had kicked into overdrive.

CHAPTER 45

DEATH

When they found the lamb's wool caught on thorns,
they assumed violence. They didn't know how gently darkness
helps shed old skins.
—Anonymous

The man standing in front of me was a notorious serial killer, but I hadn't known that, because he knew how to charm people and stay off the grid. He wasn't charming me. I understood exactly who he was. Men like us were experts at playing games, setting the stage for our prey. He was doing just that. I suspected before the night was over that I would have to fight for my life, but I was ready. A part of me had sworn that if I ever had a chance to end the son of a bitch who murdered my family, I would make him pay. Even though I'd told Ella she could help, it might not be possible. Regardless of how this all played out, I promised myself I would see her and my children soon. I refused to die at this man's hands.

"No, I don't need anything to eat or drink." I glowered at him. "Tell me about the Fletchers," I demanded again.

He cleared his throat, his brown eyes dancing with mischief. It was clear he was enjoying himself.

"I was always different than others around me while growing up. Hell, I only had a few friends that wanted to have anything to do with me. You and I are wired differently. We think differently, feel differently than most. Once I realized that, I kept to myself, but as I said, a few of the guys in school took to me, and we were friends until we graduated high school and each of us moved in different directions. It was at that time I realized that I might not ever have friends again, but I was at peace with it.

"Then, my freshman year of college, a guy in my chemistry class named Chuck asked if I wanted to hang out with him and a few others. Just a small weekend gathering around the bonfire, a few beers, some good-looking girls. I was bored at school by that time and making straight A's without studying. My time was spent in the library reading about every serial killer that came before me. I was fascinated with what I learned about them, and it felt familiar here." He patted his chest directly over his heart.

"Anyway, I agreed to get together. That Friday night, I met Chuck at my dorm, and we walked to the back of the campus and through the woods," he continued. "Eventually, we came upon a small circle of people around a campfire. Chuck introduced me to everyone, and I took a seat. They were friendly enough, but I was on high alert. I had trust issues, and it seemed strange that Chuck had asked me along when we barely knew each other. But I also understood that normal people who wanted to get to know someone invited them to hang out. So, I kept my suspicions to myself." He shifted in his seat as if what he was about to say next was hard for him to share.

"There were a few young ladies there, and they were beautiful. The other four were guys my age, and one seat was empty. It took me listening to everyone's conversation to catch up on the gossip. I learned that Cindy was the girl who normally sat in the empty chair, but she'd had a baby and didn't get to hang out with the group as often. She'd lived in Australia most of her life and intended on returning once the baby was old enough to fly across the ocean."

"What does this have to do with the Fletchers?" I asked, impatient.

"Everything," he snapped. It was the first time he showed any kind of emotion other than just being hospitable and pleasant. He smoothed his white shirt with his palm, composing himself before he continued.

"That night I didn't really learn much about the others except that they were very close friends. I didn't think much of it, but Chuck invited me again, and soon it was a few times a week that we would all hang out together. One of the other girls, Lily, took an interest in me, and we started to date here and there. It was during one of those dates that she explained why Chuck thought I might be a good fit for the group. She said each of them had a dark secret that they'd shared with each other. At first it was a sociology experiment to see if people really bonded over secrets, but then they learned to trust each other on a deeper level and became true friends. Chuck saw something sinister in me and thought I might be a good addition." The Pied Piper grinned. "After giving Lily one hell of an orgasm, she confided in me that Cindy didn't actually—" His phone rang, and he picked it up off the coffee table in front of him. "Excuse me. I have to take this." He rose from his seat and walked into another room, leaving me with my fucked-up thoughts of how to kill him once he finished telling me what I wanted to hear.

While he was gone, I looked around the living room searching for anything that might tell me more about this man, but he returned rather quickly.

"Where was I?"

"Cindy," I reminded him.

"Ah, yes. As I was saying, Lily confided in me that Cindy hadn't given birth to a baby, but she'd stolen two from a mother who had left the babies in a stroller near the park bench while she met with someone halfway across the park. In Cindy's mind, that woman didn't deserve to be a parent if she left her children unattended. Cindy had always wanted to be a mother, so she took the two boys."

"Xavier and me?"

"Yes. After Cindy stole you both, she changed her name to Emma Jo."

"My mother."

"Yes. And my new friends knew this secret about her."

"They never turned her in?" If they had, I wondered how my life would have turned out. Would I have become the same monster I was now?

"Eventually, I was trusted enough in the group to learn all of their secrets. Emma Jo's secret was peanuts to the rest of us. One man was a serial rapist, another a thief, another loved to kidnap and drug young women. The ladies also had their dark secrets. By the end of our freshman year in college, the serial rapist fell in love with Emma Jo. The weight of college and caring for her newborn and toddler had left her vulnerable and desperate, making her an easy target for Martin's advances. Around that time, she sold the baby for cash but kept you. She shared that information with Martin. Emma Jo naively believed she knew who he really was, but the truth was far darker. Martin was not a serial rapist of women, but something even more depraved. After they got married, they moved to Australia until you were in sixth grade.

Martin landed a job in Minnesota, and that's when they relocated back to the states."

As he fell silent, the realization of his words hit me like a sledgehammer to the chest. A fiery rage consumed me as I remembered my so-called father, a monster who had repeatedly violated and scarred me in unimaginable ways. A flash of memory bombarded my mind, and I resisted the urge to stagger backward with the weight of it.

"She knew what he did to me all along, didn't she?"

The Pied Piper nodded. "She told me about the time she witnessed what Martin was capable of, but she was too terrified of him to turn him in."

"So, she sacrificed me instead!" I roared. If they weren't already dead, they would be my next victims. I hadn't hurt a woman in my life outside of the games Ella and I played, but she would have been my first, and I would have refused to feel one ounce of guilt over it.

"Would you like me to continue, or have you heard enough?" he asked.

CHAPTER 46

ELLA

"Something is really wrong, Kip. I can feel it." I paced back and forth in the small office, hoping that Sebastian would come through the door at any second.

"He's okay, Ella. I'm not sure what's going on, but think about who this man is. He can deal with anything." Kip rolled his shoulders back, and I assumed it was an attempt to relieve some of his tension.

"You say that, but I can tell you're worried too. Maybe . . . maybe he just left." I swallowed over those words. "He's been having such a hard time with Death being a part of him, and he doesn't understand our relationship . . ." I blinked, trying to keep the tears at bay. "Would he do that, Kip? Would he leave me and the kids?"

Kip placed his hands on my shoulders. "Look at me, El. Even if Sebastian left, Death didn't. He'll be back, and then we will both beat his ass for being stupid."

I couldn't help but smile through my tears. "I wish he could understand how much I love both sides of him, but Sebastian is so damn hardheaded sometimes."

Kip grinned. "You don't say."

I patted one of his hands before he dropped them. "So, you suspect that he just took off to think?"

"Probably, but when he's back, we'll tell him that wasn't cool shit to do. You can decide his punishment." His chuckle warmed me and eased my anxiety.

"Thank you for being here with me and always supporting Sebastian and Death. You're an amazing friend, and I'm grateful to have you in my life."

Kip placed his palm over his heart. "It's a good thing you're married to a guy with a dark side . . ." He leaned forward, staring at me. "Because if you knew who I really was, you'd take all that back."

Startled by his revelation, I stepped away. I licked my lips before I said, "I doubt it's any worse than Death's secrets. Maybe you just need someone in your life to help you heal whatever it is you're punishing yourself over."

Kip blinked at me several times and then turned away and stared out the window. It seemed as though I'd triggered something inside of him. I cleared my throat, giving him a moment. "While we're waiting for my husband, what should we do with Xavier?"

He shoved his hand through his hair before he faced me. "If we kill him, Sebastian is going to be pissed. If we don't, then Death will be pissed. I say we let Xavier go and tell him to run, and if he makes it out of the woods, he gets to live."

My shoulders shook with my laugh. "That's not funny, but it really is. He can't even get up, much less run with his knees." Any time a soft spot for Xavier started to form, I was bombarded by horrible memories of being in the glass cage with spiders everywhere. I hated that man, and I hoped he burned in hell . . . alive. "Well, he's their brother, so I'm not sure if that changes the game or not. Plus, he'll never walk again, but I don't think it's enough punishment for what he did to me."

"Yup, his knees are fucked for life. It's not as though he were living a normal existence anyway." Kip shrugged. "Seriously, whatever you want to do is fine with me."

"Death said I could kill him." I arched a brow at my friend and rubbed my hands together. My face lit up with an ornery smile.

"But?"

I tilted my head and groaned. "I'm not sure I can do it. John was different for some stupid reason. I'll have to decide soon, though. What I do know is that he has too much information on us. He can't be released back into the wild." I giggled. The room grew quiet, and I blew out a sigh. "I hate waiting to see what might play out."

"It sucks, but I've gotten good at it with the society and taking care of Death."

I sat on the edge of the rickety desk and folded my arms over my chest. "I'm going to check in with Cami and the kids."

"I'll touch base with Ryan to see if he's heard from Bass while you're talking to her." Kip gave me a small wave, and then he left the room.

I grabbed my burner phone from my back pocket and tapped the screen. Cami's cell rang a few times before she picked up.

"Hello?" Her voice sounded strained.

"It's just me."

"Oh, good. I wasn't sure, since it's an unknown number."

"How are the kids?" A smile eased across my face as I heard Verity's screech of excitement in the background.

"They miss their mom and dad, but they're good. Dope is playing with them now. I know this might sound nuts, but Dope would make an excellent father."

My eyes popped open at her remark. "I hadn't thought about it before, but you're right. Until then, he has the twins to keep him occupied. How are you two getting along?"

"Well, the time with him has been fun. He's a smart fucking guy, Ella. Like, off the charts smart."

"I know. I hope he finds someone special. He deserves to be happy. He's spent most of his life taking care of Sebastian and keeping him safe."

Cami grew quiet for a minute. "I bet that's been really difficult on him." Her voice was full of compassion and maybe a hint of something else.

"It is, but he's loyal, which is hard to find in a friend. I'm lucky I have you." My heart skipped a beat, hoping she wouldn't change her mind about turning all of us in to the cops and FBI.

"I think this time with Dope has helped me understand why you all love and take care of Death so much. We've talked a lot about their history. How Sebastian witnessed his parents being murdered, and how Dope found him in the corner covered in blood, and when Death started to appear and talk to them. I'm not sure these guys could ever be separated, and I've realized that their connection to each other is beyond what most people could experience in a lifetime," Cami said, her tone laced with sadness.

"You miss Ryan, don't you?"

"Fuck . . . Yeah, I miss him a lot. Like, I can forgive the fact that you lied to me to protect your family, and if I get real with myself, I would have done the same, bitch."

I snorted with her confession. "It's hard putting yourself in someone else's place and trying to think differently about a situation. I guess I learned that skill while working at the attorney's office. Nothing is black and white. Shit, it's mostly gray."

"Well said. I'm glad you left me with Dope. It's been an eye-opening experience, and I understand the circumstances much better."

"Does that mean you can forgive Ryan?"

Silence filled the line, and my shoulders sagged. I understood my best friend well enough to know the answer before she even said it out loud.

"We were seriously talking about our future. If I'd married him and not known his secret, it could have put me in danger. You knew before you married Sebastian. You had a choice, y'know? Ryan took that from me, and I'm not sure if I can forgive him for it."

My heart sank for both of them. They were perfect for each other. "Give it some time. If you really love him, then maybe you guys can at least talk. It's a lot, Cami. A part of me doesn't want you with someone that's chin deep in this life, but he's not going to leave Death to fend for himself. They're family, and nothing will come between that. However, you know the secrets now, and you're involved. I can tell you from experience that when you can speak openly, the relationship gets stronger. Look at us."

Cami snorted. "It took you getting kidnapped for me to learn the truth."

I laughed. "Yeah, it's because I love you and wanted to keep you safe."

"How are you doing? Like, really doing? So much has been going on, but no one has forgotten what you lived through. I just haven't had time with you to grab our favorite ice cream and crawl in bed for a talk-and-cry day. I'm sorry. I should have done that as soon as you came home instead of falling apart on you about Death. I was a shitty friend, and I'm really sorry. I love you, and I need to know how you're doing."

My eyes misted over with her apology and concern. I swallowed over the lump in my throat.

"No matter where I am, I don't feel safe unless I'm at the penthouse. Since it's such a high-end building, the security is top-notch, and no one can even reach the elevator without first getting past the doorman, then the security at the entrance. And getting past the desk is difficult.

Not to mention you have to have a keycard to access the elevator. We're tucked away, and I'm with the guys, but I hate to close my eyes at night, even with Sebastian next to me. The nightmares are intense."

"Do you think it will help if Death . . . uh . . . disposes of the man that held you captive?"

I hesitated, wondering if I should tell her we had Xavier. If he died, then Cami would be an accomplice, and I didn't want to add to her growing list of criminal activity. "Maybe. I guess if it happens, I'll see how I feel then."

"I'm always here, even in the middle of the night. I will be glad when you come back, though."

"Me too." My mind raced with anticipation for Sebastian's return, but a sense of unease gnawed at my gut. A nervous energy pulsed through me, making it impossible to calm the churning in my stomach. I couldn't shake the feeling that something was horribly wrong.

CHAPTER 47

DEATH

Even shadows must bleed before they learn how to whisper.
—Anonymous

"If this is true, then why are you telling me all of this now?" I asked, suspicious of his every word.

"Because you deserve to know the truth."

"I don't buy that," I growled.

"You have no choice. But let me continue with Emma Jo and Martin." He crossed his legs before he continued.

"Over the years, my appetite grew, and I became known as the Pied Piper. It fit, so I was fine with the nickname. Emma Jo struggled with what my work entailed, though." He flashed me a sly grin. "Not many can understand the bloodlust and fascination of what we do, Death. But"—he pointed at me—"there's a little twist here. She appreciated what I did enough to blackmail me into killing your father."

"For what he did to me?" I asked, my voice low and deadly.

"Yes. She hated him for it, and she hated herself for being a coward and not standing up to him. Emma Jo couldn't afford my services, so she threatened to turn me in with the backlist of my victims. Since our tight-knit group held our dirtiest secrets, she had access to a few of the names, but not many. Clearly, I couldn't have that. Not to mention that if I ended Martin's life, she would hold that over my head as well. If she was willing to blackmail me once, she would do it again."

"So, you killed her first."

He winked at me. "Exactly."

"Why did you use me to help kill my father . . . Martin?" I spit out the word "father" with venom, refusing to give that title to Martin any longer. He was a despicable creature, capable of unspeakable acts against innocent children. "Why did you manipulate me into helping kill that monster? I was just a kid," I said, my voice shaking with rage.

"You were at a perfect age for me to train. Emma Jo mentioned there was something dark about you. At times, she was more terrified of you than Martin. Poor woman really stepped in shit when she stole you. No offense, but she was trapped and terrified of the man she slept next to and the young man she'd taken in as her own son. It all turned out to be a little fucked up, if you ask me."

"Why was she scared of me? I never laid a hand on her, even if I wanted to." I stared at him, trying to read his expression, but he was an expert at masking his thoughts.

"She said she began to see the moment that you weren't yourself. Emma Jo said she sensed an unspeakable evil lurking within you, a darkness that made her skin crawl. And yet, you were always a good young man, never causing any trouble. However, as you grew older, she noticed a change in you. You started watching her while she cooked dinner, your face turning cold and calculating, twisting into something sinister. She actually said that your eyes turned from blue to gray. I couldn't ignore the signs anymore. When I finally killed your parents, it confirmed my suspicions. You carried the same darkness as me, but yours manifested itself differently . . . as Death. I may be just one man, but you . . . you are two."

I didn't know how to process this information, but deep down there was a small sense of gratitude for being freed from the clutches of the monstrous man who raised me. The Pied Piper had unwittingly set me free from his cruelty. And yet, even in death, Martin's spirit haunted me with memories seared into my mind like branding irons.

"So, there you have it. Those are the answers to your questions." He slapped his leg as if he was announcing that our conversation was over. It wasn't.

"And what happened to Xavier?"

"Oh, your brother?"

I nodded, not willing to claim him as my blood.

"After he got revenge on the wretched family that took him . . . In case you don't know, he killed them, then stuffed them. They're sitting at his kitchen table even now."

"I saw."

"He had a little help. I took him under my wing since he was all alone. You weren't, though. Unlike Xavier, you had people in your life. Dope's family was good to you and so were your friends. Xavier had no one. We spent a lot of long hours talking and preparing his parents and sister for the taxidermy. It was poetic justice, if you ask me." He sneered. "As he got older, I told him about you. He was so curious about who you were that I included him as I kept tabs on you. It was rather fascinating when he became obsessed with everything about Sebastian and Death, though. He begged for a replica of the house so he could live there and feel close to you. I didn't figure it would hurt anything, so I had it built for him. Unfortunately, he had spent so much time locked up in the dark, he still felt at home in that familiar environment. He decided to live in the basement instead of the rest of the place. I figured whatever made him happy."

"And why was Ella taken?" I had heard the answer from Ella and Xavier, but I needed to know from the Pied Piper.

"Just as bait to draw you away from your friends and family. I've wanted to talk to you for a long time now." He leaned forward and rubbed his hands together. "As I already mentioned, Xavier wanted to keep Ella instead of turning her over to me. Poor guy fell head over heels for your wife. You've got a smart girl by your side. She escaped and found her way back to you."

I wanted to remind him that Ella wasn't married to me, but I thought better of it. "She's very resourceful." Inwardly, my heart swelled with pride. My queen had shown the world what she was made of. "Why now? If you've kept tabs on me my entire life, then why am I here talking to you now?"

The Pied Piper rose from his seat and approached me. I towered over him by several inches, but he wasn't intimidated.

"I've just learned that I have cancer. I'll do my best to fight it, but if I don't win, I want you to know the truth. Do what you want with it, but I do have one regret."

I scoffed at the idea that this cold-blooded killer could experience remorse. It wasn't in our nature. But then again, neither was love. Ella had been my weakness, the only person who made me feel something other than numbness in this life of violence and death. "What is that?"

He placed his hand on my arm. "You. I wish that I'd taken you as well as Xavier. I could have taught you everything I know, to keep you from killing too many men at one time, to ditch the cops off your trail, to teach you the skills that I've developed. I wanted to be in your life, but I felt it best to leave you where you were. Sebastian needed that emotional nourishment that I couldn't provide. He's a good man, and I didn't think it wise to extinguish that part of who you are."

My mind reeled as I studied his expression, trying to make sense of everything he had just revealed. Was anything he told me even true? But then again, if my real parents weren't alive, why would he lie about that? My stomach churned with conflicting emotions, and I struggled to find the words to ask him about one thing that still bothered me.

"You said my real parents were killed in a train accident. Was that a lie?"

He chuckled as he stepped back and put some space in between us. His moves made me wonder if he thought I would lash out when he answered me.

"Are you ready to return to your friends and Xavier? I really would appreciate it if you showed some mercy and turned him over to me. He won't be a problem for you any longer. You have my word. Besides, I would owe you."

"Explain to me why I should make this worth your while." I shifted my weight from one foot to the other.

His dark chuckle filled the room. "Let me see if I can put this simply. Return Xavier to me, and I'll make sure that you remain a free man. The FBI will never know you existed. Any DNA you've accidentally left behind would vanish, and you would never be charged for anything you've ever done. If you kill Xavier, then I'll lead the FBI to your door and not only see that you're charged with your crimes"—a vicious smile eased across his face—"but mine too. Believe me, there are a lot of bodies I've left around the country. You would see death row faster than most."

If that happened, Ella and the kids would be a target for the Pied Piper and his people.

"How can you even guarantee my protection from the FBI?"

His smile held decades of secrets. "When you've spent thirty years consulting on their most gruesome cases, you learn where all the bodies are buried—literally. Half of their behavioral analysis unit owes me favors, and the other half would lose their careers if certain evidence came to light. I've built this network carefully, Death. Every case I helped them solve bought me more influence, more access, more power to safeguard my own interests. Why do you think no one's caught you yet? I've been steering them away for a very long time." He paused, allowing me a moment to think about what he'd said.

"When you're dropped off at the warehouse, you'll have three hours to contact me with a decision, or the FBI will arrive shortly. You can run, but it won't do you any good. I would think carefully about your next steps." He reached in the front pocket of his dress shirt and removed a business card. "You can reach me here." He extended his hand to me.

I took the card from him. "I'll take it under consideration, but what about my real parents? Are they actually alive, or are you just trying to manipulate me? For all I know *you're* my real father."

He tilted his head and offered me a practiced, compassionate smile. "You really don't know who I am, do you?"

CHAPTER 48

ELLA

The door to the office banged open and sent me dropping to the floor as my body instinctively made itself smaller. A part of me realized I was safe in the office, but another part remembered being helpless and waiting for Xavier's footsteps on the stairs, wondering if this would be the time he decided to hurt me. My heart thundered in my chest as I forced myself to look up to face whatever threat might be coming. Seeing Sebastian stumble into the room instead of Xavier made my knees weak with relief, but my legs wouldn't stop shaking.

"Sebastian?" I hurried over to him as he held his head in his hand.

"The bastard drugged me, and my head fucking hurts like a son of a bitch."

"What?" I grabbed him, led him to the office chair, and helped him sit down. I knelt before him. "Baby, what happened? Kip and I looked for you, but we just thought you might have left me because . . ." I clenched my jaw. "Because you couldn't deal with Death and wanted to protect me."

He groaned and glanced up at me. "It had crossed my mind for sure, but once I got walking and started to sort out my thoughts, well, before I got too far, I got a fucking tranquilizer dart in my neck. The next thing I knew, Death and the Pied Piper were talking. Even though I could hear every word they said, I couldn't get past Death to talk to the man that killed my parents."

I gasped, nearly losing my balance and falling backward.

Sebastian grimaced and then he said, "Yes, I'm aware of that. I'll explain everything to her if you give me a damn minute."

"Did he hurt you other than tranquilizing you?" I ran my hands over his shoulders and biceps as I searched for any wounds.

"No. He wanted to talk . . . and Xavier."

A deep frown creased my forehead. "I don't understand." I looked around the room and located the thermos of water Kip kept in the office for us. After I hopped up and grabbed it off the floor in the corner, I flipped the top open and gave it to my husband. "Drink some water. Maybe it will help."

He drank it slowly, and his shoulders slumped forward, exhaustion coasting over his handsome features. "I'll start from the beginning, but it would be better if Kip were here too. That way I only have to tell it once."

"Okay. I'll text him to see where he's at." I fired off a text to Kip, and he arrived a few minutes later.

"Man, where the hell have you been? Ella and I were getting a bit concerned. You don't typically just take off like that." Irritation flashed in Kip's eyes.

"He was drugged and taken, but he's okay," I said quickly so he wouldn't chew Sebastian out.

"Have a seat, mate. I'll fill you both in. We have a ticking clock to decide what to do with Xavier. I can't make the decision on my own, even though Death has made it abundantly clear what he wants to do." Sebastian winced and placed his fingers on his temples, rubbing in slow circles.

As Sebastian unraveled the horrors of his past, my heart shattered into a million pieces. Tears cascaded down my cheeks in an uncontrollable torrent as I struggled to contain the scream of agony and rage building inside me. With each word, a fire of protectiveness ignited within me, burning fiercely for the innocent child who'd endured such trauma at the hands of Martin. With fierce determination, I vowed to always be there to shield Sebastian from harm and safeguard his secret at all costs.

When he explained what the offer was concerning Xavier, a vortex of anger and anxiety swirled to life in the pit of my stomach. "He can't get away with what he did to me!"

"I know, baby. He won't ever walk again, at least. Maybe that will offer you some comfort. But I'm afraid if we don't comply with the Pied Piper, life will get very dark for all of us, and I'm not willing to give you and the kids up. He's a skilled hunter, and I can't risk him coming after you a second time."

"Can't Death end the fucker?" Kip piped in.

Sebastian grew silent for a moment before he spoke again. "He said yes, but someone as powerful as the Pied Piper would have people that would never stop hunting us. We would always be looking over our shoulder. He said Xavier isn't worth what it would cost us if we killed him. Plus, he offered protection for all the shit Death has done. Basically, we're buying our freedom by returning Xavier."

My hands balled into fists. "Knowing that you would never go to prison, and we would all be protected would be worth the peace of mind. Do you trust what he told you? Does he have the power to keep us all safe?"

Sebastian nodded. "He has a far reach, apparently. Something about him . . . Well, he was a no-bullshit kind of guy. He and Death are similar in a lot of ways, and I suspect Death would have seen through his lies."

I glanced at Kip, who popped his neck, his body rigid with tension. I understood the feeling.

"I'm not sure this is our decision. I think it's Death's," I said, crossing my arms over my chest. "This is his past and future we're talking about."

"And my family's," Sebastian reminded me.

"I know. In my mind, there's no real choice here." I wanted to remind Death that he had promised I could kill Xavier, but I couldn't. I couldn't feed my fury at the expense of my family.

Sebastian nodded. "Kip? Even if Death has the final decision, I would like your opinion."

"Give the little shit back to the Pied Piper. He's not much of a payment for your future, but it affects all of us. I say drop the fucker off and let him go. It's one less mess for me to clean up."

"I feel the same way. Risking Ella and the kids isn't worth it. The Pied Piper would turn Death in." Sebastian arched a brow and grew silent again. "Death said he agrees. Let's get rid of the son of a bitch."

Sebastian leaned forward and removed a business card from his back pocket, then opened a drawer in the desk and pulled out a burner phone still in the package. "Not that he doesn't know where we are, but I still need to be smart." He ripped open the plastic.

"After the exchange, does this mean you can go back to New York?" Kip asked, a flicker of sadness in his tone.

The question sent my pulse racing with anxiety. Would we really be safe there?

"I'll talk to Ella about it later, but I think we should hang out at the penthouse for now. I would love to work at the club a little bit for old times' sake. Check the books, see Riley and you guys more before we plan the next steps."

Inwardly, I released a sigh of relief. "That would be nice. I have really missed Cami and my parents. If we can stay for a while in Portland with the Pied Piper's protection, then I would like to." My heart warmed with the idea. "Plus, the place is plenty big for our family and friends." I gave Sebastian a smile, trying to ease the tension in the room. I could deal with my emotions later. This decision was about survival.

Sebastian tapped the phone screen and then held it to his ear. "Where and when?" He looked up, our gazes connecting as he briefly chatted with the Pied Piper. Once he hung up, he stood and popped his neck. "He wants to meet you, Ella. I'm not sure we have a choice but to be ready for anything. Kip, bring the van around so we can put Xavier in the back. We'll secure and blindfold him so he can't pull any shit with us. The sooner I don't have to lay eyes on the sneaky bastard, the better." Sebastian walked over and wrapped his arms around me, pulling me against him.

"Got it." Kip gave Sebastian a salute before he left the room.

"I love you, baby. Please understand that if giving myself up would keep you and the kids safe, it would have been my first choice."

I placed my palms against his muscular chest. "I know that. I'm glad it's not coming down to that, though. I would rather be able to move on and live our lives together—grow old and raise the twins."

"Not that you need to decide right now, but maybe we need to sell the property in New York. With everything that's happened, I don't think it's the best place for us. We can stay at the penthouse and decide where we want to build our next home."

I smiled up at him, my heart melting with his idea. “I was thinking the same thing.” I pushed up on my tiptoes and kissed him. “Let’s get this over with.” I released him and slipped my hand in his. “I won’t lie. I’m a little nervous and very interested to meet the Pied Piper. I just don’t know what he wants with me.”

Sebastian’s expression filled with worry. “Me neither.”

CHAPTER 49

ELLA

Kip sat in the back of the van with Xavier while I sat in the passenger's seat and Sebastian drove. Silence filled the small space as we all wondered what the Pied Piper's plan was. There was no real reason to meet me, but I also realized men like him didn't make a move without a motive.

A light rain pattered against the windshield as Sebastian maneuvered the back road in the dark. He reached over and took my hand and glanced over at me.

"It's going to be okay, baby."

I gave him a tight smile. "We're giving the Pied Piper what he wants, so I don't think he'll try to take me again." I wished I could believe my words, but there was nothing I trusted about the man who allowed Xavier to keep me in a cage. I peeked over my shoulder and into the back of the van. Sebastian had given Xavier a higher dose of pain pills to ensure that he was compliant during his move. It seemed to be working so far, and I was a little less jumpy about the situation, but not by much.

"A Piece of Your Shadow" by Roby Fayer and Melosun played through the speakers, and I tapped my foot to the song, appreciating the distraction.

Sebastian pulled the van onto a deserted dirt road, and with each twist and turn, my chest clenched tighter in anticipation. After another half mile, he abruptly stopped and left the headlights on as the engine continued to rumble. My nerves were on edge as I watched a sleek black

SUV speed toward us, its tires kicking up clouds of dust in its wake. My heart pounded against my rib cage, threatening to burst through my skin. I took a deep breath and balled my fists, preparing for the inevitable confrontation that was about to occur.

The night pressed against us, broken only by the harsh glare of headlights—our white van against the Pied Piper's black SUV. We climbed out and Sebastian stood beside me as Kip unloaded Xavier and carried him to the man in black slacks and a white shirt. His short dark hair was peppered with gray and swept back. He appeared to be in his late sixties and exuded strength and power. Goosebumps dotted my arms, and I tried to fight the shiver tiptoeing down my spine.

The Pied Piper stepped forward, each movement calculated. His eyes never left Xavier. He tilted his head, and a man who had remained hidden behind the SUV stepped out into the light and took Xavier from Kip.

"You understand the exchange," the Pied Piper said. Not a question. A statement.

Sebastian's voice was raw. "Take him. We've done what you asked. We expect the same in return."

He shifted his gaze to me. That look. I knew that look. He saw something in me. Something he recognized. Something that made my skin crawl. Sebastian placed his palm on the small of my back in an attempt to comfort me.

The Pied Piper's approach was deliberate, each step measured like a predator calculating its strike. Up close, I could see the intricate details I'd missed before—the slight scar running along his jawline, the way his eyes seemed to dissect every inch of me.

"Ella," he said, my name a whisper that felt like ice against my skin. "You're more interesting than you know."

Sebastian's palm pressed against my back, a silent warning. Protection.

"What do you want?" I managed to say, my voice steadier than I felt.

"Walk with me, Ella." The Pied Piper held his palm out to me, and I nervously glanced at my husband.

The night seemed to hold its breath. Sebastian's fingers on my back grew rigid, a coiled spring of barely contained tension. I breathed a sigh of relief that Sebastian was with me instead of Death—he would have cut off the Pied Piper's hands before he finished blinking. Death would have never let me go alone. I needed my levelheaded husband this time.

"I'll be right here. It's okay," he said quietly, his voice trembling slightly.

The Pied Piper held his arm out to me, and I slipped mine through his, inwardly cringing as he led us away from the cars and group.

"It's a pleasure to meet the woman strong enough to marry a man like Death and Sebastian."

"I'm not sure I can say the same about the man that killed his parents, but on the other hand, you did free him from Martin."

A soft laugh escaped him. "I see he tells you everything."

"Usually, unless it puts me in danger." The twigs and leaves crunched beneath our shoes as we continued to walk, the headlights from the van lighting our way.

Sweat beaded on my forehead as I waited for him to drop the bomb of why he wanted to meet me.

"I'll get to the point. My time is valuable, as is yours." He slowed and turned to me. "Death doesn't know who I am," he continued. "I honestly thought he did, but when I asked him who joined me while Martin was bleeding out on the floor, he didn't remember. It makes sense. Sebastian was in quite a bit of shock. The first time you plunge a knife into a body and deplete the life from someone's eyes, it's terrifying and exhilarating at the same moment." He paused, offering me a kind smile. "But you know all about that, don't you?"

My heart caught in my throat. The Pied Piper's words hung between us like a razor-thin wire, ready to slice through any pretense.

"How do I know?" He chuckled, a sound devoid of any real humor. "I know everything, Ella. Every move. Every breath."

The headlights cast our shadows long and distorted against the forest floor. I could feel the weight of his gaze dissecting me.

"Sebastian believes he's protected you," the Pied Piper continued, "but protection is an illusion. Especially when someone like me decides to pay attention."

I kept my voice steady. "What do you want?"

He stopped walking and turned to face me fully. "Verity," he said simply. "Your daughter carries something . . . remarkable. A potential I've seen only a few times in my life. When she's older, I want to teach her, groom her for her future just like I did Xavier and a few select others."

"Stay away from my child," I warned, each word a knife's edge.

"Stay away?" Another soft laugh. "I've been watching her since birth. The way she looks. The way she watches. Some children have a . . . darkness. Just like her father."

My blood ran cold. Not because of his words, but because the dark part of me understood exactly what he meant.

"What are you saying?" My voice was low, dangerous. I refused to let this man, this killer, see my fear.

The Pied Piper's smile didn't reach his eyes. Cold. Calculating. "Genetics are fascinating things. Bloodlines. Predispositions." He took a step closer. "Your daughter carries something . . . special."

"I'll say it again. Stay away from Verity."

"Or what?" he challenged, his voice a razor-thin whisper.

As if on cue, the man who had taken Xavier from Kip moved slightly and revealed a glimpse of a holstered weapon. A silent reminder of the threat hanging in the air.

"I've been watching," the Pied Piper continued. "Watching Verity. Watching you both. Some children are born with certain . . . inclinations. Potential, if you will."

My heart thundered in my ears, and I strained to keep my fear and anxiety under control. "You're not touching my child," I said, each word carved from my fury.

His laugh was soft, chilling. "Touch? No. Watch? Always." He leaned in, his breath warm against my ear. "Some bloodlines are meant to continue, Ella. And Verity? She's going to be extraordinary."

I attempted to step away from him, but with lightning quick speed, he grabbed my arm.

"I can see that you intend to keep Verity safe, but who says she won't seek out Death's instruction on her own?"

"What do you want? I'll give you anything, but leave my daughter alone. You gave Death your word that we would be protected."

"And you will be, but I never promised that your children would be safe from my influence. Think about it, Ella. I can give you what even Death can't: freedom to follow your darkest desires, freedom from ever spending a day in prison, a relationship with your family and friends. I have the reach and the power."

My legs trembled with his promise. "What do you want in order to leave my baby alone?"

A wicked grin spread across his face. "I have a proposition for you. I'll reveal my true identity, and once you know, you'll understand so much more. But if you utter a word to anyone, even Sebastian and Death, your daughter's safety will be compromised and your years with her will be much shorter than if you kept that pretty mouth of yours shut." His eyes gleamed with malice as he spoke, leaving no doubt in my mind that he was capable of carrying out his threat.

I swallowed, refusing to puke all my guts out on this man's feet and let the Pied Piper know that he was terrifying me.

"Sebastian said you have cancer. You won't live long enough to come for Verity."

He threw his head back and laughed, his belly shaking. "I've just learned that I have cancer. I'll do my best to fight it, and I suspect I'll win . . . I'm too evil to die. Not even the devil wants me."

There was no debating the situation. I had to keep Verity safe at all costs. "Fine. Tell me."

He held up a finger. "Not so fast. I need your word that you won't reveal my identity to anyone. Ever."

"Why are you telling me this?"

His hot breath burned against the shell of my ear as he spoke, his voice dripping with cruelty. "Because keeping this kind of secret can break someone, toy with their mind, and I want to see what you're made of, Ella Fletcher. This will be a delicious game for me as I watch you struggle to hide the truth from your husband and friends. I. Will. Break. You. When I do, I will still have Verity, and you will be left with nothing."

A gasp escaped me, but I clamped my mouth shut. I had no choice but to listen to him, but that didn't mean that I couldn't figure out a loophole down the road. Verity wasn't even a year old yet.

"Promise me that you won't kidnap Verity. When the time comes, you'll tell us she is with you." Maybe my agreement would be enough to end this horrible nightmare for now.

His eyes gleamed with something so dark and twisted that every hair on my body stood on end.

"I will agree to that." He paused, looking me in the eye. "As for my identity." He leaned in once again, and as he whispered his answer, each word was like a shard of ice piercing through my heart. My vision clouded over in shock as the weight of his revelation threatened to crush me.

CHAPTER 50

SEBASTIAN

I resisted the urge to chase after Ella, but I was grateful I could still see her. Kip shifted from one foot to the other while the Pied Piper's men trained their weapons on us. My instinct told me that if we didn't attempt to run or fight, they wouldn't shoot. I hadn't driven out here to give Xavier over just to die.

The minutes seemed like eternity as I watched the Pied Piper and Ella talk. Although the headlights of the vehicles lit the area, I couldn't see her face or expressions. Her body remained rigid and on high alert, but I told myself that Ella could handle him. She'd spent most of her career around cold, calculating criminals, not to mention the experience she'd gained handling Death and Xavier.

"Here she comes," Kip said, his voice tight with concern.

I took a cautious step forward, eyeing the goons with the guns. Ella quickened her pace as she left the Pied Piper behind and hurried to me.

"Let's get the fuck out of here," she whispered as soon as she was within earshot.

"We're going to leave now," I announced as I slowly led Ella and Kip to the vehicle.

"Let's hope like hell they don't start shooting as soon as we reach the van," Kip muttered.

"They won't. We're safe to leave."

I didn't miss the fear that rode each of her words.

Once we were in the van, I drove away and left the Pied Piper and his minions behind us.

"I'll keep an eye out to make sure we're not being followed," Kip said.

Ella remained quiet and slumped in her seat. A soft cry escaped her as she hid her face in her hands.

"Baby, it's okay. You're safe now." I squeezed her knee. "Kip, did you leave anything important at the building we were at?"

"Nah. I gathered our duffle bags and burner phones while you were talking to Ella and before I grabbed Xavier."

"Excellent. Thank you. Buckle up: we're not ever going back there. We're heading home."

"We can go home?" Ella's question was heavy yet hopeful.

I glanced over at her. "The Pied Piper gave Death his word that we were safe. What did he say to you?"

Her jaw clenched and unclenched, and a single tear slipped down her cheek. "He reassured me that we would be taken care of."

"And you believe him?" Kip's words were clipped and distrustful.

"We don't really have a choice," she replied.

A spider crawled across the dashboard, and Ella jerked so violently that she slammed her head against the window. I quickly smashed it and brushed it away.

She rubbed her head, visibly trembling. "I can still feel phantom legs crawling over my skin at night and hear the skittering sounds in my dreams. The rational part of me knows that I'm safe, but my body remembers each moment in that glass cage."

My heart cracked wide open with her confession. I reached over and took her hand, gently rubbing my thumb along the back of hers. "You have my word that you're safe, babe. I'll stay by your side every minute if I need to."

She nodded and her shoulders relaxed a little.

Returning to our previous conversation, I said, "The Piper seems to have a large umbrella of protection, and Death agrees that we did the right thing." The van bumped along the dirt road, and I looked into the rearview and side mirrors, but I didn't see anyone else around.

"Kip, you see anyone tailing us?"

He shifted in his seat just enough to look around without being obvious. "Nope. Let's go home. I'll let you know if I see anything suspicious, but so far, so good. I'm going to call Ryan and put him on speaker. I need some proof that the Piper has the reach he says he does. Can't believe a motherfucker like that."

"Good idea," I said.

Seconds later, Ryan's phone rang.

"Hey, it's Kip, Bass, and Ella. We're driving back that way, but I need some information." Kip rattled off his questions about the Pied Piper having FBI and police influence.

"I know the name really well. From what I've seen in law enforcement," Ryan said, "the Pied Piper's reputation is real. Cases go cold when he gets involved. Evidence vanishes. Witnesses change their stories. No one can prove anything, but every cop knows not to dig too deep when his name comes up. From my experience, you can believe him."

"Thanks, man. We just needed to know if he was full of shit or not."

"He's for real. If you're dealing with him, you guys need to watch your fucking backs, though. He's smart and scrupulous."

"Thanks for the heads up," I said.

"All right, we'll catch you later. Thanks again," Kip added.

"Later," Ryan said before he hung up.

"At least we know," Ella said, trying to get comfortable in her seat.

I turned right and the van rolled onto the pavement. "Five more hours until we reach Portland. I'll hide the van, swap the plates out, then we're homeward bound."

"Thank you for taking us back. I miss the twins so much." She sniffled and wiped the moisture from her cheek.

"When we're at the penthouse, I'll take care of the kids. You just get some rest. Maybe we can go forward and put the past behind us."

"Yeah." Her tone didn't do anything to reassure me that it was possible, but I would move heaven and earth to make sure she felt safe enough to try.

The early morning sun peered over the horizon as "la di die" by Nessa Barrett and jxdn softly played through the car stereo. Ella had finally drifted off to sleep, and Kip's snore reached me from the backseat. I was exhausted myself, but I was wired from the events of the last few weeks.

Something is off with my little lamb.

I didn't disagree with Death, but I was probably overreacting. She'd been through hell, tortured mentally and emotionally, held captive, and had met the man who had helped give birth to Death. She was strong, but no one could withstand that for long.

You're not fucking naive enough to trust that the Pied Piper is out of our lives for good, right?

I stifled my laughter in order not to wake Ella. "I wasn't born yesterday, asshole."

Could have fooled me. You should have never let the Pied Piper talk to Ella. Whatever was said in that conversation fucked her up. I'm not sure you have what it takes to keep her and the kids safe.

I arched my brow. "You underestimate me."

Maybe, but you also underestimate me and what I'm willing to do for my family.

I sighed, weary from the long night of driving. "I'm not going anywhere."

Neither am I, so how is this going to work between us?

"I hate to admit it, but you come in handy at times. I don't know that things would have turned out like they did if you hadn't helped."

Death's surprise at my words bounced throughout my body.

I guess you're okay yourself . . . sometimes. Well, Ella seems fond of you, so that leaves me in a bit of a bind. If I kill you and take over, she might not forgive me.

I rubbed my chin before I replied. "Yeah, same. I'm beginning to think she really does love both of us. In my eyes, we have no choice but to make this work the best that we can."

Silence was his only reply for a full minute.

He snarled. *Agreed.*

"Guess it's settled, then."

Not quite. There's something else.

The rest of the ride home was quiet except for the voice in my head. I parked the van and stared at my wife, overcome with gratitude for her. Not just any woman could put up with me, with both sides. Yet here she was. She'd put her life on the line to save me and our children. I wasn't sure it was possible to love someone as much as I did my beautiful Ella.

CHAPTER 51

ELLA

The moment Sebastian opened the penthouse door for me, my heart skipped a beat with joy. Alaric and Verity were sitting on the floor playing with Dope and Cami. But even the familiar comfort of home couldn't stop my instinctive scan of the corners, looking for eight-legged shadows. I'd done the same thing at every stop on our drive, checking every room before I could relax. Sebastian had noticed but hadn't said anything, just quietly checked the spaces with me.

"You're back!" Cami yelled and jumped off the floor, nearly barreling me over with her hug.

I stiffened at the sudden contact, my body betraying me again. Dark spots danced at the edges of my vision as memories of being restrained flooded back. Cami immediately stepped away, understanding dawning in her eyes.

"I'm sorry, I should have—"

"No," I cut her off, forcing myself to breathe normally. "I want hugs. I want normal. My brain just . . . forgets sometimes that I'm safe." I reached for her hand and squeezed it gently. "Try again? Slower this time?"

The second hug was gentler, and I focused on the familiar scent of her shampoo, on the present moment, on being in a safe place. The flashback receded, but the tension in my neck remained.

A smile pulled at the corners of my mouth with her embrace. "It's super good to be here. Hopefully, for a while too."

Cami released me but held on to my shoulders. "Does that mean what I think it does?"

I nodded, a silly grin slipping into place. "We're staying for a while, which means we will have more time together. I don't think I would be able to sleep at the house in New York."

"Shit, I wouldn't be able to sleep with you there either. I would be worried about you and the kids every second of every day." Her eyes cut over to Sebastian. "You, on the other hand, I wouldn't worry about since you, uh . . ." She cleared her throat. "Y'know. Jekyll and Hyde your way through situations." She gave him a small grin.

Relief washed over me. Maybe we were making some progress with Cami accepting Sebastian and Death.

"Ma-ma!" Verity squealed and lifted her arms.

I hurried over to her and scooped her off the floor, peppering her sweet little cheeks with kisses. Her infectious giggles warmed me as I held her closely. "Mama's home, baby girl."

Alaric released a wail, and I set Verity down and picked up my son. "Hi, baby. How's my boy?" He laid his head on my shoulder and grabbed my shirt in his little hand. "I love you too." I rubbed his back as he buried his face in my neck.

"Looks like everyone is happy that you're here, including me," Dope said, standing.

"How were the kids?" Sebastian asked, giving Dope a slap on the shoulder.

"Busy. They kept us busy. My ass is tired." He chuckled, beaming at the twins.

"You two look like you need some coffee," Cami said as she headed to the kitchen.

Alaric and I joined her and left Sebastian and Dope to catch up.

"You look exhausted. How are you holding up?"

I brushed the stray hair from my eyes and smiled. "I'm super glad to be back, and even happier to stay for a while. I've missed Portland."

Cami gave me a concerned look as she placed a coffee cup beneath the spout of the espresso machine. "What about Sebastian? He's back on Death's stomping grounds. Isn't he worried?"

"No. We'll manage it like we always do." I couldn't tell her we had immunity for anything that Death did. The thought speared my chest like a thousand needles because the price was too high. I would never give Verity to the Pied Piper. Never.

Cami waved her hand in front of my face. "Where'd you go?"

"Sorry. Just a lot to process. Xavier won't be a problem any longer." I needed to let her know that I wasn't in danger from him at least.

Her brows shot up. "Did . . . Is he . . . ?"

"Alive? Yes, but he won't ever walk again. We traded him to the man that was behind my kidnapping for our freedom and protection." That was all I was willing to tell her.

Her lips formed an O. "That's good news, then. I won't ask any more questions, because I get the feeling I don't want to hear the answers."

I sat at the table and adjusted Alaric on my lap. He stuck his fist in his mouth, slurping loudly. "I won't tell you anything that would hurt you. Trust me on that one."

She started the next cup of coffee and leaned against the granite counter. "I know, and at first it pissed me off, but I was just upset about Ryan and . . . Death." She shook her head. "I'm not sure I'll ever get used to calling him that."

"It will grow on you and so will he. All I can say is that no one better fuck with you or there will be consequences." I shot her a knowing look and grinned.

"Oh hell, Ella. Seriously? He can't go around"—she moved her finger across her throat like she was slitting her neck—"deleting everyone that annoys me. No one would be left in this city."

I giggled, grateful for the lighter conversation.

"It's so not funny."

"It really is." I blew on my coffee and took a sip. Cami disappeared and delivered Sebastian his cup. We were definitely gaining some ground with her accepting him.

She returned a minute later and sat at the table with me.

"Have you talked to Ryan?"

Cami pursed her lips as sadness flashed in her gaze. "Yeah."

"And?" I couldn't help but remain hopeful that they could work things out. I understood where Cami was coming from, but it was hard to see her so unhappy. Him too.

"I told him it was over. I just can't sleep next to someone that has a hidden life. If he got caught, I would go down with him too. It's dangerous, and you and Sebastian keep me busy enough trying to dodge the shit you two stir up."

Cami's expression was sad and lost, and my heart ached for her. Even though she tried to hide it, she was clearly devastated by Ryan's betrayal. I suspected it was harder to leave someone when you were still madly in love with them. If I could, I would erase all her pain just to see her happy again. She deserved nothing less.

"Not sure I can disagree with that logic. I know that he kept you out of his work to keep you safe, but if I were in a serious committed relationship with Sebastian and learned about Death the way you did, I would be upset and most likely end the relationship too." I didn't tell her that I'd contemplated running, but I knew that Death would track me down, so it was a moot point. Honestly, I hadn't ever wanted to leave him. I was just scared about a life with a serial killer. Now, I was running from a different monster, the Pied Piper.

We continued to chat over coffee until it was time to put the kids down for a nap. I needed one as well, but I knew I wouldn't sleep unless Sebastian held me.

I kissed the kids goodbye as Sebastian and I left to check on Velvet Vortex, the bar and restaurant he and Kip owned together. It was a relief to do something normal for a change, and I was looking forward to having a nice meal and a few drinks with my husband.

The moment I stepped into the elevator, my stomach clenched. The enclosed space, too similar to the glass cage, made my palms sweat and my breathing shallow. Sebastian must have noticed because he immediately pulled me against him.

"Count with me, baby," he whispered. "Five things you can see."

I focused on his voice, on the grounding exercise we'd developed. "Your blue shirt. The floor numbers. Your wedding ring. The elevator buttons. My reflection in the mirror."

By the time we reached the lobby, my heart had stopped trying to escape my chest, but my legs still trembled.

"Let's get you outside in the fresh air." He led me out of the building and to the garage where he kept the BMW. I inhaled deeply, filling my lungs with the healing touch of the outdoors. Sebastian gave me a few minutes to settle down before we got into the car.

"It's good to be back home." He reached over the console and squeezed my hand. "I wanted to let you know that I've upgraded everything at the penthouse," Sebastian explained. "Dope installed military-grade surveillance and motion sensors on every floor. The elevator needs both keycard and biometric access now. No one gets within fifty feet of this building without us knowing. I hope it helps."

"It does . . . a lot. Thank you." I nibbled on my lower lip and then said, "As much as I love upstate New York, I think it would be best to sell the place. I'm so sorry. I don't think I can go back there."

Sebastian frowned. "You don't have anything to apologize for, baby. I didn't protect you the way I should have."

"You can't keep blaming yourself. We had no idea we were being watched."

"We do now," Sebastian muttered, anger in his voice. "Ella, I know something happened with the Pied Piper when he took you to the side to talk. Please tell me. You've been acting strange ever since."

The glass of the passenger window blurred with tears that were about to spill, my fingers trembling against the cold surface. Every word caught in my throat like shards of broken glass—each potential revelation was a dagger that could slice through the fragile peace we'd fought so hard to maintain. Sebastian couldn't know. The weight of my silence pressed against me, a suffocating burden that threatened to crush my lungs.

My daughter. My beautiful, vulnerable daughter. The thought of exposing her to even a whisper of additional danger made my heart seize with a primal, raw terror that cut deeper than any physical wound. I'd become an expert at swallowing pain, at burying truths so deep they might never see the light again.

The Pied Piper's identity burned in me like a fever, a toxic knowledge that could destroy everything. And yet, I would endure. I would protect. No matter the personal cost, no matter how much each unspoken word felt like a betrayal, I would keep my family safe. Even if it meant carrying this darkness alone, consuming me from the inside out.

I blinked hard, swallowing the storm of emotions, and prepared to wear my mask of calm. Again.

"I'm processing it all. I went through a lot, and we're just now settling down enough for it all to hit me like an avalanche. I almost lost you and the kids—lost my entire life." The pain and the memories pressed against me like a cement block on my chest. "As for the conversation with the Pied Piper, I just wanted to make sure that he could be trusted. I'm still not sure, but he promised to take care of us again. He said he wanted to meet me and that I was special for being able to marry you and hide your secret. I also asked about Xavier, and he promised he would never bother us and that Xavier was under his care. It was interesting because he seemed to really care about Xavier. The rest of the time he was devoid of any emotion."

"Other than living at the penthouse where we're safer, I'm not sure what else to do to help you heal. I fucking hate it. I hate watching you hurt and pretend to be all right when I know you're struggling, Ella."

His words were a protective shield. He saw me. His love wrapped me in a warm blanket and reminded me that he would be by my side every step of the way. Even when he wasn't physically with me, I knew Sebastian would remain close by. If he wasn't, then Kip and Dope would be with me. Yet, even amidst the relief they provided, I found solace in moments of solitude, and I longed to make peace with them. But it was a small price to pay for never being imprisoned in a glass cage again.

I was painfully aware that time could not be rushed, but today, this minute, I had the privilege of being with an incredible man who would move mountains for me. Taking a deep, calming breath, I lifted my chin defiantly, ready to embrace the night with my husband, my soulmate. Together, there was nothing we couldn't conquer. We had already proven our strength and resilience through countless trials.

CHAPTER 52

DEATH

The flock remembers a lamb that was led astray.
The shadows remember a soul that finally found its way.
—Anonymous

"Where are you taking me?"

Ella's laughter echoed through the air, a stark contrast to the quiet terror that still lingered in our minds after her kidnapping. The scent of spring blossoms filled our senses, a reminder of the world moving on while we did the same one day at a time.

After Ella's abduction, Sebastian and I had made a pact to spend more of our days with our family to make sure they felt safe and loved. Despite not being able to switch back and forth at will, we were always aware of each other's presence and could sense each other's minds.

"This way, little lamb." I slipped my arm around her waist and led her to the rose garden in Portland. Cami had taken care of Ella's hair and makeup under the guise that I was taking Ella on a special date, and I was. The tricky part had been to blindfold her and have Cami help her get dressed. Their giggles had filled the bed and breakfast we'd rented out. Sebastian and I weren't sure how we were going to keep all of this a secret from Ella, but Kip, Dope, Ryan, and Cami had been excited to help. At one point, when we were all making plans while Ella was giving the kids a bath, the tension between Ryan and Cami had reached new heights. I had glowered at them and said, "This is Ella's day we're planning. So whatever is still between you two, fuck it out, and get over it."

"Oh, shit. My heel just sank into the grass." Ella tugged on my arm, stopping me while she tried to work her shoe out of the dirt while blindfolded.

"I've got it." Cami hurried to her best friend and freed the shoe. "There you go." She brushed off her hands and gave me a big grin. We'd come a long way, and I was grateful for Ella's sake. The only reason Cami was important to me was because she was my little lamb's best friend, and the kids loved her too. It was good enough for me, and I'd made a huge effort not to terrify her. Every once in a while I couldn't help myself, though.

"Be still, little lamb," I said, before I scooped her up in my arms and carried her the rest of the way.

"I might like this," she whispered against my ear and nipped at my neck.

"You're making me hard. Stop. We will have plenty of time for that later."

"Oh, so serious." Her joking tone was peace to my ears.

"You have no idea," I muttered, wishing I could adjust myself, but we had an audience. I slowed when we reached our destination. "I'm going to set you down." I lowered her until her feet touched the ground and she gained her balance.

"Ma-ma!" the kids squealed in unison.

"Can I see now?" she asked, her question brimming with curiosity.

I removed her blindfold carefully in order not to mess up her hair. Cami had threatened my life if I didn't protect her work of art. I had resisted the urge to tell her that Ella was already a work of art, but for once I kept my mouth closed.

Ella's green eyes filled with wonder as she looked around. Dope wore a black suit with a white dress shirt and blue tie. Kip also wore a black suit, but his tie was crimson and matched mine. Cami and the twins stood on the opposite side of the men, dressed in red and black. Even though it was spring, the colors were fitting, plus I had insisted on them.

"What's happening?" Her gaze landed on the few seats, and her smile grew. "Why is everyone so dressed up?" She glanced down at her red dress and gasped. "Death, what's going on?"

No white for my Ella—I knew better than anyone the stains we both carried. How fitting that I chose the color of blood, the shade that had marked every significant moment of our shared history.

I lowered to one knee. "You married the wrong man," I growled as I reached into the inside jacket pocket and produced a wedding ring set.

I lifted the lid, and the two-carat princess-cut diamond sparkled in the sunlight. Sebastian and I had agreed on the engagement band, but the smaller diamonds on each side were carefully chosen by me.

"Marry me, little lamb. Make me whole."

The seconds ticked by as she stared at me in awe, love and astonishment flashing over her beautiful face. "Of course I'll marry you, Death," she whispered.

She extended her hand, and I carefully removed her current wedding set and slipped them into my pocket.

Dope cleared his throat and rocked back on his heels. "Are we ready to perform the ceremony?" He grinned as if he had just ended world hunger.

Standing before her, I felt the familiar sensation of being co-conscious with Sebastian, both of us present in this moment. The crimson of her dress caught the light, and I appreciated how she wore something that acknowledged both sides of who we were—both Sebastian and me.

When it came time for our vows, I felt myself emerge fully, my voice carrying the deeper timbre that Ella had learned to recognize as mine. "I came into existence to protect Sebastian, to carry his pain. But you, Ella—you saw me as more than just a protector. You understood that I wasn't simply a fragment of darkness. You recognized me as my own self while still loving the whole of who we are."

My hands—our hands—reached for hers, steadier than Sebastian's would have been in this moment. "I've spent years existing in the shadows of Sebastian's life, emerging only in moments of necessity. But you brought me into the light. You showed me that I could be more than just the keeper of his trauma. That I could love . . . that I could build something of my own while still remaining part of him."

As I lost myself in her presence, I was drawn to the light she carried within her even as it illuminated the shadows that clung to me like a second skin. And as I looked into Ella's eyes once more, I knew without a shadow of doubt that our journey together would be paved with unspeakable horrors and twisted pleasures beyond imagining. She was *my queen*, my scarlet lamb, and I would lay down my life for her. My throat tightened with emotions so deep for this woman, I wasn't sure how to manage them. I turned my attention back to the ceremony.

"I vow to protect you not just as Sebastian's protector, but as someone who loves you in my own right. I won't promise that things will be simple—living with our system never is. But I swear that both of us, Sebastian and I, will love you with everything we are." The space between my consciousness and Sebastian's blurred as I finished, "In every moment, whether I'm present or within, whether you're speaking to him or to me, you are part of us both. This I vow, as Death, as part of Sebastian, and your husband."

Looking into her eyes, I saw no fear, no hesitation, only love of both sides of who we were. Ella was unafraid of the darkness that lurked inside me, and a sense of euphoria washed over me. The cold grip of my past sins loosened its hold as I gazed into her trusting face, filled with a love so pure it felt like a blade slicing through my twisted soul. Her unwavering acceptance of my duality, the light and the shadow intertwined within me, was a balm to my tormented spirit.

"I have a confession," she said, her cheeks reddening slightly. "I wrote vows for you a long time ago." Her fingers tightened around mine.

The corners of my mouth lifted. "I'm ready to hear them, little lamb."

She cleared her throat before she started. "Death, when I first fell in love with Sebastian, I knew I was falling in love with all of him, but you were an added bonus. Some might call what we have complicated, but to me, it's beautifully simple. I love every part of who you both are. When you emerge, I don't see darkness or fear. I see strength, safety, and a love so fierce it takes my breath away." Her voice wavered slightly, but her gaze remained steady on mine. "I vow to be your safe harbor, just as you've been ours. When you surface, you'll never need to hide or retreat. I promise to love you as your own self, while honoring the beautiful complexity of who you and Sebastian are together. I won't ever ask you to be less than what you are—a warrior, a part of the man I love." A tear slipped down her cheek, but her smile was radiant. "I vow to stand beside both of you. To be strong when Sebastian needs softness and gentle when you need rest. To understand your silences and your storms. To never make you choose between being his protector and being yourself."

She reached up to touch my face, a gesture so tender it made even my hardened heart ache. "This is my promise to you, Death. To love you wholly, to accept you completely, and to walk beside you both in this beautiful, complex life we're building together."

I felt Sebastian stir within our consciousness, equally moved by her words, as our shared love for her created a perfect moment of harmony between us.

I slipped the wedding rings on her finger, then Kip offered her a new band for me. It was two-toned white and yellow gold, which symbolized both Sebastian and me.

Ella's eyes misted over as she looked up at me.

I lowered my mouth to her ear and whispered, "Little lamb, you're the flicker of light in my dark, dark world. The color in my grayscale existence. I yearn for you like the night yearns for the stars."

As we were pronounced husband and wife, a chilling realization crept over me. She was now entwined with me not just in love but in sin. A twisted smile tugged at the corners of my lips before I leaned in and kissed her. In that instant, I realized that she was mine in every sense of the word, bound to me not just by love but by the darkness that stained my soul.

As the last rays of sunlight painted the sky in deep crimsons and golds, I felt myself beginning to recede, letting Sebastian emerge fully to share the experience. In that space between, where our consciousness merged, we were united in a single thought. She was ours, and we were hers, in all our broken, beautiful imperfection.

Ella's fingers intertwined with ours, and I caught her secret smile. The one that said she knew exactly who she was looking at in this moment of transition. She'd once told us that loving us was like watching the sun and moon share the same sky, each essential, each beautiful in their own right.

As Sebastian took control, his love flowing alongside mine, I carried this truth with me into our shared depths. Some people spend their whole lives searching for someone to accept their darkness. We'd found someone who not only accepted it but saw it as an essential part of who we were—guardian and protected, darkness and light, Sebastian and Death.

In the end, that's what love really was. Not the absence of shadows, but having someone who will walk with you through them, hand in hand, unafraid.

CHAPTER 53

DEATH

In the valley of the shadows, the lost lamb learns that darkness, too, can be a kind of belonging.
—Anonymous

My queen had been breathtaking during our wedding, and now I couldn't wait to present her with my wedding gift in Washington state near the San Juan Islands.

"Where are we going?" she asked as the truck crept down the narrow dirt lane. The dense foliage of trees hid the road so well that I'd almost missed it myself. But it was perfect for what I needed.

"You'll see." I arched a brow at her, my gaze running up and down her gorgeous body.

I turned left and drove off the path into a secluded area where we wouldn't be found. Turning off the engine, I looked over at her, unbuckled our seat belts, and then opened my door, ignoring her questioning gaze. Reaching behind the seat, I retrieved a bag I'd hidden before our trip.

I flashed her a wicked grin as I set the bag on the floorboard near the brake and gas pedal. "Face me and spread your legs, little lamb."

Once Ella was situated, I tugged on her ankles and pulled her across the bench seat toward me, sending a rush of desire through my entire being. With each pull, her dress rode higher and higher on her thighs, revealing more of the black satin thong that taunted me. My fingers hooked onto the sides of the material, and I slowly eased it down her legs.

I glanced up at her, then I buried my face in her pussy and ran my tongue along her clit.

Her moans of pleasure filled the car as I teased her nice and slow.

"You always know how to make me feel good." She grabbed my hair and lifted her hips off the seat.

I nipped and licked until I brought her to the edge, then sat up and wiped her juices off my chin. I opened the bag and removed the remote-control mini vibrator. I chuckled as I inserted it into her slick cunt, then fumbled with the remote and turned it on.

"Oh." Her eyes widened as I played with the speeds before deciding to leave it on low.

"You'll keep that in until I tell you otherwise. Understand?"

"Yeah." Her response was breathy, and her pupils dilated with desire.

I held my hand out to her as she climbed out of the car on my side. Her palm rested on my shoulder as I knelt to assist her with putting her thong back on. After she was situated, I rose and gazed down at my stunning wife. "Are you ready for your wedding gift?"

She placed her palms on my chest and beamed up at me. "You are my wedding gift. I don't need anything else."

I ran my knuckles along her soft cheek. "I made a promise I was unable to keep, but I think this will make up for it."

She tilted her head into my touch. "If you insist." Ella flashed me a sweet smile.

"Follow me." I grasped her hand firmly and guided us along the trail, the sun shining down and illuminating our path as we made our way deeper into the forest. The abandoned building was barely visible, hidden amongst the overgrown trees and bushes. Even when we were close to the entrance, it was hard to spot. I reached into my pocket and retrieved the key, then swiftly unlocked the padlock.

"Watch your step."

"Maybe I should have worn better shoes." She carefully chose where to walk and entered.

"I have boots for you here." A sinister grin eased across my face.

She giggled, and I could tell she had an idea about her present, but there was still something she didn't know. That was the real surprise.

Holding hands, we strolled to the back of the building until we reached the room I had in mind. The creaking sound of the door opening was so loud it would have alerted anyone nearby that we had arrived. I flicked on the light switch and waited for our eyes to adjust before closing the door behind us.

Ella looked up at me with a quizzical expression. "Who is that?" She pointed to the man suspended on a hook from the ceiling.

Ropes wrapped around his torso, pinning his arms against his body, and a dirty gag was stuffed into his mouth. I walked over to a button and pushed it, and the hook lowered until his feet touched the floor.

"Can I get closer?" Ella asked with a hint of excitement in her tone.

My cock twitched with the idea that Ella wanted to dive into the dark waters with me. "Of course."

She approached and circled him, looking him up and down. "You look familiar." My little lamb removed the dirty rag from his mouth, and he licked his parched lips.

"Hello, Ella. It's been a long time." His voice was raspy and hoarse from lack of water.

I located the thermos and cup I kept in the corner and poured a little bit of water. "Here, little lamb. You'll want his throat nice and wet so his screams will be heard." I sneered at him as I gave it to her.

She placed the cup to his mouth and tipped it up, allowing him a few sips before she returned it to me.

"I don't remember who you are. Should I?" She glanced at me and then at him.

"Tell her," I growled.

He swallowed, his eyes shifting between us. "Jameson. We knew each other when we were kids . . . We spent some time at John Bordeaux's house after school."

Ella's mouth dropped in shock. "We were friends," she whispered. She whirled on her heel. "Death, there's been a mistake. He shouldn't be here. Jameson helped me turn John in to the authorities."

I placed a finger beneath her chin. "There's no mistake, little lamb. He's here just for you." I slid my hand around her waist and to her back to place a calming palm on her. She would need it in a moment.

"Jameson has been looking for his father." I waited for that to sink in.

"Who's his father? I don't remember ever meeting his parents, but it was years ago, and I had John to deal with."

Jameson cleared his throat. "I can't believe that after all of this time you haven't figured it out." He laughed as if he didn't have a care in the world and wasn't about to meet an incredibly unpleasant death.

Her gaze narrowed on him, and she approached him until she was almost in his face. "Tell me."

"If I'm going to die, then I might as well have some fun first." He gave her a big grin. Jameson had no idea what he was doing. Pissing off my little lamb was dangerous territory.

I walked across the room and retrieved one of the knives and a pair of boots I had laid out on the table.

"Ella." I motioned for her to join me. "Put these on."

She nodded and slipped off the black flats that complemented her black-and-white dress. Soon it would be stained in crimson, and the thought of her covered in blood made my cock painfully hard.

Once she changed her shoes, I reached in my pocket and turned up the vibrator. Her eyes closed and a soft moan escaped her full lips.

"That's it. Feel the pleasure coursing through you as you think about taking his life, Ella."

Her fingers bunched her dress at the waist, and I adjusted the speed to low once again. She took the knife from my hand, her gaze wild with lust and the darkness I hadn't seen in a long time.

Her chin tipped up as she returned to Jameson. She placed the tip of the knife to his neck and pressed it into his skin until a bloom of blood marked him. "What have I not figured out?"

Jameson's eyes bulged with a mixture of fear and adrenaline as the cold blade dug into him, ready to cut through flesh at any moment.

"Who I am," he stammered, his voice shaking uncontrollably.

I leaned against the wall, my arms crossed over my chest, and watched with a sick satisfaction.

"Tell her," I commanded, my tone dripping with venom. A twisted smirk spread across my face as I anticipated the chaos that was about to unfold.

"I'm John's son," he confessed, his words trembling with both shame and defiance.

"What?" Her voice cut through the air, filled with shock and anger. "John never mentioned having a son, or any children at all."

"Keep going," I growled, my patience wearing thin. My little lamb deserved to know.

"He had me," Jameson continued, his voice cracking under the weight of his guilt. "I lived with my mother, which made it easier for me to help lure innocent kids to his home." The words hung in the air like a toxic cloud, poisoning the room with their sickening truth.

"You were bait?" Ella staggered backward with the news. "I thought we were friends. You helped me turn him in. We made sure he was distracted so I could slip out of the house."

"Kind of. If you recall, John was long gone by the time the cops came to arrest him."

Ella's expression fell, then morphed into one filled with rage.

"You lured all of us into his basement," she said, venom lacing each of her words. "You pretended that he hurt you too, but now that I think about it, I never actually saw him touch or record you." Her hand shook, and the knife jabbed into his neck. "It was all a lie. Everything that came out of your mouth was a goddamn lie, and you supported him." With a loud roar, she ran the blade down his chest and cut through the ropes that bound him. They dropped to the cement floor with a heavy smack. Due to lack of blood flow and poor circulation, Jameson's legs couldn't hold him, and he collapsed.

"Little lamb, Jameson was looking for his father after we killed him. He got a bit too close for comfort, and once I learned the truth about him, I thought he would make up for Xavier."

Ella flinched with his name.

"Thank you," she said softly, never taking her attention from her prey.

"What are you going to do with him, little lamb?" I stroked the remote in my pocket, ready to turn it up as her fury escalated and the darkness consumed her.

With a quick move, Ella raised her foot and delivered a kick to Jameson's chin, sending him sprawling backward. "That's for the innocent kids you lured into the devil's den." She circled him, her muscles tense and ready to pounce. "Do you know how good it felt to kill your father? His screams echoed through the warehouse as I plunged the knife into him over and over." Her chest heaved as she recalled the experience and shared it blow by blow with Jameson.

The color drained from his cheeks as he realized he wasn't dealing with the sweet little girl he used to know. The vulnerable, powerless girl. I suppressed my chuckle and continued to watch the show unfold.

Ella laughed as she knelt in front of him and unbuttoned his pants. She reached in and grabbed his limp dick and pulled on him.

"Gonna get me off one last time before you kill me? You always were a cock hungry whore."

I chuckled, understanding exactly what she was about to do. My little lamb continued to impress me.

In one swift motion, she sliced off Jameson's dick. His agonized screams reverberated throughout the room, and she quickly shoved his severed dick into his mouth, silencing his cries of pain. I turned up the vibrator just a little, rewarding her with the ecstasy she craved.

Blood spurted from his open wound, and Ella reached over and sliced off one of his ears and placed it on the floor next to him.

Snot and tears streamed down his face as he attempted to plead with her around his cock. As much as I wanted to jump in and assist, this was about Ella and allowing her the safety to embrace her darkness, lean into it, and feed the beast that she'd kept contained for so long. I couldn't give her the Pied Piper and Xavier, but Jameson would help her heal a little more. It would empower her so she never feared any man again. That was my gift to her. Power. Pleasure in the pain.

She stood and circled him slowly.

As I watched Ella stand before the man who had lured her to a pedophile, a delicious chill ran down my spine. Her eyes, usually filled with warmth and kindness, now burned with a fiery rage that made me smile.

Ella's slender fingers curled around the knife, the blade glinting in the faint light as she stepped closer to Jameson. The room was heavy with a tense silence broken only by the sound of her slow, deliberate footsteps on the cold concrete floor. I could see the raw determination in her expression mingled with a hint of vulnerability.

With every step she took, I felt a surge of conflicting emotions within me—anger at the man and a twisted sense of satisfaction at the thought of justice being served.

And then it began. Ella's movements were swift and precise, each cut drawing forth a gush of crimson that splattered against the walls like macabre art. She didn't flinch at the sight of the blood pooling on the floor or spurting onto her face and body, her gaze unwavering as she inflicted pain upon the man who had caused her so much suffering.

I stood there, rooted to the spot, unable to tear my attention away from the scene unfolding before me. The air was heavy with the metallic scent and the echoes of muffled screams. It was a dance of death and vengeance, with Ella as its ruthless conductor.

And yet, there was a strange sense of poignancy to it all. As Ella continued her slow, steady progress around the man, each cut more calculated than the last, I couldn't help but feel as though I were witnessing not just a moment of reckoning, but a transformative act of self-discovery.

Her once soft, delicate fingers now bore the marks of deep scarlet stains, and yet they seemed to glow with a newfound strength and purpose. Her eyes, those warm pools of compassion that had always drawn me toward her, now burned with an intensity that held the very essence of life and death.

The room around us—cold, concrete, and unyielding—seemed almost alive with the energy of their struggle. Every movement, every breath, every flicker of emotion was magnified in that dreary space, as if some unseen force was using this moment to carve itself into our very souls.

And through it all, I found myself standing there in silent reverence. This wasn't only about revenge or retribution. It was about two souls dancing on the razor's edge.

In those moments, I saw not a woman seeking vengeance or justice, but rather one who was attempting to reconcile her past with her present. To find solace in the knowledge that she could rise above her trauma and transform herself into something stronger, more resilient.

As the man's screams finally faded into silence, Ella stood there panting and drenched in blood, her once delicate features now etched with fierce intensity. She looked at me for what seemed like an eternity.

I tapped the remote control and turned up the vibrator.

"Death," she said as she sank to her knees in Jameson's blood. "Oh god." She bunched her blood-soaked dress and pulled it up to her waist, exposing her thong to me. With a quick slice of her knife, the black satin material fell into the puddle beneath her.

"That's it, scarlet lamb. Experience the adrenaline rush and exhilaration from the kill pulsing through your veins."

Her mouth parted as her eyes closed, and her free hand sneaked down her lower belly and between her legs. She rubbed her clit, her gaze connecting with mine again.

"That's it. Play with that pussy while you're covered in another man's blood."

Unable to stand it any longer, I unbuttoned and lowered my zipper, freeing my hard cock. Her attention locked onto my dick, and her tongue darted across her lips.

Her eyes gleamed as she continued, taunting me with her disobedience. "Are you defying me?"

She bit her lip while she pleasured herself.

"There are consequences for disobeying me, Ella." My voice was low and deadly as I approached her. Once I closed the gap between us, she reached up and tugged my jeans down to my knees and then she wrapped her hand around my cock. Staring down at her bowing before me and covered in blood nearly sent me over the edge of oblivion.

She gave me a sinister grin as she stroked me, and then she brought her knife up to my thigh and pressed the tip into my skin. I stilled, wondering if she had sacrificed her fucking sanity when she'd killed Jameson.

Her tongue flicked across the head of my cock, and she sucked, slowly, as she dragged the knife closer to my balls.

"You need to stop, little lamb. You're playing with fire."

She batted her long lashes at me as the sharp blade teasingly brushed against my sensitive skin. My pulse raced with fear and arousal as I watched her toy with the idea of cutting me. Ella laughed, enjoying the power she held over me, before dragging the weapon down my thigh, leaving a thin trail of blood in its wake. Her dilated eyes widened with desire as she licked off the crimson drops, savoring the metallic taste on her lips.

"Bleed for me, Death," she demanded, her voice dripping with sadistic delight.

She continued to cut my legs, each one met with an eager lick from her blood-stained tongue. But I couldn't deny how incredibly turned on I was by her reckless behavior. My scarlet lamb was meeting me on a new playing field, and I craved more of her dangerous games.

Ella's attention shifted to my groin again, and with a grin, she ran the knife's edge along my pulsing vein. I sucked in a sharp breath at the sight of my blood throbbing beneath the blade. She leaned closer, her attention fixated on the life that flowed from me, and I could see the hunger in her.

"You are mine," she growled, her voice rough as she bit down on my thigh. I cried out in a mix of pain and pleasure as she marked me with her teeth, leaving a red imprint on my skin. My heart pounded as I felt her possessive claims on me. Her dominance over me was both frightening and exhilarating, and I found myself craving her touch more than ever.

The moment she moved the blade and pressed it to the underside of my dick, I grabbed a fist full of her hair and jerked her back.

"You're flirting with the devil, scarlet lamb."

She smiled up at me before she said, "I know."

Respect and curiosity for her bravery swirled inside my chest, but she had to submit. I pried her mouth open and shoved my cock into it. "Choke on it, my little slut." Shoving all the way into the back of her throat, I cut off her air supply. As the seconds ticked by, tears filled her eyes and snot dangled from her nostrils. Her nails clawed at my legs as her expression pleaded with me to let her breathe. Her face reddened as I held my ground, forcing her to remember who she bowed to. Her eyelids fluttered, then I pulled out. She coughed and gasped for air, glaring at me.

I reached out and smoothed her hair, comforting her. "You did well, scarlet lamb. I never expected you to push my limits." I cupped her chin and forced her to look at me. "I am the only man allowed to break you. I am your god, and you will bow and worship me."

Her gaze softened, and I suspected she was remembering the first time I said that to her.

"Do you want me to fuck you?"

She nodded, swallowing over her tears.

"That's my good cum slut." I helped her stand. My fingers danced along her inner thigh, and I turned off the vibrator with my free hand.

"I'm taking this out of your cunt." I removed an anal vibrator from the pocket of my jeans as she held onto me for balance. "Turn around and bend over."

She willingly obeyed. I wedged her legs apart, allowing me better access. I slipped the new toy into her soaking wet pussy and fucked her slowly with it. Once it was wet again, I placed it against her tight asshole and slid it in. After it was situated, I turned it on low.

"Oh. My. God."

"My blood whore loves it in the ass, don't you?"

"Y-yes." She trembled as I ran my cock over her slick cunt before

I grabbed her hips and held her in place as I forcefully shoved inside of her.

"Tell me what it was like plunging the knife into Jameson." I continued to fuck her as she gave me details of how it felt to stab him over and over until the life drained from his eyes.

"Your tight pussy is even tighter with the toy in your ass." I picked up my pace as I buried myself deep inside her. "Will you kill again, little lamb? Will I fuck you next to another body and in their blood?"

"Yes!" she screamed, nearing the edge of her orgasm.

"Look at him, Ella. Look at the work of art laying on the floor next to you. His mouth slack and his eyes lifeless."

She turned her head and looked at Jameson's mutilated corpse while her cunt gripped my throbbing cock as I pounded into her.

"I-I can't wait any longer," she gasped.

I slipped my hand between her legs and located her swollen clit, rubbing it.

"Come for me. Come on my dick, little lamb."

Her scream bounced off the walls, and with wild abandon, she writhed against me as if possessed, driving me deeper into her with each thrust. Her body convulsed, begging for release as I ravaged her mercilessly. Every nerve inside me ignited with desire as I plunged into her, feeling her tightness grip and pull at my throbbing shaft. In one final explosion of passion, my balls tightened, and I emptied myself inside of her eager cunt, filling her with every last drop of my hot cum.

Slowly, I pulled out of her, and I removed the toy before she straightened. She turned and as she reached for me, I saw the pain in her eyes, a reflection of the emotions that had driven her to kill. It was then that I realized that this was not just about vengeance. It was about survival, about finding a way to heal from her unspeakable trauma.

We remained silent as I reached out and enveloped her in my embrace, feeling every bit of fear and pain she had endured flow into me. We stood there for what felt like hours, clinging onto each other as if our lives depended on it. It was a moment of raw vulnerability, a testament to the strength of human connection amidst darkness and chaos.

Slowly, we disentangled ourselves and looked around at the aftermath of what had just transpired. It was as if time had slowed down, each tick and tock amplified by the weight of our actions. And yet, there was a sense of resolve that emanated from us both, a determination to move forward together despite everything that had happened.

I tipped her chin up and placed a kiss on her mouth. "I hope you liked your wedding gift."

She laughed. "It was amazing. Thank you."

We stood in the middle of the room, kissing. Her blood-soaked clothes stained mine with a life that no longer deserved to exist.

Finally, we broke our embrace. "One last thing."

She arched a brow at me as she followed me to the table that held the weapons and cleaners. To the right was a small container that I'd covered with a white towel and placed a gold bow on top of. "For you." I motioned for her to lift the cloth.

My little lamb lifted the covering and revealed a glass jar with two eyeballs floating in a clear solution. She gasped, her hand flying to her mouth, before she laughed and grinned up at me.

"The man that drove to your house and distracted you while another jabbed a needle in your neck . . . I give you his eyes. He will never be able to see you or hurt you again."

Ella's brows rose and then she giggled. "You plucked out his eyes for me?"

"I did. It will be a forever reminder of who holds the power, little lamb. We do. Always."

"Yes," she agreed. "Y'know, most girls like jewelry."

"Not my girl."

She threw her arms around my neck and pressed her eager mouth to mine.

"I love you, little lamb. You will always be my queen."

"Always."

I rubbed her back before I spoke. "Kip and Ryan will be here shortly. Let's get cleaned up and leave."

She nodded eagerly, and I led her out of the room and to a small bathroom we used to clean up. After our shower, I toweled her dry and handed her a change of clothes. Ella laughed as she realized how prepared I was.

Forty minutes later, I'd collected my tools and left the cleaning supplies for the guys.

"Are you ready?"

"Yes." She beamed at me as we made our way out of the building and into the remaining moments of sunlight.

"Where to next?" she asked as we walked to the truck.

The hair on the back of my neck rose as I spotted our vehicle. I slowed and placed my finger to my lips, silencing her. Her shoulders tensed as we both looked around, holding our breath as we surveyed our surroundings. No one had followed us here, but I was well aware that we were always being watched.

"I don't see anyone," she whispered. Ella squeezed my hand, and I understood what she was telling me. She didn't see anyone, but she sensed them.

The sound of fresh twigs snapping caught our attention, and we waited on edge and ready to fight. Clapping rang through the forest before we saw him appear.

"A beautiful show, Ella. Congratulations." The Pied Piper appeared in front of us almost out of thin air.

I stepped ahead of my wife, my eyes narrowing on him. "What do you want?" I snarled.

"Relax, Death. I just wanted to see what this young lady is made of. Very impressive stuff, I might add. Next time you should check your table for a hidden camera."

I growled, knowing damn well I'd scanned every inch of that place before I brought Ella. The son of a bitch must have snuck in during my wedding.

Ella's body stiffened against mine, and I reached behind me and kept my palm on her leg.

"We're just leaving." My fingers flexed as they itched for my knife. If I needed it, I knew that Ella would remove it from the back of my jeans and place it in my palm. After all, I had promised not to kill the motherfucker the last time I saw him. I never promised about the next time.

"Don't get all riled up. I just wanted to congratulate the happy couple on their nuptials." He took a few steps forward. "And this." The Pied Piper reached into the front pocket of his slacks and removed a white envelope, then handed it to me.

"What is it?" I asked, not trusting anything he did.

"Look inside."

Ella peered around me as I opened it and lifted out a piece of paper.

"The deed to the replica of your childhood home is now in yours and Ella's names. Not your real names, of course, but it's yours. Tear it down, live in it, do whatever you need to do. Xavier won't need it any longer."

"Why?" Ella asked. "What motivated you to give us the rights to it?"

The Pied Piper smiled. "Because to move forward into the people you're meant to be, you have to destroy the past and create a new future. This house meant pain for both of you. Now you have the power to do with it as you wish." A car pulled up next to ours, and the Pied Piper nodded. "That's my ride. Again, congratulations on the wedding. I'll be seeing you around." He gave us a wolfish smile and a small wave goodbye.

We stood still as we watched him climb in the car, then drive off.

"Death?"

I stared at the paper in my hands. "That was unexpected."

"It was . . . but—" She peered up at me, her idea evident in her eyes.

"Is that what you want?" I dragged my knuckles down her cheek.

"Yes," she whispered. "Do you?"

"Definitely." I gave her a wicked little grin, and then we hurried to the car.

We'd taken an unplanned trip back to Minnesota and to the replica of my childhood home. My little lamb and I had gathered what we needed, then went to work. At first, she was stressed, but as we worked, she began to smile. We kept the conversation light and began to plan our future for us and our children.

Hours later, we stood outside of the house, staring at it.

"I hope this gives you some closure, Death. All the pain, all the horrible memories for both you and Sebastian. Maybe this will set you free."

"It's not only my hell anymore, but also yours too, little lamb. Maybe we will both find peace."

I grasped her hand tightly, our fingers intertwined as the final remnants of gold, blue, and pink painted the sky with the sinking sun.

"Are you ready?" I asked.

"Yes. I'm ready."

I reached into my pocket and pulled out a brand-new burner phone. There was one last thing I had to do before we left. Once it was done, I replaced the cell and took a deep breath.

"See you in hell, motherfuckers," I sneered.

Ella and I dropped hands, and together, we circled the house like vengeful demons as we unleashed streams of fire that devoured everything in their path. As the flames raged higher, I signaled for Ella to move away from the inferno and tossed the last gas can into the blaze.

Sirens cut through the night as they grew closer, signaling it was our time to leave. They had been my one call before we torched the place.

In that moment, nothing else mattered except watching our past crumble to ashes in front of our very eyes. As long as Ella and I were together, we could face anything—even if it meant that we were monsters ourselves.

BONUS SCENE

Curious big brown eyes peered at me over the worn mahogany of the pew directly in front of Sebastian and me. I pressed my lips together to suppress a laugh as the frustrated mother, her dark hair escaping from a messy bun, tugged on her son's wrinkled blue button-down shirt and hissed for him to face forward. Sebastian's large palm settled on my thigh, his fingers creating heat that burned through the thin floral fabric of my sundress.

He leaned closer, and the sandalwood notes of his cologne wrapped around me like a hug as he pressed his lips against my cheekbone, utterly disinterested in the droning message. I couldn't blame him. Our only purpose in this vaulted sanctuary was to identify the next desperate mother and children for the Safe Horizon Society's help.

"These ancient pews are bloody torture devices," he murmured, his rich Australian accent rolling through me like warm honey.

I turned to face him, noting how crimson flooded his skin from his collar to his cheekbones. He cleared his throat, his blue eyes darkening beneath furrowed brows. His lips grazed the sensitive curve of my ear, his stubble scratching deliciously, as he whispered, "Death wants to fuck you against the cold marble altar once this place empties."

My pulse quickened instantly, a liquid heat pooling between my clenched thighs. I smoothed my suddenly trembling hands over my dress. "Business first."

I was still adjusting to the fact that Sebastian and Death were communicating with each other; I would catch fragments of those midnight whispers from the hallway, Sebastian's voice tight with frustration while Death's came in a hollow, echoing timbre. Sebastian struggled with that side of him, but I loved both men—the warm-eyed husband who brought me coffee in bed and the masked serial killer whose touch left me begging for more.

The polished oak pew creaked as we slid onto our knees, the worn velvet kneelers cushioning our descent while incense hung heavy in the air. As the congregation bowed their heads and murmured prayers in unison, Sebastian and I scanned the rows of people for Patricia's copper hair. For eight long weeks we'd watched her arrive with bruises hidden beneath high collars, clutching the tiny hands of her twin daughters in their matching Sunday dresses. Today we would finally approach her face-to-face about escaping the man whose wedding ring she wore like a shackle. My heart ached for those little girls with their identical braids and scuffed patent leather shoes.

Finally, the mass finished, and the congregation began to leave.

"There," Sebastian murmured as he nodded toward a familiar figure—Patricia. She stood gracefully, her hands firmly clasping those of her twin daughters, one on each side, their small faces peeking out from beneath matching hats.

We rose from our seats and waited as the crowd thinned more before we moved against the stream of people flowing toward the exit. Our steps were deliberate as we navigated toward the front of the church. Patricia's eyes darted nervously, scanning the sea of faces with an anxious edge. Her husband was out of town for the weekend, but he had a nasty habit of returning home unannounced, like a storm without warning. The last thing we wanted was to draw attention to her and the girls and increase the risk they already faced.

"Hi, I'm Ella." I reached out for her hand, noting how her fingers trembled before she briefly shook my hand and then withdrew them into the sleeves of her oversized cardigan. Her deep brown eyes, ringed with shadows of sleepless nights, darted between my face and the exit door. "It's nice to meet you."

Behind me, Sebastian leaned against the far wall, arms crossed over his chest to make himself smaller despite the impossible task. The fluorescent lights cast his six-foot-two frame in stark relief against the beige wall, his shoulders spanning nearly the width of the door—a guardian presence I found comforting but that made her press herself deeper into her own small frame, as if she could make herself disappear.

"It's okay. He's the founder of the Safe Horizon Society and my husband." I squeezed her trembling hand. "He'll protect you and the girls."

She nodded, her tongue skating nervously across her chapped lips. Her eyes kept darting toward the doorway where her daughters played with worn dolls on the faded carpet. "Greg is leaving on another business trip for about five days. I don't think he'll be able to come home early."

"When?" I kept my voice low, steady.

"In two more weeks." She twisted her wedding ring, the small diamond catching the overhead lights.

"Okay. We'll plan for that time. Please know that we'll have eyes on you in case we need to move faster, okay?" I shifted my weight from one foot to the other; my heels were pinching my toes.

"Yeah. Thank you." Her voice cracked, eyes glistening. "I-I can't thank you enough. The girls are getting older, and it's time."

I understood her careful choice of words, the way she censored herself with the children just feet away. One slip of the tongue, one careless mention of escape plans, and they might innocently repeat everything to Greg. The bruise peeking from beneath her sleeve told me why we kept them in the dark. Safety demanded secrecy.

After we spoke briefly about the details, I discreetly handed her a burner phone, emphasizing the crucial importance of keeping it hidden from prying eyes. She exhaled a deep sigh of relief as she accepted it, her fingers trembling slightly with the weight of what it represented.

"Just having someone to call if there's . . . ," she began, then her voice trailed off as her eyes flicked toward the children playing nearby before she continued, "an issue helps."

I offered her a warm, reassuring smile. "We'll be in touch once we have a meeting place arranged. All you need to do is pack whatever essentials you can fit in the trunk of the car and keep a low profile in the meantime."

Her eyes glistened with tears. "Okay. I can do that," she replied, her voice barely above a whisper.

I kept the remainder of our conversation brief, sensing the urgency in our situation, and then said my farewells to her and the girls, their innocent laughter a stark contrast to the tension in the air. I quietly walked to the side of the room, where my husband stood waiting, and I joined him with a heavy heart.

Sebastian pulled me against him in a warm embrace, his arms wrapping around me with comforting strength as I rested my head against his chest, trying to regain my composure. The rhythmic beating of his heart was soothing in the tense silence.

"It'll be okay, Ella," he murmured softly, his voice soothing my fears about the family. "We're giving them a safe fresh start. I know it's hard to see them so scared, but keep the end game in mind."

I tilted my head up and noticed the flicker of steel in his eyes. He winced as the muscles in his jaw tensed visibly.

"Goddammit. Really?" he muttered under his breath, bowing his head in frustration. Gently, I placed my hands on each of his temples and massaged lightly with my fingers as I tried to ease the tension and soothe the pain as Death began to emerge.

Gradually, he raised his head. The connection between us was palpable as our gazes locked, a silent understanding passing between us.

"Little lamb." His voice was low, gruff. The sound vibrated through my bones like distant thunder.

"Hi." I smiled at him, my heart immediately feeling better with his presence, as if the stained glass windows had suddenly let in more light.

"The people have cleared the sanctuary." He gave me a wicked little smile as his head tilted toward the altar at the front of the room, its marble gleaming under the soft glow of candles.

"You know the priest is still around." I sunk my teeth into my bottom lip as his hand, warm and calloused, trailed beneath my dress and up the inside of my thigh, leaving goosebumps in its wake. My breath hitched as his fingertips massaged my clit through the thin fabric of my black lace thong, sending electric pulses up my spine.

"Then we should be quick about it."

He moved my thong out of the way, the fabric sliding against my swollen flesh, and teased my sensitive skin with deliberate, knowing circles.

"You're wet, little lamb. Are you ready for me to bend you over the altar and hear you beg your god for more as I fuck you deep enough to make the saints blush?"

I giggled nervously as he took my hand, his fingers entwining with mine. He led me down the aisle, our footsteps echoing through the vast, empty chamber. The scent of wood polish filled my nostrils, and the stained glass windows cast kaleidoscopic patterns on the stone floor. Once we reached the altar, I looked around the room, my attention scanning the wooden pews and the balcony above, but we were still alone.

"Anyone could walk in at any given moment," I whispered, my voice barely audible, as if the very walls might hear me.

He wrapped his hands around my waist, his touch firm yet gentle, and lifted me effortlessly onto the edge of the altar. The cold marble sent a shiver up my back, or perhaps it was his touch that ignited my senses.

"Are you nervous, Ella? Or do you like being at the mercy of my cock and risking being seen? Is it a turn on for you, little lamb?" he murmured, his voice a low rumble like distant thunder. His eyes, dark and intense, bore into mine, searching for the truth hidden within their depths.

"I'm not sure," I admitted, my voice barely a whisper. "We've never fucked in a public place, much less a church." My heart pounded in my chest, a drumbeat of anticipation mixed with a bit of anxiety.

His mouth crashed down on mine, a storm of passion and desire. He possessively threaded his hands through my long hair, his fingers tangling in the strands. He pulled my head back and deepened our kiss, his tongue exploring my mouth with an urgency that left me breathless. His free hand pulled my legs apart, his touch firm and insistent, and he moved my dress up around my thighs. The cool air of the church was a stark contrast to the heat of his touch. He allowed himself the access he craved as his fingers traced the delicate lace of my undergarments.

"I'm about to make you pray, my little whore," he growled, his voice a primal promise that sent a wave of heat pulsing through my veins. "Get ready to beg for absolution."

His hand cupped my jaw, thumb pressing against my cheek, as he angled my head back to study me. The altar was smooth beneath my thighs, but the weight of his stare singed hotter than any candle. He tugged my dress higher, the material bunching around my waist and baring me completely. I felt exposed—every inch of me was at his mercy while the saints' faces and hammered gold around them blurred at the edges of my vision. His other hand yanked my thong down in a swift motion that made the lace burn against my skin.

"Spread your legs." His command was a whisper, but it echoed off the dome of the sanctuary, as though God himself just spoke. I obeyed, knees falling open, pulse stuttering as he stepped between them. He pressed the hard outline of his cock against me, grinding it into the slickness of my folds, just letting me feel the threat of it, the promise. I whimpered, my hips rolling involuntarily, desperate to be filled. I'd never ached so shamelessly, never wanted to be watched, devoured, and ruined the way I wanted it now.

He hooked his fingers under my knees and pulled me even closer to the edge, the marble biting into my ass. His hands were bruising, but every squeeze made my cunt throb.

"Look at you, little lamb. So fucking hungry for it." His words sent a bolt of humiliation and pride through me, the two warring in my chest. He leaned down, mouth grazing my ear. "You want to be fucked in your god's house, don't you?"

"Yes." It was a confession, the purest I'd ever uttered.

He lined up at my entrance and thrust in hard, bottoming out in a single, unyielding stroke. The stretch was brutal and exquisite. I cried out, only half muffled by his palm over my mouth. It was too much and not enough, and I couldn't remember how to breathe. He began to fuck me, each stroke deep and sharp, the slap of skin on skin a filthy percussion beneath the murmur of candle flames. My head knocked back against the altar, eyes squeezed shut, but he grabbed a fistful of my hair and pulled until I met his gaze.

"Keep your eyes open. Watch me ruin you."

His cock filled me completely, dragging against every nerve ending inside me. The sounds were obscene—slick, wet, desperate—and I could only imagine what it would be like if someone walked in and saw me being fucked and worshiped on the altar. The thought made me clench around him, made me want to claw at his back or bite his neck. He must've felt it, because he grinned, teeth flashing, and slammed into me even harder.

He leaned in, face inches from mine, sweat beading at his temples.

"Are you going to come for me, little lamb? Are you going to soak this altar with your sweet little cunt?" His words stoked my desire, each one making me tighter, needier, more helpless against the build of pleasure. He reached between us, and his thumb found my clit, then pressed down in tight circles. Every thrust forced my spine against the marble, and I thought I might splinter, body and soul, right here on the altar.

His hands pinned my thighs wide open, and I could see past his shoulder to the staring face of the crucifix above the altar. The thought should have filled me with shame, but all I could feel was his cock inside me, the blunt force of his hips, the obscene slickness pooling between my legs. My fingers scrambled uselessly for purchase, nails scraping along the edge of the altar. He kept hold of my hair, forcing me to meet his eyes—those gray, hungry eyes—and the way he looked at me made me feel like the only thing in the world that mattered.

He pressed his forehead to mine, his breath ragged while his body strained. There was nothing gentle, nothing forgiving. Every motion was a demand, a claim, a rough liturgy he was writing into my flesh. He worshipped me, but he did it by wrecking me, by making my body echo with the rhythm of his hips and the sting of his teeth when he bit my shoulder to keep from crying out.

I wanted to tell him I'd never felt so alive, so dirty, so loved, but all that came out was a high, helpless moan.

"Come for me, Ella," he said, and the sound of his voice seized me as the world blanked to white stars and hot, shivering pulses that started at my cunt and spread through every part of my body. He didn't slow, kept fucking me through it, relentless, and the aftershocks were almost too much. I could hear myself, my little strangled moans, half cry and half laugh, but I couldn't stop.

He pulled out and spun me around, bending me over the altar so my cheek pressed against the cold marble. He kicked my ankles apart and entered me again, harder this time, one hand in my hair and the other pressed between my shoulder blades, pinning me in place. He built a rhythm, fucking me with brutal efficiency, and I felt another orgasm building, raw and greedy and unstoppable. My thighs trembled, knees nearly buckling, but his grip kept me upright and exactly where he wanted me.

He felt it, the way I clenched down around him, and he laughed—a low, triumphant sound that vibrated straight through my chest.

"Good girl," he said, rough and reverent all at once. "Come for me again."

I did, shattering on the altar, vision sparking and heart pounding like I'd just been baptized in fire. He kept fucking me through it, relentless.

I heard his breathing shift, the ragged edge of effort and surrender. I thought of all the people who'd knelt before this altar, all the tears and prayers and silent pleas, and realized in some desperate, hysterical corner of my mind that this was its own form of worship. His hips slammed into me, his cock swelling inside, and I felt it: the final loss of control as he came, deep, pulsing, marking me.

He stayed like that for a moment, pressed tight to my back, both of us gasping, sweat cooling on our skin. When he finally let go, I nearly collapsed, my arms braced against the altar for support. He turned me around and set my feet on the floor as he pushed the hair out of my face and kissed my forehead with a tenderness that made my eyes sting with unshed tears.

"You are so fucking perfect," he whispered.

I pulled my dress down over my thighs and tried to smooth the wrinkles, but there was no hiding the way my body shook or the flush on my cheeks. He tucked himself into his slacks and then he smoothed my hair and cupped the back of my neck with so much reverence that I wondered if he was afraid I might shatter if he touched me too roughly.

We heard a door at the back of the church, the faint clatter of keys. I stiffened, panic flaring in my chest, but he just leaned in and brushed his lips against my ear.

"Confession, little lamb?"

I couldn't help it. I laughed, wild and breathless, and followed him as we hurried down the aisle, the scent of sex clinging to the air as we hurried out of the building.

Once we spotted our car under the flickering streetlight, he pressed me gently against its cool metal side, his lips playfully nipping at my lower lip. "I love you, little lamb," he murmured, his voice a deep velvet whisper. "I will always be your god, but you will forever be my queen."

ABOUT THE AUTHOR

J.A. Owenby is an international bestselling author of dark romance novels that ooze with angst and twists. She grew up swearing like a sailor in the backwoods of Arkansas before her adventures took her to stormy Washington, where she resides with her husband and three cats. Owenby's friends describe her as "delightfully twisted," and she loves fan mail and wine.